PROTECTOR

HEROES OF RENEGADE

RENEGADE
WARRIOR
PROTECTOR

PROTECTOR

JENNIFER PIERCE

Protector
Heroes of Renegade: Book 3

Copyright © 2026 Sunrise Media Group LLC

Print ISBN: 978-1-966463-78-8

This book is a work of fiction. Names, characters, places, and incidents are either products of the author's imagination or used fictitiously. Any similarity to actual people, organizations, and/or events is purely coincidental.

Unless otherwise indicated, all Scripture quotations are taken from the Holy Bible, King James Version.

For more information about Jennifer Pierce please access the author's website at jenniferpiercewrites.com.

Published in the United States of America.
Cover Design: Sunrise Media Group LLC

And we know that all things work together for good to them that love God, to them who are the called according to his purpose.

ROMANS 8:28 KJV

ONE

SAMANTHA WILLIAMS PULLED THE FIRE HOOD over her head, slid her arms into the self-contained breathing apparatus harness, adjusted the shoulder straps, and fastened the belt as Ciaran "Murph" Murphy cut the siren of Engine 4 and eased it to the curb. Once they were stationary, everyone deployed from the truck without a word about Sam's phone call just now.

The vibration from her elderly, busybody neighbor's call still tingled against her palm. If her crew saw the tension in her face, they might ask what was wrong. Normal people wouldn't be thrown by something as simple as running late; they'd wonder why it affected her so much.

Greer slammed the door shut. "Ready?"

"Am I ever not?" Sam tried to find a smile and go back to being their teammate rather than the guardian of a teenage girl. Right now they had a fire to fight. There was nothing she could do about the fact that Isabella had left for school later than usual. Harmless, really—what teenager didn't oversleep on occasion? But Sam's pulse spiked anyway. In their world, even small details could draw attention, and attention led to questions—questions she could never answer. Isabella relied on her to keep her safe, and Sam knew any slip could put them both at risk.

Sam donned her fire helmet, leaving the mask unsecured for now, and shook out her gloves before she jogged around to the hose compartment, grabbed a section, and let the roughly twenty pounds fall onto her shoulder.

This was always when she found her focus. When the weight of *this* job—and not motherhood—hit her. If she wasn't all-in, nothing-else-matters with the job of being a firefighter, someone could die.

Sam used her left hand to grab a loop of the hose behind her and maintain control. It would let her know if there was resistance because someone stepped on the line, if it got snagged, or if she'd reached the end. Then she could start dropping line from her shoulder.

She focused on running the line perpendicular to the engine and up to the front of the old commercial building. Was this another arson or just faulty wiring?

Mason Greer followed behind her, making sure the line wouldn't kink once the water flowed. Then he'd help advance the line into the building.

Captain Cole Bennett and Zachary Holt had already forced entry through the front door, giving her and Greer access to the fire.

She laid the nozzle on the ground long enough to put on her mask. Sweat had already started to form across her brow from the fire's heat. Once the mask was on, the flow of oxygen replaced the thick smell of smoke. All she needed now was the—

"Water!" Murph yelled over the radio.

Time to put out the flames.

Sam led the attack line through the building, dousing the flames while Greer supported the hose from behind. The fire grew in intensity as they neared the center of the building. As if someone had started the main fire as well as little ones on their way out. Another one for the Renegade arsonist.

If someone had asked her years ago where she would be right now, fighting fires in Renegade, Colorado, with a new identity would not have been her answer. No. She'd still be Madison Johanson the nurse. Probably working twelve-hour shifts in a hospital somewhere. Making sure her little sister had a better life than she'd had—three meals a day, weather-appropriate clothing, shoes that fit and weren't falling apart. Things the average person would consider necessities but which had been luxuries for Madison. No one else was going to do it for Anna—now Isabella.

Samantha shoved thoughts of her neglected childhood from her mind. No use bringing up the past when it was as dead as Madison. There was a job to be done—a job that meant saving lives and using her training to stay safe so she could get home, where her real job began. The one where she raised her sister better than their mother had raised Madison.

She'd done a bang-up job of that, considering they were in WITSEC now. One traumatic childhood traded for a slightly less traumatic childhood. At least Isabella had someone to fight for her.

Her teammates shouted out their progress as they pushed deep into the bowels of the abandoned building until the flames were extinguished.

"Keep the line charged while we do the overhaul. Williams, get ready to hit it if it lights back up," Captain Bennett ordered before inspecting the largest burn area. "This where it was the heaviest?" He pointed to a heap of debris in the middle of the open space.

"Yes," she responded.

He held the thermal imaging camera up to the area and then ran it around the room. "Thermal's clear."

Sam followed the crew as Captain Bennett thoroughly inspected the rest of the structure.

"Building's cold. Let's clean it up."

They filed out of the structure and started cleanup.

Sweat rolled down her back as she folded the hose. She couldn't wait to get back to the station and shed her turnout gear.

"Excuse me." A small voice sounded from behind Sam as she rolled the hose.

Sam turned and found a little girl with blonde pigtails and tear stains on her cheeks. She knelt down. "Are you okay?"

The little girl shook her head, sending her pigtails swinging. "My mommy said if I ever need help, to find a policeman or a fireman."

"Your mommy is very smart. Are you lost?" Sam looked up as a woman in khaki capris and a green T-shirt jogged up.

"Emily, there you are. Let the firefighters do their jobs."

"But Mommy, you said if I ever needed help, to find a policeman or fireman."

"I did, but I meant an emergency. This isn't an emergency."

Emily nodded furiously. "It is too."

"Not the type of emergency that I meant." The woman turned to Sam. "I'm sorry. Her kitten is stuck in the tree. I was looking for our ladder, and I guess Emily had other plans."

Sam smiled at Emily. "You came to the right place. Saving kittens from trees is our specialty."

Emily jumped up and down, clapping. "Yay!"

Emily's mother shook her head. "You don't have to. I'm sure the kitten will be okay until my husband gets home and can help dig the ladder out of the storage building."

"Nonsense. Let me put this hose up, tell my crew, and see what we can do."

Emily threw her arms around Sam's leg and squeezed. "Thank you!"

Sam patted the little girl on the back, then made her way toward the engine and ran into Greer. "Hey, there's a kitten stuck in a tree. I'm going to go see if I can help."

"That's so cliché. I'm in." Greer turned. "Cap, we're going to go do a citizen assist."

Captain Bennett looked around, most likely assessing the progress of cleanup, then gave a thumbs-up. He'd never let them go if cleanup wasn't mostly done, unless it was a medical emergency.

She started back to Emily and her mom and realized Greer was jogging right behind her. "I don't need your help."

"Oh, I'm not helping. I'm just coming for the entertainment. Cats are evil on a good day. Trap them in a tree and add in some fear and they become psychos. Once I'm done laughing, I'll tend to your wounds." He clapped her on the back.

She rolled her eyes. "Cats aren't that bad. In fact, some people love them."

"Talk to me after you've contracted cat-scratch fever." He fell into step next to her, then let out a low whistle as they got closer to Emily and her mother. "Wow."

Sam shoved him. "Oh no. We are professionals. We're saving a cat and making a little girl happy. There will be no flirting."

"I can't make any promises." He flicked his hair out of his eyes.

She gave him a side-eye. He may have sounded serious, but the twinkle in his green eyes suggested otherwise. "She's married."

"Disappointing." Greer was a good guy. Definitely a flirt, but it was mostly harmless. The fact that he looked like a young Elvis, minus the pompadour, didn't make it hard for him to charm the ladies. Rectangular face with full lips and black hair. He even had older ladies fawning over him.

He was the guy you went to shoot pool with after work. But not the guy you invited to help you move house, because it would take hours longer than necessary. And he was never serious about anything except fitness and nutrition.

"Okay, Emily. This is my friend Greer. Let's go see if we can get your kitten." Sam made it a point not to introduce him to the mother. And not just because she didn't know the lady's name.

They followed the duo.

"You really don't have to do this. The kitten will be okay until my husband gets home. It's not the first time he's done this." The woman brushed hair back from her face.

"It's not a problem at all."

Emily ran up to a tall cottonwood tree full of deep green leaves. "He's up there!" She pointed past the lower, thinner branches to the thicker, sturdier ones fifteen feet up.

Sam studied the tree. Definitely climbable, but not so much in her turnout pants, which were stiff and didn't allow the maneuverability she would need. She shrugged off her jacket, unfastened the waist of her pants, and loosened the suspenders while kicking off her boots so she could strip down to her duty uniform.

"Here we go. You climb that tree like a spider monkey!" Greer laughed.

"You really don't have to do this," Emily's mother said.

"Nonsense. Climbing trees is like riding a bike, right? You never forget how to do it."

Sam grabbed the lowest branch and tested its sturdiness before starting her ascent. The rough bark cut into her feet through her socks as she climbed. She maneuvered up the branches and made her way to the kitten. It mewed softly as she approached.

"Hey, little guy. Let's get you down from here. Emily misses you." She slowly reached forward, trying not to scare the animal any more than he already was.

The fluffy white kitten sniffed her fingers.

Sam had to wonder if this was a tactic she could use with Bella. Would the teen respond to gentleness? Sam didn't even know where to start with the girl, but she had to figure out something.

"That's a good boy." She inched her fingers closer, but the kitten stepped back. "It's okay. I'm here to help you."

She reached forward a little more, and the little guy didn't move. She gave him a small pet on his head, and he immediately purred.

"Come here." She scooped the kitten up and cradled him to her chest. He stayed still as she descended the tree.

Emily waited with arms wide open for his safe return. "Thank you!" She hugged her kitten.

Sam crouched. "You're welcome, Emily."

"That was awesome." Greer clapped her on the shoulder. "Were you in the circus before moving to Renegade?"

Sam's stomach tightened as she straightened. "I guess you'll never know."

She never talked to anyone about her past, and she never would. Her and Bella's safety depended on no one ever finding out who they really were or how Madison had testified in federal court and sent a dangerous man and all his cronies to prison for life.

If anyone discovered her past, she and Bella would be moved out of Renegade so fast their heads would be spinning.

For the sake of this life she had built, no one could ever find out her secrets.

***

Adrenaline coursed through Deputy US Marshal Liam Roberts's body as he shifted his weight from foot to foot, ready for the hunt. But this wasn't a fugitive apprehension task force. Nope. He'd given up that career, become the guardian of his niece, and taken a job at the Marshals' office in the city of Renegade. He looked around the room, taking in his new coworkers, who were busy gearing up, all wearing some fashion of blue jeans, tees, and running shoes.

This was a far cry from his old life.

But if he didn't make this work, he'd be ruining more than one future.

Liam looked down at his black slacks and button-down shirt. Not his fugitive-hunting apparel. He'd been in his new office all of two minutes before his new boss, Supervisor Daniel Howard, had told him to grab his gear and meet in the conference room for a briefing about a fugitive apprehension.

He already had his vest and duty belt on by the time the others filed into the conference room. A whiteboard filled the entire right wall. Pictures of criminals were taped along the board, with notes written all around them. A table that seated eight was centered in the room. Instead of sitting, everyone stood behind a chair. Just as anxious to get the hunt started as he was.

Except he shouldn't be this excited. He'd kissed the late nights kicking in doors and arresting bad guys goodbye. The adrenaline-filled life of fugitive apprehension didn't mesh well with single parenthood. A role change in his personal life had required a role change in his career. Now he was supposed to spend his days guarding the courthouse, transporting criminals, and handling witnesses—all with the caveat that he could be called for fugitive apprehension if needed.

Not what I expected on the first day, Lord.

Maybe after Sophia turned eighteen and went off to college, he'd go back to that life. If it was still available. He'd been told Renegade was where good marshals went to die career-wise. Apparently, no one ever transferred out of Renegade.

Which was a small price to pay, seeing as his sister sat in prison because of him. He'd made a decision as a teen that had sent her running down the wrong path and straight to a life of crime. He'd made something of himself, becoming a marshal on the straight and narrow, trying to absolve himself of his guilt. His sister hadn't been so successful, no matter how he'd tried to help her.

In the end it had been a no-brainer to become Sophia's guardian. After all, it was another way he could make amends.

No way would he have let her disappear into the foster care system. But he couldn't help feeling like God had thrown a wrench in where Liam had thought his life was going. He'd hoped to one day become a father; he'd just expected to start at the beginning—with all-nighters, diapers, and spit-up. The works. Not to be thrown immediately into the hormones and high school stage. And doing it as a single man, at that.

"Okay." A broad-shouldered man wearing stonewashed blue jeans, a simple black shirt, and a US Marshals ball cap yelled over the activity, pulling Liam from his thoughts. "We've got John Vickers. Number eight on the list."

The US Marshals' Most Wanted list: the fifteen criminals the Marshals considered the most dangerous. There were some real bad guys, and occasionally gals, on that list.

Supervisor Howard stepped up. "Before we get into the details, let me introduce you to our newest team member." He gestured to Liam, and all eyes turned to him. "This is Liam Roberts. He'll be our new WITSEC and court-security guy. He comes to us from the fugitive apprehension team in Virginia."

Supervisor Howard went around the room putting names to the new faces, starting with the broad-shouldered man. Ethan Butler.

Next, Howard gestured to a man in his mid-forties, close-cropped dark-brown hair graying at the temples. "Nick Stanton."

He then pointed to a woman with warm-toned skin and light-brown hair slicked back into a bun. "Emma Kennedy."

"Cody Albright." A man sporting a two-day beard was next.

"Finally, Jodi Glover." She was the shortest member of the team but not by much. Blonde hair tucked through the back of a US Marshals ball cap.

Each team member acknowledged him in some fashion, whether a wave or head nod.

"Okay, Butler, fill us in on Vickers." Supervisor Howard turned the room over to Butler.

"He's wanted on multiple counts of capital murder. Known to be armed and violent. The last encounter law enforcement had with him, he said he'd die before going back to prison. Word is he's here in Renegade. One of my informants just called and said he's at the Blue Moon Motel on Jefferson." Butler crossed his arms over his chest.

Great. Fantastic way to start his first day. Fugitive with a suicide-by-cop attitude.

"On a scale of Rendell to Lowe, what are we talking about?" Albright asked.

"Lowe."

Albright grimaced.

They threw around names like he should know who they were. "Someone want to fill in the new guy?"

"Rendell said he wouldn't be taken alive, but once we showed up, he gave up without issue," Glover supplied.

"Then cried for his momma." Albright chuckled.

"Silas Lowe was the complete opposite." This time Kennedy chimed in.

"*Was* being the operative word." Albright's jaw stiffened.

Lowe had obviously meant what he'd said and hadn't survived the encounter. Which one of Liam's new teammates had been the one to pull the trigger?

Butler tapped his upper thigh. "Roberts, you're with me. Stanton and Kennedy, set up on Lincoln. Albright and Glover, you'll set up on Pine. We go in slow and keep our distance until we know it's him. Once we've verified it is Vickers, we'll make the arrest. Let's go."

The other four agents filed out of the room while Butler hung behind. "Follow me." He didn't wait for a response. Just turned and walked away.

Liam followed him to the secure elevator to the first floor, where they exited into a secured parking lot. Butler climbed into a black pickup truck that was backed into a spot right by the exit. Liam climbed into the passenger seat.

Butler threw the truck in Drive and tore out of the parking lot.

"What's the plan?" Liam looked in the side mirror to see two black SUVs following behind.

"You heard it. Verify and arrest." Butler glanced over. "Figured you'd know by now what you're doing, Mr. Fugitive Task Force."

"Right, but what's the plan on the arrest? How's the hotel set up?"

Each department executed arrests differently. With Butler as the lead on this case, he'd be making the decisions.

Still, Liam pulled up a map of the area on his phone and took a look at the layout.

Butler gave him a side-eye and gripped the steering wheel tighter. "The hotel is in the shadier part of Renegade. It's on the corner of the lot. Stanton and Kennedy will be set up a block north to maintain visual on the back of the motel. Albright and Glover will be a block to the east, watching the front. You and I will be half a block west."

Sounded like Butler had a good perimeter set up.

"Once we verify it's Vickers, we'll make a decision on how to take him down."

"Okay." That's all he needed to know.

Because he was new in town, he had studied maps and knew general locations and roads, but he wanted to know what the maps wouldn't tell him. The things he'd learn working with this team and operating on the streets of Renegade.

His phone rang in his hand. The words *Marshal Samuel Dennison High School* filled the screen.

"I have to take this."

Butler nodded.

He slid the Answer icon across the screen. "Liam Roberts."

"Good morning, Mr. Roberts. This is Vice Principal Woodworth. I'm calling you regarding Sophia."

His stomach sank. "Is there a problem?"

"Well, yes. Sophia was caught with several young ladies vaping in the bathroom this afternoon when they were supposed to be in class."

Liam closed his eyes and took a deep breath. Skipping class and vaping in the bathroom? Next she'd be skipping school entirely. After that, how long would it be before she ended up like her mother?

"She was given lunch detention. We just wanted you to be aware of the situation. We know she's new to Renegade, and had hoped she would start off on the right foot, but this isn't it. Her records from Virginia indicate she's been in some trouble before the transfer. We'll be encouraging her to take this fresh start more seriously."

And so would he.

Liam cleared his throat. "She was having some difficulties in her home life that caused issues. We're working on making sure that trouble isn't repeated here."

"We're aware. Just know that we are a compassionate and understanding administration. If you need any assistance with locating services in Renegade, please let us know. We only want what's best for our students."

"Thank you. Sophia and I will talk tonight." He disconnected the call and shook his head. "That kid."

Renegade was a fresh start for him and Sophia. New lives in a new town. The past was behind them. More hope for a better future for Sophia. Starting over was going to be hard, and they'd both have to make adjustments. They were each nursing broken hearts. For different reasons though.

That hope didn't stop the little voice in his head questioning everything and worrying about the future. Liam knew he needed to take those thoughts captive and trust God's plan, even though it didn't make sense. It was hard, but he was trying. God would give them the strength to overcome the past and move forward.

"Did you get your business squared away?" Butler glanced over.

"For now."

"Good, because we're here." Butler eased the truck to the curb and killed the engine.

Silence filled the truck. Adrenaline coursed through Liam as he studied the motel, waiting for Vickers to make an appearance.

Tried to feel like himself, a marshal on a fugitive apprehension team.

Rather than a father with no idea what he was doing.

TWO

A N HOUR AND A HALF AFTER THE CALL HAD gone out, Sam collapsed in one of the dayroom recliners. One building secured, one cat rescued. All in a day's work. She sighed and lifted her hands to reset her ponytail.

Greer breezed into the dayroom. "Did you hydrate?"

"I just sat down." She let her arms drop to the recliner arms. "I'm not getting up again unless the bell goes off."

"You know hydration is important. Especially in our line of work. Equipment and gear maintenance." He lifted a finger. "Debriefing, reports." He lifted two more. "Hydrating while waiting for the next call." He lifted a fourth finger.

"Yes, Dad." She huffed as she stood. "Statistically speaking, the next call will be a medical call."

"You still need to be hydrated." He shot her a look. "Besides, statistics are changing thanks to a firebug making their home in Renegade."

"Fine." He was right, even if she had no intention of saying that out loud. "Do you think the fire we just put out was started by him or her?"

There had been a string of arsons in commercial buildings over the past few weeks. So far there had been no rhyme or reason to the fires, and thankfully, no one had been hurt.

But that could so easily change.

She, of all people, knew how quickly everything could shift trajectory.

"Most likely, but I'm not an investigator. I just put out the fires. We should probably eat now. No telling when we'll get another chance." Greer turned his head toward the bay door and yelled loud enough for those in the bay to hear him. "Who's ready for some food?"

"Depends on who's on kitchen duty." Sam started after him into the kitchen portion of the open-concept room.

Greer turned around and walked backward. "Um, that would be me." He smiled proudly.

Mason Greer was the station's youngest firefighter at twenty-four. He was also the station health nut. That wasn't a bad thing—health was important, sure. But some of the things he'd had them try had been a bit sketchy.

"I think I'll pass on the swamp-water protein drink." She followed Greer. "That slimy drink tasted like a dirt-covered rotten apple sprinkled with ash."

She was more of a pizza and side salad kind of girl.

He rolled his eyes and passed into the kitchen. "Wheatgrass has antioxidants, is good for your immune system, and boosts energy."

The dayroom, where she'd been sitting, was basically a living room. There was a couch, loveseat, and a couple recliners arranged in front of a television. A kitchen island separated the two portions, and the long dining table seated everyone if they all squeezed in.

She wrinkled her nose. "I'd rather eat chalk than wheatgrass."

"I got you, Sammy. You can have my bacon sandwich." Dean stuck a half-eaten sandwich in her face.

She flinched back. Where had he come from?

Caleb Dean was the antithesis of Greer when it came to nutrition. His diet consisted of bacon and more bacon, and yet he seemed to remain fit despite the cholesterol clogging his arteries. He stood a couple inches taller than her, and while he wasn't quite as muscle-bound as Holt, you could tell he worked out.

When it was Greer's turn to cook, he tried to balance out the meal and make it healthier for his coworkers. He'd tried to sneak some turkey bacon onto Dean's breakfast plate one morning. That had not been a great morning. For anyone.

Sam figured the balance between the two men was somewhere in the middle ground—where she tried to live. Just your quiet, average life. *Nothing to see here.*

She pushed the sandwich in Dean's hand away and frowned. "Where's the bacon? All I see is mayo."

Greer looked over from behind the counter, where he poured some oil into a pan. "Dude. We've been back from the call all of five minutes. How do you already have a bacon sandwich?"

"It's an emergency bacon sandwich. I always keep one ready to go. You know, just in case." Dean shrugged his shoulders and took a bite of the sandwich, causing mayo to dribble down his chin.

"Exactly what kind of situation requires an emergency sandwich?" Greer crossed his arms over his chest.

"That's the point! You never know." Dean slung his arm around Sam's shoulders. "That's why you've always gotta have one ready, right, Sammy?"

She shoved him away, and he finished the sandwich, licking his fingers like a little kid.

Sam gestured to the glob of mayo on his chin. "How does your wife put up with you?"

"She looks forward to his shifts." Zachary Holt breezed in and sat on one of the stools around the kitchen island. The guy had light-brown hair that he usually kept covered with a ball cap, was six-two, and looked like he could crush bricks with his bare hands. Despite his scary appearance, he was a giant teddy bear. "That way she has some peace and quiet."

Sam lifted an eyebrow. "With two little kids at home? Unlikely."

Dean hopped up to sit on the counter. "She said the only way this marriage is ending is if one of us dies. And since she doesn't look good in orange, she can't kill me unless she figures out the perfect crime." He shrugged.

"So instead, she feeds your bacon addiction, hoping you'll have a heart attack one day," Holt interrupted. "She's in it for the death benefits."

"You're just jealous that I can eat what I want and still have this fabulously fit body." Dean gestured to himself and sent Holt a kissy face.

"Barf." Sam went to the coffeepot. If Dean was the antithesis of Greer, Holt was the military upgrade. His muscles had muscles.

"I have no desire for a dad bod like what you're rocking." Greer turned around and started pulling food from the refrigerator.

Dean sucked in his practically nonexistent stomach and then let it out. He was in shape, as they all were. They had to be to do this job. The team was only as strong as its weakest link.

As the lone female of Station 4, she'd been prepared to fight for their respect when she'd arrived four years ago, but they'd welcomed her to the family. She trusted each of these men with her life, and they trusted her with theirs. Now she didn't want to go anywhere else.

"Williams." Captain Bennett's voice came over the speaker system. "Telephone call. Line two."

Her stomach clenched as she jogged to the lobby for a little privacy. The only telephone call she would be getting at work would be from the school. Was Bella sick? She'd have to take time off to go get her sister and run her home.

She snatched up the phone. "Sam Williams speaking."

It might have been years, but part of her would always hesitate before she called herself Sam and not Madison.

"Ms. Williams. This is Vice Principal Woodworth. I'm calling regarding your sister Isabella."

"Yes, ma'am. Is everything okay?"

A list of illnesses rolled through her mind. It wasn't quite flu season yet. Maybe strep or a sinus infection. Bella had seemed fine last night. Had she woken up ill? Maybe that was why the neighbor had noticed she'd been late this morning.

"Physically, she's fine, but she is in trouble. We caught several young ladies vaping in the bathroom this afternoon when they were supposed to be in class. Isabella was one of them."

Vaping was no better than smoking in the girls' room. Hadn't she taught Bella better than that?

"Since this is her first offense, we've only given her lunch detention. We just wanted you to be aware of the situation."

"Yes, ma'am. I'll have a discussion with her tonight. Thank you for calling."

Isabella had been a good kid all her life. Was this the start of a teenage rebellion, or just a misunderstanding? Sam intended to quash this as quickly as possible so it didn't disrupt the tenuous hold they had on the peace in their lives.

She headed back to the kitchen and ran into Dean in the hallway by the noticeboard, which was covered with safety posters someone had drawn mustaches all over.

"Everything okay?" He frowned.

"It will be once I talk to that sister of mine." She gritted her teeth. "I taught her better than that."

"Uh-oh. What happened?" Dean sidestepped to lean against the wall.

Sam moved with him and checked no one else was nearby. She didn't want to talk about this in front of the others. "That was the school. Bella skipped class to vape in the bathroom."

"Typical teenager doing typical teenage stuff? Might not be a big deal."

"I'm hoping she was just in the wrong place at the wrong time. I'll know more tonight when shift is over." It couldn't be more than that, right? Isabella knew she had to mind her p's and q's. She knew how essential adhering to the rules was. Their lives depended on it. Depended on anonymity and flying under the radar. Right now, it was a simple note in her school file, but if the behavior persisted and the police got involved, that would create official reports.

No one in WITSEC who had followed the rules had ever been located—or worse. It was when people broke the rules that their lives were endangered.

Part of following the rules meant staying out of trouble. Vaping in the bathroom was no big deal, but it could lead to a big deal if she kept hanging out with those girls.

"Ah, teenagers. Gotta love 'em. I know you like rules and all, but she's a kid, and kids make dumb mistakes. They push boundaries and see how far they can get before it breaks." Dean folded his arms over his chest.

"What do you know about teenagers? Your kids are little."

"Uh, I *was* a teen. And I watch TV. She's at that age where she's learning about the world. She's moving from being a kid to an adult."

"She's fourteen. She's not an adult, Dean. She's a kid I'm responsible for."

"To you, she isn't an adult. But in her mind, she's close. She's going to make some dumb decisions in her life. Didn't you when you were her age?"

"It's hard to find the time to make dumb mistakes when you're working a full-time job and raising your sister."

Or that had been the case up until she'd graduated nursing school. Then she'd started dating Matteo "Matt" Marino and made the dumbest decision she could. He knew a guy, Corvino DeLuca, looking for a private nurse. She took the job without a second thought. The pay was good, and it beat long hospital hours. Look how that had ended. "I want better for her."

"All parents do. When she makes those mistakes, use them as moments to teach her. Yes, the decision was bad, and there are consequences as a result, but what can she learn from this? Don't just be someone telling her what to do all the time. Help her grow as you do."

She hadn't thought about it that way. How could she turn this into a learning situation? There was definitely a "be careful who you hang out with because they tend to rub off" lesson here.

She'd been around Matt for months and hadn't turned into a mobster. But this wasn't the same—not even close. Back then, she hadn't known who he really was. Not until the FBI had shown up and shattered the illusion. After that, everything had shifted— watching where he went, who stopped by, memorizing names and faces, tracking movements like her life depended on it. Because it had.

She'd been so young and desperate, especially with Bella to think about. The hours had been decent, the paycheck better than anything else around.

And DeLuca had been recovering from some illness when she was hired—less crime boss, more grumpy patient in silk pajamas. She hadn't seen much, not at first. But according to the FBI, what she had seen was enough to close the gaps in their investigation. Enough to make her the missing link.

She'd been there for the quiet meetings. The whispered conversations. She hadn't known what was said behind closed doors, but she'd known who had walked through them. And that was all the Feds had needed to get a conviction.

She'd been so naive. Focused on doing her job and caring for her sister. Occasionally, their mother had made an appearance, and Sam would have to deal with whatever mess she'd brought along with her.

Sam and Bella weren't going to live like that here in Renegade. Not if Sam could help it.

"Hang in there." Dean clapped her on the shoulder. "It'll get better."

Sam sighed. "I hope so."

<hr>

Thirty minutes had passed since they'd pulled in front of the rundown motel, and Butler hadn't said a word. Which just gave Liam plenty of time to craft the speech he was going to give Sophia later about not vaping and not making friends with the bad crowd.

The silence didn't bother Liam. He was used to stakeouts, where conversation depended on who he was working with. There was a variety of different types of people. It appeared that Butler was the silent type. Was he silent because he was thinking through every possible scenario, or was he just introverted? Liam was certain of one thing: Butler wasn't the type to crack jokes to lighten the mood. No, that appeared to be Albright, who'd been sharing one-liners since they arrived.

"You know, we're basically government-funded stalkers," Albright cracked over the speaker.

Butler grabbed the radio. "Can it and focus."

"Aye, aye, Captain," Albright replied from his spot on Pine Street.

"Is there anything I should know about this area that's not on the map?" Liam looked out the window and studied the motel.

Ethan continued to watch the motel. "That treed area behind the motel is fifty yards of mud. The rain and snow melt off drains there, and it hardly ever dries out. If we end up back there, you're gonna lose your shoes. It will be easier to skirt the boundary and catch the guy as he emerges from the other side."

"Good to know."

"Also, don't expect anyone in this neighborhood to help you. These people ain't seen nothing and don't know nothing."

It didn't surprise Liam. Most people didn't want to help law enforcement. They'd rather break out their cell phones and record what was going on. Going viral was more important than helping.

"Do we want to send Kennedy knocking? 'Oops, wrong door'?" Stanton's voice crackled over the radio.

Liam responded. "I was thinking the same thing. Get eyes on him and speed up the identification."

"Not right now," Butler replied. "We don't want to burn the motel, and this guy is armed and dangerous."

"So send me," Liam said to Ethan directly. "No one knows who I am."

Before Ethan could shoot down that idea, the door to the room they were watching opened, and a man stepped out. He jogged to an old beat-up car and opened the back door.

Ethan lifted the radio to his lips. "Positive ID. Vickers is in room twenty-four. Hold your positions."

Liam watched Vickers rummage around in the back seat of the car before returning to the room.

"Did anyone see inside? Is he alone?" Albright asked.

"I can't tell from this angle," Butler said.

Other than a small strip of light from the sunshine, all Liam could see beyond the door was blackness. He couldn't make out any other figures in the room.

Butler looked at him. "Okay, go now and see if he checked in alone, and I'll keep watch."

Liam removed his ballistic vest. It was a risk, but if Vickers happened to look his way and see *US Marshal,* they'd lose their edge. He didn't want their cover to be blown.

He made his way to the motel office. The bell above the door rang as he entered.

"Can I help you?" A middle-aged man who'd seen better days sat behind the counter.

"Deputy US Marshal." Liam showed the man his badge. "The man who checked into room twenty-four. Did he check in alone?"

The man glowered at him but looked at his computer screen. "Room twenty-four booked by a John Smith yesterday. He was alone when he checked in."

"Thanks." Liam started to leave, but then turned back around. "I wasn't here. Got it?"

The man nodded. "I just work here. I don't make it my business to know nothing 'bout no one."

Liam walked back to the truck and climbed in. He grabbed the radio. "Confirmed Vickers checked in alone yesterday under an alias."

Butler lifted his radio. "Doesn't mean he's alone now though. Stanton and Kennedy, get in position behind the motel. Albright and Glover, you're with us."

"We're in position," Kennedy responded.

"Let's go." Butler pulled into the parking lot, blocking the car Vickers had been in moments before.

The four of them jumped from their vehicles. Liam pulled his weapon. Albright grabbed the ballistic shield from his SUV and led the way as they approached the door.

They took position, Albright closest to the door on the left, near the window, shield at ready, Glover behind him. Butler to the right of the door against the wall. Liam took position next to him.

"Ready?" Butler asked.

Everyone nodded.

He reached over and banged on the door. "US Marshals! Open up!"

They listened and waited.

Nothing.

Butler banged again. "US Marshals! Open up, or the door is coming down!"

"We got a runner!" Stanton yelled over the radio from behind the building.

Butler and Liam both twisted around and took off to join the chase.

Liam turned the corner of the motel in time to see the fugitive disappear into the treed area Butler had told him about, Albright and Glover on his heels.

"Fugitive has entered the rundown patch of trees," Liam notified Stanton and Kennedy.

Kennedy responded, "We'll meet him on the other side."

"I'll go right, you go left," Butler commanded.

"US Marshals! Stop!" Albright yelled from the copse of trees.

Liam spotted flashes of the chase and entered the tree line just as Albright tackled Vickers. The two men tussled on the ground. Glover was a few paces behind with her gun ready, just in case.

A gunshot rang out. Albright fell back and grabbed his shoulder. Vickers surged to his feet and aimed his gun at Glover. She slid to a stop, raising her weapon with deadly precision.

Another shot rang out, and Vickers collapsed. Butler's trigger finger was faster than Glover's.

Butler advanced on the subject. "Cover me."

Liam and Glover closed in, weapons trained on the fugitive. Butler kicked the gun out of reach, holstered his weapon, and rolled the wounded man to his stomach to secure his hands behind his back.

Seeing Ethan had the suspect handled, Liam holstered his

weapon and raced to Albright. Blood leaked from between Albright's fingers.

"Hold on. I've got you." Liam put pressure on the wound, causing Albright to grimace and groan in pain.

"Shots fired. Fugitive in custody. Officer down. We need medics times two," Glover yelled into the radio.

The response came a second later. "Ten-four."

Glover pulled gloves from her pants pocket and then started life-saving measures on Vickers by pressing down hard on the wound to slow the bleeding. "You're not dying here. Not on my watch. You have a date with a judge and a panel of twelve of your peers."

"Stanton, you sweep right. I'll take the left. Make sure there's no accomplices," Butler ordered.

Liam turned his full attention to Albright. "How are you doing?"

Albright gritted his teeth. "I've been shot. How do you think I'm doing?"

"Right, but tell me if you get tired or cold." Liam prayed that both men lived.

Vickers needed to live just as much as the marshal. Not only because he needed to pay for his crimes but to give him the opportunity to know God. He was definitely a bad guy, but he was a bad guy loved by a good God.

God saw all sin as equally condemning, unlike man, who determined there were levels of sin. It was a hard thing to reconcile in his line of work. Liam was better than the fugitive in the eyes of man, but not in the eyes of God. Not without the blood of Jesus covering him.

Liam held the pressure firm, jaw tight. The fugitive was in cuffs, the scene was secure, but his prayer wouldn't stop repeating: *Not today. Don't let death win today.*

Sure, he'd been thinking that giving up a fugitive-apprehension career to move to Renegade and raise Sophia was a kind of death. At least, the death of the life he'd thought he would have.

But today had shown it wasn't completely gone. Liam had to choose life—for himself and for Sophia.

But would she do the same?

THREE

SAM RINSED HER PLATE AND ADDED IT TO THE station dishwasher, still thinking about the call from the school, even though she'd determined to solve that problem later. It was Greer's turn to cook but her turn to clean up.

Despite her reservations, the chicken caprese sandwiches Greer had made were delicious. She had seriously questioned his sanity when he'd pulled out Greek yogurt and basil pesto and started to mix them. But it worked. So well.

She closed the dishwasher door. "I'm shocked to say this, but good job, Greer."

"High protein and tasty." He leaned against the counter. He'd said that since she wouldn't let him help with cleanup, he'd at least hang around and keep her company.

The others had already filtered out of the kitchen to the dayroom, or wherever else they wanted to spend what downtime they might have.

Just as she was deciding what to do next, the alarm pealed

throughout the station, followed by the mechanical voice announcing a medical call and an address.

"Let's go." She shut off the water, dried her hands on a towel, and ran to the engine. It was a medical call, so no need for turnout gear—though she tossed it in, just in case.

Murphy had the engine started, and Lieutenant Fischer was climbing in the front when she made it to the rig. Once she and Greer were in, Murphy pulled the truck out of the engine bay and onto the busy street. He flipped on lights and sirens, and they sailed past waiting traffic.

"Two patients with gunshot wounds. One of them a federal agent," Lieutenant Fischer advised.

Sam watched through the window as the scenery changed. It was amazing how a couple of blocks could change the area from a nice neighborhood to a dilapidated, crime-infested area. Kind of like the stark contrast between her old life and her new life.

Murph pulled the engine up next to a copse of trees behind a rundown motel known to the station for drug overdoses. Instead of the usual handful of civilians walking away, determined not to get involved, she spotted at least three unmarked police cars, blue lights flashing, and a couple Renegade squad cars.

She hopped down from the engine and grabbed the medical bag. One of the men standing in the parking lot wore a vest with *US Marshal* emblazoned on it.

The Marshals were here.

Of course, that explained the federal agent who'd been shot. Unease filled her gut. She had a job to do and a life to live. Working on the marshal in charge of her case could be risky. If her US Marshal handler, Ethan Butler, was hurt, she'd have to pretend she didn't know him.

The broad-shouldered marshal marching toward her confirmed he wasn't the one injured. Working on patients was hard enough, but knowing them made it tougher.

She didn't *know* know Deputy Marshal Butler, but still, she didn't want anything to happen to him. Not that she wanted anything to happen to someone else either . . .

She took a deep breath, casting the circling thoughts from her head. She needed to focus on the patient, whoever it might be.

"What do we have?" Lieutenant Fischer asked Deputy Marshal Butler.

"One of my guys has a GSW to his shoulder, and the fugitive has a GSW to the chest." He didn't even look at her.

"Greer, you take the marshal. Williams, you take the fugitive."

"Yes, sir." Greer peeled off from the group and headed in the direction Deputy Marshal Butler pointed.

Lieutenant Fischer had unknowingly made the best decision. Just as they weren't aware of her real name, none of her coworkers knew she was a licensed nurse. Or Madison Johanson had been, at least. She had more training than Greer, even though they both had the same paramedic qualification. But she couldn't go beyond the bounds of what a paramedic could do without serious consequences. Like losing her certification and license. She had to follow the rules.

She wasn't a nurse anymore.

She wasn't a lot of things.

She followed Butler to a man lying on the concrete in the supine position, cuffed hands beneath him. His shirt had already been cut away, and a woman wearing a US Marshals vest held some sort of cloth over the wound to apply pressure.

He appeared alert and oriented. How was that possible?

Sam dropped the medic bag, pulled gloves from her pocket, put them on, then knelt. She looked the man in the eye. "I'm Sam. I'm a paramedic, and I'm here to help you. What's your name?"

"John," the man said.

"Hello, John." She turned her attention to the brunette female. "What do we have?"

She could clearly see the gunshot wound, but she needed to know if there had been any other trauma or possible injury.

"One shot to the chest. Entry wound only."

Sam quickly looked the patient over and didn't detect any obvious signs that suggested an open pneumothorax. If the lung had been punctured, they would have bigger problems than just blood loss.

"Keep pressure on the wound. I'm going to apply a chest seal." She grabbed the packet and opened it. "Okay, let me see the wound."

The marshal lifted the cloth and sat back.

A small entry wound with minimal bleeding. Where was all the blood? He'd taken a bullet to the chest, an area of the body full of major arteries and organs.

Just because he was fine now didn't mean he'd remain that way. The man sitting in front of her was a ticking time bomb. She would need to watch for cardiac tamponade. If John's heart was being constricted by internal bleeding, he would require immediate intervention. Something even Madison Johanson wasn't qualified to do.

Using the gauze that was included in the packet, Sam wiped the man's chest free of blood and then put it on the wound. "Hold this."

The marshal held the gauze while Sam removed the protective film from the seal. She looked at the man. "When I count to three, I want you to exhale as much as you can and hold it. Can you do that for me?"

The man nodded his head.

"Okay, one. Two. Three."

The man exhaled. Sam grabbed the gauze from the marshal and wiped the wound again, then applied the seal and pressed around the edges, making sure it adhered to the man's skin.

She turned to him and smiled. "Good job. You can breathe

normally. I'm going to roll you so I can check for an exit wound, and I'll be placing a pulse ox on your finger."

With the assistance of the marshal, she rolled the man and checked his back for wounds, then checked his oxygen levels.

More sirens sounded behind her. The ambulance was close.

"Okay, I'm going to check the rest of your vitals now." She wrapped a blood pressure cuff around his right upper arm.

The paramedics arrived, and she gave them the rundown to transfer care, then grabbed all her stuff while Greer finished transferring care of his patient.

Several more police cars had arrived. A few officers milled about, but most had gathered by a truck. Deputy Marshal Butler was busy talking to the group.

She counted five people in US Marshals vests. Three men and two women. She could see a couple had blood on them. She grabbed a packet of cleanup wipes and a biohazard bag, then took them to the group.

"Excuse me." All eyes turned to her. "I thought you might want to clean up."

She opened the pack of wipes, then pulled a couple for the woman and handed them over. She turned to the man whose vest identified him as Roberts and offered him the wipes. He seemed to have the most blood on him.

"Thanks." He accepted the wipes and started cleaning the blood from his hands. He was roughly half a foot taller than her. His chestnut-brown hair was tapered short with a soft wave on the top, and he sported a neatly trimmed beard.

A thrill of attraction spread through her body. He was definitely easy on the eyes.

Tearing her gaze from him, she offered the wipes to the others standing in the huddle, but they all declined.

She opened the biohazard bag and waited for the marshals to finish cleaning up.

They deposited the used wipes in the bag.

"Thank you," Roberts said, holding her gaze a moment longer than necessary. Warmth spread through her chest.

Roberts hadn't been around her GSW, so the blood on his hands must belong to the injured marshal. For someone who had been involved in this shooting and tending to a wounded colleague, he was steady and calm. A chill raced down her spine. This was a man you didn't want to mess with.

She swallowed. "You're welcome." She sealed the bag and returned to the engine.

"Ready?" Murph said from the driver's seat.

"Good to go." She patted his seat.

Murph pulled the engine out and headed back to the station.

Sam looked at the watch on her left wrist. Fourteen hundred. Isabella would be out of school and back at the house in two hours. Good thing today was her first twelve-hour shift of the week. She'd be home tonight, and they could talk about the incident at school.

Once she got the truth out of Isabella, things could get back on track.

No way would Sam allow this to be the beginning of everything going downhill.

Liam stepped into his new office and dropped into his chair, one that was much nicer than he was used to. It was going to take a few days to get used to having his own office, but maybe this whole move wouldn't be so bad.

His gaze settled on a basket wrapped in cellophane with a dark-blue ribbon tied at the top that had been sitting on his desk when he arrived. He hadn't had a chance to see what it was. Now was as good a time as any.

A knock sounded on the wood frame behind him. Not even a moment to collect himself from the crazy first day so far.

"Roberts." Supervisor Howard stepped in.

Liam spun his office chair and stood. "Yes, sir."

"Tough start to the day." He gestured to the empty seat next to Liam's desk. "May I?"

Liam nodded and returned to his seat.

"Good job out there. Tell me what happened." Supervisor Howard crossed his right ankle over his left knee.

Why was he asking for a rundown of what happened? He'd come to the scene and talked with Butler. Either this was his standard practice following an incident like this, or Supervisor Howard suspected there was more to the story than he'd been told.

"Butler and I were in his truck, watching the motel. Vickers stepped out of room twenty-four and retrieved something from his vehicle. Butler positively identified him. I went into the motel office to find out if Vickers had checked in alone. I confirmed he had but under an alias."

He paused a moment to get names straight in his mind. "Albright and Glover watched the back in case he snuck out. Butler, Stanton, Kennedy, and I knocked on the door and prepared to breach if necessary. He didn't answer. Albright alerted us that Vickers was sneaking out the back window. He and Glover pursued.

"Butler and I split up, each taking one side of the urban tree lot. I heard Albright yelling and saw movement close to where I was. I went into the trees to assist. Albright tackled the fugitive. They tussled on the ground. There was a gunshot. Albright fell back. Vickers stood up and aimed his gun at Glover. Butler shot him before Glover could."

Supervisor Howard nodded. "As always, there will be an internal investigation into the shooting. In the meantime, Butler is on paid administrative leave pending the outcome."

"Yes, sir." It didn't matter that Liam thought it was a good shoot, it still needed to be investigated properly.

Supervisor Howard opened his suit jacket and produced a piece of paper. "Here's your password for the computer and all the important phone numbers. You've already gotten your key card, so you're good to go."

Liam took the paper. "Thank you, sir."

"Since Butler's on leave, I'm going to need you to familiarize yourself with his WITSEC cases and be prepared to handle anything else that comes up. We've got a guy on our radar, Torres, but he's still working out the details with the US Attorney, so he's not in the program yet. I have that file for now." He handed Liam a manila folder. "That leaves the Williams sisters, Samantha and Isabella. Everything you need to know is in this file. I don't have to tell you this is for your eyes only as their case officer. You're on courtroom duty starting tomorrow, so take the rest of today to familiarize yourself with the WITSEC case and the courthouse."

"Will do, sir."

Supervisor Howard tapped the desk before standing up and seeing himself out.

Liam used the new credentials to log in to the system. He checked his email and then turned his attention to the manila folder, starting to look into Butler's witnesses when his stomach rumbled. He tugged over the basket and read the card, a small welcome from Aubrey, the receptionist, and untied the bow. Under the coffee mug and tumbler, both personalized with his name, he found several energy drinks, a box of painkillers, and an assortment of homemade cookies and muffins.

He opened one of the cellophane-wrapped muffins and took a bite. Blueberry spilled over his tongue, and his eyes widened. These were perhaps the best blueberry muffins he had ever tasted. He needed to remember to tell Aubrey thank you.

He turned back to the witnesses. Madison Johanson, now

Samantha Williams. Twenty-nine. Her sister Anna Johanson, now Isabella Williams, was fourteen. In the program because Madison/Samantha had been employed as a private nurse for Corvino DeLuca.

Liam blew out a breath. That was a name he'd heard before, and nothing good ever followed it.

Corvino DeLuca was the head of the DeLuca crime family in New York City. DeLuca had ties in guns, drugs, and human trafficking.

He studied the photos in the file. *Samantha.* Dark-blonde hair and brown eyes. An oval-shaped face, high cheekbones, and full lips.

His heart rate kicked up. She was the attractive firefighter who'd responded to the scene today. He'd had to tear his gaze away from her and focus on what his coworkers had been talking about.

Isabella had brunette hair and brown eyes. A square face with low cheekbones. Despite the differences between the two, there was still a resemblance.

Another knock on the wood frame.

Liam turned and found Butler standing at the door.

"Supervisor Howard said you're taking over my witnesses. Any questions?" Butler took the seat Supervisor Howard had occupied moments ago.

Liam slid the goodies basket toward Butler. "Want a treat?"

Butler shook his head. "But if I were you, I'd hide the cookies. If the others catch wind, you're in trouble."

"That good?" Liam eyed the chocolate chip cookies.

"Better."

"Noted." Liam turned back to the folder on his desk. "I see why she's in WITSEC, and I recognize her as one of the firefighters who responded at the motel earlier. How'd the FBI convince her to testify?"

Butler said, "At first, she refused, scared of retaliation, but her mother got into some trouble, and the FBI offered to go light on her if Madison agreed to testify. The only stipulation Madison had was that the younger sister came with her."

Liam couldn't blame her for being reluctant. Anything related to the Mob was dangerous. Some of the torture stories he'd heard about people who'd talked scared him, and he'd seen a lot of things in his career.

"She's been in Renegade six years. No trouble from her or her sister."

"Got it."

A lot of criminals who agreed to testify and enter WITSEC used the opportunity as a new beginning. Dropping their old ways and taking the straight-and-narrow path, never getting in trouble again. But some didn't. Instead, they continued on with their crimes or came up with new ones. It was difficult to tell who would do what.

For an innocent witness, entering WITSEC was often a lot harder. They'd done the right thing and then had their entire lives upended as a result. The Williams sisters had given up everything for the sake of justice, and now it was up to the Marshals to make sure they were protected.

"Anything else I should know?"

Butler tapped his fingers on the desk. "You're joining a solid team. I know you're here for WITSEC and court security, but with me and Albright out, you'll probably have to pitch in on the fugitive task force." He clenched his jaw and took a deep breath. "Good luck."

Liam suspected there was more the man wanted to say but held back as he left the office.

He logged out of the system to take a walk around the courthouse and get his bearings before he started his security assignment tomorrow.

He spent the next hour visiting every office of the courthouse, introducing himself to those he would come into contact with on a regular basis, like Judge Stephen Mullinax and his staff. The layout of the courthouse was different than Virginia. Everyone he met seemed the same though. Friendly and welcoming.

He'd known the names and faces in Virginia but hadn't really known all the people, because he'd spent most of his time in the Marshals' headquarters or pounding pavement. Renegade would be the complete opposite, and not only because it was twice as big as Richmond, with a population pushing 500,000.

This building would be his home away from home.

After he'd checked all the boxes on his first day on the job, he could go home and talk to Sophia about the telephone call he'd received earlier. This issue with the school needed to be nipped in the bud.

He took the private elevator up to the second floor and made his way to his office. He'd grab his bag and head out. But first, he needed to thank Aubrey for her welcome gift. If she was still here.

He found her in the break room, rinsing out the coffeepot and preparing it for tomorrow. She wore a white pencil skirt and heels to match the fitted dark-green blazer. Her red hair was pulled back into some fancy knot.

"Ms. Richardson." He shoved his hand in his pants pocket.

She turned and smiled. "We're going to be seeing a lot of each other. Please call me Aubrey."

He nodded. "Aubrey, I wanted to thank you for the gift basket. I appreciate it."

She smiled brightly. "I figured you'd need the coffee cup and the energy drinks to stay awake during court duty."

"Yes, that can have its boring moments." He grinned at the joke. Nothing in their job was boring. They had to be vigilant at all times. "What about the painkillers?"

Her smile faltered. "It was a joke about having to deal with Ethan Butler."

"He that bad?" Liam crossed his arms over his chest.

"He's just grumpy sometimes. Mostly when he's trying to locate a fugitive." The chagrin in her expression melted away. "Do you have some free time this evening? I could take you to meet his witnesses, since you're taking them over while he's on leave. I'm familiar with all of Renegade's witnesses, and it might be easier on them if someone they know is there when you're introduced."

Liam furrowed his brow. "You know who the witnesses are? That's unusual."

Aubrey smiled tightly. "That's how Supervisor Howard wants things done. I do the menial things so the marshals can do the important things."

"Okay . . ." Interesting take on the job.

"I just do what I'm told." She shrugged. "So, did Butler fill you in?"

"Yeah, he gave me a rundown of their case." He hadn't expected to meet them today, but if she was willing to make the introductions, then he'd be happy to do it now. It shouldn't take too long. "Let's go."

She handed him a stack of papers she'd picked up off the table. "We're going to need these."

He looked at the papers and noticed a missing poster for a lost cat. "Mr. Whiskers?"

"Yeah, it's a plausible way to interact with the witnesses and not give away who we are or why we're there. It's what they're expecting. My precious Mr. Whiskers has escaped, and I'm devastated by it." She sniffed. "We'll go door to door handing out flyers in the neighborhood. That way, no one is the wiser."

She was a smart woman.

He tapped the stack of papers. "I guess we need to go find Mr. Whiskers."

FOUR

SAM UNLOCKED THE DOOR AND HUNG HER KEYS on the designated hook on the wall to the left. Bella's keys weren't hanging where they should be. "Bella?"

She turned and flipped the deadbolt, then tossed her bag down next to the recliner and toed off her shoes before wandering down the hall.

"Bella, you didn't hang up your keys."

She was constantly reminding the teen to do simple things. Keys got hung on the key hook so they didn't get lost in the tornado of clothing littering her bedroom floor.

Bella's bedroom door was open, and the light was off. Unease filled her gut. It was after six. She should be home.

Sam flicked on the light in case Bella had lain down and fallen asleep after school. It had been known to happen. Although not so much now that she was in high school.

Bella's bed was a mess, the comforter was halfway off, and three different shirts lay crumpled on top.

How were they sisters?

Sam liked her things to be neat and orderly. Everything had its space. Keys on the hook. Clothes in the closet. Bed neatly made every morning.

No sign of Bella's backpack either. She pulled her phone from her pocket and started to dial Bella's number but was interrupted by the doorbell.

That better not be the police bringing her home.

Wow. That was a huge jump from vaping in the bathroom. She dismissed the thought. *Long day much?*

Sam peered through the peephole to see who it was and spotted her landlord on the porch. She stepped back, undid the deadbolt, and opened the door. "Dr. Torres." She didn't know what kind of doctor he was. She just knew he'd introduced himself as a doctor when they'd met the first time.

"Good evening, Ms. Williams." Dr. Torres smiled. He was a slender man in his fifties with some gray threaded through his black hair.

She looked past him, hoping to see Bella strolling up too, but it was just the doctor. "What can I help you with?"

He never stopped at their house—especially not in the last month or so. Maybe something was wrong? He didn't micromanage, pretty much left them alone. Of course, she'd been a good tenant and not given him a reason to make appearances. Except for the time the water heater had gone out.

He ran a hand through his hair and glanced around, as if nervous. "I just wanted to stop by and let you know that I'll be going out of town for a little while and to give you some contact information for the man who will be handling all of my rental properties while I'm gone. His name is Daniel White."

"Sure, come in and I'll get a piece of paper and pen." She stepped to the side to let him in, then scanned the street again. Couldn't this have been a telephone call? She needed to find her sister.

They'd lived here six years, and this was the first time he'd shown up unannounced.

"No need for you to write anything down. I've got it all right here." He held out a piece of paper the size of a postcard, his smile a little too brittle.

She took the paper and read over it.

"Just keep paying your rent like normal. But if you have any issues or maintenance needs, give Danny a call." He tapped the paper in her hand. "He'll help you out."

"Okay, I will." She kept the frown to herself. That would be the worst-case scenario, right after she looked for how-to videos on the internet or asked one of the guys from the station for help. She didn't want strangers in the house with Bella here. It wouldn't be the first time she'd had Dean come fix something.

"While I'm here, is there anything that needs to be taken care of before I leave town?" He looked around the living room, probably checking for evidence they'd gotten a dog or something. Why else would he be nosy?

She didn't have time for this. Not with her sister MIA right now. "Nope, everything is fine." She shook her head. "I should go. My sister will be home soon."

"Good. Good."

"Knock, knock," a woman's voice called from behind Dr. Torres.

He stepped out of the way, revealing the woman the voice belonged to. Aubrey, the Marshals' office admin, stood next to the handsome marshal from the motel shooting.

Lead filled her stomach, and her vision blurred. Why were they here? Had something happened to Bella?

Sam swallowed. "Is—"

"Hi." Aubrey's bright smile seemed intended to reassure. "Sorry to intrude on your evening, ma'am, but my Mr. Whiskers escaped, and I was hoping you'd seen him." She thrust a missing cat poster into Sam's hand.

The lead melted away, and Sam took a deep breath. She'd been told early on that if the Marshals needed to make contact with her for a reason unrelated to her case, they would use a missing cat.

"I'll just be on my way." Dr. Torres stepped up to the doorway.

"Have you seen Mr. Whiskers?" Aubrey handed Dr. Torres a poster. "I live a block over, and this goof"—she nodded to the marshal—"left the front door open and he escaped." She sniffed. "I'm so worried."

Dr. Torres studied the poster and shook his head. "No, I haven't seen him. Sorry."

"Please call the number if you do." Aubrey pleaded with her eyes.

"I will. Goodbye, Ms. Williams. Remember, if you have any issues, contact Danny." Dr. Torres tipped his head and exited her house.

"What about you?" Aubrey asked. "Have you seen Mr. Whiskers?"

Sam studied the flyer. "I haven't."

Aubrey let out a squeaky cry as a tear rolled down her cheek, then started to sniffle before turning into the marshal's chest.

His eyes widened as he awkwardly wrapped an arm around her. "It's okay." He patted her shoulder.

"You poor thing." Sam stood back, watching Dr. Torres get in his car. "Why don't you come in, and I'll get you a tissue."

"That's so kind of you." Aubrey slowly entered the house, the marshal on her heels.

Once everyone was inside, the marshal shut the door.

"Sorry to surprise you, but we're having a staff change in the office, and I wanted to introduce you to your new handler." Just like that, Aubrey's tears were gone. "Samantha, this is Deputy US Marshal Liam Roberts. Deputy Marshal Roberts, this is Samantha Williams."

The marshal stuck his hand out. "It's nice to meet you again."

She shook his hand. "I hope everything is okay with Deputy Marshal Butler and the other injured marshal."

Aubrey smiled. "Deputy Marshal Butler is fine, just taking some leave for a few days. And Deputy Marshal Albright will be fine too."

"That's a relief." Sam had wanted to ask about the man she'd treated but knew she wouldn't get any answers. Various laws protected his health information. She didn't understand how he'd survived until the ambulance arrived. Had he made it to the hospital? It wouldn't be the first time the unexplainable had happened. Like the drunk driver with severe injuries who survived when the victim with seemingly minimal injuries didn't.

"Is Bella here?" Aubrey asked, pulling her from her thoughts.

Sam gritted her teeth. "No, she's out of the house."

It wasn't a lie, but she wasn't going to tell them she had no idea where her sister was. That would make her irresponsible. Another thing to add to the conversation she was going to have with Bella.

"That's okay. You can tell her about Deputy Marshal Roberts." Aubrey smiled.

"I have the telephone number that was assigned to Deputy Marshal Butler, so the only thing changing is the person that answers." Deputy Marshal Roberts smiled reassuringly. "Everything else is the same. Call me if you need me."

Aubrey shifted on her feet. "Sorry, I hate to ask, but can I use your restroom?"

"Sure." Sam pointed to the bathroom.

Aubrey handed the stack of flyers to Deputy Marshal Roberts and walked away.

Deputy Marshal Roberts stood tall, projecting calm authority. "I want to assure you that even though I'm new to Renegade, I'm not new to law enforcement or the Marshals. I have a bachelor's degree in criminal justice. I entered the police academy the day after I turned twenty-one. And I worked as a police officer until I was hired by the US Marshals six years ago." He kept his eyes on her, steady and attentive. "Do you have any questions for me?"

Sam studied the man in front of her. She had questions for him, but she highly doubted he'd answer them.

Sam shook her head. "Not at this time, no."

"Paperwork is two-dimensional. It tells us who you are but not *who* you are. Is there anything specific to you or your sister that's not listed in your files that you want me to know? Are there any questions or concerns about your situation?"

She took a deep breath. "It's probably nothing, but Bella is usually home by now, and as you can see, she's not. She didn't answer her phone when I called."

Concern filled the marshal's face. "Is that typical for her?"

"No. She knows the rules. She's supposed to come straight home from school."

"Does she have any extracurricular activities that might have run late? Any friends she likes to hang out with? Perhaps they lost track of time."

"No extracurricular activities. She has friends. It's possible she could be with one of them."

"Any reason to believe she could be in danger because of your past? Threats or anything of that nature?"

She shook her head again. "No." Sam was confident Bella would have told her if she had received any.

"Okay. So it's possible that this is just her losing track of time or something simple like that."

Possible? Yes. Uncharacteristic? Also yes.

"I'm here to protect you and Isabella. How do you want me to respond to this? I can and will scour the city for her if that's what you want, or I can stay in the background and let you handle this until you tell me otherwise. It's your decision."

While this wasn't like Bella, she had gotten into trouble at school today, so her being late could be tied to that. "Thank you. I'll wait a bit and go from there."

"Be sure to let me know if or when you need me. Even if it's the middle of the night. In the meantime, I'll pray for you."

Sam clenched her jaw and fought the urge to roll her eyes. She'd given up on prayers a long time ago. As far as she could see, they didn't do anything. And she needed Bella to get her butt home.

The bathroom door opened behind her, and Aubrey rejoined them and took the flyers from Deputy Marshal Roberts.

"If you don't have any more questions or concerns, we'll be on our way." Deputy Marshal Roberts slid his hands into his pockets.

"No. We're good for now."

He turned and opened the front door. "It was nice to meet you."

"You too." Except it wasn't. It was a reminder of her past failures and how she'd ended up in Renegade.

She watched the two walk down the sidewalk to the next house, then pulled the phone from her pocket and unlocked it. Her thumb was hovering over Bella's contact picture when she saw her coming from the opposite side of the road.

Sam narrowed her eyes as Bella strolled up the walkway. "Where have you been?"

Bella sighed and entered the house. "I was with my friend."

"The same friend that you were caught vaping with at school?" Sam shut the front door and locked it. She slid the deadbolt over and then engaged the chain lock, just like she'd done every night since finding out who she'd really been working for.

Bella dropped her bag on the ground with a thud. "Her name is Sophia, and we weren't vaping."

"Then why did I get a telephone call from the school?"

"Because we were in the bathroom with the girls that *were* vaping, but we weren't. Guilty by association." Bella dropped onto the loveseat.

"Why were you in the bathroom when you were supposed to

be in class?" Sam moved to stand in front of Bella and crossed her arms.

"Sophia had to go between classes, and the stalls were all full, so we waited. The girls started vaping while she was in the stall. I wasn't going to leave her in there alone."

"Did you tell the teachers that?"

Bella's eyes widened. "Of course not! Snitches get stitches. They don't have WITSEC in high school."

Nausea roiled in Sam's stomach. "I'm not a snitch. Is that what you think?"

Sam had done the right thing when she'd testified, and they'd been *rewarded* with a new name and a new life in a new town. But they were safe here. They were protected from the Mob guys who wanted them dead. Bella was right that she would've had to face the girls at school afterward if she'd told the principal what they'd done.

"This is about more than just being a snitch, Bella. You're not pointing the finger at them when they were caught red-handed. You're clearing your name. If you don't come forward, the teachers will believe that you were vaping too."

"I'd rather the teachers believe that than to cross the Renegade Rebels."

Sam groaned. It had been a while since she'd been in high school, but it seemed nothing had changed. There were still cliques and drama. "Bella."

"I'm not doing it." The teen crossed her arms over her chest.

Sam took a deep breath. "Fine. I'll call the school and tell them."

"For the love of Pete, it's just detention, not the end of the world." She stood up and faced Sam. "Don't you dare call the school and get involved. I don't need you trying to solve all my problems. You'll only make it worse."

Bella stormed to her bedroom and slammed the door.

Sam sank into the recliner. She didn't want to argue with Bella anymore. Not tonight. Not about this. Not when the ghosts of their past were still haunting them. They'd survived Sam's testimony against the Mob. Surely they could survive high school.

What could she do? This could be the beginning of the end if Sam didn't encourage her sister to stick to the straight and narrow. Follow the rules. A tiny step in the wrong direction and it could snowball into more trouble before they knew it. Like official reports on school files, which were just as dangerous as doing well in sports and getting their pictures in the media.

There was so much more at stake than whether Bella was considered a snitch or a cool kid. If she didn't watch herself, she would be noticed.

And if they were discovered, it could lead to their deaths.

Liam stared out the windshield, Sam's image sticking in his mind. She was beautiful, no doubt. But closed off, like she didn't want to let anyone in. Could he really blame her though? She'd had a hard life, and going into WITSEC had only made it harder.

The look on her face when he'd mentioned prayer told him she either wasn't a believer or wasn't on good terms with God at the moment. The last six months of his life couldn't really be compared to her story, but he couldn't imagine facing it alone. Without God to get him through. He couldn't begin to fathom how Sam felt.

"I wish you could have met Isabella. She's smart as a whip." Aubrey's voice pulled him from his thoughts. She looked at the clock on the dash and finished buckling her seatbelt. "That took longer than I expected."

"Okay, I'll take you back to the office."

"That would be fabulous." She smiled.

He turned from the Williamses' street onto another main street. His attention was caught by a high-school-age girl carrying a blue-and-purple chevron-patterned backpack. A backpack he recognized. What was Sophia doing over here?

"Um, see that girl?" He pointed to Sophia.

Aubrey leaned forward. "Yes."

"That's my niece. She's supposed to be at home." He gripped the steering wheel.

"Oh." Aubrey pursed her lips.

"Yeah." Liam rolled down the passenger-side window and pulled the SUV up next to his niece. "Sophia?"

Sophia stopped and stared straight ahead. At what, he couldn't be sure. It was just another residential street. No one out and about.

Liam leaned his left arm on the steering wheel. "Just because you stopped moving doesn't mean I can't see you. I'm not the dog."

He looked at Aubrey. "Sophia has a Chihuahua named Blossom. She'll look right past you if you stop moving. It's like her eyesight is failing and she can only see movement. Which isn't the case, according to the vet."

Audrey rolled her lips between her teeth to smother a smile. "Sophia."

Her shoulders slumped, and she turned to the SUV, a grimace across her face. "I guess I'm busted."

"Yeah, you are. Get in."

Sophia opened the back door and climbed in, tossing her backpack on the seat. "I can explain."

He eyed her through the rearview mirror. "Oh, you will. Later." He turned to Aubrey. "Aubrey, this is my niece, Sophia. Sophia, this is my coworker, Aubrey Richardson."

Sophia leaned forward and thrust her hand between the seats. "Nice to meet you, Aubrey."

Aubrey twisted in her seat and shook Sophia's hand. "Likewise."

Liam drove back to the office. He wanted to give Sophia the third degree about school and ask why she hadn't gone straight home, but decided to spare Aubrey the sighs and eye rolls that were Sophia's MO.

"That's me right there." Aubrey pointed to a small car parked in the employee lot. "Good night, Deputy Marshal."

"Good night." Liam watched as she climbed into her car, and waited for her reverse lights to come on before he drove off.

"So, she's super pretty." Sophia didn't give him a chance to speak. "Were you on a date?"

"You think I have time for dating?" He didn't, but it went even deeper than that. His life had flipped upside down in the last few months. Could he really open himself up again? Risk letting someone in when everything felt so fragile?

"I know, I know. New town, new job, new dependent. I get it. I ruined your life." She slumped back into the seat.

Liam jerked the steering wheel to the right and pulled the car to the curb. He turned around to face his niece, who was staring at her fidgeting hands in her lap.

"Look at me when I say this."

She slowly raised her face until she was staring at him. He could see the unshed tears in her eyes, and his heart constricted.

"Sophia Daniella Roberts, you did not ruin my life. You mean more to me than you can even imagine."

"What about Giselle? She left once you got custody of me." She folded her arms over her chest. "You probably hate me for that."

"Giselle leaving was not your fault. Things had been rocky for a while." It had been a long time coming, but that didn't make the pain any less. "It just so happened that our relationship ended at the same time. So both of us got a fresh start."

Giselle would probably have blamed the breakup on Sophia, but the truth was, once Sophia had begun playing a bigger part in his life, it'd become clear he and Giselle wanted different things.

"A fresh start where you're a bachelor saddled with a teenager."

"You say saddled. I say gifted. God knows what He's doing." At least, he was trying to trust that was the case—even when it was hard and what God was doing didn't make sense.

"Why would God's gift to you mean my mom is punished?" Her eyes narrowed. "You know that doesn't make sense."

"Soph, your mom's going to jail isn't a punishment from God. It's a legal consequence for the crimes she committed. Every choice you make has a result, and not all results are good. That's why you need to make sure you're making the good choices."

She sighed. "Whatever."

"I can only imagine what you must be feeling. But we'll get through this together." He gave her a reassuring smile and turned back around, pulling onto the street and heading home. "Speaking of choices. Want to tell me about your day? Like the telephone call I got from the school today, and why I found you walking down a street alone when I'm pretty certain I told you to go straight home from school."

Sophia sighed, and he watched from the rearview mirror as she rolled her eyes, just like he predicted she would. "My friend and I weren't vaping in the bathroom. I had to pee, and she waited while I did. The line was long, so we were in there past the bell. The teacher came in and marched us all to the principal's office. She didn't even want to hear our side of the story."

He narrowed his eyes at her.

"It's the honest truth." Her gaze darted around, an action that indicated she could be lying.

She'd gotten into some trouble at her old school when her mother had first been arrested. Mostly mouthing off and being disrespectful. There'd been a few verbal altercations with students who were giving her a hard time about her mom.

He understood how she felt. Being talked about was frustrating, especially when what was being said wasn't true. But the teen had to learn to control her temper and her mouth. If she stuck it out with him, he could repay his sister for taking the blame for him, and ensure Sophia had a chance to thrive.

"Soph, if your friend was vaping, it's okay to let her take the fall. You don't have to go down with her. It's putting you on a slippery path."

"I already know all of this. You've given this lecture before." She crossed her arms over her chest and looked out the window. "I'm not gonna wind up in jail because I had to pee."

"What were you doing in that neighborhood?" He'd revisit the vaping later.

"My friend lives over there. She wanted to show me around, so we went walking."

"Who's your friend?"

The phone rang before she could answer. Thomas Mahar's name flashed on the screen on the dash. Liam had known Tom for years. When Liam's sister was arrested, Tom was the person Liam had gone to first. Tom had helped him navigate the transition from uncle whose niece was staying with him to guardian of said niece.

Tom had called him this morning to pray over him before starting the new job. He was probably calling to see how the day had gone. Liam pushed the button on the steering wheel.

"Hello, you're on speakerphone," he warned. Not that Tom would say anything that Sophia shouldn't hear.

"Hey, Sophia. How's it going?" Tom and his wife, Beth, had become close to Sophia since Liam had been awarded guardianship. Part of that was because Sophia had been a frequent guest at their house while Liam was on fugitive apprehension, working his last few weeks while waiting for the transfer to Renegade.

"It's okay." She turned to stare out the window.

"It has been an eventful day." Liam clicked the turn signal and directed the vehicle onto their road.

"That's why I called. Making sure you didn't die of boredom going from an adrenaline junkie to desk jockey." Tom chuckled.

"Nope, still kicking." Thank God Albright and the fugitive were still kicking too. "Look, we're about to pull into the house, and I need to figure out dinner. Can I call you back in a bit?" He also wanted to talk to Sophia some more.

"Yeah, no problem."

"Okay, talk to you later." He hit the button on the steering wheel to disconnect the call.

He'd barely stopped the SUV in the driveway before Sophia was out and racing to the front door.

Maybe more talking wasn't on the menu for tonight.

Nothing about their new life in Renegade made sense. He was in over his head parenting a teenager. Tom's call reminded him to give it to God and lean on Him. God was working everything out to their good.

Liam closed his eyes and sent up a prayer, handing it all over to the One who saw how this ended.

FIVE

S AM PULLED THE PENCIL FROM HER MOUTH AND marked the number of boxes of nitrile gloves in the supply closet. They'd need to order two more boxes of extra large, three boxes of large, and one box of medium. She set the clipboard and pencil on the shelf and moved on to inventory the gauze.

Anything to keep her mind off Bella and yesterday. Or the handsome marshal who'd shown up at their house. She shook her head, pushing his face from her memory. There was no room for a man in her life, especially the man who was in charge of her safety.

The story about the vaping was plausible, but was it the truth?

Sam had no reason to doubt Bella, but what if she was lying? Their lives depended on both of them minding their p's and q's. All it took was one small mistake, and the perfectly crafted life the US Marshals had created for them would crumble. Was she overthinking? Would a simple issue at school snowball into DeLuca finding them? She couldn't be sure. She'd never thought going to work for a sick man would end with her in WITSEC.

"Williams." Greer's voice out of nowhere startled her.

Sam's hands slipped, and the boxes of gauze rained down on her feet. She sighed as she squatted to clean up the mess she'd made. "Where did you come from?"

"Well, when a man loves a woman and they get married—"

She reached out and grabbed his pant leg, making sure she grabbed leg hair, and gave a quick pull.

"Ouch." He jumped back.

"I know that part." She looked up at him from her crouch. "I just meant you scared me."

Greer bent over and rubbed his shin. "You're so violent."

She rolled her eyes and gathered the gauze. "Did you need something? I'm busy."

He grabbed the clipboard and looked at it. "Isn't this Dean's chore this week?"

"Maybe." She stacked the gauze back in the closet. "I needed something to do."

"In that case, you can do my chores as well, yeah?" He tossed the clipboard back on the shelf. "I don't mind."

The station siren blared. "Engine 4, respond to a commercial fire alarm. Marshal Samuel Dennison High School."

Sam's breath caught. Bella's school.

She raced to the engine and donned her turnout gear.

Once everyone was loaded, Murph pulled the truck onto the road.

Lieutenant Fischer turned to them. "Looks like an alarm activation from the pull station on the west side of the building. Evacuation in progress. No sign of smoke or fire."

Sam's leg bounced on the engine floorboard. It was just a pulled alarm. There was no danger. "That's Bella's school."

Greer clapped her on the shoulder. "I'm sure she's good."

Sam stuck her helmet under her arm and nodded. "She better be."

Murph turned the engine onto the school's road, and Sam studied the structure, looking for any signs of fire. "Everything looks normal."

Except for the students calmly filing out of the school and congregating in class groups on the field so their teachers could do roll call. Sam strained to see if Bella was among them.

Fischer shoved his door open. "Williams, take the panel. Greer with me and Captain Bennett on three-sixty. Murph, you man the engine."

The ladder truck pulled in, and its crew unloaded, having gotten their instructions from Captain Bennett.

Sam hoofed it past a line of students streaming out the main entrance, none of them her sister, and made her way to the school office. Using the universal key she kept clipped to her belt loop with a carabiner, she unlocked the panel and flipped the plastic cover. She juggled the helmet and squeezed her radio. "Pull activation Zone 3, west side of the building. No smoke alarms tripped."

"Three-sixty complete and clear," Captain Bennett said. "Williams, silence the alarms. Let's clear the building. Engine, take the west. Ladder, take the east."

Sam silenced the audible alarms, then met Lieutenant Fischer and Greer at the entrance. Captain Bennett would be with the school personnel.

"We'll sweep out." Lieutenant Fischer gestured down the hall, indicating they'd start here and work out. He readied the thermal imaging camera and took the lead, sweeping to determine if there were any hidden fires, like in walls or lockers. Meanwhile, Sam and Greer followed behind, listening. Greer carried the Halligan and axe as they moved along. If a thermal area was detected, they would have the iron tools to gain entry to the area to check for certain.

The trio walked methodically through the west side of the school. No smoke was visible, so every few feet, Sam took a deep breath, sniffing for the smell of fire.

They reached the end of the hall. "No thermal indicators, and no visible or olfactory indicators," Lieutenant Fischer relayed to the ladder team. "West wing cleared."

Even with the building evacuated and the hall cleared, unease settled in Sam's stomach. Putting eyes on Bella would be the only way to relieve it.

"Ten-four. We're checking the auditorium now," Dean advised.

"Williams, you go reset the panel, and I'll go talk with the captain," Lieutenant Fischer instructed.

"Yes, sir."

Sam repeated the process of opening the panel and did the necessary steps to reset the system. She was locking the clear protective case when the principal and school resource officer entered the room.

"We can look at the surveillance and see who pulled the alarm," the resource officer said as he passed by Sam and into his office, leaving her standing in the lobby with Principal Duncan.

Sam had confidence in the SROs in Renegade. They'd know who had set off the alarm before the engine pulled out of the lot.

"Sam Williams?" Principal Duncan asked.

"Yes, ma'am." Sam stopped and looked at the principal, who was in her forties, dressed in a silk blouse and black trousers.

"I thought that was you." The woman smiled.

Principal Duncan knew Sam and her team because Station 4 had been to the high school a couple of times on career day and for other school activities. She couldn't recall a time they'd been here on an official fire call though.

"Please thank your team for responding. We greatly appreciate it."

"Our pleasure." Sam meant it. It was not only their job but something they took pride in. The ability to keep Renegade's youngest citizens safe.

"Ms. Duncan," the SRO called from his office. "I've got the video pulled up."

"Excuse me. I have an issue to deal with." Ms. Duncan gave a tight smile and disappeared into the SRO's office.

Sam locked the panel box and exited the office.

Students filed slowly back into the building. Sam moved against the flow and made her way outside to where the others had reconvened at the engine.

"Good job, everyone." Lieutenant Fischer often praised his team after a job was finished.

Sam shucked her turnout coat and tossed it on her seat.

"Here comes the principal." Greer nodded to the approaching woman.

Sam turned around to find a scowling Ms. Duncan.

The principal looked at Sam's boss. "Lieutenant Fischer, would it be possible to have a moment with Ms. Williams?"

Was the panel not properly reset? Sam replayed the reset in her mind. No, she'd done everything she was supposed to do.

"Uh-oh, someone's in trouble," Greer whispered beside her.

She rolled her eyes. "For the love of Pete, Greer. We're adults."

"Yeah, adults being called to the principal's office." He snorted. The man actually snorted.

"As long as another call doesn't come in, we've got a few minutes." Lieutenant Fischer nodded his approval.

"Ms. Williams, follow me, please." Ms. Duncan turned on her heel and walked back into the school.

Dread filled Sam's stomach as she followed the principal like the troublesome kid Greer had insinuated she was. "May I ask what's going on?"

"Unfortunately, it appears that the fire alarm was pulled by two students. One of whom was your sister."

Heat flushed Sam's body as her nails bit into the palm of her hand. "Are you certain it was Bella?"

Isabella knew the importance of Sam's job—every firefighter's job—and that false alarms were a waste of time and resources. Sam had lamented it a couple of times over the last few years. She thought Bella had more sense than that.

"There is video of Bella and another student around the fire alarm, talking, before the alarm was pulled. Bella opened the cover, and the other student pulled the lever."

Sam pinched the bridge of her nose. "Unbelievable."

The principal entered the office waiting area, giving Sam no choice but to follow. Bella was seated in the chairs next to another girl about her age with shoulder-length strawberry blonde hair that accentuated her full cheeks.

The girl sat stiff and silent, staring straight ahead, while Bella sat hunched over, not making eye contact with anyone.

"Isabella, in my office please." Ms. Duncan led the way down the hall to her office. Sam and Bella fell in line behind her.

"Have a seat, ladies." Ms. Duncan shut the door and took her seat. "Isabella, would you like to explain to us why you pulled the alarm?"

Sam turned her full attention to her sister and waited for her response.

Bella looked down at her hands clasped in her lap. "I don't know."

Sam narrowed her eyes at her sister. "A—Isabella! What do you mean you don't know?"

Bella didn't bother to look up from her hands. "I don't know."

"'I don't know' isn't an answer," Sam ground out. Of all the people in the world to pull the fire alarm, it had to be the sister of a firefighter. "There's an explanation, and I want it now."

Bella just shrugged.

"Are you sure you don't want to tell us anything about what happened?" Ms. Duncan prodded.

Sam glanced at Ms. Duncan, who had a knowing look on her

face. There was more to this than she had told Sam in the hall. The other girl sitting outside the office was probably the real trouble-maker.

"I pulled the fire alarm. That's all." Bella looked up and met Ms. Duncan's gaze.

"Very well, then. Please have a seat in the lobby while I talk with your sister."

Bella stood and left the room. The door clicked behind her.

"I'm sorry about this. Bella knows better than to pull the alarm."

"It is my belief that Bella was coerced into pulling the alarm." Ms. Duncan folded her hands on her desk.

Sam sat back in the seat. Was Bella covering for the girl sitting next to her? Was this the same friend that had gotten her into trouble yesterday?

Sam closed her eyes and sighed. It was time for the "be careful who you surround yourself with" talk again.

Liam stood by the wall to the left of the defense table in the Renegade Federal Courtroom, close enough to lunchtime that his stomach was rumbling. But that's what happened when breakfast got skipped because a certain teen forgot to get more cream cheese for the bagels.

It had only been three hours since he'd clocked in, but it felt like he'd already pulled an eight-hour shift. Time was passing slowly. That was the difference between high-stakes, adrenaline-filled fugitive apprehension. What was it Albright had said yesterday? They were government-funded stalkers? He had crossed the bridge to government-funded babysitter.

The defendant, dressed in prison garb, hands attached to the chain circling his waist, sat next to his attorney.

As court security, Liam divided his attention between the

defendant and the gallery, watching for anything suspicious. Like signs the defendant was going to try to escape or a spectator was going to do something dangerous.

The hearing droned on, sounds whomping together around him until it all washed into one mass. Liam didn't spend too much time trying to understand the legal jargon that was thrown around by the attorneys.

One of the double doors to the courtroom opened. He tensed and waited for whoever it was to enter.

Henry "Hank" Green, another older marshal assigned to Renegade, stepped in and took a seat at the back of the gallery.

Liam reached up and tapped the coiled earpiece. The courthouse radio traffic had continued throughout the hearing, so he wasn't in here because of a threat, or Liam would know about it.

Maybe he had a personal stake in this hearing or the one that was going to come up next.

Liam focused back on the defendant and others in the room. Judge Mullinax banged the gavel on his desk, ending the hearing.

The defendant and his attorney turned to speak with each other. Hank made his way over.

Liam stepped forward, preparing to take the defendant out of the courtroom and back to holding.

"Deputy Marshal Roberts," Hank said. "Supervisor Howard sent me to take your place."

"Is something wrong?" Changing marshals in the middle of the day was uncommon.

"Everything is fine here, but the school called for you. Said it was important." Hank grabbed the defendant's arm as he stood from the table.

Liam looked at the phone on his belt. One missed call from the school. He had never even felt it vibrate. His pulse raced.

"Before you panic, Aubrey confirmed that it was not a situation that couldn't wait until you were done with this hearing." Hank led the defendant to the courtroom's secure exit.

"Thank you." He pulled the phone from his belt and checked the voice message that had been left. *Please call me back.*

He dialed the school's number. "This is Liam Roberts, and I'm returning Ms. Duncan's phone call." He ran his free hand through his hair.

"One moment, please." He was placed on hold, and digitized elevator music belonging in the 1990s started to play.

After a few moments, an unfortunately familiar voice answered: Principal Duncan. "Mr. Roberts?"

"Yes, ma'am."

"I'm afraid I'm going to have to ask you to come pick up Sophia. She isn't sick or injured, but she is in trouble. Your niece pulled the fire alarm today, causing the school to evacuate and the fire department to respond."

Liam rubbed his hand down his face. "She did?"

"We can discuss it in more detail when you arrive, but I'm afraid I'm going to have to suspend Sophia for three days."

His stomach turned. "I'll be there as soon as I can."

Liam disconnected the call and stormed down the hall to the Marshals' office. He pushed through the door.

Aubrey looked up from her computer screen. "Everything okay?"

Liam shook his head. "My niece has gotten herself into some trouble, and I need to pick her up from the school."

"I'm sorry to hear that." She frowned.

"Me too." He used his key card and let himself into the secure portion of the office. He walked down the hall to Supervisor Howard's office to let him know he had to leave for the day.

Two days on the job and he was already having to take personal time off.

It took twenty minutes to get to the high school, and Liam used all of that time to pray for wisdom and discernment for everyone involved. His chest tightened at the sight of a fire engine parked in the bus lane.

What had Sophia been thinking?

He locked the SUV and marched inside. Sophia sat in a lobby chair next to a girl whose brown hair hung down and obscured her face. She appeared to be about two inches shorter than Sophia and roughly the same weight, but that was a crude estimate since she was seated and slumped over a bit. Neither of them looked happy.

Because they'd been caught?

He opened the lobby door, and the girls looked up. He knew the other girl's face. He'd seen it on his computer yesterday afternoon. Isabella Williams.

Voices from his left drew his attention to a narrow hallway, where a woman in a blouse and slacks walked side by side with Samantha Williams.

Liam and his niece had been in town less than a week, and Sophia had managed to get herself tangled up with one of his witnesses. He closed his eyes and took a deep breath.

"Thank you, Ms. Williams," the principal said.

"Yes, ma'am." Samantha stopped in her tracks when she saw him in the lobby. Then she wiped the shocked look from her face and turned to her niece. "Bella. Let's go."

"Mr. Roberts, you and Sophia can follow me." Principal Duncan gestured down the hallway.

At the mention of his name with Sophia's, Samantha's head whipped in his direction.

He ignored Sam's stare and looked at Sophia. "Let's go." He jerked his head in the direction of the principal.

Principal Duncan closed the door once everyone was in the room. "Please, have a seat."

Liam glanced at Sophia, who sat in the office chair, arms crossed over her chest, a frown pulling down her face. He took the vacant seat next to her.

Principal Duncan took a seat at her desk and faced Sophia. "Would you like to tell us why you pulled the fire alarm today?"

"Because I could," Sophia grumbled.

"Sophia." Liam gritted his teeth.

"What? She asked for a reason."

"It's time to be serious." He fisted his right hand.

"I am being serious. I pulled the fire alarm because it was there and I wanted to. So punish me and let's move on." She settled into the chair.

"Sophia, you can wait in the lobby." Principal Duncan waited for Sophia to excuse herself and close the door behind her.

"I'd like to apologize for this. I don't know what's going on with her." Liam rubbed his hand on his thigh. "I mean, I know, but I don't know how to handle it. This all stems from her mother's arrest and the upheaval it has caused."

"I understand she's had a very difficult time lately. Something no teenager should have to deal with."

"I agree, but that doesn't change the fact it's a situation she *has* to deal with. Hard isn't an excuse." He couldn't do anything about the past. All he could do was help her now and make sure both their futures were better.

"Have you considered getting Sophia some counseling?"

"It has been suggested to me, yes." A few of his friends in Virginia had mentioned it. He hadn't had the time to find anyone since the move.

"Mental health is an important part of human well-being. None of us like the stigma associated with it, but if a person was sick or broken, treatment would be sought to heal them. Mental health is no different."

Liam said, "It is something I'd like to pursue if it will help her. We're new to Renegade. Do you have any suggestions?"

"I do have a list of counselors who work with the school. They come in and do therapy sessions on-site, so students don't miss too much of their classes. It's also discreet, so the students don't have to feel embarrassed."

"I appreciate it." Liam relaxed a little.

"Now, back to today's events. Because of the seriousness of the action, Sophia will be suspended for three days. We have video footage of the two pulling the alarm."

Interesting.

"That being said, I'm not certain that they weren't coerced into doing this."

"You think someone forced them into it? Or dared them?"

"The footage shows the two of them meeting with a group of students just before pulling the alarm."

Sounded like they needed an investigation. "And have you questioned those students?"

"I can't give you any details, but we are looking into the possibility. Obviously, Sophia has decided not to incriminate anyone else. Maybe that's something you can get her to talk to you about."

Would she talk to him if she was in trouble? He hoped she would. "We'll sit down tonight, and I'll see if I can get her to open up to me."

"I'd appreciate it if you would let me know what you're able to find out. If it involves others in my school, I want to address it."

"Yes, ma'am. I certainly will."

"Even though she is suspended, Sophia will still have access to her online classroom and is expected to maintain her studies." Ms. Duncan slid a piece of paper across her desk. "This is her login information, which she should already have."

She opened one of her desk drawers and pulled out another sheet of paper. "This is that list of counselors."

Liam accepted the papers. "Thank you."

She smiled. "Thank you for coming in. Please let me know if there is any other way we can assist you and Sophia."

"I will." Liam opened Principal Duncan's office door and walked the short distance to the lobby. Sophia had returned to the seat she'd occupied when he arrived.

"Time to go." He used his no-nonsense marshal voice to convey how serious he was.

He and Sophia were going to have a come-to-Jesus meeting tonight.

SIX

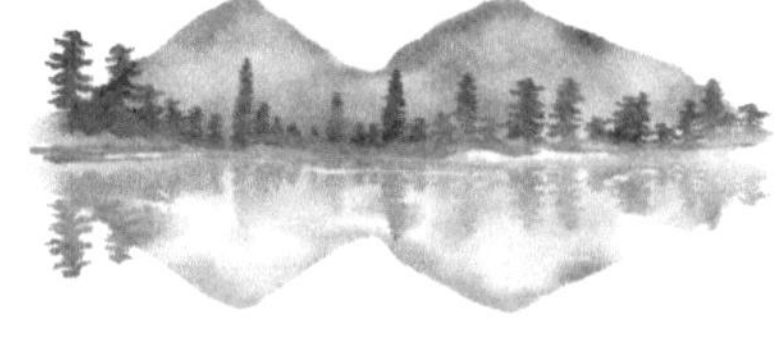

BELLA. WHAT AM I GOING TO DO WITH YOU?" SAM pulled her phone from her turnout pants, pulled up the Renegade Ride app, and looked for a ride back to the station. Estimated wait time—ten minutes.

Engine 4 pulled out of the school's lot, and Bella leaned against the wall as Sam laid her turnout coat on the sidewalk. She'd told Lieutenant Fischer what was going on, and he'd given her the rest of the day to handle the situation.

There was one problem with that—they were stranded at the high school. Bella couldn't ride back to the station on the engine, and Sam couldn't leave her here alone.

"Do you know how dumb that was? You wasted time and resources. What if there was another emergency, a real one, and we couldn't get to it because we're here dealing with teenage shenanigans?" Sam stared at her. "And let's not forget how embarrassed I was when I found out someone pulled the alarm and that someone was my sister. I'm a firefighter, Bella."

The doors to the school opened, and Liam and his daughter stepped out. He wore a scowl that probably matched Sam's.

She stopped reading Bella the riot act. Now was not the time or the place to discuss this. She needed to cool down, and they needed privacy.

"Sophia." Bella stood up straight.

Sophia slowed and opened her mouth.

"Truck, Sophia." Deputy Marshal Roberts stopped in front of Sam.

The friend Bella had gotten into trouble with was the daughter of a US marshal. Not just any US marshal, *their* US marshal.

Well, he wasn't theirs—he was just their handler.

At least she wasn't the only one to face professional embarrassment. It couldn't be too fun to have a criminal for a child when you were in law enforcement. But now she knew who the bad influence was between the two teen girls. Things were starting to make sense again.

Sophia rolled her eyes and stomped off to the SUV parked in front of the school.

Liam called after her: "I'll be there in a minute." He looked from Bella to Sam, then stuck his hand out. "Liam Roberts."

Bella stood up straight and gawked at him. "You're our new marshal?"

Sam shot Bella a look to shut her up. Sam had told Bella about their new handler last night. Most of the WITSEC business was done between Sam and Deputy Marshal Butler, but Bella had needed to know there was a change in case anything happened. She had the emergency number like Sam did.

Sam studied Liam's hand before she took it. Even though they'd met last night, no one knew that. In a life filled with secrets, she had to keep up pretenses, because anyone could be watching them. "Sam Williams."

He looked around the parking lot and then down to her turnout pants and the turnout coat next to her. "Do you two need a ride?"

"We're fine. I've called a ride." Even if she hadn't, under the circumstances, accepting a ride with him wouldn't be wise. It would only give the two girls time to conspire and get their stories straight.

Sam already knew exactly what had happened. Sophia was a bad influence.

Liam looked at Bella and then back to her. "May I speak with you? Over there." He gestured away from Bella.

"Yes." She turned to Bella. "Do not move."

Bella grunted.

They walked far enough away that Bella couldn't overhear their conversation. Liam turned his back to Bella and faced Sam. "I have no idea what's going on here." His voice was low.

"This is uncharacteristic for Bella." Sam leaned a little to the right to keep her sister in line of sight.

"Sophia had been in a little bit of trouble before we moved here, but nothing like this."

So his daughter *was* a troublemaker.

As if he could read her mind, he narrowed his eyes at her. "She's had a rough six months. Her mother just went to prison, and now she's living with me. Up until this point, it's all been attitude and back talk."

She felt sorry for Sophia, but just because she'd had a rough time didn't excuse her behavior.

"Bella hasn't been in trouble at all." She crossed her arms over her chest.

Deputy Marshal Roberts rubbed his hand down his face and sighed. He pulled his wallet from his pocket and produced a business card. "I'll be talking to Sophia and getting to the bottom of this. I'd appreciate it, if you find anything out from your sister, that you'll let me know. My personal cell phone number is on there."

She took the business card and looked from it to his face, which was etched with worry—the same worry she felt for Bella every single day. The professional wall between them thinned. "I'll let you know what I can find out. If your daughter is more forthcoming as well, please let me know."

He looked to the SUV and then back to Sam. "She's my niece. Not my daughter."

Interesting.

"Have a good afternoon." He walked past her to his SUV.

Sam returned to Bella.

"So . . . he's hot." Bella all but drooled at the retreating marshal.

Sam would not give Bella the satisfaction of being distracted. No matter how handsome the marshal was. And he was, but that was hardly the point here. Her sister had messed up in a major way, disrupting everything and putting them on the Marshals' radar in a way they shouldn't be.

"The fire alarm, Bella. Really?" She gestured at her turnout pants and coat on the ground. "You wasted the department's time today. For what?"

She shrugged her shoulders.

Sam's eye twitched. Bella was pushing it with this tactic of not telling her that she'd been peer-pressured into doing it by her new friend.

A car turned into the parking lot, and Sam's phone beeped. "Our ride is here. I want you to think about today long and hard on the way home. We are going to talk about this." She picked up her turnout coat and stormed off to the waiting car.

Bella didn't say a word the entire time. Not in the Renegade Rides car. Not at the station. Not on the car ride home. She went straight into the house and to her room.

Sam grabbed a couple bottles of water and gave Bella a few moments to get settled. They were going to sit down and talk about this. She just hoped her sister would be forthcoming.

She knocked on Bella's door.

"Come in." Bella's voice was muffled.

Sam opened the door and found Bella curled up on her bed, hugging a pillow to her chest. Tear stains on her cheeks.

"May I?" Sam gestured to the bed.

Bella sat up and moved over.

Sam handed her a bottle of water and took a seat. "We need to talk about the fire alarm."

"I'm not going to change my story." Bella took a drink from her water and put it on the nightstand.

"Is whoever you're protecting worth it?"

Bella glanced at Sam and then hugged the pillow back to her chest. "I'm not protecting anyone. I wanted to see what would happen if we pulled it."

"You know there are cameras all over the school, right?"

"So?" Bella scoffed.

"Principal Duncan knows who you talked to before pulling the alarm. The same girls that were vaping in the bathroom yesterday. Did they tell Sophia to do it?"

"No. We did it because we wanted to." She fell back onto the bed, her legs dangling off.

The water bottle crackled in Sam's squeezed hand. "You're not doing yourself any favors with this. Sophia and these girls aren't your friends. They're only using you."

"You don't know what you're talking about."

"Are they blackmailing you?" Sam's gut tightened. "Because whatever it is, we can deal with it."

Bella sat up straight. "What are you even talking about?"

"If they have incriminating photos or details about you and are threatening to release them, we can figure it out."

Bella huffed. "That's not it."

"Then what is it?"

Bella opened her mouth, closed it, then hugged her pillow tighter. "I have nothing else to say."

Sam sighed and held out her hand. "Well, until you decide you want to tell me the truth, you're grounded. Hand over your phone and laptop."

Bella groaned. She pulled her phone from her pocket and then retrieved her laptop from the small desk in the corner.

"You're grounded to your room. You can only go to school and back. *When* you can go back to school." Sam went to the door. "Tonight, you can have your computer back. For homework *only*."

Bella remained silent.

If she could just get her sister back on track, things would be fine. Sam wished there was an instruction book on raising teenagers, but she knew one thing: Bella was done hanging out with that bad influence.

"Sit on the couch. We're going to talk." Liam opened the door, and Sophia stomped inside.

The teen flung herself down onto the couch. Blossom came running into the room and jumped up into Sophia's lap.

Liam lowered himself to the coffee table in front of Sophia, leaned forward, and rested his forearms on his thighs. "I know what you told Principal Duncan and what Principal Duncan told me. Now *you* tell me what happened."

Sophia's face hardened as she crossed her arms over her chest. "I wanted to see what would happen, so I pulled the alarm."

Liam clenched his jaw. "You and I both know that's not the truth."

"The truth is subjective."

Liam took a deep breath. "Why are you protecting these people?"

"I'm not protecting anyone."

"It's on video, Soph. You talked to a group of students, then you and your friend Isabella pulled the alarm."

"They asked for directions to science class."

Liam closed his eyes and counted to ten. "From the new girl, who's been at school less than a week?" This was not going as planned. "I can't help you if you won't help yourself."

"I don't need your help."

"You think you're grown, but you're not. You're fourteen, Sophia. If you keep going like this, you're going to end up like your mother. Is that what you want?"

Sophia's face reddened. "Then I guess I'm just like my mother. Why did you even bother to take me in? You should have just sent me to juvie and saved yourself the trouble." She grabbed Blossom, stood up, then raced to her bedroom.

Lord, help me. I have no idea what I'm doing. Give me guidance.

He stood up, then walked to Sophia's door and knocked. "Soph, that's not what I meant. Open the door and let's talk."

"I don't want to talk right now." Her voice cracked.

Liam grabbed the door handle and started to turn it. But stopped. She didn't need him barging in on her and forcing her to talk. That wasn't going to do anything but make the situation worse. She needed time to calm down. And honestly, he needed time to figure out how to approach this. He'd give her some more time. But eventually, they were going to talk.

He thought about calling Tom and asking him for advice, but he didn't need to burden his friend with any more of his troubles. What he needed to do was see what kind of help he could get here in Renegade. He pulled the list of counselors from his pocket and stationed himself on the couch with the laptop.

An hour later, he had researched all of the suggestions and narrowed them down to a few prospects. He'd let Sophia make the final decision. She was the one who would interact with them.

He knocked on her door. "Sophia."

Silence.

He knocked again.

The door opened. Sophia stood on the other side, wrinkles pressed into her face where she must have slept on something.

"Can we talk?"

"I don't have anything else to say."

"Well, I do." He jerked his head to the front room. "Five minutes."

She sighed and disappeared into her en suite bathroom.

He sat on the couch and waited for her to join him.

Exactly five minutes later, she plopped down next to him.

He stared straight ahead. "I'm sorry about earlier. I do not think you are your mom. I'm sorry if that's what you thought I meant. I don't want to see you end up like her. Soph, you're smart, and you have a bright future ahead of you. Don't let some loyalty to people you barely know get in the way of that."

She looked so much like her mother at the same age. The age when she'd first gotten into trouble. And it hadn't even been her fault. She'd taken the blame for something she hadn't done, and that had set her on a path that'd led to her current predicament.

He looked at her. "You've been through a lot for someone your age. I'm worried about you, and I don't know how to help you. It has been suggested that you see a counselor."

She chewed her bottom lip.

He handed the list to her. "All I ask is that you look it over and think about it."

She gingerly took the paper from him.

"I know you're not telling me the complete truth about what happened at the school. But you did pull the lever, and you've been suspended from school. And for that, you're in trouble here as well."

She sighed.

"No electronics except for schoolwork. I'm home for the rest of the day today, but tomorrow, your phone will stay on the kitchen counter and be used only for emergencies." He narrowed his eyes. "Real emergencies."

She pulled her phone from her pocket and handed it to him.

Unfortunately, they lived in a day and age where landlines were almost nonexistent. Since he hadn't had one installed yet, he didn't want to leave her without a means of communication.

"You can use your laptop right now to look at those suggestions." He nodded to the list lying on the couch next to her. "Then you can write apology letters to Ms. Duncan and the fire department for wasting time and resources."

He stood and headed toward the kitchen, giving Sophia some space. When he looked back, her jaw was clenched and she was fidgeting with the list of names. He kept going. Hopefully, she'd come to him if she wanted to talk.

Were there any books or articles that detailed the cost of running on a false alarm call? If he could sit Sophia down and show her exactly how much it would cost the citizens of Renegade for her dumb stunt, that would be something he could use to teach her about the consequences of her actions.

Maybe Samantha Williams could answer those questions.

Their lives had crossed in an unofficial capacity thanks to two teenage girls acting out. No, despite the fact he'd given her his personal cell number, she was still his witness, and he should limit contact to official business.

This wasn't covered in his training.

God, why did You bring me here?

He prayed silently for wisdom and guidance.

Because if he failed, if this spiraled out of control . . . the safety of Sophia and his two witnesses was at risk.

He couldn't let that happen. Not on his watch.

SEVEN

SAM STIFLED A YAWN AS SHE DUNKED THE OVER-sized sponge in the sudsy bucket of water in the engine bay.

She'd been thinking about how the stunt Bella had pulled yesterday could affect their future. How long would it take to pack their belongings?

Since entering WITSEC, Sam had made every effort to live as a minimalist, so if they ever had to leave at the drop of a hat, there wasn't much to pack. If they had to move and change their identities because Bella got into trouble, the Marshals would remind them of that fact at every turn.

Thinking about picking up and leaving filled her with grief. She'd have to cut ties with her colleagues, people she considered family. They'd be safe, but she'd be brokenhearted.

Even though the sun was shining and there was a nice breeze, perfect for washing the engine, a sense of foreboding hovered over her. She felt much like that donkey who kept losing his tail in the old stories. She wasn't a psychiatrist, but she was pretty certain he suffered from clinical depression.

She attacked the front bumper of Engine 4, water splashing on the driveway. Nothing distracted a person like scrubbing bug guts off their engine. Not the worst option, though running on the treadmill or doing some weightlifting would be better. Only, it was wash day, and there was still a job to do. Exhausted or not. She'd worked on less sleep.

As punishment, Sam had given Bella a list of chores to keep her busy. She was getting more than just a suspension from school. It was not a vacation—Sam would make sure of it.

Murph walked around the front of the engine with the water hose. "If you scrub that any harder, you're going to wear a hole in the chrome." Murph was six foot two with red hair, green eyes, and pale skin. Not a fiery red. More of a subdued, darker red.

Sam sighed. "Sorry. I was thinking."

"Isabella?" He rinsed the soap from the bumper she'd just scrubbed.

"Yeah." She tossed the sponge in the bucket and shook the excess water from her hands. Sam looked at her watch. "You think Captain Bennett will be done soon? I might talk to him about some sort of community service for Bella to do. Something around the station that can help her understand the seriousness of what she did."

"Anything you want to talk about?"

"No." She patted him on the shoulder, then grabbed the bucket and took it back to the bay. She'd grab some microfiber towels to dry the engine. Water spots were unprofessional. They took pride in their station and their equipment. The better care they took of everything, the longer it lasted.

The station alarm sounded.

Murph raced back into the bay with the hose. She set the bucket to the side, out of the way, and raced to her turnout gear, lined up against the wall.

"Williams, you're sitting this one out," Lieutenant Fischer yelled across the empty bay.

She'd just plunged her feet through her pants and into her boots.

Was she being punished for what Bella had done? That couldn't be it. She'd been on other fire calls since the incident.

"Why?" She hitched the suspenders over her shoulders.

Lieutenant Fischer stopped in front of her, his face an emotionless mask.

She couldn't discern anything about what was going on in his head, but he looked her in the eye. She wasn't going to like what he had to say.

Finally, he spoke. "The call. It's your house."

Her coworkers gearing up and rushing to the engine faded to the background as her throat constricted. "I have to go."

"I'm sorry, but you can't. Take your car and meet us there." He turned to the engine.

"Please, sir. I won't do anything once I'm there, I promise. Just let me ride along. I'll get there faster that way." If she had to drive herself, she'd be way behind the engine. It could speed, and people moved over for red lights and sirens. "Bella is home alone."

His face hardened as he stared her down. "Get in. But you stand on the perimeter, do you understand?"

"Yes, sir." She climbed into the engine, then pulled the phone out of her duty pants and dialed Bella. Straight to voicemail. She slammed it against her thigh. "Come on, Bella."

Bella was technically grounded from her phone, but Sam had left it at the house in case of emergencies. Surely she would see it was Sam calling and answer.

She dialed again.

Voicemail.

Greer reached over and cupped her shoulder. "Everything is going to be okay. We got this." Determination covered his face.

She gulped.

They might have the fire, but what about Bella?

At the end of the day, all they had was each other. If she lost her sister, she would have nothing worth holding on to.

Sam couldn't explain it, but the ride to her house blinked by. Yet, at the same time, it felt like it took an hour.

The house was fully engulfed. Her stomach sank and her eyes burned. Her living room was perfect fodder for a flashover. An enclosed room with synthetic, combustible materials.

How it started and what was going on weren't the most important things at the moment though. Where was Bella?

Sam's gaze swept the bystanders as Murph staged the engine. Bella wasn't among them. She dialed Bella's phone again, but with the same result.

The teen's voicemail connected. "Hey, it's Bella. Why are you calling me? Send a text." Followed by a beep.

"Bella." Sam's voice cracked. "Call me immediately." She scanned the street in both directions. Maybe the teen had gone for a walk or something.

While her coworkers unloaded and started fighting the fire, Sam went to each person standing around and asked if anyone had seen Bella.

Nausea grew with each no.

Sam held her stomach and watched the flames devour her home. Black spots danced in her vision. Where was her sister? She bit her lip until a metallic taste filled her mouth.

Finally, the flames were put out, and the guys were able to make entry into the house. She rushed toward her front door, but Lieutenant Fischer grabbed her around the waist and held her back.

"You can't go in there. You know it."

She fought his grip. "I've got to see."

"Samantha. Stop." He wrapped her in a restraining bear hug. "Let them do their jobs."

"It's not their house or their sister." She screamed and fought harder. "Let me go."

His hold on her tightened. He picked her up, spun around, and carried her to the road.

She kicked her legs and struggled to free herself. "You know something!"

She tried to twist and look her superior in the eye. Why hadn't she bothered to put on a radio? She'd know everything by now if she'd heard the update on what they'd found inside.

"I'm sorry, Sam." He set her on her feet. He didn't have to say the words, because she heard it in his voice.

"No!" Her knees buckled and she crumpled to the ground. "It's not her!"

The tears she'd been fighting since the call had come in flowed down her face as her heart shattered in her chest.

"I'm sorry, Sam. There's a body in the house."

"Your Honor, we request a continuance." The prosecutor leaned his fists on the table in front of him, sweat on his hairline and the back of his suit collar.

Deep into their third hearing of the day, the judge looked as tired as Liam felt.

Liam adjusted his tie. It had been a long time since he'd had to wear one on a regular basis, and this was going to take some getting used to. But at least he wasn't in the hot seat.

The defense attorney jumped to her feet, glaring at the prosecutor. "On what grounds?"

"The witness has failed to show up as he promised." The

prosecutor pushed his glasses up his nose. "I assure you we're looking for Dr. Torres, Your Honor."

Liam's head whipped around to glance between Judge Mullinax and the prosecutor. Torres? The guy whose file Howard had. Samantha's landlord. That couldn't be a coincidence, right?

Where was the guy?

"Wasn't he under the protection of the US Marshals?" The judge leaned forward, glancing at Liam as if he should've told his boss to hand over the file regardless.

"He was supposed to enter WITSEC today after providing his testimony. Every effort is being made to locate him."

"We object." The defense attorney addressed the judge. "A delay in proceedings violates my client's right to a speedy trial."

"In the interest of both justice and maintaining the defendant's rights, I'll grant a continuance. You have three days to produce your witness."

"Yes, Your Honor," the prosecutor said.

Liam didn't want to be in the assigned marshal's shoes. The internal investigation would be a nightmare if something more than a flat tire or cold feet had happened to the witness.

"I want an update," Judge Mullinax addressed the prosecutor.

The door to the secure entrance opened, and Hank slipped in and crossed to Liam. "You're needed upstairs. There's an issue with one of your witnesses."

One of his witnesses? Liam nodded and exited the way Hank entered. He followed the secure hallway to the Marshals' office.

Supervisor Howard was waiting for him when he entered. "Roberts, Renegade PD called, and the Williamses' house is fully engulfed in flames. You need to get there now."

"I'm on my way." He turned around and took the security elevators to his vehicle.

He responded Code Three, lights and sirens, to ensure he made it to the house quickly. There was no telling what had caused the fire, but this wasn't just a house. Not to Sam. Not to Bella. Not to him. If something happened to Bella . . . Sophia would fall apart. And honestly? He might too. He'd never had a witness die, and didn't want to be the first marshal with that distinction.

His phone rang. *Private Caller*. He clicked the button on the steering wheel. "Roberts."

"Uncle Liam?" Sophia's voice was barely audible over the sirens.

"Sophia?" He turned the volume up. Why wasn't she calling him from her cell phone? He'd taken the phone privilege from her but had left it at the house for emergencies.

"Can you come pick us up?"

Loud music played in the background.

"Who is us, and why aren't you at home?" He clenched his jaw.

He was on duty and on his way to an emergency situation, but his niece needed him. How was he supposed to choose? It wasn't like he could call someone else to pick her up. They were new in town. He didn't have any friends or family here. After visiting the Williams sisters with Aubrey a few nights ago, he had the feeling she wouldn't mind, but he didn't want to impose. This was his problem.

"Me and Bella are at the corner of—" She paused. "Oak and Fourth Street."

"Isabella Williams is with you?" The decision was made for him.

"Yes."

"Are you two safe? Did you sneak out of the house?" And yet she'd called him, even knowing how much trouble she would be in. Something was wrong, but she'd done the right thing.

"We're fine." She sounded exasperated. "We're at a gas station. They let us use the phone."

And she didn't think he'd want to know why?

"Stay where you're at. I'll be right there." He killed the lights and sirens and busted a U-turn, gripping the steering wheel until his fingers were numb.

What were the two girls doing out in the first place? He couldn't speak for Isabella, but Sophia was grounded. And why was Isabella's house on fire? Unease swirled in his gut.

He pulled the vehicle into the parking lot of the gas station, jumped out, and headed to the entrance.

Sophia and Isabella pushed through the glass door and met him in the parking lot.

"I'm sorry, Uncle Liam." Sophia at least had the good sense to look ashamed.

"Get in the vehicle." He marched back to the driver's side.

The girls slid into the back seat of the SUV, tossing their backpacks on the floorboard.

"Buckle up." He pulled out of the parking lot and activated the lights, foregoing the sirens so he could question the girls. "I need to know right now where you two have been and how long you've been gone."

In the rearview, the two girls looked at each other. Something passed between them.

"This is extremely important. Do not lie to me. This is more than just breaking the rules and sneaking out." He slowed at a stoplight and made sure all vehicles yielded to him, then accelerated quickly.

Sophia sighed. "We met at the skate park a couple hours ago."

"Isabella, what were you doing before you left your house?" He glanced at her in the rearview mirror, wondering if she'd left the stove on or something.

"Um, nothing? I mean, my sister gave me some chores. I did a few of them. I was supposed to be back in time to finish them before she got home, but—"

Sophia nudged her, and Bella stopped talking.

Liam made a mental note to dig into that later. First, he needed to determine what she knew about the fire. "Were you burning candles or did you leave the oven on?"

He slowed at another intersection.

"No, why?"

"Because when Sophia called me, I was on my way to a fire at your house."

He was opening a can of worms in front of Sophia. She would surely have questions as to why he knew their house was on fire and why he would be responding to it. He'd have to think about an excuse to give her later. Right now, information was needed.

Isabella leaned forward. "Is everything okay?"

"I don't know anything other than there is a fire. Did you notice anything odd or unusual in the neighborhood when you left?"

"No." She shook her head. "Oh my gosh, does my sister know?" Isabella's eyes widened.

"I assume so. Why don't you call her and let her know we're on our way?"

Isabella looked at her lap. "We didn't take our phones with us."

That explained the gas station phone, but not why they'd called him.

"Why did you leave your phones at home?" But he already knew the answer.

"So if you checked my location, it would show I was still at home," Sophia answered.

"What were you doing there instead of being home?"

"Oh no." Isabella leaned forward and stared out the windshield.

Several fire engines lined the block. Hoses were strewn about, and firefighters were busy doing their jobs. Smoke hung heavy in the air. Bystanders lined the sidewalk, watching the commotion.

Liam pulled his SUV to the blockade, threw it in Park, and turned to address the girls. "Stay in this vehicle and do not leave. Do you understand?" He looked at both girls and waited for them to acknowledge his instructions.

"Yes, sir," they said simultaneously.

He jumped from the vehicle, pulled his shield from his belt, and flashed it to the officer manning the perimeter. "Deputy US Marshal, where's incident command?"

The officer pointed to a trio of firefighters gathered on the sidewalk in front of the house. He recognized the commander from the shooting at the motel. This was Sam's team. They'd been the ones to respond to her house.

He scoured the scene as he made his way to the trio, trying to find Sam, but there was no sign of her. Of course, some of the firefighters were still in full turnout gear, and he couldn't see their faces through their face shields.

One of the men saw him approach, an older guy with dark curly hair. "Can I help you?"

"Deputy US Marshal Liam Roberts." He showed the man his badge. "I'm checking in on a situation that may involve people I'm concerned about. Nothing official here—just hoping you can help me out."

Liam had to dance a fine line. He needed to determine what was going on without alerting anyone to the Williams sisters' status as witnesses. If people assumed they were personal friends because the teens were also friends, this would be a whole lot easier.

"Captain Bennett. Good to meet you." He motioned to the house. "Residential fire. There's a body inside and clear signs of an accelerant used. We'll know more after the investigation that will confirm whether it's arson."

Had Sam come home early from her shift? His thoughts turned to Isabella in his SUV. Were they looking at a murder investigation? He blinked rapidly at the scene in front of him.

"Do we have an identity on the victim?"

It was surely too soon to know for certain, but the question had to be asked.

"Not an official one. One of our firefighters, Samantha Williams, lives here with her fourteen-year-old sister Isabella. Right now, Isabella is unaccounted for." The man's voice cracked. "Sam is over there. Devastated."

Liam whipped his head in the direction the captain pointed. She sat on the curb, wrapped in the arms of another firefighter, who'd shed his coat.

"Isabella Williams is not inside that house." He turned to go to the duo seated on the curb.

"How do you know?" Guarded hope filled the captain's face.

"Because she's in the back seat of my SUV." He walked toward where Samantha was seated. "Ms. Williams?"

The man looked up and glared at Liam. "Now's not the time." His arm tightened around Samantha, whose face was buried in his chest and shoulders, shaking with sobs.

"It's not Isabella." The words rushed out of his mouth. He needed to end her suffering. Because he knew what it was like to lose someone. His sister had gone to prison, but it was still a type of grief—Sophia didn't have her mother in her life, and he didn't have his sister here with them.

Samantha whipped her head around and stared at him with bloodshot eyes. "What did you say?"

"Bella is in my SUV."

Samantha pushed herself free of the man and stood up, looking around wildly. She grabbed his forearm. "Take me to her. Now."

"This way." He led her to the vehicle.

Before they could reach the blockade, the door opened, and Isabella stepped out.

"Bella!" Samantha raced to her sister and grabbed her in a bear hug. "I thought you were dead."

Isabella wrapped her arms around Sam. "Yeah, well . . . I wasn't home."

"Where have you been?" Samantha pulled away and framed Isabella's face with her hand. "I called. You didn't answer."

"I'm sorry. I didn't know." Tears streamed down Isabella's face.

Samantha pulled her back into a hug. The two sisters stood embracing each other, sobs racking their bodies.

Liam turned away, not wanting to intrude on their private moment.

If Samantha and Isabella Williams were standing in front of him, then who was dead inside their house?

The hair on his neck stood on end. He turned back to them, scanning the area. This had to be considered a targeted attack. "I'm sorry to interrupt," Liam said, "but for the sake of your safety, we need to get you both out of here."

EIGHT

SAM RELUCTANTLY LET GO OF HER SISTER. SO many emotions bombarded her as adrenaline flowed through her system. Bella was safe.

She opened the SUV door. Bella climbed in, and Sam followed her. Once they were buckled, Sam pulled Bella to her and wrapped her arms around her. "I love you."

"I love you too," her sister whispered back.

Deputy Marshal Roberts climbed into the driver's seat and set the SUV in motion. His niece sat in the passenger seat up front, staring out the window. She sniffed and wiped her face with her sleeve.

Sam reached up and patted the teen on the shoulder. "We're all okay."

"It's okay, Sophia." Deputy Marshal Roberts reached over and awkwardly patted the girl's forearm.

"I know." She pulled her arm away.

The poor man was way out of his league. Sophia didn't need a pat—she needed a hug. It was a lot for someone her age to take in.

Sam squeezed Bella tighter. Thankfully, they were both alive and unharmed. As much as she wanted to be angry about Bella sneaking out, today, at least, she was glad the teen had been disobedient. Who knew what would have happened if Bella had been home? There could so easily have been a second body added to the scene.

Sam wouldn't go there. It hadn't happened, so there was no use in dwelling on it. She needed to focus on what they were going to do now. Everything they owned had just gone up in flames. They only had the clothes on their backs.

She knew what needed to be done immediately—contacting the landlord's guy, Danny, and making a claim on her renter's insurance—but what did this mean for them and WITSEC?

"Deputy Marshal Roberts?" She looked at the stoic man in the driver's seat, finding herself oddly reassured by the steady presence. Not that she'd ever been the kind of woman who needed a man around so she could feel safe. It wasn't like that with marshals anyway.

He glanced at her in the rearview mirror, those blue eyes warm. "You can call me Liam."

"Liam, you wanna tell me where we're going?"

"To the Marshals' office to figure everything out."

She nodded, then laid her head on top of Bella's and closed her eyes. Then realized she'd left the scene without speaking to anyone. She needed to let Lieutenant Fischer know she'd taken off, so he wouldn't worry about her.

She sat up straight. "Does the Captain know it's not Bella in the house?"

Liam nodded. "I spoke with him before I found you."

She pulled her phone from her duty pants and sent a text to the group chat, letting them know she and Bella were okay and that she'd be in touch.

Liam pulled the SUV into the courthouse parking lot and around to the back. Without a word, he led the way through a private entrance and up to the US Marshals' office.

"Samantha and Isabella, have a seat in here." Liam opened the door to an empty conference room. "Sophia, with me."

Sam watched Liam and his niece walk out of the room and disappear down the hall.

The room he'd left them in had a conference table and eight chairs. There were posts about the Marshals Service on the walls. A television was mounted in the far corner.

She wasn't sure how long they had before Liam came back, but she needed to get the truth out of Bella.

"I need you to tell me everything that happened today." Sam looked her sister in the eyes. "Don't worry about if I'm going to be angry or if you're going to get into trouble. That doesn't matter right now. What matters is figuring out why someone set our house on fire."

Bella's eyes widened. "Like they did it on purpose?"

Sam nodded. She was going to leave out the part about the dead body for now. "Start from when I left this morning."

Bella sat in one of the rolling chairs and put her hands in her lap. "I got up at six thirty like I normally do. I started working on some of the chores you'd left for me to do. I got the refrigerator cleaned out and the dishes done. Then Sophia called." She bit her lip. "I know I wasn't supposed to answer, but I did."

Sam kept her face neutral, not wanting to show anger or disappointment. If she kept her emotions off her face and out of her body language, maybe Bella would be more forthcoming.

"She said her uncle was making her write apology letters to the school and fire department."

Interesting. Sam hadn't thought about that as a punishment. She tucked it away for future use.

"Don't get any ideas." Bella rolled her eyes. "We hung up, and I did some more of the chores. The kitchen was done." She reached up and grabbed a strand of hair and started twisting it around her finger. A nervous habit she'd had since she was a little girl.

"Go on." Sam nodded.

"There was a group text from our friends. They had ditched school and wanted us to go hang out with them at the skate park. We thought since we weren't in school anyway, we might as well go for a little bit. I told them I had to be back in time to finish my chores."

So she'd deliberately disobeyed the rules and gone to hang out with friends. And those friends were skipping school.

"You met these friends at the skate park?" Sam kept from bouncing her leg, a nervous habit she had picked up years ago after losing control of her life.

"Yeah, Sophia and I met them at the park, and we hung out for a bit."

"How did you end up in the back seat of the marshal's SUV?"

Isabella rolled her lips between her teeth just like Sam did sometimes.

Sam sat still and silent, willing Bella to continue with the truth.

"They wanted us to go somewhere else, so we rode with them. Then they wanted to do something we didn't want to do, so Sophia called her uncle because we didn't have a way to get back across town."

"And he picked you up?"

She nodded.

"What did these friends want to do that you didn't?"

Bella pursed her lips.

"Come on, Bella. You didn't do it, so you can't get into trouble for it." Sam leaned forward.

Bella shook her head.

"Knock, knock." Aubrey Richardson stepped into the office with a couple bottles of water and wrapped muffins. "I know it's been a rough day. I thought you might need a drink and snack." She set the goodies on the table.

"Thank you," Sam said.

Bella reached out and grabbed one of the muffins, then picked at the plastic wrapping.

"Deputy Marshal Roberts will be with you in a moment. Do you need anything else?" Aubrey asked.

Right now? They needed a lot. Because they had nothing. Sam's stomach sank. Where were they going to live? "No, we're okay for now."

Aubrey smiled. "Okay, just let me know if you need anything."

Sam turned back to Bella once the administrative assistant was gone. "Did you have any friends over while I was out?"

She shook her head.

"This is serious, Bella." Sam might regret telling her this, but the teen needed to understand the seriousness of the situation. "There was a dead body inside the house."

Bella's mouth fell open, and the muffin she'd picked up fell from her hand and landed on the conference table. "No. I promise. No one came over."

"When you left to meet your friends, was there anyone in the neighborhood you didn't recognize?" Sam couldn't restrain her leg any longer and let it bounce.

Bella closed her eyes and thought a moment. "No, I didn't see anyone." A tear slid down her cheek. "Are we in danger again?"

Sam had asked for honesty, so that's what she was going to give her sister. "I don't know."

Liam shut the door to his office, leaving Sophia alone. No matter how he tried to ask her about everything that had happened, she only said that they had met up with some friends at a skate park and moved on to a place nearby, where he'd picked them up.

She'd called him because their friends had wanted to go somewhere else and Bella hadn't wanted to go.

He knew the story from there. He'd grill her more later, but right now, he had to deal with the Williams sisters. And before he could do that, he needed to go see his boss.

He knocked on the closed door of Supervisor Howard's office. "Come in."

Liam opened the door and stepped inside the medium-sized office. Everything was neat and tidy, including the man behind the desk. Papers in a stack beside the keyboard. No coffee mug.

Howard said, "Roberts. What do you know?"

"I have the Williams sisters in the conference room. The fire chief said the blaze at their house is a result of arson and that there was a dead body inside."

Supervisor Howard let out a whistle. "Do the sisters know anything?"

"I haven't talked with them yet."

"Why not?"

"A situation has come up, and I wanted to speak with you before I went to them."

"Oh?" Supervisor Howard raised his eyebrows.

"Remember the telephone call I got from the school about my niece the other day?" When Supervisor Howard nodded, Liam continued. "She and a friend pulled the fire alarm at school. That friend was Isabella Williams."

Supervisor Howard's face hardened. He'd been out of town the last couple of days, and with Deputy Marshal Butler on suspension, it meant everyone was pulling double duty.

"You were in a meeting this morning, and I got the call about the fire before I could talk to you."

"Can't say that I've ever run into something like this in my career." Supervisor Howard steepled his fingers in front of his chin.

"There's more. I was on my way to the Williamses' house when my niece called. She and Isabella Williams were together and needed a ride from a gas station on the corner of Oak and Fourth."

Supervisor Howard sighed.

"I wanted you to be aware of this before I went in. I understand if you need to assign a new marshal to the case."

"Under normal circumstances, I think that would be prudent, but unfortunately, I don't have anyone else to assign them to. Butler and Albright are out, and Glover has a full schedule with her witnesses and working fugitive apprehension." Supervisor Howard stood. "Does your niece know details about the Williams sisters?"

"I haven't told her anything, sir. However, I picked them up on my way to the house fire, so she might be wondering how I knew their house was on fire and why I was going there."

"Has she asked yet?"

Liam shook his head.

Howard put his hands behind his back and walked to the window. "I'm sure we can spin a believable tale to explain that." He turned back to Liam. "Go talk to the sisters and see what you can find out. Report back to me."

"Yes, sir."

Liam exited the office and made his way to the conference room.

Isabella sat with her head on her arms on the table, but Liam didn't figure she was asleep. Sam was beside her sister, massaging her temples. His heart ached for them.

He knocked on the doorframe. "Ladies."

Two sets of eyes focused on him.

"Sorry to keep you waiting." He pulled out a chair and took a seat. Standing over them could intimidate them. Something he didn't want to do. So he got on their level. He looked from Samantha to Isabella. "Can you tell me about this morning?"

Sam shifted in her chair. "I got up at five like I usually do and ran on the treadmill. Left the house at six and was at the station by six fifteen. I did not see anything suspicious when I left. I haven't noticed anything suspicious or out of the ordinary in the last few weeks. Other than Bella's school trouble and getting a new marshal."

Yeah, she'd done this before.

She folded her arms over her chest. "I've followed protocol like I have been the last six years. No contact with anyone in our past, and I stay away from social media."

"Okay." Liam turned his attention to Isabella.

She huffed. "Same. I didn't see anyone unusual when I left. Yes, I've gotten into trouble the last couple of days, but I haven't talked to anyone I used to know, and I haven't told anyone about us being in WITSEC."

"Not even Sophia?" Liam held his breath.

"Not even Sophia. I know the rules." She, too, crossed her arms.

He released his breath. At least his niece was still in the dark on that one.

Samantha looked at her sister. "Vaping in the bathroom and pulling fire alarms unnecessarily are also against the rules, but you still did that."

"For the last time, I wasn't vaping." Bella sighed. "Pulling the fire alarm is different. It won't kill us in horrible ways."

"People have been trampled to death during fire alarms, Isabella." Samantha put her palms on the table.

"Sorry."

"Okay." Liam wanted to interrupt before this got too far off topic. "Have either of you received any threats recently? Weird or unusual telephone calls, text messages, or emails?"

Both shook their heads.

"Are either of you seeing anyone?"

"As if." Isabella pouted. "She won't allow me to date."

"You're too young. You need to focus on school." Samantha pinched the bridge of her nose.

Liam agreed with her, but fighting that battle with Sophia was another story. He looked at Samantha. "How about you?"

"No. I'm forever single thanks to my poor decision-making skills." She sighed.

Something he had in common with her. Choosing Giselle had been one of a list of poor choices he'd made.

Was Sam referring to the decisions that had led to her going into WITSEC? Or had there been more boyfriends?

"Can you clarify that for me?" He tried not to sound personally interested in the answer. Just professionally. "Are you saying you have some ex-boyfriends that could potentially be a problem?"

"No. I was talking about Matt Marino."

Liam filed that one away. "Do either of you have a reason to suspect that your covers have been blown?"

Samantha looked at Isabella. "I have no reason to believe that. Bella?"

The teen shook her head. "I promise, the only thing I've done that's against the rules is the fire alarm and sneaking out."

"What happens now?" Samantha asked him.

"Right now, there's no proof that this incident is in any way related to your past. Apparently, there's an arsonist running around in Renegade. This could be as simple as the arsonist making a mistake and paying dearly for it."

Still, if he was going to do his due diligence with this, Liam would need to do a deep dive into the DeLuca case to see where those pivotal players were these days.

Sam sighed. "The Arson Investigation Unit will know more once the body in the house is identified."

Liam nodded. "I'm leaning toward this being an isolated incident and not related to your case. I don't want to risk blowing your covers or moving you until we have proof otherwise. So for now, it's just an unfortunate occurrence."

"An unfortunate occurrence," Sam deadpanned.

Liam's face heated. "I'm sorry. That was a poor choice of words."

"I understand what you mean." She smiled weakly. "I'm assuming since we're playing that angle, it will be up to me to handle our living arrangements and property loss."

"I can help you as much as possible in an unofficial capacity." Unfortunately, no US Marshals services or funds could be used.

Hopefully, the investigation wouldn't reveal a targeted attack. Or, for their sakes, a personal one.

Sam stood and rubbed her hands on her turnout pants. "Can you take us to the station, or do I need to figure that out on my own as well?"

He grimaced. "I said the Marshals wouldn't help right now, but I can still do a few things. I can take you to the station. And if you'd like, I know a church that has a donation closet that can help you and Isabella with some clothes and toiletries for now."

It wasn't much, but every little bit helped.

Sam's face pinched.

"It's Orange Street Church, isn't it?" Isabella piped up.

"It is," he answered.

"I've been there a couple of times. The people are really nice." She smiled.

Sam's brow was still furrowed, but she nodded. "We'd appreciate it if you could connect us with the church."

She didn't really seem all that appreciative—more like reluctant. Did she have an issue with that particular church or just church in general? If so, maybe this would be a step in the right direction.

"Let me grab Sophia, and we can be on our way." He turned and looked at Isabella. "Just because she's my niece doesn't mean she knows anything about how the three of us are connected. My job is strictly confidential. I haven't told her anything. I expect you to keep it the same, okay?"

It wasn't that he didn't trust Sophia. He honestly didn't think she would do anything to purposely put her friend in that kind of danger. But he'd seen it happen before. In his line of work, a simple slip of the tongue could have deadly consequences.

Bella nodded solemnly. "Yes, sir."

As soon as they were in his vehicle, Sam pulled out her phone and started messing around on it. He assumed she was trying to locate a place to stay. Heaviness filled his stomach.

The teenagers whispered quietly in the back seat. Liam wanted to call the church, but his phone was connected to Bluetooth, and he didn't want to have the conversation broadcast on speaker phone. Especially when he'd decided he would donate a little bit of extra funds to help the closet with the monumental task it was about to undertake.

"Uncle Liam?" Sophia asked from the back seat.

He glanced at her in the rearview mirror. "Yes?"

"Why don't we have Sam and Bella stay with us?"

NINE

SAM BIT HER LIP TO KEEP FROM LAUGHING. Sophia's question had caught Liam just as off guard as it had her. Mr. Straightlaced Marshal was *flustered*, and it was disarming how she'd noticed.

"Uh—" He glanced at Samantha, a deer-in-the-headlights look on his face.

"Our house is perfect," Sophia said. "Bella can stay in my room with me, Sam can sleep in your room, and you can have the couch. Bella and I are the same size, so we can share clothes and everything." Excitement tinged her voice.

"Except underwear. I want my own," Bella added.

Sam had to agree about the underwear, but not about the roommate status. "I don't think that's a good idea." Sam saved Liam from being the proverbial bad guy. "The two of you have gotten into trouble together recently." She turned in her seat to look at the teens. "Plus, I'm sure your uncle has a lot on his plate as a US marshal, and he doesn't need two extra people running around his house. I won't make him sleep on the couch."

"Oh, he doesn't mind. That's the gentlemanly thing to do." Sophia waved her hand in dismissal.

Liam coughed. The poor man.

The phone vibrated in Sam's hand. She looked at the message from Dean.

Saved by her bestie.

"Thank you for the offer, but we're going to have to pass. We've got another place to stay."

If this whole situation wasn't such a tangled mess, she might have considered it. But for both her and Liam, there were professional lines that needed to be maintained. Not to mention the two girls had gotten into trouble together recently.

"Where are we staying?" Bella asked.

"Dean and Cass are going to let us stay at their house."

"Joy." The word was coated in sarcasm.

"I thought you loved Charlie and Bobby." Sam typed a quick thank-you to Dean.

"I did. When they were *babies*. Now they're annoying four-year-olds. Did I tell you Charlie had a frog in his pocket the last time we were over there?"

"No, but I was there when Cass found it." Sam smiled at the memory of her friend pulling the frog out of her son's pocket.

Bella might not enjoy the boys as much as she used to, but they would be a good distraction in the midst of everything going on right now.

Liam pulled his vehicle into the station parking lot. The bay doors were open, and her coworkers were standing at the entrance, waiting for her arrival. Dean must have told them they were on their way.

Liam parked the vehicle in front of the public entrance.

Sam climbed out of the SUV and waited for Bella to join her before trudging toward the bay.

"Sam." Dean was the first to approach her. He wrapped her in a hug. "Cass will be here in a few minutes."

"She doesn't need to pick me up. I have a car, and I know where you live. She didn't have to come all the way over here." Dean and his family lived thirty minutes away, outside of town. She didn't need to be stranded there with her car here.

"It's no trouble. Plus, the boys have some energy they need to burn, and what better place than the firehouse?"

Isabella joined them.

"Bella, you gave us all quite a scare." He gave her a quick hug.

"I'm sorry." She hugged him back.

"We're just glad you're okay." Dean stuck his hand out to Liam. "I'm Caleb Dean."

Liam and Sophia had followed them into the station.

"Liam Roberts." He shook hands with Dean. "My niece, Sophia."

If Sam wasn't mistaken, that handshake lasted a fraction of a second too long as they sized each other up.

Dean and Cass were the first people she and Bella had met when they'd moved to Renegade. Dean had taken her under his wing when she'd started at the station. He was like the older brother she'd never had.

"Thank you for bringing Bella home earlier. We thought she was the one inside." Dean gritted his teeth.

"No problem." Liam stuck his hands in his pockets. "Any idea whose body it was?"

Dean shook his head. "Not yet. We put the fire out and went back on call. Fire marshal, police, and forensic pathologist are still out there."

Sam's throat constricted. Everything they owned was gone. They literally only had the clothes on their backs. Her knees buckled, and she grabbed one of Liam's arms to keep from falling.

His muscles tensed beneath her palm. "Whoa." He steadied her with the other hand. "Are you okay?"

No, she wasn't okay. Far from it. "Must be the adrenaline wearing off."

"Come on, Sam, let's get you inside." Dean grabbed her other arm and led her into the dayroom.

Greer jogged over and handed her a bottle of water. "Here. Can I get you anything else? Have you eaten?"

She loved her crew. They were the family she'd never had. Sure, there was constant ribbing and friendly competition, but when one of them needed something, they all stepped up.

She shook her head. Food was the last thing she wanted right now. The thought of it made her nauseous.

"What about you, kiddo?" Greer asked Bella.

"I could use a snack." She shrugged.

Bella seemed to be taking today's events in stride, which was good. Of course, she hadn't been exposed to as much emotional trauma as Sam. She hadn't spent what had felt like an eternity thinking her sister was dead. Grief had a tendency to drain people. Emotionally and physically.

Bella followed Greer into the kitchen.

Liam cleared his throat. "If you're good, Sophia and I are going to leave."

She nodded. "We're good. Thank you."

He dipped his head in farewell and turned to Dean. The two men shook hands again before Liam and Sophia walked out of the dayroom.

Dean knelt in front of Sam. "Are you sure you're okay?" Concern filled his features.

Her chest tightened, and she took a deep breath, struggling to release the tension. "I'm just tired."

"Sam." Cass rushed into the dayroom, her dark hair streaming behind her. She wore her usual slim jeans with a black T-shirt.

Dean stood up to face his wife, then looked at the bay door. "Where are the boys?"

Cass waved toward the bay, her smartwatch snug on her wrist. "Out there, bothering Holt and Tate."

Zachary Holt and Logan Tate, the firefighters who manned the ladder truck, would entertain the two boys just fine, but Sam wouldn't let them loose in a gas station with a hundred dollars.

"Cass, why don't you drive Sam and Bella home with you? Me and one of the guys will bring her car after shift."

Sam sat up. "You don't have to do that. I can drive."

Dean shook his head. "You think you can now, but I don't think you should."

He was most likely right. She'd had an adrenaline dump, and if her knees buckling were any indication, the crash was coming.

Sam stood up. "Let me at least take off my pants and boots."

"Easy there, this is a public place, and there are children present." Tate galloped into the dayroom with Charlie on his back.

She smiled half-heartedly.

"Giddy up, horsey." Charlie kicked Tate's side.

Tate whinnied and galloped away.

Sam shook her head and went into the bunkroom.

An hour later, she'd had a shower and was now sitting on the couch in the Deans' spacious living room, wearing a department T-shirt and sweatpants she'd swiped before leaving the station.

The aromatherapy mister on the wood-and-glass coffee table emitted lavender. Cass's way of taming the boys for bedtime.

"Here you go." Cass handed her a glass of wine. "I figured you might need this."

"You have no idea." Sam took a sip and leaned her head back.

"So, did that hot guy with the teen I saw walking out of the station have anything to do with you?" Cass wiggled her perfectly trimmed eyebrows, her long brown hair now in braided pigtails.

"Unfortunately." Sam lifted her head and took another sip of wine before resuming the lounging position, propping her legs up on the coffee table.

The image of Liam standing in the dayroom before leaving flashed in her mind. Black slacks, white button-down with the sleeves rolled up to his elbows. He'd tossed the tie and unbuttoned the top two buttons of the shirt at the Marshals' office. The man was handsome, no doubt about that.

"'Unfortunately?'" Cass looked at her expectantly. "You say that like it's a bad thing."

"His niece and Bella have been getting into trouble together at school." She still needed to do something about Bella sneaking out, but she didn't have it in her right now. Bella was alive because she'd disobeyed. It went against everything Sam held dear—but how could she be mad about that?

Cass said, "Shame. But at least he's easy on the eyes."

"Aren't you married?" Sam rolled her head so she could give Cass the evil eye.

"Doesn't mean my eyes stopped working." She stuck her tongue out. Then she stood up from her spot on the recliner, sat down next to Sam, and wrapped an arm around her. "I know today has been rough. I just want you to know that I'm here for you. If you need anything, just ask. I mean anything. You and Bella are welcome to stay here as long as you need."

"Thank you." Sam swallowed the lump of emotion in her throat, closed her eyes, and thought about this afternoon.

Her house had burned down, with a body inside. Liam wasn't convinced that it was related to DeLuca. And she wasn't entirely convinced either. She had followed all of the Marshals' instructions. Bella had misbehaved the last couple of days, but Sam was sure she wouldn't do anything to jeopardize their safety.

So why had the house been set on fire?

And who was dead inside?

Thanks to the fire, she didn't even have the telephone number for the man the landlord had said would take care of anything that came up.

Her eyes burned. She squeezed the bridge of her nose.

The phone in her pants pocket started to vibrate, then the generic ringtone that came with the phone started to play.

She pulled the phone from her pocket and saw *Orange Street Church* flash on the screen. She sighed. Liam had kept his word about contacting the church.

The things she was willing to do for her sister.

Liam and Sophia drove in silence. After leaving the fire station, he'd gone back to the office to do the paperwork associated with today's events. Sophia had sulked in the office chair next to his desk. Now they were on their way home.

He didn't relish leaving Sam and Bella. But they were with friends who would keep an eye on them. Not to mention the people at the church, who would take care of their physical needs. He needed to leave their safety in the Lord's hands.

"Sophia."

"Huh," she mumbled.

"We need to talk some more about you sneaking out of the house."

"Do we have to?"

"Yes. Not only was it against the rules, but it's dangerous." He'd seen a lot of things in his career.

"Whatever." She laid her head on the window.

"You're new in town. You don't know these kids from school. What if they're into something dangerous?"

"Seriously, they're just teenagers like me."

"Yeah, teenagers who were vaping in the bathroom, talked you into pulling a fire alarm, and were sneaking out. If they told you to jump off a building, would you do that too?"

Was he seriously using something he'd heard from adults when he was her age?

She sighed. "No."

"You don't have to give in to peer pressure. You can say no. It doesn't make you a loser or dumb."

"Are we really having this conversation right now?" She turned in her seat to look at him.

"Yes. What exactly were you guys out doing?" His knuckles were white from gripping the steering wheel.

"For the last time, we were just hanging out."

"And why weren't they in school?"

"What do I look like, their parents?" She huffed.

There was more to this story than she was saying. They hadn't just skipped school to hang out.

"What is it going to take to make you realize you're going down the wrong path?" How could he get it through her head that the road she was on would only lead to more trouble?

"How many times are we going to have this conversation?" She crossed her arms over her chest.

"As many times as it takes for you to start making better choices."

He pulled into their driveway.

"I wish Mom was still here. She wouldn't be so uptight."

Pain shot through his chest. That's because his sister had been too busy making her own bad decisions to worry about what Sophia was doing.

"I'm only doing what I think is best for you. I don't want to see you end up hurt or in jail."

"Whatever." She jumped out of the vehicle and ran inside.

Liam leaned his head against the steering wheel. *Lord, help me.*

I don't know what I'm doing. Give me knowledge and discernment. Help me reach her. In Jesus's name.

He sat up and noticed Sophia's backpack was still on the floorboard. Should he search it? She was a minor, and he was her guardian. She didn't really have any expectation of privacy. Except, searching her bag could make everything worse. But what if she was hiding something?

No. He wouldn't snoop just yet. He leaned over and grabbed the bag, knocking it against the steering wheel as he got out of the car. Metal cans clanged inside.

Now he had cause to be suspicious. He unzipped the bag and found several cans of spray paint.

His stomach sank. Just like he suspected. They had been doing more than hanging out at the skate park. He zipped the bag back up and carried it into the house.

He tossed it on the table. "Sophia, get in here."

Sophia slogged in. "What now?"

"Tell me about these." He unzipped the bag and dumped the contents on the table.

Sophia's face paled.

"Why do you have spray paint? In most states, you have to be eighteen to purchase this."

"Why are you snooping in my stuff!"

Sophia had the audacity to be angry? Really? "I wasn't snooping. You left your bag in the car, and I picked it up. It made noises it shouldn't have, so I looked in it." He grabbed a plastic sack and started picking up the cans. "Believe it or not, I am responsible for you. Not just making sure you're fed and clothed but also making sure you behave and learn right from wrong. I don't want to see you get hurt or in trouble."

She rolled her eyes.

"Sit down. Now." He pointed at the kitchen chair. "You are not going anywhere until you tell me the truth."

He pulled a chair out, sat down, leaned back, and crossed his ankle over his knee. This wasn't just about spray paint or rules. It was about keeping Sophia safe—the way he wished someone had kept his sister protected when she'd needed it most. His faith grounded him here, reminding him that God's hand was in the messiness, but that didn't mean he could step back and do nothing.

She plopped into the chair, slouched down, and crossed her arms over her chest. And remained silent.

The only sound filling the kitchen was the ticking of the old clock above the pantry.

Liam remained perfectly still. Sophia, on the other hand, squirmed in her seat and fidgeted with a string on her jeans.

"I have all night." He stared at her. "You forget what I do for a living. I've sat a lot longer and in less comfortable spots. This is like a vacation."

She gritted her teeth.

Minutes ticked by. It was a battle of wills. Sophia was sorely mistaken if she thought he would give up the will to keep her safe.

She sighed. "Fine."

He tilted his head and waited for her to talk.

"We met at the skate park, and the others did some graffiti. But nothing bad or serious. Only on the metal trash cans and picnic tables."

"It was not your property to do anything to, so it is kinda serious. It's a crime, Soph."

Sophia let her head drop to her chest. "I know. That's why when they said they wanted to move on to an abandoned warehouse, I scooped up the cans and we ran."

He narrowed his eyes at her. Was she telling the truth? "And I should believe you because . . ."

"Ask Bella, she'll tell you." Sophia looked at him wide-eyed, begging him to believe her.

"I will. But first, tell me everything, starting from the vaping incident." He leaned forward and placed his forearms on his knees, willing to use every bit of his training. But not on one of the Marshals' most wanted. No, he was going to use it on a fourteen-year-old.

Because it might be the only way to get through to her.

"I've already told you all of that. We weren't vaping. We pulled the alarm. There's nothing else to add." She bit her bottom lip.

"You know you'll get into more trouble if you keep lying. Just tell the truth and get it over with." Could she not see that she was only making this worse for herself later?

"I did tell the truth. We weren't involved in the vandalism." She huffed.

This was impossible. They were just going to sit here and go round and round and only frustrate each other more.

"Go to your room. You can add another two weeks of grounding for sneaking out."

She stood up and turned to walk out the door.

"Soph." He stood, and when she turned around, he hugged her tightly. "I love you. Please know that you can talk to me about anything."

"Okay." She turned and went to her room.

Liam took the time to photograph the spray-paint cans and made notes. He needed to document everything related to them in case this turned into more than just teenagers being teenagers.

When he was finished, he paced the kitchen as thoughts swirled in his mind. Was he making the right decisions when it came to Sophia? What about when it came to the Williams sisters?

Liam had no idea what he was going to do.

TEN

SAM LAY ON THE BED IN THE DEANS' SPARE room and stared at the ceiling. The sun was slowly rising, casting light into the room and onto the TV sitting on the dresser, which hadn't been turned on. Despite the adrenaline crash and relaxing glass of wine, she'd barely slept. Unlike Bella, who lay beside her, snoring.

Several times throughout the night, Sam had rolled over and stared at her sister. For ten minutes yesterday, she'd thought Bella was dead.

Her chest ached at the memory. It hadn't happened—she needed to remember that. Bella was safe beside her. People would say God had been watching out for Bella with how everything had played out. Getting her out of the house.

But if God was watching out for Bella now, then where had He been when Sam was a child and fending for herself because her mother was too drunk to remember she had a daughter? Where had God been when Sam started working for the Mob with no idea she was in over her head?

Why hadn't God been watching out for her?

There was so much that needed to be done today. Getting in contact with her landlord's guy and getting some necessary clothes and toiletries were at the top of her list. But she didn't have it in her to get up. Instead, she rolled over and watched Bella sleep.

Sam may not have carried the girl in her womb, but she loved Bella like she was her own child. She'd been there since the day Bella was born. And yesterday, she'd come too close to losing her. Tears burned Sam's eyes. She closed them and took deep breaths. She'd cried enough last night.

Her thoughts turned to the fire and the dead body. Who was it, and why had her house been chosen? Had it been meant as a warning? Had the Mob found her and Bella?

Sam didn't think so. The Mob didn't do things like that. If those people knew where they were, Sam and Bella would already be dead or captured. The Mob didn't taunt. They acted. Either take out the threat or torture it to teach a lesson.

Bile rose in her throat.

A door shut somewhere down the hall. There was no use lying in bed thinking. She needed to get up and start doing.

She stood up and wrapped her hair in a bun on top of her head, then closed the bedroom door behind her as she followed the light down the hall to the kitchen. The scent of fresh-brewed coffee thickened as she got closer.

Dean was standing at the coffeepot, pouring himself a cup. He glanced up at her before setting his cup down. "Sleep well?" He pulled another cup from the coffee-mug tree, poured some in it, and handed it to her.

She accepted the mug, wrapping her hands around it. "No."

Dean slid the coffeepot back onto the burner and picked up his own mug. "Didn't think you would." He leaned his hip against the counter and took a small sip of his coffee. "My mother is going to come watch the boys this morning, so Cass can help you with whatever you need."

Thickness filled her throat. "They don't have to do that."

"They want to. You and Bella are family."

Sam swallowed the lump in her throat. "Thanks. I have an appointment at the Orange Street Church clothes closet at nine."

Dean quirked an eyebrow. "Church?"

He knew she avoided church, although he didn't know why.

"Well, Bella seemed excited about it." She shrugged.

Dean smirked.

"Don't read anything into it."

"Never." He pushed off the counter. "I gotta get to the station." He clapped her shoulder. "I know it's rough, but it will all be okay."

Sam rolled her eyes. "Yeah."

"Cass should be out shortly. She's enjoying some quiet time before the monsters wake up"—he looked at his watch—"in ten minutes or so."

Sam chuckled. They weren't that bad. At least, not when Sam was around.

"Help yourself to whatever you want in the kitchen. *Mi casa es su casa.*"

"Thanks. I really appreciate it. Hopefully, we'll be out of your hair soon enough."

"Don't worry about it." He set his empty cup in the sink.

Normally, Sam would be on her way to the station as well, but Captain Bennett had given her the day off to deal with this disaster. Since she was here invading their space, she might as well make everyone breakfast.

She opened the refrigerator and pulled out bacon and eggs, making a mental note to replace everything she used in case they had particular plans for the items. She found some pancake mix and food coloring in the cabinet and busied herself starting breakfast.

"Whoa," a tiny voice said from the kitchen door.

Sam turned and found Charlie rubbing sleep from his eyes. Luckily, the boys weren't identical twins. Charlie had blond hair, whereas Bobby's was brunette.

"Good morning, Charlie." She looked at the microwave clock. Dean hadn't been kidding. Ten minutes.

"Are those pancakes?" Bobby pushed past his brother. He stepped up to the counter and peered at the plate. "Why are they green? Did they mold already?" He tilted his head.

Sam suppressed a laugh. "No. I added food coloring to make them special."

"Charles, put your hand down," Cass barked from the kitchen door as Charlie reached for a pancake. "Wait until everything is done."

She sidled up next to Sam. "You didn't have to cook breakfast for us."

"It's the least I can do after everything you've done, and will do, for me and Bella."

"Dean told you? He has a big mouth." She frowned.

"You know you love him." Sam flipped the bacon in one pan and turned her attention to a green pancake on the griddle.

"Let me help." Cass took the spatula and dealt with the pancakes. The two women worked in tandem, finishing the pancakes and bacon, and Sam made fluffy scrambled eggs for everyone.

"I should probably go wake Bella up. She'd sleep till noon if I let her."

Cass looked dreamily at her boys. "I can't wait for that day."

Sam shook her head as she walked down the hall to the bedroom. She opened the door. "Bella—"

Bella jumped and let out a squeal.

"I'm sorry. I didn't mean to scare you. I thought you'd be asleep."

"I wasn't." Bella's voice was strained.

Sam stepped into the room and sat on the bed next to her sister. "Is everything okay?"

Bella nodded. "J-just getting ready to come out."

Sam wrapped her arms around her sister. "We're going to be okay."

Another set of traumatic circumstances to heap on someone so young. Would Bella ever get to live a normal life?

Bella shrugged out of the embrace. "I need to go to the bathroom." She quickly disappeared out the door.

Okay, odd. But who wouldn't be a little off after the last twenty-four hours? Sam returned to the kitchen, where Cass already had the boys seated at the bar with plates of food. "I hope you don't mind that I already served them. They were turning savage."

Sam ruffled Bobby's hair. "I don't believe it."

Charlie shoved a forkful of eggs into his mouth. "What's a savage?"

"Charlie, don't talk with your mouth full," Cass warned.

The boys were already done eating by the time Bella made it into the kitchen.

"I made you a plate." Sam pointed to the plate of food on the counter.

"I'm not hungry." Bella sat down at the bar and laid her head on her arms on the counter.

"You need to try to at least eat a little bit. We've got a lot to do this morning."

"I'm not hungry," she mumbled again into the counter.

"Okay." Sam couldn't remember the last time Bella had skipped breakfast. It must be the stress.

"Here." Cass returned with a pile of clothes and laid them next to Bella on the counter. "They'll probably be a little big, but they'll do until we can get our shopping on."

"Yay," Bella groaned as she grabbed the clothes and disappeared.

"Sorry about her." Sam set her fork down.

"Don't be. It's a lot. Just give her time." Cass started cleaning up the mess her boys had made.

"Let me help." Sam stood.

"Nonsense. Finish eating and go get ready. My mom should be here any time."

An hour later, Sam walked up and down the aisles of clothing in the church's clothes closet. She hadn't thought the clothes would be in this good a shape or that there would be such a good variety. No, she'd expected rags and junk.

They'd been welcomed warmly and given the rules. Pick out five outfits and grab the necessary toiletries. There were all kinds of shampoos, conditioners, and soaps to choose from. A wide variety of everything.

A backpack containing brand-new, unopened packs of underwear and socks, along with toothbrushes and toothpastes, was given to them, and it would be used to carry their new toiletries and clothes.

Sam quickly grabbed two changes of clothes and a pair of pajamas. She'd buy her own clothing later, but she wasn't going to deny that she needed a few things to get by on before she could do that.

Cass trailed behind Bella, holding the clothes she picked out.

"Ma'am, you're not done shopping, are you?" An older lady peered at the few items in Sam's hands. She had to be in her seventies, a long white braid over her shoulder.

"Yes, I don't need much." Sam looked at the things in her hands. "I'm just here for my sister."

"Nonsense. There are plenty of clothes here for you to take as well." She patted Sam's arm.

Sam bounced from foot to foot.

"Nervous?" the woman asked. "Don't be. You're not the first person to walk through those doors full of uncertainty."

Sam forced a tight smile, preparing herself for the usual platitudes.

The woman looked from Sam to Bella and back. "She looks like she's a shopper. Would you like a drink while you wait for your sister?"

"You have no idea. She'd shop until she dropped if I let her." She smiled, a genuine one this time. "I don't need anything right now."

"Why don't you humor an old lady." The woman smiled sweetly.

Sam didn't want to be rude. She looked at Bella, who was admiring some dresses. Cass was with her. Everything would be okay.

"Yes, ma'am." She followed the woman to a small café area just off the clothing section.

"Have a seat." The woman went behind the counter and grabbed a couple bottles of water and a plate of cookies. "My name's Barbara."

"Sam."

"I won't pretend to know what you're going through right now. That's your story." Barbara took a seat. "But I know you've been through a lot. It's okay to be overwhelmed."

Sam opened her mouth to respond, but Barbara held up a hand. "You don't have to explain, and I'm not going to ask. If you want to tell me, I'll listen, but that's not what we're about." She nudged the plate of cookies closer to Sam. "We're called to help others and to spread the good news of Christ."

Sam had believed that good news once. It had been such a relief to learn there was a God in heaven who saw her, who loved her and had come to save her. But in the end, what had that knowledge actually changed for her?

She tapped her fingers on the tabletop.

"I'm guessing you have your doubts about God."

Was her discomfort that obvious? "You'd be correct."

"I was in your shoes once. Not that I know your whole story, but I've doubted God plenty in my life. I've seen some evil things, child." Barbara reached over and patted her hand. "But I've also seen miracles."

The woman's hand was warm over hers, not ice cold like she'd expected an older woman's hand to be. If this woman had seen evil, how could she continue to believe in a good God?

Barbara gave Sam's hand a light squeeze, then let go. "Just like Romans 8:28 tells us, bad things happen, but God will use those bad things for good. Take Joseph, Job, Moses, the bleeding woman, and Mary Magdalene, for example."

Sam folded her hands in her lap. Some of those names sounded familiar, but she couldn't remember much of their stories. Except maybe that Joseph was the one with the colorful coat.

"All great stories that you'll find in the Bible, but the most important one is that of Jesus. He was crucified for our sins, ensuring we have eternity with God." The old woman stood, then went back to the counter and picked something up from behind it.

She placed an old, worn Bible in front of Sam. The cover was ratty, and the pages were crinkled. It had been well read.

"Take it. Read it. Start with the gospel of Mark. Come back if you have questions."

Sam gasped. "I can't take this."

It was much too personal. She hadn't asked for this. It felt far too much like giving a person something dear. Who would do that with a stranger?

"I insist. Consider it a loan." Barbara smiled. "Read over it, and bring it back when you're done."

Sam blinked back tears. The weight of the Bible in her hands felt heavier than it should have. "Thank you."

———

Liam had spent last night seeking the Lord in prayer and asking for guidance on how to proceed with Sophia and Samantha and Bella. He'd prayed protection over all of them.

He'd gotten up early this morning and dragged Sophia out of

bed. She was going to spend the day at the Marshals' office, so he would at least know where she was.

Sophia parked herself in his extra office chair while he did a deep dive into the Williams sisters' case. None of the major players were missing, so they, at least, could be ruled out as the dead body in the house. That didn't mean it wasn't someone connected to the Mob. It just meant he had to do more digging.

He turned his attention to the owner of the property, Dr. Cameron Torres. Liam dug into the file a little, realizing it was the same guy Howard had mentioned. Dr. Torres had been scheduled to testify and, shortly thereafter, go into WITSEC himself. He was the missing witness from the hearing the other day. There weren't any updated notes in the file saying he'd been found. Could he be the guy in the fire?

If so, that would open a whole other can of worms. He made a mental note to touch base with Howard to see if the boss could give him any insights. If the boss wasn't in, maybe Glover knew something about Torres. He looked at his watch. She was out on a fugitive hunt right now—catching bodies.

Since Hank was covering his shifts at court security, Liam decided they should make a run to the fire station to see if he could get any information from them and talk to Samantha about her landlord.

"Let's go." He pushed back from his desk and stood.

Sophia didn't move. She slumped in the chair, staring at the wall. "I used to walk dogs after school," she muttered. "Now I follow a US marshal around like one."

"You brought this on yourself." He grabbed his keys. "I can't trust you to stay home, so you're tagging along."

He led the way down the secure entry and exit this time. This morning he'd made her go through the full security check. It was an experience she'd needed to have. Once they were through, he'd leaned over and said it was much worse in jail. He should have her sit in on one of the criminal trials. Let her see exactly what would happen.

He hadn't let her attend any of the hearings with her mother. He'd wanted to spare her, but in doing that, had he done her a disservice? Yes, seeing her mother go through all of that would have been rough, but would they be in their current predicament if he had let her see it, experience it? Had he inadvertently started the ball rolling that would crash her life like it had her mother's?

Liam's left wrist ached at the childhood memories. The glass of milk he'd accidentally knocked over. His father's rage and the wrist fracture as punishment. He'd simply fallen—that was the story the ER had gotten, anyway. Broken bones healed, but experiences were relived over and over. If Liam hadn't let his sister take the fall for the car, their father wouldn't have turned on her the way he had. He'd been cruel before, but after that, Kayleigh could do no right. And when you spent your whole life being treated like a criminal, maybe it wasn't such a leap to become one.

Lord, forgive me.

"Where are we going now?" Sophia's question pulled him from his thoughts.

"To the fire station."

Sophia's eyes lit up. "Do you think Bella will be there?"

He shook his head. "I doubt it. But if she is, it doesn't mean anything. You're staying in the vehicle."

"Ugh." She crossed her arms over her chest.

"Don't worry. I'll crack the windows."

She turned and narrowed her eyes. "I'm not a dog."

"I know that." He smiled at her. "Seriously though, you will stay in the car. I won't be long."

Her face softened. "Okay."

He pulled the vehicle into a parking spot in front of the fire station lobby and left it running.

Cool air blew over him as he opened the lobby door. A man

in his thirties, dressed in duty clothes, sat at the welcome desk. Liam didn't recognize him from his last few encounters with the station's crew.

The guy's bushy eyebrows rose. "Welcome to Station 4. How may I help you?"

He pulled his badge from his belt and showed it to the man. "Deputy US Marshal Liam Roberts. I need to see Captain Bennett, please."

"Just a moment." The man stood and disappeared through a double-paned glass door.

A few minutes later, the man returned, Captain Bennett on his heels.

"Deputy Marshal Roberts." Captain Bennett stuck his hand out.

Liam shook it.

"Follow me."

Captain Bennett led him into the open area and down a hall to a large office with a leather couch, a US flag on a pole in the corner, and half a dozen commendations hanging on one wall.

Captain Bennett shut the door behind him. "What can I do for you?" He took a seat behind a mahogany desk.

The station must have a pretty nice budget. Liam was not going to be jealous of this man's desk—or the cushy chair he got to sit in. "I wanted to stop by and see if you'd been able to find out anything about the fire at Samantha Williams's house."

The captain leaned back in his chair. "Is this a Marshals matter?"

Liam needed to make sure Samantha's cover remained intact. "Not officially. You see, Isabella and my niece, Sophia, are quite close." Not exactly a lie. They knew each other enough to get into trouble together. "Anyone close to my family is close to me."

Liam was not here on official business. The captain didn't have to share any information. He could tell Liam to take a hike, and

Liam would have to. He just hoped the man would be forthcoming with information.

This wasn't just about the case—it was about protecting the life Sam had built here and proving to himself he could keep those he cared about safe. Success here meant more than a clean file; it meant trust, redemption, and finally, finding peace.

Captain Bennett studied him. "I understand." He sat up and pulled a manila file over in front of him. "Since Sam is part of our station, we aren't handling the investigation, but I can tell you what they've told us." He opened the folder and moved a couple of pages about. "It was definitely arson. There were traces of accelerant all over the house and several ignition points. Whoever did this wanted the house to burn, and with it, the body."

"Any idea whose body it was?"

Captain Bennett shook his head. "The remains are with the forensic pathologist now. We're still trying to get in touch with the property owner. Sam said he stopped by a couple nights ago and said he was going out of town. So far, he hasn't returned any of our calls. She was given a number for someone should she need anything, but unfortunately, that burned with the house."

Liam pulled a card from his wallet. "I'd appreciate it if you'd let me know if anything happens. As a professional courtesy."

Captain Bennett accepted it. "Professional courtesy?"

"Yes, gotta look out for my niece's friends." Liam stood. "Is Samantha here today?" He rubbed his hands on his pants.

"Of course you do." The captain gave him a knowing smile. "She's out today. I'll let her know you stopped by."

He probably thought there was something between Liam and Sam, or that Liam at least wanted something to be there. He was going to allow him to think that. If he thought this was a personal thing, it worked in Liam's favor.

Would it really be so bad if everyone thought they were together? It might actually make his job easier.

As they walked toward the lobby, Dean, Sam's new roommate, sauntered up.

"Deputy Marshal, nice to see you again." He stuck his hand out.

Liam shook it. "How's Samantha doing?"

Dean's grip tightened. Interesting.

They released hands.

"About as good as one can expect. My wife is helping her get things sorted today."

"I'm glad she has people around to help her." Liam tried to gauge Dean's feelings about Samantha. Yeah, he was married, but that didn't mean there weren't feelings there, even if the guy never acted on them. Liam had seen all kinds of things in his line of work, and at this point, he was rarely surprised.

"Yeah, it is. You work with people enough, they become family. She's like the little sister I never knew I wanted."

Liam relaxed a little. "I can only imagine."

He wouldn't know exactly the relationship firefighters developed, because he didn't spend the same amount of time with his coworkers as they did. But it didn't mean he didn't know what camaraderie was. Marshals might not live together for hours, but they did spend hours together and watched each other's backs. Shared life-and-death situations. Similar, but different at the same time.

"I'll let her know you dropped by." Dean waved as he wandered off.

Liam climbed into his vehicle, relieved Sophia was still in it.

She turned slightly in her seat. "Now where?"

"One more stop and then back to the office."

"I should have brought a book." She leaned her head back against the headrest.

"I can arrange that." Surely there were some books floating around the office. Was she too young to start studying the Marshal manual?

He shook his head and pulled out of the parking lot.

The drive to the coroner's office only took ten minutes, hardly giving him enough time to figure out how to be a father to a teenage girl.

"You're going in there?" Sophia's face paled. "There are dead people in there."

"Unfortunately. It's a part of the job." He opened the door.

"How many dead bodies have you seen?"

"Too many." He stepped out and turned to face her. "Stay in the car. Lock the doors."

"Yes, sir." She saluted him.

He shook his head and shut the door. After showing the receptionist his badge, he was escorted to the coroner's office.

"Deputy Marshal Roberts." A petite woman in her early forties, dressed in scrubs, stuck her hand out.

He shook it. "Dr. Falleur."

"What can I do for you today?"

"I was wondering about the body found in the fire yesterday. Do you have an identity yet?"

He had a pretty good idea who the victim might be, and if so, the Marshals would need to investigate how a witness set to testify had been killed.

Hopefully she was willing to say, even if it wasn't technically his case to work. He had a little more freedom with the forensic pathologist than he did with the fire captain. She was less likely to ask probing questions since she was used to dealing with law enforcement.

She rounded the desk and tapped the screen of her tablet. "The body was too burnt for a visual identification. I can tell you it's a man. Luckily, his right hand was curled in a fist under his body. I'm dehydrating his fingers. Hopefully, it'll be enough to get prints."

Then they had to hope that his prints were in the system. If so, it wouldn't take long to determine the victim's identity. Then they'd be a step closer to finding out if Samantha's cover had been blown.

And whether he had to upend her entire life just to keep her safe.

ELEVEN

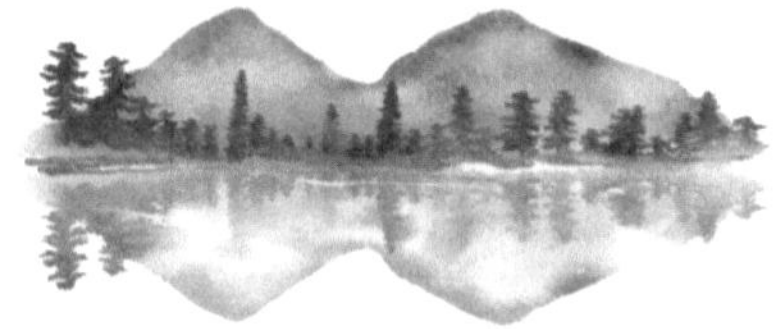

S AM PUSHED OPEN THE STATION DOOR AND held it for Bella. "Come on, sleepy head. Another new day awaits."

Bella dragged herself inside the station and slumped into one of the recliners in the dayroom. "It's so early."

"Bella, you only woke up thirty minutes early." Teenagers were so dramatic.

Sam went to the coffeepot, refusing to admit she was probably as tired as Bella. It was difficult to get quality sleep with her sister tossing and turning beside her.

Bella groaned and pulled the hood of her hoodie over her eyes. She burrowed into the recliner.

"Good morning, ladies." Greer walked into the dayroom, duffel bag slung over his shoulder.

"Why is he so cheery?" Bella pulled her knees to her chest and wrapped her arms around them.

"Because, Bella." Greer gently tapped her on the head. "It's a beautiful day."

She pulled her hoodie back and glared at Greer. "Are you on drugs?"

He grinned. "Nope, they test us."

"Come on, Bella, you can go back to sleep in a bunk room."

The teen groaned and stood, following as Sam walked through the dayroom and down the hall that led to the bunk areas. The station was a fairly new build, so that meant they each had their own small room. A nice cozy room big enough for a twin XL bed, a nightstand, and a wardrobe. Sam chose the bunk room closest to the dayroom so she could keep an eye on Bella.

She could have let her stay with Cass, but Sam wasn't quite ready to leave her alone for too long. The pain and agony of thinking she was dead was still too fresh. If she could see Bella, she'd know she was okay.

Sam tucked her duffel bag in the wardrobe and grabbed a set of bedding. "Here you go." She handed the sheets, blanket, and pillow to Bella, then left to let her make the bed and get some rest.

She normally didn't bother with a bunk room while she was working the day shift. There were occasions she'd make use of it, but most of the time, she spent her free time doing chores around the station.

She skipped the early-morning hubbub in the dayroom. She didn't have it in her to see all the pitying looks or answer all the *How are you doing?* questions.

Everyone clocked in and started the morning checks. They always checked the equipment at the beginning of shift. They'd check it again before the shift ended and make sure everything was restocked and cleaned if needed. The next shift would do the same.

It might seem redundant for both shifts to check, but they couldn't be too careful. A simple mistake could be devastating. This helped minimize as much human error as possible. Perfection was the goal.

"So, the station had a visitor yesterday." Greer stood next to her, checking his SCBA. "A certain US Marshal visitor."

She wanted to be anywhere but here right now. She focused on her tank but didn't respond. He had her telephone number. Why was he checking up on her at the firehouse?

"Came in and talked to Cap." Greer was fishing.

"Probably asking about the fire." She put her SCBA back in the engine.

"That wasn't the only thing he was asking about." He bumped her shoulder. "Wanna tell me about the man with the badge?"

She shrugged. "There's nothing to tell you. His niece is the girl getting into trouble with Bella. Probably trying to do a background check on me and my parenting." She was grasping for a plausible explanation.

"Uh-huh, sure." Greer put his SCBA up. "That's why he looked disappointed when he was told you were off for the day."

"I guess you'll just have to ask him yourself the next time you see him."

"Oh, so you plan on seeing him again, do you?" He nudged her, grinning.

"That's not what I meant." She rolled her eyes at him.

"Whatever you say."

"Shhh. Do you hear that?" She stopped and pretended to listen intently for something.

Greer's brows furrowed as he concentrated. "Hear what?"

"The whistling?" She tilted her head.

He listened longer.

"Never mind, it's just the wind tunnel between your ears."

"Ouch, that hurt."

"You know I love you." She smiled sweetly and moved on to checking the hoses on the engine.

Once the equipment check was done, Sam went to the bunk room to check on Bella. She was still snoozing.

Sam stood in the doorway and watched her sleep. Her chest tightened. What were they going to do now? She'd still been unable to get in touch with her landlord. She had some money in savings, but not enough for the first and last months' rent and a deposit for a new place to live. Not to mention purchasing new clothes, furniture, and all household necessities.

That was if they didn't have to pick up and move again. Something Sam didn't want to do. Not just for Bella's sake. Sam liked it here. Renegade was her home, and her RFD brothers were family. A loud, boisterous family, but a family all the same.

A hand rested on her shoulder. "Everything okay?" Lieutenant Fischer asked quietly.

Sam closed the door to let Bella sleep. "Yes. Just thinking."

"I don't want you worrying about the next steps. Station 4 and all of RFD are here for you."

Her throat clogged with emotion. "Thank you."

She would expect nothing less from her friends. Not out of selfishness but based on their history. There had been several times in the last six years that RFD had banded together for one another.

When the previous fire station chief was diagnosed with cancer, they'd held fundraisers to help with the finances, done work around his house, like mowing the lawn. Little things that made his life easier. When Cass had the twins and they spent time in the NICU, the RFD family had been there.

"Have you heard anything new on the fire?" she asked Lieutenant Fischer. She'd spoken to him briefly yesterday, so she knew the investigation was being handled outside Station 4.

"Nothing new. You'll be the first one I tell when I do." He patted her back as they walked to the dayroom.

The call alarm wailed. "Engine 4, med call." The dispatcher gave the address.

Sam and Lieutenant Fischer rushed to the engine. Turnout gear was stowed inside, and everyone climbed in.

"That's Mr. Bonetti's address. The sheet says chest pains." Lieutenant Fischer filled them in on the call information.

"Mr. Frequent Flier himself." Greer nudged her knee. "Twenty bucks says he declines a ride."

"Greer!" She punched him in the arm. "You are not betting on the poor, lonely old man."

"What? His calls always end up with him declining to go to the hospital once he's calmed down. You know it's just his anxiety with a touch of hypochondria."

Mr. Bonetti was getting older, and Sam dreaded the day that it really was something serious. Hopefully, that wasn't today.

"You're a horrible little man," Murph said from his seat.

"Who you calling little?" Greer sat up straighter.

Compared to Murph, Greer *was* little. Murph was six-six compared to Greer's five-eleven and three-quarters. Maybe if he did the pompadour thing, he'd break the six-foot barrier.

"That's enough, children. Greer, you take this one," Lieutenant Fischer instructed.

Murph staged the engine in front of Mr. Bonetti's house. Sam looked around, her pulse quickening when she didn't see him. Normally he met them on the porch or in the driveway. But there was no sign of him.

"Greer."

"I know." Greer's voice held a note of worry.

They piled out, grabbed the medical bags, and made their way up to Mr. Bonetti's door.

Greer rapped on the wood. "Mr. Bonetti. Renegade Fire Department."

He waited a minute, but Mr. Bonetti didn't answer.

"Help." A weak voice could be heard from somewhere in the house.

Sam dropped the medical bag and dug in the potted fern for the key to the front door. She didn't want to cause damage getting in if they didn't have to, and Mr. Bonetti had told them more than once where he kept his extra key.

She unlocked the door and let Greer take the lead.

"Mr. Bonetti, where are you?" Greer paused and listened.

"In the kitchen." Mr. Bonetti's voice was so weak.

Adrenaline pulsed through Sam's veins.

Greer rushed into the kitchen and stooped down in front of Mr. Bonetti on the kitchen floor.

"Hey, Mr. Bonetti. How are you doing?" Greer assessed the patient.

"My chest hurts." He panted, his hand clutching his chest.

Chest pains, shortness of breath. Could be a heart attack. But could also be a number of other things as well.

"We need a twelve lead." Greer started wrapping the blood pressure cuff around Mr. Bonetti's arm.

Sam pulled the supplies needed to start an EKG from the med bag. She raised his shirt and started placing the electrodes on his chest and abdomen with steady hands.

"BP is one eighty-five over one-fifteen."

Sam studied the monitor. "I've got irregular rhythm. No ST elevation."

"Mr. Bonetti, are you allergic to aspirin?" Greer asked.

They knew the answer, with as many times as they had been to see him, but the question still had to be asked.

"No." His voice was weak, and he was clammy.

"Renegade EMS." The relieving EMS crew shouted from the front door.

"In the kitchen." Mr. Bonetti's voice was weaker than normal.

The EMS crew wheeled a stretcher in, and Greer started the handoff. Mr. Bonetti was loaded into the ambulance, and it sped off.

If the Marshals forced her and Bella to leave Renegade, she would never be able to work as a firefighter or a medic. She would have to give up everything she'd built for the last six years. Now wasn't the time to sort out her feelings about God. It was time to do what she knew.

Stick to the plan.

Liam studied his computer screen, still running down known associates of the Mob. He'd even looked into the Williamses' mother, a real piece of work.

A long list of alcohol-related offenses and shoplifting, liquor—all minor stuff. Until shoplifting had turned into breaking-and-entering and burglary. Sheila Johanson should be doing time, but she'd managed to weasel out because the Feds wanted DeLuca and used that to their advantage by leaning on her daughter.

Were Samantha and Isabella better off because of it? In his opinion, yes—they were safer now. The Marshals knew what they were doing. Witnesses who followed all the rules had a one-hundred-percent success rate in relocation. So far, it looked like Samantha and her sister had done exactly that. Neither had social media, and a review of their IP activity showed nothing unusual or concerning.

Sheila Johanson really wasn't a good mother. No wonder Samantha had insisted Isabella join her in WITSEC. There was no one else to care for her. The arrests dated back to Samantha's own childhood. Looked like he wasn't the only one who'd grown up rough.

But that was the only thing that was common. She'd been neglected. He'd been beaten. Which was worse? They both had physical and mental effects. The guilt from that one lie as a teen had rooted deep, shaping every decision since—discipline, control, the need to make things right—all of it born from what he'd let happen to Kayleigh. Luckily, Sam was like him and put her past behind her, moved forward to better things.

Unlike his sister, who'd been in and out of juvie until she turned eighteen and was now in prison.

Sophia's birth had put her on a better path for a long time. But then she was back to old habits. While she hadn't directly been involved with her boyfriend's criminal dealings, the law didn't care if the drugs were actually hers. It just cared that they'd been found in her possession.

His cell phone screen lit up, pulling him from his thoughts. The phone vibrated against his desk as it started to ring. *Renegade Coroner.*

He slid the answer icon. "Roberts."

"Deputy Marshal Roberts, this is Dr. Falleur at the coroner's office. I've got an identification on the burnt body."

Liam grabbed a sticky note and an ink pen. "Great. Who is it?"

"The man's name is Dr. Cameron Torres."

Liam couldn't say he was shocked. Now that they had a positive identification, they'd have to figure out how Samantha's landlord had ended up dead in her house and why. He prayed the cases weren't related to her past in a way that compromised her security.

"Thanks. What about COD?"

"I haven't completed the report yet. There is a single gunshot wound to the head. Appears to be an execution-style murder, probably with the fire to destroy evidence."

Liam's stomach sank. The Mob was notorious for its execution hits. However, there was still no proof that this was related to Samantha and Isabella's past.

He'd need to talk to Howard about Dr. Torres.

"Anything else you can tell about the body?" Was this a simple execution, or had there been torture before?

"The burns are extensive, but I didn't see any other indication of physical trauma in the X-rays. No broken bones or stab wounds."

That ruled out torture. "Thank you. I'd appreciate it if you forwarded me a copy of the report once it's complete."

"Of course." The forensic pathologist hung up.

He found Glover's number in his cell phone and hit Call.

She answered on the third ring.

"Are you busy?" He had to ask, even if she was doing surveillance on another fugitive believed to be in the area.

"Just staring out the window, waiting for our guy to show his face."

"I've got some bad news for you." He tapped his fingers on the desk.

"Of course you do. I knew this couldn't be a social call." She sighed.

"Your witness, Dr. Cameron Torres, has been found."

"He's dead, isn't he?"

"Unfortunately, yeah. He's the body in my witnesses' house."

"Oh. Wow." She whistled. "Okay. I'll start making the calls."

"What can you tell me about Dr. Torres?"

Yes, he had access to the files, but there were things that didn't make it into the notes. Thoughts and gut feelings he'd need from her to build a complete picture.

"Not your run-of-the-mill white-collar criminal, which was why he hadn't gotten a deal yet. The US Attorney knew he was holding back about this shadow syndicate that some people think is operating in town."

First Liam had heard of it. "You don't think there is one?"

"I want evidence."

"And that's what Torres should've given?"

"Assuming he had any. He initially decided to roll on everyone, but then wouldn't give up what he knew. Except to say that the syndicate was using his medical research to create a recreational drug, or the formula for it, and that it's started hitting the streets. But he'd also run up gambling debts and then dabbled in some real estate schemes to pay off his creditors. Unfortunately, the guys he got tangled up with were high-level and connected."

Liam grimaced. "They got to him before he could testify."

"Sounds like it." She sighed. "Howard isn't going to like this."

"I'm going to go check in with Ms. Williams and see what I can get from her. I'll let you know what I find out."

"Thanks."

"No problem." He disconnected the call and started looking through the file on Dr. Torres.

His screen lit again. This time it was the number he had saved for when his sister called.

He slid the Answer button and listened to the mechanical speech that always played before talking to an inmate.

"Liam." His sister sounded tired.

"Hello, Kayleigh."

"I know you're probably working, but I just had this . . . feeling. I needed to check on you. Everything going okay?" Her tone was lighter than it used to be, but he could hear the weariness behind it.

Mother's intuition.

"Things have been better." He leaned back in his chair.

"Oh no. Is Sophia okay?"

"She's fine. She got into some trouble at school, and she snuck out the other day while I was at work."

Kayleigh chuckled. "Ah, the teenage years. I remember thinking I knew everything back then. Guess I didn't turn out to be the best example."

She wasn't the only one. They'd grown up fighting their own battles—just in different ways. Far from what was portrayed in television and movies, and not worth reminiscing on.

She sighed. "What exactly has she done?"

Liam gave her the rundown of the last few days, his own failures weighing him down. He'd failed Kayleigh.

"I wish I was there." She sighed.

She wasn't the only one. He was used to dealing with hardened criminals, not a hormonal teenager. "Maybe you can call her tonight and talk to her?"

"I will. Enough about Sophia. How are you holding up?"

"We got moved in and settled in the house, and the job transfer went off without issue. I did have to help with a fugitive apprehension on my first day, but since then, it's been court and my other duties." He picked up a pencil and started tapping it on his desk.

"That's good, but *how* are you?"

"Kayleigh, I'm fine."

"It's okay to admit you're not fine. Your life has been turned upside down because of me. You're suddenly a parent, thrust into raising a teenager. You didn't even get the fun parts."

"I was there for some of the fun parts," he countered. He'd made sure to see his sister and niece several times a year.

"It's not the same." A sigh came over the line.

The phone beeped, and a mechanical voice advised she only had five more minutes on her card.

"I'll get you some more minutes." It was the least he could do.

"Thanks. Can I ask you a question?"

"Anything." He meant it. He would do anything for her.

"I've been going to Bible study," she said after a beat, almost shyly. "Trying to figure this whole faith thing out. For the first time in a long time, I've got a little peace. Took me coming to prison to find it."

Liam's gut tightened. He was glad that she had found Jesus, even if it was behind bars. "I'm proud of you, sis."

"I know I've asked a lot in the past several months."

"Kayleigh, I'd give my life for you. You know that."

She took a deep breath. "Please forgive me," she said quietly. "For being an idiot. For thinking I was untouchable. I know what my choices did—to you, to Sophia. I can't fix it from here, but I can start trying."

Emotion clogged his throat. "Kayleigh, if anyone should be apologizing, it's me. If I had just taken the blame for wrecking Dad's car . . . maybe your life would've gone differently."

She let out a short laugh. "What?"

"You took the fall. That was the start of everything. If I'd let him take it out on me—"

"Liam!" Her voice cut sharp. "Don't you dare blame yourself. I was already heading down the wrong path long before that night. You didn't break me. Life did. Choices did. But not you."

He swallowed hard.

"I'm grateful," she said. "For everything you've done—for me and Sophia. Don't ever doubt that."

"I won't," he whispered, even though the guilt still pressed in.

"I don't blame you for anything, and you shouldn't blame yourself either. Love you, little bro."

"Love you too." He disconnected the call and took a few minutes to add money to her commissary card, then set the phone down, Kayleigh's words still burning in his ears. *Don't you dare blame yourself.*

Easier said than done.

TWELVE

S AM JUMPED FROM THE ENGINE AND GRABBED the medical gear for cleaning. Dean was standing next to the ladder truck, checking gauges.

"Bella up yet?" She swung the bags over her shoulder.

He shook his head. "Not yet. How's Mr. Bonetti?"

Her stomach sank. "Today wasn't one of his typical episodes. This could be a life changer for him."

"Do you think it's the one that will send him to long-term care?"

"I hope not. I'll miss seeing him." Even if he was okay nine-ty-eight percent of the time.

Once she was finished, she went and checked on Bella. The bunk room door was closed. Sam looked at her watch. Bella had had plenty of rest. Time to get up.

She opened the door. The bed was empty. She hadn't seen Bella when she'd passed through the dayroom.

Could she be working out? Sam laughed to herself. Not likely.

They'd had a treadmill and some smaller weights at home. Sam couldn't recall a time seeing her use either of them.

Sam made the rounds of the station and couldn't find her. She asked the guys if they'd seen her. No one had.

She'd snuck away yet again.

Sam clenched and unclenched her fists, squelching the urge to scream. It wouldn't do any good. She couldn't call her, because they hadn't replaced her cell phone yet. She didn't need one if she was grounded from it and with Sam all the time.

That had obviously been a bad decision.

How much more of this could she take? She'd tried everything to make sure they were safe. She'd crossed all the t's and dotted all the i's. Given Bella space. Kept her close. Nothing was working.

What if Bella wasn't the only problem?

An ache spread through her chest. She'd deal with that later.

She wandered into the bay, where Dean and Tate were huddled around the ladder truck.

"Have you guys seen Bella?" Sam asked.

Dean turned to her and wiped his hands on the rag hanging from his pants. "She's not in the bunk room?"

Sam shook her head. "Nope. Or the dayroom, kitchen, workout room, conference room, or outside. I was hoping maybe she was hanging out in the ladder truck."

"I haven't seen her since this morning," Tate said. "I thought she was still asleep in the bunk room."

"I'm gonna kill her." She gritted her teeth. Odds were that she was with the marshal's niece. The trouble had started when she'd moved to town.

"You probably shouldn't threaten murder when there's a cop here." Tate gestured behind her.

She turned just as Deputy Marshal Roberts walked into the bay.

"Speak of the devil," she mumbled.

Once he spotted their group, he nodded. A solemn look on his face. Her anger quickly melted away. She bit her lip and wiped her hands on her pants. Every time he showed up, he had bad news. Was this about Bella?

She met him in the middle of the bay. "Deputy Marshal Roberts. Is everything all right?"

He pressed his lips into a thin line. "Is there somewhere private we can talk?" He looked over her shoulder.

Sam turned. Dean and Tate had remained at the ladder truck but watched the two of them with curiosity.

She moved around him. "Let's go in the conference room."

Once they were both in the room, Sam closed the door and turned to him.

"Is everything okay?" He lightly touched her forearm.

The question and gentle touch coming from him were unexpected. Not that she thought he shouldn't ask her how she was doing, but it was the way he'd asked. Like he genuinely cared. He stood there, waiting for her to answer. It wasn't just a comment thrown out to fill the silence.

Why did it make her want to tell him everything?

She couldn't afford this right now. It was better to bottle it all up and shove it down in the dark abyss. "I'm good. Is this about Bella?"

"No. We've identified the person found in your house, and I have some questions for you."

"Oh." She slumped into a chair.

"Can you tell me about your landlord, Dr. Torres?" he asked.

"It was Dr. Torres?" She sat up straight.

Liam nodded. "We got the official identification today."

She blew out a breath. "I didn't know him that well. I know he was a doctor of some sort. We had a typical landlord-tenant situation. I paid the rent. Something broke, he fixed it. We've only talked a handful of times in the six years since we've lived here."

"Over the years, did you have any issues with people looking for him at your house or contacting you about him?"

She shook her head.

"Did he ever do any surprise inspections or maybe monthly pest treatments?"

"He had a key to my house, but he always gave me twenty-four hours' notice before coming over. He knew I was a firefighter and my hours were different."

"Have there been any times you went home and thought something was odd or off? Like someone had been in your home without you knowing?"

She thought back over the years and couldn't think of anything like that. "I never had any reason to believe someone had been inside without us knowing about it."

"Do you know what he was doing in your house?"

She massaged her temple with her left hand. "I have no clue. He'd told me he was going out of town for a while. I hadn't seen or heard from him since." She looked at the marshal. "You're sure it's him?"

"His identity was verified with his fingerprints."

"This proves that the fire and murder aren't related to me and Bella. Our covers are safe?"

Liam drummed his fingertips on the conference table. "It leans in that direction but doesn't mean we can let our guard down. Just in case he happened to be in the wrong place at the wrong time."

Nausea filled her stomach. Bella could have been in the right place at the wrong time.

"Bella ran off."

"What do you mean 'ran off'?"

"I made her come with me to the station today. She was sleeping in the bunk room when a med call came in. She was gone when we got back."

"Have you called her?"

"No. I haven't replaced her cell phone yet. I thought she'd be with me the whole time, or with the guys if I got called out, and it could wait another day or two." Hindsight was twenty-twenty.

"Can you show me where she was sleeping?" He stood.

"Yeah, but I don't know what you think you'll find. She took her backpack with her."

"Humor me."

She exhaled. "Fine." He wasn't going to find anything.

She led the way from the conference room, across the dayroom, and into the bunk area. Her neck burned with the stares of her friends and coworkers. His repeated visits to the fire station would undoubtedly raise unwanted questions. Although, right now, all she cared about was finding Bella.

"See." She opened the door. It looked exactly like it had a few minutes ago.

He stepped inside and looked around the room, under the bed, and in the trash can. He quickly checked through the wardrobe and then turned to her.

"May I?" He gestured to the door behind her.

She stepped out of the way and let him shut the door to inspect the area.

"There's nothing here. I told you." She crossed her arms over her chest.

"There's plenty here. You just don't see it." He turned and settled his blue eyes on her. "No signs of a struggle or that she left in a hurry. The bed is made but not rumpled, so she most likely didn't sleep in it. This was planned, and she was just waiting on the perfect time to make her slip."

"Did they teach you that in marshal school?" she deadpanned. All things she had figured out on her own.

He cleared his throat. "She went out the window."

Sam looked at the window. Sure enough, it was unlocked. Sam gritted her teeth. "That girl."

He stepped back over to the bed and pulled the nightstand away from the wall, revealing a charging cord plugged into the outlet. "I thought she didn't have a phone anymore."

Sam narrowed her eyes. "She doesn't."

He pulled the cord and handed it to her. "Actually, she does. Unless this belongs to someone else."

"No. We're anal about making sure the rooms are cleaned after every shift." What was going on with her sister? Getting into trouble at school, sneaking out, now an unknown phone.

"There's something else we need to talk about. It could be related to why she took off today." Liam shoved a hand in his pressed navy slacks.

She'd ask if the day could get any worse, but she knew it could. There was no sense in tempting fate. Instead, she sighed. "What?"

"The night of the fire, I found cans of spray paint in Sophia's backpack."

"Great." She sighed again. She'd been doing that a lot the last few days. It was like the next thing was always worse than the last. "So, they weren't just out hanging out with friends."

"It took a while, but I got the story out of Sophia. Our girls weren't actually vandalizing, but they didn't stop it. Until the group decided to move on to another location. That's when Soph grabbed the cans and they ran." He rested his other hand on his belt, above his badge.

"So you think that's where she's at now? Hanging out with those kids?" Sam fisted her hands on her hips. "Where's your niece?"

He looked taken aback. "My niece is at home."

"Are you sure about that? Because Bella didn't start getting into trouble until Sophia showed up."

"Are you trying to say my niece is the problem?" He stood straight, jaw clenched.

That's exactly what she was saying. "Yes."

"Look, Sophia has had a rough go of it the last six months.

Yes, she got into a little trouble before we moved, but that was all about her attitude. Nothing like this." He waved his arm around the room. "Vaping, vandalizing, sneaking out of windows."

"A rough go of it?" Sam's blood boiled. "At least she has her real name and real life." She made sure to keep her voice low, but this guy wasn't going to tear her down.

Liam worked his jaw back and forth. "I could make the same assumption as you about the girls. Isabella could be the mastermind behind all of this."

She opened her mouth to argue. "There is no way Bella is to blame."

"Are you sure about that? Willing to stake your life here in Renegade on it?"

Bella knew the rules. She knew them inside and out. But knowing the rules and following them were different things. She knew not to sneak out, but she'd done it anyway. Twice. Maybe Liam was right. Maybe Bella was encouraging this behavior.

"And are you certain it's all on Bella? Honestly?" She needed to know his thoughts. Was she wrong and losing control of Bella?

"Honestly, I think what we have is two girls who have been through a lot and are vulnerable. Someone noticed and manipulated them. Taking the cans of spray paint and running off is proof they're not *bad* girls. They knew what they were doing was wrong and stopped before it got worse."

Sam rolled her lips over her teeth. He had a point. "Okay. So what do we do now?"

Liam pulled his phone from his pocket and made a few swipes. "Based on my tracking app, Sophia's still at home."

"We both know that doesn't mean a thing." They were smart enough to have left their phones at home before. Just not smart enough not to get into trouble.

She'd been so focused on Bella being the innocent one, she'd never considered any other angle. Was everything Sam had worked for over the last six years slowly slipping away?

Liam hadn't resorted to putting all the blame on Bella. Not like she had done to Sophia. He was steady, competent, capable. He'd looked at the situation objectively and turned what could have been a disastrous argument into something where they could work together for the good of the girls.

A small warmth threaded through her chest, and she quickly shoved it down, unwilling to think about what it meant.

Liam stared at Sam. She was scared. She acted like she was holding it all together on the surface, but the furrowed brows, the tight line of her lips, and her rigid posture said otherwise.

That was why she'd lashed out. He couldn't really blame her. He wanted to lash out, to blame anyone but Sophia, but the truth was, it didn't matter who'd started it—the girls had each followed. They'd made their own choices.

He broke his gaze from Sam and looked at the blinking dot that represented Sophia's phone. It was exactly where it should be, but she'd deceived him before.

He switched over to his contacts and hit her name. It rang and rang. He inwardly groaned. He thought he'd gotten through to her last night. Apparently, it had gone in one ear and out the other.

"Hello?" Sophia answered.

The tension in Liam's shoulders disappeared. "Hey, Sophia. I'm with Isabella's aunt. Isabella left the fire station and didn't tell anyone where she was going. Do you know where she might be?"

"Yeah, she's here."

"Sophia, I thought I grounded you." He pinched the bridge of his nose. Isabella sneaking out of the fire station and to his house didn't really help prove his case that Sophia wasn't the problem in this messed-up equation.

"I know. I'm sorry, but she needed me." Concern laced her voice.

His pulse picked up. "Is everything okay?"

"For now. Can you come home?"

He looked at Sam. Something was not all right. "Are you safe?" He brushed past Sam and opened the door, making a beeline to his vehicle.

"What's going on?" Sam followed him.

Liam didn't miss the looks from her coworkers as they sped through the dayroom.

"Yes. It's nothing like that. We just need to talk to you about something."

He could hear Isabella's voice in the background but couldn't make out what was said.

"We're on our way." He used the fob, unlocked the vehicle, and opened the door.

"Lieutenant!" Sam yelled as she veered off from Liam.

There was silence over the phone.

"Sophia." His tone was sharp.

"Just you," she said. "I had to leave the room. Isabella's scared, and I don't think she'll say anything if her sister shows up."

Sam climbed into the passenger seat and started buckling up.

Liam stroked his chin. "Okay." He disconnected the call.

"Isabella is at your house? Is she hurt?" Sam looked at him, concern filling her features.

He nodded. "They want to talk to me." She wasn't going to like this. "Alone."

Her eyes widened. "They don't want me there?"

"Sophia said Isabella is scared, and she's afraid she won't talk to me if you show up."

Her shoulders slumped and her face fell. He'd just delivered an emotional punch. He knew how it would feel if the girls didn't want him there.

"I'm sorry." Like that would make it better. "I'll go talk to the girls and let you know what's going on. I promise."

Sam stared out the windshield. "She doesn't want me there?"

He reached over and laid his hand on her forearm. "Don't let your thoughts go crazy. I've seen it before. Kids are more open and honest with someone they don't know that well, because they're not worried about that person being disappointed in them."

Sam turned to look at him. "I'm supposed to just let you go, and I stay here?"

"Do you trust me?" He studied her face. "I'm the one here to keep you and Bella safe."

"I don't even know you."

"I understand. I'm asking a lot of you right now. But trust me. Let me go see what I can find out."

The emergency alarm started blaring.

"Go do your job. I'll call you after I've talked to them."

Her coworkers flooded into the bay.

"Okay." She got out of his vehicle and jogged to the engine, then started preparing to go out.

Liam put the vehicle in Reverse. "Lord, we need You now. Give me strength to deal with whatever is coming and knowledge on how to handle it. Give Sam the peace and comfort only You can. Be with Isabella and Sophia and give them strength to face this. In Jesus's name."

All kinds of scenarios went through his mind on his way home. None of them good. He pulled into the driveway, took a deep breath, and said another prayer before climbing from the vehicle and going inside.

"Sophia. I'm home." He shut and locked the front door.

"We're in here," Sophia yelled from her bedroom.

He turned into her room and found the two girls huddled

together on the floor, next to Sophia's bed. Tear stains streaked Isabella's face.

His heart constricted. Whatever was going on was serious. He squatted down in front of the girls. "Everything is going to be okay."

Whatever the situation was, they'd handle it.

Isabella shook her head.

Sophia nudged her. "We have to tell him."

Tears rolled down Isabella's cheeks. "I know."

She reached into her jacket pocket, pulled out a phone, and handed it to him. "Here."

Sophia moved a bit and produced another phone identical to the one Isabella had. She swiped the screen a few times and handed the phone to him.

A text message from an unknown number was displayed on the screen.

Unknown Number

Keep your mouth shut.
Or else. 🔥 🔥 🔥

Liam looked at Sophia and then at Isabella.

"We both got one," Sophia said.

Liam tensed as he looked over the phone. It was a typical pay-as-you-go phone that could be bought at a gas station. Nothing fancy. And not the phone he'd purchased for Sophia. He took a deep breath. He didn't need to go at this the wrong way, or the girls would clam up.

"Okay. We can deal with this." He stood. "Let's go into the kitchen." He stood and left the girls alone.

"See. I told you," Sophia whispered.

He grabbed three cans of soda from the fridge and set them on the table. Then he sat and waited for the teens.

A few minutes later, they shuffled into the kitchen and sat at the table.

"Okay. Tell me everything from the beginning."

Sophia looked at Isabella and waited. When it was clear she wasn't going to say anything, Sophia took a deep breath. "There're some kids at school. The ones that were vaping in the bathroom."

Liam nodded and waited for her to continue.

"They're the Renegade Rebels. They're cool."

He fought to keep his eyes from rolling. Typical high school social hierarchy.

"Well, when we got caught with a few of them in the bathroom, we refused to say who we saw provide the vape. They thought that was cool and started talking to us more."

She looked at Isabella. "The day we pulled the fire alarm, Sabrina, the leader, said that her boyfriend was leaving for boot camp. He graduated last year. She said her parents wouldn't let her say goodbye to him, and he'd be gone for more than six months. She wouldn't get to see or talk to him until after he got out."

Isabella took over. "She asked us if we could help her sneak out to go see him one last time. We agreed."

Liam knew where this was going. To be young and naive again.

"We pulled the fire alarm so she could sneak away during the evacuation." Isabella wrapped her arms around her middle.

"Go on," he encouraged.

Sophia fidgeted in her chair. "The next day, they texted us and asked us if we wanted to hang out. They told us to leave our phones at home. So we met them at the park."

Liam schooled his face.

"They said we were cool for covering for them both times." Sophia shrugged.

Bella took over the explanation again. "We were hanging out and having fun, and one of them pulled out spray paint and started tagging things at the park. They wanted to go to another secluded place and do more painting."

Bella looked at Sophia.

Sophia wrapped her arm around her friend. "We need to tell the truth. Get it all out there."

Bella nodded. "We followed them. They gave us a couple cans, and we sprayed some dumpsters. Tori—Sabrina's best friend—and her boyfriend disappeared for a few minutes. Probably to make out. When they came back, they gave us the cell phones they'd bought at the grocery store. Said since we left ours at home, we needed a way to stay in touch with them while we were out."

As an adult, Liam could see the signs in the story. These friends had been testing them. Seeing how trustworthy they were, pulling them deeper into their world.

He had questions but didn't want to interrupt in case they stopped talking. It was best to get it all out, and then he could go back in and ask those questions to fill in the blanks.

"One of the guys that was with us kept playing with a lighter," Bella continued. "He'd grab long pieces of grass or leaves and set them on fire and watch them burn."

"It was weird the way he watched the flames," Sophia added. "Like he was hypnotized."

Bella nodded. "Anyway, he said he wanted to watch something burn. He lit a piece of trash on fire and threw it in the trash can." She swallowed. "Sabrina called him an idiot and put the fire out with her bottle of water. She told him to save it for later. That's when I knew we needed to get out of there. So while Sabrina and Tori argued, we snuck off."

"So you called me from this cell phone?" He looked at the two cell phones on the table.

The girls nodded.

"What happened after you left?"

"You found the spray cans and yelled at me for having them," Sophia said.

"I didn't yell." He pinned Sophia with a stare.

"Anyway," Sophia continued. "We decided we didn't want to be a part of their stuff anymore, so we ghosted them."

Apparently, they hadn't taken that too well. "Is this the first threatening message you've gotten from them?"

"You can read the texts." Sophia nodded at the phones.

He had every intention of doing so.

Maybe Sam had every reason to be scared—the girls were getting themselves into some pretty sketchy stuff. A slippery slope.

But did it connect to the fire at their house and the doctor's death? Liam didn't know, but he was determined to find out.

THIRTEEN

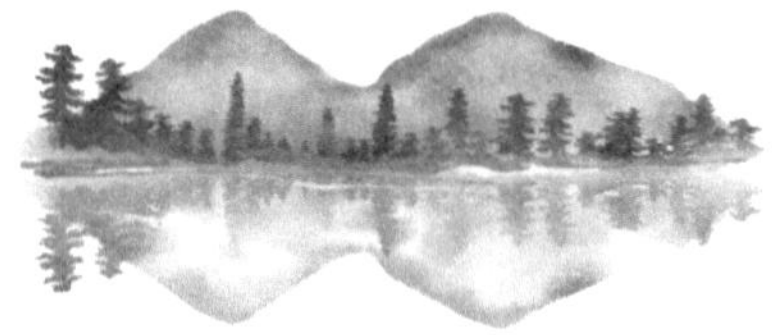

SAM FOCUSED ON THE ORANGE GLOW THROUGH the thick, rolling smoke billowing out the windows of the flooring store. Forearms burning, she aimed the pressurized water at the heart of the fire. Sweat rolled down her back as the heat enveloped her. She stepped forward, the flames hissing as the water hit its target. She fought with all her strength until the fire was out.

"This is the fifth commercial fire." Greer put the Halligan back in its place. "Another arson. The arson investigators need to hurry up and catch the people doing this."

"Yes, they do." She tossed the fire hose on top of the engine, into its spot.

"I wonder if they'll find any spray-paint markings around this fire like the others."

Sam stopped and turned to Greer. "Spray paint?"

"Yeah, the other four fires had spray-painted graffiti in the vicinity." Greer slid the rolling door shut on the engine. "The investigator thought it might be connected. Don't you read the department memos?"

"I've been busy."

Liam had said that Sophia had been caught with spray paint in her backpack.

Anxiety knotted her stomach. It was just a coincidence. Nothing to worry about. Besides, the girls were with him now. They couldn't be involved in this fire. But still. "When was the last arson fire?"

Greer looked up and to the right, thinking. Then his face softened. "The one that was the same day as the fire at your house."

"Was there graffiti there?" Please say no.

"Yeah. Around the block from the store."

Sam was going to be sick. She tugged her phone from her duty pants under her turnout pants. No missed calls or text messages. Her thoughts flitted from the fire at her house to the arsons and the girls. Were they all connected?

Once the scene was cleaned up, everyone loaded into the engine, and Murph pointed it back to the station.

Sam nudged Greer with her elbow. "Do you know if they found graffiti around my house as well?" Her right leg bounced on the floorboard.

"I don't think so. You think your house might be related to the others?" He tilted his head a little.

"I don't know. I was just curious, I guess."

"It's always possible they could be related, but all the others have been commercial buildings, and no one died."

He was right. The fires were probably unrelated. "Maybe it was a copycat."

Murph pulled up in front of the station, and Sam and Greer hopped out to stop traffic so he could back the engine into the bay.

Sam's phone chirped from her pocket as she reentered the bay.

Once she had removed her turnout gear, she dug the phone from her bag. There was a text from Liam.

Liam
The girls are fine. Call me when you get off.

Sam
Thank you.

Everything was okay for now, but would it be once she told him about the spray paint at the scenes of the arsons?

She walked through the dayroom and into the kitchen, grabbed a bottle of water, and chugged it. She didn't need another lecture about hydration.

"Hey, Sam." Dean joined her in the kitchen area. "Are you fraternizing with the enemy now?" He grabbed his own bottle of water.

"Excuse me?"

"I'm not sure we can keep you on the team if you're turning into a badge bunny." The words may have been meant as a joke, but his tone suggested otherwise.

Sam scoffed. "What are you talking about?"

But she knew exactly what he was talking about. She just needed to deflect until she could think of an appropriate excuse. Her life and Bella's life could hang in the balance. The truth wouldn't work.

"Deputy Marshal Liam Roberts has been around the station couple of times. Is there something going on there?"

This wasn't like the lighthearted teasing she would have expected from him. "What if there is?"

He shrugged. "Nothing. I just don't want to see you get hurt, that's all."

Was that really all?

The alarm wailed again.

Dean was saved by the bell.

They were called out for two more med calls before the shift was over.

Sam tossed her duffel bag into the back seat of her car and dialed Liam's number.

He answered on the second ring. "Samantha."

"Right. Is Isabella okay?" She chewed on her bottom lip.

"She's fine, but we do need to sit down and talk."

"How bad is it?" She leaned her head back against the head rest.

"It's not great, but it's not bad either."

"Text me your address. I'm on my way."

"Okay. I was just about to order some pizza for the girls. Any special requests?"

Depending on what he had to say, she probably wouldn't be able to eat. "No, thanks." The phone beeped in her ear, indicating she'd received a notification. "I got your address."

"We'll see you when you get here."

"Goodbye." She disconnected the call and looked at the address he'd texted. She needed to remind herself that it couldn't be too bad or either he would have called her earlier, or she'd be picking Isabella up at the US Marshals office.

She pulled her car into the driveway behind the black SUV and put it in Park. Everything was going to be okay. She took a deep breath, exited the vehicle, and walked up to the front door.

It opened as she approached. Liam stood in the opening, blue jeans hanging low on his hips and a blue thermal shirt with sleeves pushed up to his elbows defining his torso, unlike the button-down shirts she was used to seeing. His hair was tousled as though he'd been running his hands through it.

Cassie was right. He was good-looking.

Her stomach fluttered. Now was not the time to be admiring this man. It was wrong on so many levels. In another life, where he wasn't a marshal and she wasn't his protected witness, Sam might have been tempted to run to him and jump, see if he would catch her. Take a chance and see what might happen in his arms.

"Good evening." He stepped to the side to let her enter.

She ducked inside, avoiding getting too close to him. A hint of citrus and sage filled her nose. Had he always smelled like that?

The door clicked shut behind her, snapping her to attention. "Right this way."

She followed him into the empty kitchen. "Where's Isabella?"

"She and Sophia are hanging out in Sophia's bedroom." He pulled a chair out for her. "Have a seat. Can I get you something to drink? The pizza should be here in ten minutes."

She shook her head. "I'm fine."

He opened the refrigerator, pulled out a bottle of water, and set it in front of her. "Just in case."

Her knee started to bounce under the table. "What did you find out?"

He sat down in the chair across the small table from her. His gaze was entirely focused on her. "It appears that our girls haven't been completely honest with us up until this point."

She sat up straight and met his gaze. "I was afraid of that. What did you learn?"

"There's a group of individuals who go to school with them called the Renegade Rebels."

"I've heard of them. According to Bella, it's a group of popular students with bad reputations."

"Well, the girls that were in the bathroom vaping are part of that group. They spun some sob story about the leader, Sabrina, needing to sneak out of school to say goodbye to her boyfriend before he left for six months of basic training."

He was talking, but all she could do was watch his lips move. Ugh. Why now? This was about Isabella being a dumb teenager, not Sam and her dumb teenage crush on their marshal.

"Which brings me to today." He pulled his phone out, swiped a few times, then turned the phone to her.

A photo of a threatening text message filled his screen. Sam tried to swallow the lump in her throat.

"This is why Isabella snuck away from the fire station and ended up at my house with Sophia. This is the result of them ignoring the text message about where they went."

Sam closed her eyes and took a deep breath. "We might have bigger problems." She opened them and met his solemn expression with one of her own. "There was graffiti near all the arsons. I think these kids are arsonists."

Liam knew there were so many ways this could get worse, but he didn't know if he was prepared to hear it. "What's that?"

"Greer told me that spray-painted graffiti had been located in the vicinity of each of the first four commercial fires. There was another commercial arson today. Greer said this was number five. The fourth one was at a store, the same day my house burned."

Liam blew out a breath. "Okay."

He stood up and paced the kitchen. Definitely didn't look good for the girls.

He ran the entire conversation with the teens through his mind.

Finally, he turned and rested his hands on the back of the chair he'd just vacated. "I don't think the girls were involved in the fires. They're scared. This text"—he tapped the cell phone on the table—"was an eye-opener for them."

"I think we need to tell them this new information and see what they have to say."

"I agree." He went to the kitchen door. "Sophia. Isabella. Can you come in here please?"

The girls shuffled into the kitchen. Their smiles faltered when they saw Sam.

Isabella wrapped her arms around her middle.

"Have a seat, please." Sam pulled out the chair to her right.

Isabella took a seat and stared at her hands in her lap.

"Sophia, you too." Liam eyed his niece.

Sophia took the seat on the opposite side of Isabella, while Liam took the chair to Sam's left.

"Isabella. You've been lying for almost a week," Sam told her.

"I know. I'm sorry," Bella said to her lap.

"Look at me, please." Sam kept her voice calm and neutral.

Her sister obeyed, eyes shining with tears.

"We can get through that. Okay?"

Bella nodded.

"It's time to be completely honest."

"Yes, ma'am. I will."

"Sophia, that goes for you too." Liam looked pointedly at his niece.

"Yes, sir. We will." She reached over and grabbed Isabella's hand.

"Bella, you've heard me mention some arsons in Renegade." Sam focused her attention on her sister.

Bella nodded.

"Well, at every fire, there has been spray-painted graffiti."

Bella's eyes widened.

Sophia jerked her face to Liam's. "It wasn't us."

He exhaled with relief. It was a long jump from the things they'd admitted to doing to intentionally setting fires.

"We didn't have anything to do with fires," Bella echoed.

"You understand how we would have a hard time taking your word for it with the lies you've been telling." Liam studied the two teens in front of him.

Tears spilled down their faces.

"I know, Uncle Liam, but I swear it wasn't us."

Bella stared at her sister, pleading with her eyes. "We did the fire alarm and some graffiti, but we didn't have anything to do with fires. When that guy set the trash can on fire, we left."

Sam looked between the two girls and then to Liam. "I think they're telling the truth. Finally."

"I think so too." He tapped his hand on the tabletop. The doorbell rang, interrupting the tension. "That's the pizza. Soph, will you get some paper plates while I get the pizza?"

Sophia nodded and wiped the tears from her face.

Liam walked to the front room to collect the pizza. When he returned to the kitchen, he found Sam embracing the girls.

"It's okay. We'll get everything figured out," she told them. "But we need you to be honest with us from now on, okay?"

Both girls nodded into her arms.

Something in his chest shifted, and he now saw Samantha in a whole new light. This woman, with her tough exterior, worked a physically demanding and often heart-wrenching job. But she hadn't let it make her callous. She still cared about the people she loved.

He pushed those thoughts away and entered the room.

"Pizza's here." He was overly cheery. There would be plenty of time for them to discuss what was going on, but right now, everyone needed a break from the heaviness. "Let me say a blessing, and then we can eat." He set the boxes on the table.

Sam's brow furrowed, but she didn't say anything.

He bowed his head and closed his eyes. "Dear Lord, thank You for this day. Thank You for Your mercies that are new every morning. I pray that You bless this food to the nourishment of our bodies and bless the hands that made it. Be with us each and every day and guide our steps. Amen."

Bella and Sophia echoed the amen. Sam remained silent. He wanted to dig into that, but now was not the time.

At first, the kitchen was quiet, then Samantha started asking

Sophia questions, like what kind of hobbies she had. The conversation flowed between bites.

Sam was genuinely interested in what was being said, focusing on each person who spoke. The conversation hadn't been started to fill the silence, and she wasn't dismissive when questions were answered. She asked like she really wanted to know. The complete opposite of Giselle.

He listened as they laughed and talked about their favorite movies and television shows. Sam surprised him when she mentioned a classic cartoon. One he loved as well. Nothing like a talking dog solving mysteries.

His gaze kept going back to Samantha. Wisps of her dark-blonde hair had escaped from its braid and framed her face. Her right eye crinkled more than the left when she smiled. Her laugh was like a balm, softening the hard edges of his day.

Another shift in his chest. He was noticing too much. Not good.

He stood up, gathered the trash from the table, and stuffed it in the can. He needed fresh air. He pulled the full bag from the can and took it outside to the garbage bin he kept next to the garage door.

He looked at the sky filled with blues, pinks, and purples as the sun set. God was an amazing artist.

The front door opened, and he turned to see who was joining him. Sam shut the door behind her, shoved her hands in her pockets, and met him in the driveway.

She looked at him, dead in the eye. "Thank you."

The urge to reach out and touch her was strong. *God give me strength*. He shoved his hands in his own pockets to keep them under control. "No problem."

"I really mean it." She sighed and looked away. "The last week has been stressful. Bella has been acting so out of character." She turned back to look at him. "And to be honest, I kind of blamed Sophia."

Liam started to say something, but she shook her head.

"I didn't want to believe that Bella would make those kinds of decisions without someone influencing her. It turns out I was wrong about who was doing the influencing. And for that, I owe you and Sophia an apology."

He gulped. "Thank you. Don't be too hard on yourself. I might have thought Bella was a bad influence once or twice." He gave a small smile.

One she returned. She rubbed her hands up and down her arms. With the sun going down, the temperature was dropping. "Do you think the fire at my house has anything to do with the girls and the friends they've been keeping?"

"My first inclination is no. They were with the group of kids when your house was set on fire. Not to mention that none of the other fires included murder. But that doesn't mean there aren't other players in our group of firebugs."

She shivered.

He unlocked the SUV, pulled out a windbreaker, and handed it to her.

She paused for a second, accepted it, and slipped it on. "Thanks."

Did she even notice that her touch on his hand lingered?

Liam wanted to draw her close and give her a hug. They'd both had a crazy day, but things were looking up. Only the silver star badge on his belt and a quiet check in his spirit stopped him from doing what he wanted to do.

He cleared his throat. "I plan to look into the names that Isabella and Sophia gave me and see if I can pull anything. I'll get in touch with RPD too. Those kids may not be involved with your house, but it is likely they are, or know who is, involved with the other arsons."

She squeezed her eyes shut. "Does it make me a bad person that I don't want to do that? That opens the possibility of them forcing the girls to testify. I just don't want them to have to go through what I went through. Not to mention them digging into Bella's and my past and discovering our secret."

He reached over and cupped her shoulder. "It's the right thing to do, and I'll be with you guys every step of the way."

"That's something else we need to figure out. You can't keep showing up at the fire station. The guys are asking questions. I can't tell them the truth."

"Why not? I'm helping you with Bella. That's all." He let his hand drop.

"But it's not all. I think we've turned a corner on the acting-out problem, so that excuse is gone. Now we have to move on to the bigger issue. Are we safe?" She bit her bottom lip.

"I don't know that for certain. My gut says you are, but that's not proof. Until we have solid evidence one way or another, you have to be careful."

She nodded.

"Can we not be friends? Friends visit each other. Hang out. Things like that." He shrugged his shoulders.

Even if he could see it leading to something more, he needed to tamp down the attraction. Not only was it unprofessional, but she didn't seem to have a positive view of God.

Still, until they knew more about the arson and murder at her house, he would need to be in frequent contact with her. He could touch base with her via phone, but he would need to occasionally see her in person. And since she didn't have a home, it would have to be around someone she knew—or at least in public, where someone she might know would spot her.

"The only way they'd believe us hanging out together is if we were dating." She crossed her arms over her chest.

He choked on air and started coughing. How did she know he'd been thinking about that exact thing?

She narrowed her eyes at him. "Relax, I wasn't serious. I'm not even sure they'd believe it then."

He thought about what she'd said as he regained his composure. It wasn't that bad an idea. Definitely a good reason for him and Sam to be seen together and talking to each other so much. He had been going to suggest using the girls' friendship as an excuse, but that would only get them so far. "You know, that could work."

She looked at him, dumbfounded. "You're serious?"

"Think about it. People in new relationships can't get enough of each other. Always calling or texting each other. Finding ways to be together. If we're *dating*, people won't read too much into it. They'll be like 'Okay, honeymoon phase' and move on with their lives. Anything else we come up with will have an expiration date. I mean, even if our girls are BFFs, your coworkers will think it's odd that you and I spend so much time together."

The more he talked, the wider her eyes grew.

"Plus, there's Sophia. We can't tell her the truth. This will be the easiest thing to explain to her."

Sam closed her eyes and took a deep breath. "If we do this, we don't need to tell Bella the truth either. She needs to believe it's real too. I don't think she'd let it slip. We've been in WITSEC six years, and she's kept her mouth shut so far. Given the last couple of days, maybe it's best to keep her in the dark as well."

She made a good case, and he was almost convinced it might work.

If he could keep from falling in love with her in the process.

FOURTEEN

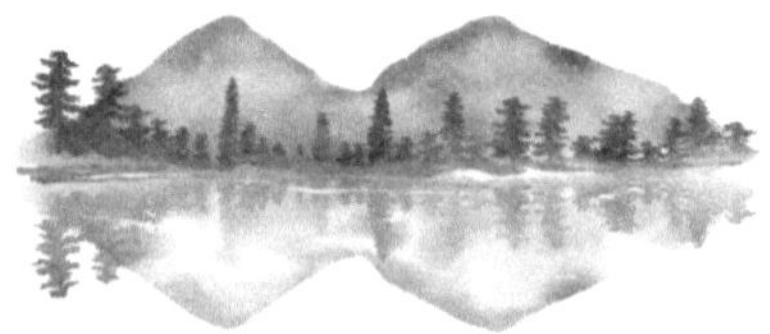

Sam stood in Liam's driveway, wearing his US Marshals windbreaker, thinking about what it might feel like to have his arms around her. The cologne he wore hung heavy on the jacket.

Her phone chimed in her pocket. She pulled it out and checked, more grateful than she realized for the interruption. A message from Dean.

She sighed.

"Everything okay?" Liam looked her in the eye.

"Yes, just big brother Dean checking in on me."

"That's another reason the fake dating thing would work. If your friends think you're dating a marshal, they'll assume you're safe and won't be hovering over you."

She just had to open her big mouth. She'd only been thinking out loud when she'd mentioned dating. She'd worked at the station long enough that her coworkers knew her idiosyncrasies. They knew her life revolved around Bella, the station, and the small family she'd created there.

Pulling away from the team because of a new relationship had the added benefit that one of her friends wouldn't get caught in the crossfire if something happened.

She bounced on her feet, her mind whirring with all kinds of thoughts. What she needed was a good run, and she fully intended to get one tonight on Dean's treadmill.

The run would let her think. Long and hard. Weigh the pros and cons of this charade. Was she willing to risk her heart to spend so much time with Liam? The reward would outweigh the risk. Besides, it was only fake dating. No one had said feelings would be involved. This was just another way to find out what was going on.

She pulled the windbreaker off and handed it back to Liam. "Let me think about it."

"Okay." He tossed the jacket in the SUV and locked it up.

"We should be going." She turned and trudged back into the house. "Bella, it's time to go."

The girls moaned from Sophia's bedroom, then they raced out.

"Can Bella stay the night?" Sophia grabbed Liam's arm.

"Please," Bella pleaded with Sam.

Liam looked from the begging teens to her and back. "Not tonight. I don't know about Bella, but Soph, you're grounded. Plus, I have to work tomorrow."

"Ugh." Sophia dropped his arm and started to pout.

"Bella, you're grounded as well. Don't think I forgot about that little stunt you pulled today either."

She scrunched up her face. "I'm sorry."

"Maybe we can revisit the idea of a sleepover in a few weeks."

Sophia and Bella squealed at the same time, then hugged each other like Sam had said yes and not maybe.

Liam looked at Sam and mouthed *Thank you.*

She could only imagine what Sophia was going through. Probably very similar to Bella's experience when they moved to Renegade.

"Thank you again for everything today. Do I owe you anything for dinner?"

Liam shoved his hands in his pockets and shook his head. "My treat."

"Oh, well, thanks again." She turned and herded Bella to the car.

There was so much to say right now, but Sam didn't know how to go about it.

"Don't think that we won't talk about everything. I just want to wrap my head around it all. The more I think about you sneaking off, the angrier I get, and I don't want to be angry when we talk." She reached over and grabbed Bella's hand.

"I'm sorry." Bella squeezed her hand.

"Please don't do that again. You can come to me for anything. I mean it. Anything." She looked at her sister and made sure she heard what had been said.

Sam had made her fair share of mistakes in her life. She wanted better for her sister.

Bella leaned over, turned on the radio, and changed it to a station playing Christian music. Not Sam's choice, but it could be a lot worse. It wasn't long until she found herself tapping along to the beat on the steering wheel.

She pulled into Dean's drive and put the car in Park. Even though Dean had given her a key, she still knocked on the front door before letting herself in.

"Nobody's home." Charlie giggled from underneath the coffee table.

"Okay, funny boy, it's time for a bath." Dean walked into the living room with a wiggling Bobby in one arm. "Hey, Sam."

"Run, Charlie," Bobby squealed from his position. "Save your-self!"

"Oh no you don't." Cass yanked Charlie from under the coffee table. "No stinky boys in my house."

"Um, while you two take care of that . . ." She waved her arms at the commotion. "Do you mind if I hit the treadmill?" Cass was a runner just like Sam. It was one of the things that had bonded them.

"Sure. You know where it's at," Cass said as she and Dean carried the boys down the hall.

Sam and Bella followed behind, veering off into the room they were staying in. Sam changed out of her work clothes and into the department sweats she'd swiped the day of the fire.

"I think I'm just going to go to bed." Bella flopped down on the mattress, spread-eagled.

"Sounds good to me, but save room for me in the bed, 'kay?"

"I'll think about it." Bella rolled over onto her stomach and rested her head on her arms.

Sam shut the door to the spare room behind her and hit the treadmill. The methodic pounding of her feet eased the tension she'd been holding in her body.

She focused on her breathing. In through her nose and out through her mouth.

Her life was spinning out of control.

There were so many questions that needed answers, and she didn't have them. There was nothing she could do to fix the situation. Normally, when something went wrong, she could reason, plan, and create a solution. Sick or injured patient? Implement a treatment plan until EMS arrived. Building on fire? Implement a plan to extinguish the flames. Issues with inventory? Figure out the cause and correct it. What was she supposed to do about this? She couldn't fix it.

Pain stretched from her calves and up her legs as she pushed herself further. Maybe if she pushed herself to the limit, she'd sleep peacefully tonight and not fitfully like she had been since the fire.

After three miles, she did a cooldown before she showered and collapsed into bed.

High-pitched giggling drew Sam from sleep hours later. She didn't know how long it had been.

She rubbed her eyes and rolled over. Every muscle in her legs ached, but her run had achieved its purpose. Once her head had hit the pillow, she'd been out, and there had not been one thought about a beguiling US marshal and his nice-smelling jacket. She opened her eyes to the empty bed.

More giggling echoed through the door. Sam looked at her cell phone.

10:00 a.m.

She dropped her phone on the nightstand. She couldn't remember the last time she'd slept this late. Her day off was already half over. She pulled herself from the bed and shuffled to the bathroom. Once she was dressed and presentable, she followed the giggles down the hall and into the living room. In the middle of the room, there was a giant fort.

Cass smiled at her from the cushionless couch, a book on her lap. "I hope the boys didn't wake you."

"It's way past time for me to get up."

"Sam?" Bella's head popped out of a small opening.

"Morning," she greeted her sister.

"You needed the rest. I'd say have a seat, but trust me, it's not that comfortable." Cass gestured to the lumpy spring portion of the couch.

"Thanks, but I was actually thinking about taking Bella shopping for more clothes and things."

It was her first day off since the fire that she had time to do more shopping. The first trip had just been for necessities. This one would be for more. Bella would be getting a budget though.

Sam's savings wasn't a lot, but this was also a learning moment for the teen.

"Shopping!" Bella scrambled out of the makeshift fort, the boys on her tail.

"We wanna go!" Charlie grabbed one of Bella's legs while Bobby grabbed the other.

"Not gonna happen, boys." Cass stood up. "This is boring shopping. Besides, you have a birthday party to go to."

"Party!" the boys yelled simultaneously and took off running down the hall.

"You two march right back in here and help clean up this mess," Cass yelled after them.

"We can help too," Sam offered.

Once the living room was returned to normal, Sam and Bella loaded up in the car.

"Sam?" Bella asked.

"Yeah." She glanced at her sister.

"I know I'm grounded and everything, but do you think we could take Sophia shopping with us?"

Was that a good idea? Would letting the girls get together while they were in trouble negate the fact that they were grounded?

In normal circumstances, Sam would stick to her guns and say no. Except, this wasn't normal. It had been a rough week for Bella, and she could use a friend with her as she replaced everything she owned.

Having someone there to help take her mind off the reason she was shopping would be a good idea. Plus, it would give Sam some time to get to know Sophia. Not just so she could know who her sister was getting into trouble with, but also so she could maybe have a positive influence on the girls and there wouldn't be any more trouble.

"I don't think that will hurt."

Bella squealed in her seat.

Sam closed her eyes. Hopefully, the day wouldn't contain too many more squeals.

Liam pulled his SUV into the outlet mall parking lot. He was meeting Sam and the girls in ten minutes. Sam wanted Sophia to go clothes shopping with them, despite the trouble the girls were in. He'd suggested meeting them for lunch, and they could work on the couple thing. The sooner they started spending time together, the better.

The story would sell better if the girls came to the conclusion on their own instead of Liam and Sam just outright telling them.

He'd tried to speak with Supervisor Howard this morning, but he was a hard one to pin down. A multitude of meetings had taken up his morning. Aubrey had told Liam to call Howard now, in between meetings.

Liam dialed the supervisor's number.

Supervisor Howard answered on the second ring. "Howard."

Liam pulled the SUV into a spot and shoved it into Park. "Supervisor Howard, this is Liam Roberts. I need to speak with you about the Williams sisters."

"I've got five minutes before my next meeting. That enough time?"

"It will have to be." Liam rubbed the back of his neck. "It turns out that my niece and Isabella Williams aren't just getting into random trouble. The people they've been hanging with could possibly be related to the arsons around Renegade."

Supervisor Howard whistled. "I'm going to guess that's not the only reason you called."

"Both girls received threatening text messages yesterday from said people. I've already been in touch with Renegade Police Department and the fire marshal."

"Good. Do we have reason to believe that the group is responsible for the Williamses' house fire?"

"I don't have anything to confirm or deny. Personally, I don't think they are related, but I'm not going to discount it." Liam tapped his fingers on the steering wheel.

"Good idea."

"Samantha is worried about all of the attention she has been getting from me. In a professional capacity, that is. Between the fire at her house and the girls getting into trouble, she's afraid her friends and coworkers are going to start asking questions and her cover will get blown."

Now for the tricky part. "We tried to come up with some explanations last night. Everything I can think of doesn't lead to long-term contact between us, or as much as we would need to ensure their safety. Then she mentioned a fake relationship."

Yep, he'd done that. Thrown her under the bus. Actually, it *had* been her idea. He was just running with it.

Supervisor Howard exhaled into the phone. "As in dating?"

Liam leaned his head back. "Yes. I know the rules frown upon getting personally involved with a witness, but we won't actually *be* involved with each other romantically."

But they would be spending a lot of time together.

"I don't know. That's a fairly thin line you're suggesting you dance on."

"I know, sir, but it makes the most sense. It can easily be explained. We met because of the girls. We hang out because we like each other and the girls are friends. It doesn't raise any suspicion with the people she's around. I can keep an eye on them and dig into what could be going on. Everyone wins."

Supervisor Howard was silent.

He was going to nix the idea.

"I'll green-light this for now. But if anything happens—I mean anything—it's your career that's in jeopardy."

Liam swallowed the lump in his throat. "Yes, sir."

"This conversation never happened." His tone left no room for argument.

"Understood." Liam gave a curt nod, even though Supervisor Howard couldn't see him.

The weight of the situation settled heavily on his shoulders. There was so much riding on this. The safety of his witnesses, his niece, and his heart.

Lord, am I doing the right thing?

Peace settled over him. Whatever happened, good or bad, God would be with him.

He opened the SUV door and made his way to Timberline Toasties.

Being new to the area meant he didn't know much about the local cuisine outside of the major food franchises, but Sam had raved about the sandwich shop known for its variety of grilled cheese options and paninis.

Liam's mouth watered as garlic, butter, and roasted chicken wafted from the door of Timberline Toasties as customers came and went. Sam and the girls were waiting for him outside.

Sam was wearing a pair of blue jeans with a simple green T-shirt and a pair of black ballet shoes. Her blonde hair wasn't slicked back into a braid. Instead, she had it piled on top of her head in a messy bun.

He was overdressed in his black slacks and cream-colored long-sleeve button-down shirt.

"Uncle Liam!" Sophia waved.

He joined the girls. "It sure smells good." He rested his hands on his hips and looked through the window into the restaurant.

"It tastes even better." Sam pulled the door open. "Shall we?"

He stepped around her and opened the door. "Ladies first."

"Since you bought dinner last night, I'm buying lunch." Sam led the way to the counter.

"That's not necessary." She didn't need to feed him and Sophia when she had so much more to worry about.

"I insist. Please don't make a big deal of it."

"Can you do that?" He rubbed the back of his neck. "I mean, you've got pretty big expenses coming up."

She smiled at him. "I'm sure. We're going to be fine."

He studied her for a moment. What would she do if he argued with her about it? If they were going to treat this like a first date, then shouldn't he pay?

She laid her hand on his forearm. "I'm serious, we're okay. I want to buy you lunch."

"Okay." He looked at the menu. "What do you suggest?"

She could buy lunch, but he'd buy dessert later.

FIFTEEN

S AM SLID INTO A BOOTH AND MADE ROOM FOR Bella. Only, Bella slid in across from her, followed by Sophia. Leaving the space next to Sam as the only available spot for Liam to sit.

Sam swallowed as Liam moved into the seat. Heat radiated from his body. Or was that her imagination? Everything was going to be okay. This was what they wanted. The girls needed to figure out on their own that she and Liam were dating. No better way to start than by sitting next to each other.

The girls chatted away. Completely ignoring the two adults sitting with them.

Liam turned to Sam. "How is it going?"

"I can't complain." She smiled. "Not that it would do any good if I did."

"True." He unwrapped his straw and slid it into his cup. Then he wadded up the paper and tossed it at Sophia's head. It hit her on the cheek.

"Hey." She turned and narrowed her eyes, then stood her straw on end and slowly started pushing the paper from the top of the straw down toward the table. Once the paper was scrunched up, she put the straw to her lips and blew, shooting the paper at Liam. The wad of paper flew past him and landed on the table behind them.

He looked over his shoulder. "Good thing no one is sitting there."

He grinned, lifted his left arm, and reached across the back of the booth to grab the paper. The movement brought his chest closer to Sam. All she could do was stare at the pearl-like button on his shirt. Her breath hitched at his nearness. Citrus and sage was quickly becoming her favorite fragrance.

He righted himself and tossed the paper on the table. "Behave."

Sophia's mouth dropped. "You started it."

Sam regained her composure and took a drink to quench her suddenly dry mouth. What was wrong with her body?

"Fine."

"Sam." A pimple-faced teenager called her name.

"I'll get it." Liam stood up and retrieved the two trays with food.

"Blessing?" Sophia cocked her head and looked at her uncle.

"Always. You want to do the honors?"

Sophia nodded and bowed her head, followed by Liam and then Bella.

Sam watched the three people sitting with her. Where did they get their faith?

"Heavenly Father, thank You for today and for our friends. Thank You for this food and the hands that made it. I pray that we find Samantha and Bella some good deals and everything they need. Amen."

"Amen," Liam and Bella repeated.

Sam picked up a french fry and pointed it at Sophia. "You can call me Sam."

"Okay, Sam." Sophia smiled and then took a bite from her

pepperoni panini. A dreamy look crossed her face. "This is amazing."

"You should try mine." Bella pushed one of the cut halves on her plate toward her friend.

"Do you want to switch, half for half?" Sophia offered.

Bella shrugged. "Sure."

"Try it with the soup." Bella slid the bowl of cheddar tomato soup toward her friend.

These girls were going to become the best of friends, even though they'd gotten off to a rocky start together with the rebels from school. Sam was certain that if she and Liam could keep them away from those delinquents, then their problems would be solved.

Well, the problems with the girls and their recent penchant for getting into trouble.

Liam nudged her with his elbow.

She looked at him. Did he expect her to offer to split her lunch with him? Oh, she hoped that wasn't the case. She wasn't a huge fan of patty melts, and bacon was her favorite part of the pig.

He leaned in a little closer. "Thanks for lunch."

Her cheeks warmed. "You're welcome. Thanks for letting Sophia hang out with us today."

His mouth lifted into a languid smile.

The warmth from her cheeks spread through her body like the fires she fought as an unexpected rush of attraction settled in her chest.

She quickly turned her focus to her sandwich. Attraction to the man sitting beside her was not something she needed to mix into this equation. Her life was complicated enough.

Liam wadded up his napkin and tossed it into the empty plastic basket his sandwich had been served in. "I've got some time to kill. I thought I'd go with you to a couple stores. Maybe get some dessert before I head back to the office."

Sam's stomach stuttered. Not good. She needed to spend less

time with him, not more. She pasted on a smile. This was for their safety. Everything she did was to protect Bella. "Sounds good."

When everyone was finished eating, they cleaned up their mess and headed to the first store, one completely dedicated to teenage girls. Bella and Sophia disappeared among the clothes.

Liam nudged Sam's shoulder with his, bent down next to her ear. "Why is the music so loud?"

As if to answer his question, a group of girls squealed as they found whatever they'd been looking for. He hadn't even realized it was already past time kids were getting out of school.

He nodded. "I understand now."

"First time in one of these stores, huh?" Sam laughed.

He grimaced. "Are they all like this?"

"If it's aimed at teenagers, yes. Fortunately, this is the only one in this outlet mall." Part of the reason she'd chosen this one.

The girls bounced between clothing racks and jewelry displays.

"I now have a favorite outlet mall. Tell me the others so I can avoid them." He laughed.

"You'll want to avoid Ridgeline. I think that one was designed by teenagers. It's *the* place to hang out."

"Noted." He shoved his hands in his pockets. "So."

"So?" She quirked an eyebrow at him.

"Tell me about you. I know what's in your file and what I've observed. Tell me who the real Samantha Williams is."

Her stomach sank. There wasn't a real Samantha Williams. She was a lie, created to protect everything Madison Johanson loved.

The girls bounced up, saving Sam.

"Find anything?" she asked.

"Not really." Bella shrugged.

They moved on to a sporting-goods store. One that carried athletic clothing and shoes. Sam managed to avoid any more personal conversations with Liam.

They moved on to a discount department store. The one Sam

expected to spend the most time in. Bella and Sophia were loading their arms with things to try on.

"Sam." Liam tapped her on the shoulder.

Dread knotted in her stomach. He was going to dig again. She took a deep breath, preparing herself for the conversation. Could she politely decline to answer?

"I saw something in the men's section I want to check out." He tilted his head. "Would you mind if I went to have a look?"

Relief flooded through her. "No, go ahead."

"I'll be right back." He walked off, taking long strides.

She caught herself staring. It was hard to ignore the way his slacks fit.

"Sam." Bella's voice pulled Sam's attention back to where it needed to be. She turned. Bella was in a pair of stonewashed jeans, paired with a light-purple sweater that hung off the shoulder. "What do you think?"

Where had the little girl in pigtails gone? The girl standing in front of her was more woman than child now. Sam's heart clenched. "You look beautiful."

Bella smiled and disappeared back into the dressing room.

Sam turned to look at a clearance rack conveniently placed by the dressing rooms.

A teenage boy dressed in black pants and a black hoodie stood off to the side, the hood pulled up, hiding his face in the shadows. She'd seen him in every store they'd been in so far.

She picked up a shirt and studied it, masking pulling her phone from her pocket, then slid the shirt back on the rack and picked up another one. She opened the camera app on her phone and slowly made her way around the rack until she was at an angle she could see the kid's face.

She lifted her phone up and pretended to be texting, but snapped a photo of him instead.

She quickly sent it to Liam.

Sam

____

I think we're being followed.

She saw the moment he read the text. She waited for the three dots to appear, but they didn't.

A moment later, an arm snaked around her waist. "Hey, babe."

Liam's calm, steady voice startled her.

He lifted a shirt from the rack, turned her so her back was facing the kid, and held the shirt up.

"I think this brings out the color of your eyes. You should try it on." It may have looked like he was focused on her, but she could tell his gaze was on the teen behind them.

"I've seen him in each of the stores so far," she whispered. "It could be nothing. But why is he in the women's clothing section?"

"I don't know, but I intend to find out." He put the hanger back on the rack and marched toward the teen.

Liam stared the kid down as he made his way toward him. "Why are you following us?"

The kid's eyes grew wide, and he looked around wildly.

Liam kept marching toward him, determined to find out what was going on.

He darted off.

"US marshal. Stop!" Liam shouted as he gave chase. He raced past gawking shoppers and grabbed the kid before he could make it out the door.

"What's your name?" Liam stared the kid in the eyes.

He was about sixteen or seventeen. Five-eleven or six foot. Average build.

"I don't gotta say nothing to you." The kid jutted out his chin.

Liam clenched his jaw. "Why are you following us?"

"It's a free country. I can go where I want." He tried to rip his arm out of Liam's grasp.

"I'm going to ask you again. Why are you following us?"

The kid's eyes narrowed. "Maybe I liked what I saw." He licked his lips lasciviously.

Liam's free hand fisted at his side. The kid was trying to get a rise out of him. It wasn't going to work. "Try again. Without the attitude this time."

"I'd rather not." He smirked.

"Were you spying on us? Who sent you?" Liam leaned in closer.

"I was looking for a present for my mom."

Liam wasn't going to get anywhere with this kid.

"What's going on here?" a security guard interrupted.

Liam kept a grip on the kid's arm. "I'm Deputy US Marshal Liam Roberts. This kid has been following us all afternoon. It's suspicious. I'm trying to determine why."

The security guard fisted his hands on his hips. "Identification."

Liam inhaled deeply and reached for his badge, clipped to the other side of his body.

The kid took the momentary distraction to shove Liam hard, yank free, and run out the front door.

Liam grunted and chased after him, but he was swallowed up in the crowd of shoppers. He pushed forward, hoping to catch up, but it was no use. The kid was gone.

He could keep chasing, but what if the kid wasn't alone? Liam needed to make sure Sam and the girls were safe, then he could hunt the boy down.

Sam and the girls stood by the entrance with the security guard. She looked at him expectantly. He'd let her down.

"I lost him in the crowd." Admitting his failure left a bitter taste in his mouth.

"Did he say anything to you or the girls?"

Sam shook her head. "No. They didn't see him. I showed them the picture. They recognized him."

Liam looked at the girls.

"It was Aiden. He was the one that set the trash can on fire." Sophia crossed her arms over her chest.

Liam needed to get his hands on the security footage, see if he could find out where the kid went. Maybe he'd be lucky and get a license plate. That could wait though. First priority was getting everyone out of here and somewhere safe.

"I think it's time you make your purchases and we get out of here."

Sam nodded and took the girls to the sales register.

Liam pulled his badge from his belt and showed it to the security guard. "I'm going to make sure they get somewhere safe. While I'm gone, can you pull the video footage for me? I want the common-area footage and individual footage for the stores we've been in." Liam gave the security guard the names of the stores they had visited. "I want to see where he came from and where he went."

The security guard nodded. "I can do that."

"Good. I'll be back for it."

Sam and the girls joined him. "Ready?" He placed his hand at the small of Sam's back, and she jumped. He leaned into her. "Relax. Doting boyfriend escorting his girl and their girls out."

Her cheeks tinged as she nodded. She leaned a little closer. "Where exactly are we going?"

"I'm going to follow you back to Dean's." He hadn't decided what he would do with Sophia yet. He knew that Samantha and Isabella would be safe at Dean's house because he'd already checked into all of her coworkers. Perhaps he could take Sophia to the office, and she could sit with Aubrey.

He was woefully unprepared to be in a parenting situation right now. He used to be able to take off for wherever whenever and not have to worry about anyone but himself.

"You don't need to follow us back. We'll be okay." Sam stared straight ahead.

He leaned into her. "I'm not necessarily worried about something happening as much as I am about someone following you, finding out where you're staying, and coming back later."

"Right." She sighed. "Because my life isn't complicated enough."

He rubbed his hand up and down her back. "It will all be okay."

"You don't know that."

"No, but I know the One that does."

"Yeah, I'm not impressed with His track record." She sped up and passed the girls, running from the conversation.

His heart ached for her. She'd been through so many hard things that she couldn't see beyond them to what God had done in the midst of it.

Lord, help me help her.

SIXTEEN

SAM WAS NOT GOING TO HAVE THIS CONVERSAtion with Liam in the mall parking lot. Not here. Not ever.

"Samantha," Liam said.

"I don't want to talk about it."

He held up his hands in mock surrender. "I get it. But that's not what I was going to say."

The girls stopped next to him and looked between the two of them in confusion.

Sam fisted her hand on her hip. "Then what?"

"My SUV is right here. Get in, and I'll take you to your car."

"Right." She let her arm fall.

The girls piled into the back seat, tossing Bella's shopping bags between them.

Liam climbed in and started the engine. "Which way?"

She pointed in the direction of where they'd parked. "It's over there."

He pulled the SUV in front of her car. "Stay in here while I have a look." He hopped out, not bothering to wait for an answer.

She chewed her nails as he walked around the car. He peered inside, then dropped to his knees to look underneath.

Sam turned to the girls, who were chatting in the back seat as if this was completely normal. What she wouldn't give to be oblivious to what was going on right now.

He stood up and walked around to the passenger-side door and opened it for her. "We're good to go. Hop in and I'll follow you."

"Since we're going to the same place, can Bella ride with us?" Sophia asked, suddenly paying attention to what was going on.

"That's up to Samantha." He looked at her.

"Call me Sam." She peered back at the girls. "I don't care."

"Thank you," the girls said simultaneously.

Liam shut the door behind Sam and walked her to her car.

"What are we going to do about this?" She gestured to the outlet mall.

"You aren't going to do anything. I'm going to come back and take a look at the surveillance footage. Then see if I can light a fire under RPD to get me the info on this Aiden kid."

She nodded.

"We should get going. I've got to take Sophia home before I can come back."

"Since I've got to come over to your house this evening, what if she just stays with us this afternoon? She'll keep Bella occupied." Sam didn't want to play twenty questions with Bella when they got home.

Liam studied her. "Are you sure you want to do that?"

"If I didn't want to, I wouldn't have suggested it."

He nodded. "Will Dean be okay with it?"

She'd forgotten she was going to someone else's house and would need to ask permission to invite guests over. "I'll call him on the way and make sure it's okay."

"Sounds good." He stuck his hands in his pockets. "Lock your doors when you're inside."

She nodded and climbed into her car.

Once they were on their way, she dialed Dean's number. Hopefully, he wasn't out on a call.

"Hey, Sam."

"Put out any fires today?"

Dean was covering for one of the other team members today. She wouldn't bet on it, but he'd probably picked up the shift to avoid the birthday party the boys had today. She couldn't blame him. Screaming kids all hyped up on sugar weren't her favorite.

"As a matter of fact, we've put out two. I was the hero. Like always."

"Sure you were." She laughed. "Listen, I was calling to ask if Bella's friend Sophia could hang out with her at your house today. I would have called Cass, but she said the boys had a birthday party, and I didn't want to add to her chaos."

"The marshal's kid?"

Was there a change in his tone?

"His niece, yes. We had lunch together, then took the girls shopping. Some kid was following us. Liam confronted him, but he got away. Liam's following us to your house now."

"Is everything okay?"

"Yes. We're fine. Just, after the week I've had and the threat to the girls, I'm a bit unnerved." She hoped that's all it was, but deep in her gut, she knew it wasn't. "I figure if Sophia could hang out with us, it would keep the girls busy and out of trouble until I meet up with Liam tonight."

"Uh-oh. Do I smell a romance?" Dean teased.

Sam's face heated. Her normal reaction was to go into why a romance would not be happening, but this was a ruse. One she needed to keep herself and Bella safe. "It's possible we might be seeing each other."

"I knew it!" Dean yelled. "Greer owes me twenty bucks."

"You guys seriously bet on my love life?"

"No one said a word about love, sweetheart."

Sam growled. "Whatever. Can Sophia hang out or not?"

Dean laughed. "That's fine."

"Thanks. Don't get into too much trouble."

"Me? Never."

She disconnected the call and pulled into Dean's driveway, and Liam pulled in behind her. Everyone got out and met at the front of Liam's SUV.

"Here." She handed Bella the key to the house. "Y'all go inside."

Bella took the key, and the girls disappeared inside.

"I called Dean, and he's okay with Sophia staying." She sighed. "And now he knows that there's something going on between the two of us."

Liam smirked. "Come on, dating me isn't that bad. I'm quite the catch."

"I'll have to take your word for it."

His face fell, and he quickly cleared his throat. "I better get going. I need to get that footage."

Something she'd said had hit a nerve. She wanted to apologize but didn't know how or why, so she just nodded. "Okay."

She watched him climb into his SUV before she turned around and went inside.

The girls had already disappeared into the room she and Bella had been sharing. She checked on them quickly, then decided to sit down and watch some mind-numbing television.

She channel surfed for a while before finding a movie she'd seen a million times and watching it anyway. It was comforting. She knew everything that was going to happen, and there were no surprises. As the movie started, she scrolled on her phone, looking for a new place to live.

Realistically, she'd want something in the same area so Bella could stay at her current school. Plus, it was conveniently close to the station. It had to have at least two bedrooms. In a perfect world, there'd be three—then she could have a workout room slash study room for Bella. Three-bedroom houses in her price range were going to be hard to find.

Suddenly, the window to her right exploded, and glass rained down on the carpet. Muffled pops and loud thudding filled the front room.

Sam dove for the floor and crawled away from the window and toward the hall. Bullets whipped above her, destroying anything in their path and lodging in walls. She dialed 911 as she crawled.

Bella's and Sophia's screams and the pounding of Sam's heart drowned out the chaos as she made it to the hallway.

"911. Where's your emergency?"

Sam gave the dispatcher Dean's address. "Someone is shooting into the house."

She moved the phone away from her mouth and waved at the girls, who stared from the floor in the spare room, faces pale. "Stay down and crawl to me."

"Do you know how many shooters there are?" the dispatcher asked.

"I didn't see anyone."

"Are you in a safe place? Away from all windows?"

"We're heading there now." She led the girls to the hall bathroom. It was centrally located with no windows. She dragged them both past her, then shut the door. "We're safe."

"Are shots still being fired?"

The gunfire had stopped. "Not right now."

She'd watched enough television shows and movies to know that that didn't necessarily mean the attack was over.

"Officers are on their way. Stay on the line with me, okay?"

Sam motioned for the girls to get into the bathtub, where they huddled together and cried. She climbed on top of the bathroom counter, away from the door in case bullets came flying through it.

She looked wildly around, trying to find anything she could use to defend herself. There was nothing but bath toys and toddler things. A rubber duck wasn't going to save the day.

Liam would know what to do. He wouldn't be huddled up on a counter, waiting for them to come to him. He'd chase them down and make them regret showing up. That was what he was trained to do. She was trained to fight fires. Not the same thing.

"The officers are two minutes out. Can you tell me what's happening now?"

Two minutes wasn't long, but it was too long when someone's life was on the line.

She shushed the girls, pulled the phone away from her ear, and listened for sounds. "I don't hear anything," she whispered into the phone.

"Okay, officers are on the scene. Sit tight. They're going to check the perimeter, and then they'll come to you. Remain on the line with me."

"Okay." Sam climbed off the counter and made her way to the girls. "The police are here. Just a few minutes longer."

The girls sat up and wrapped their arms around her.

"Okay. They're entering the house. Stay where you are until they knock on the door."

Shouts and commands from officers echoed on the other side of the door.

Sam gripped the phone and forced her breathing to slow.

"Officer Johnson is coming to get you, okay?" the dispatcher said.

"Renegade Police Department!"

The girls whimpered at the man's booming voice.

"He's here," Sam told the dispatcher.

"Okay, I want you to let him know you're in there and follow his directions."

"Thank you." She disconnected the call. "We're in here alone."

"Okay, open the door slowly."

She stood and unlocked the door, then slowly opened it. Three armed officers stood on the other side, weapons pointed down.

Her body trembled as she raised her hands.

Liam slid the CD containing the outlet-mall footage into his work computer. The footage outside the sandwich shop popped up on screen. He watched as their group left the sandwich shop, then followed their steps to the first store and waited to see when Aiden would show up. He fast-forwarded the footage ten minutes and stopped when they all walked out of the store.

The guy didn't enter the store after them.

He restarted the footage. A few beats passed, then Aiden slunk out of the store and turned the same direction the girls went. He'd already been in the store when they got there. Without seeing all of the footage, it looked like a coincidence turned into an opportunity.

The phone in his hand vibrated, followed by the generic ringtone. He looked at the caller ID. Sam.

His stomach clenched, and the hair on the back of his neck stood on end. "Sam?"

"Is this Deputy US Marshal Liam Roberts?" an unfamiliar male voice asked.

"It is. Who is this?" He paused the video.

"This is Corporal Johnson with the Renegade Police Department."

Liam hit the door in a full sprint, racing to his car. "What's going on?"

"Everyone is okay, and no one is injured. But there has been a shooting. Samantha Williams asked me to call you."

"Tell her I'm on my way there now." He disconnected the call and tossed it in the passenger seat as he started the SUV. He slammed it in gear and activated the lights and sirens.

Lord, I know he said no one was hurt, but please keep them safe.

Police cars lined the street he'd left an hour ago. He turned off his lights and sirens, jammed the SUV into Park, and hopped out.

He ripped his badge from his belt and flashed it at the nearest officer. "Where are the woman and two teenagers that were in the house?"

"They're in my unit." She turned and pointed to a unit in the middle of the melee.

He jogged to the cruiser and pulled open the door.

Sophia jumped at the suddenness. "Uncle Liam!"

She scrambled out and threw her arms around him. He crushed her to him. "Sophia. Thank God you're all right." He pulled back and looked her over, then hugged her again.

Sam slowly climbed from the unit, Isabella behind her. He gathered the two of them into the hug as well.

"Thank You, God, for Your protection," he whispered into the huddle. He pulled his head back. "Is everyone okay?" He made eye contact with each of the girls in his arms.

Isabella's and Sophia's faces were splotchy, and their eyes were rimmed with red. The paleness of Sam's face only made the bags under her eyes more pronounced.

She said, "We're good."

"Sam!" Someone yelled from over behind the barricade.

They all looked to the commotion. Dean was standing next to an officer, pointing at their huddle.

Sam pulled from Liam's embrace and jogged to her friend, who grabbed her in a bear hug, practically lifting her off her feet.

The officer let him through the perimeter. Dean immediately pulled Isabella to him. "Oh, kiddo." She hugged him back.

Dean looked at Sophia, still in Liam's arms. "I'm glad you're okay." He reached out and patted her on the arm.

"I'm so sorry," Sam apologized to her friend.

Dean turned to her. "Did you shoot up my house?"

She shook her head.

"Then you have nothing to be sorry for."

"I brought them to your house." She gasped. "What if Cass and the boys had been home?"

"You can't think like that." Dean framed Sam's face in his hands. "They weren't home. No one was hurt."

Liam spoke up. "I'm positive we weren't followed back to the house earlier." He was an experienced law enforcement officer. He knew how to spot a tail, and there hadn't been one.

"See," Dean said. "Plus, we don't even know if this is related to you. It could be a coincidence."

"Does this type of thing happen in your neighborhood often?" Sam crossed her arms over her chest.

Dean rubbed the back of his neck. "No. I was just trying to make you feel better."

She quirked an eyebrow at him. "We can't stay here. I'm not going to put your family in any more danger."

"Where else are you going to go?"

Liam stepped forward and wrapped his arm around Sam's shoulders, pulling her close. "They'll stay with me."

Sam stiffened under his arm.

His offer surprised him too. But this was strictly professional. No other reason.

"Moving in together. Isn't that really too soon?" Dean narrowed his eyes at Liam.

Sam tilted her head up and looked at Liam.

"Relax. She's not *moving in* moving in." He looked at Sam.

"You'll just be staying until you find a new place and whoever it is gets caught. It makes the most sense."

She just stared at him.

"Why would you go anywhere else when you have built-in security with me?" He leaned down and kissed the tip of her nose.

Her eyes widened even more, which had to be anatomically impossible.

He turned to face her, eclipsing Dean from her sight, and gently grabbed her shoulders. He hoped he could communicate what needed to be said with his facial features.

If they wanted to keep her cover intact, this was the best way to do that.

She started to nod. "You're right. Plus, it will be good for the girls."

He smiled. "It's settled, then." He turned back to face Dean and pulled Sam to his side again.

Dean stared Liam down, his jaw clenched.

Interesting reaction to wanting to keep Sam safe. The guy was married, and they worked on the same firefighter team, watching each other's backs. Liam figured it was a big-brother type reaction.

Dean's face softened a bit when he looked at Sam. "Fine. You're an adult. You can do what you want, but—" He turned to Liam and squared his stance. "You hurt her"—he nodded to Sam—"or her"—he nodded to Isabella behind them—"and you'll have to deal with me."

The threat was strangely comforting. It meant Samantha had people in her life who would protect her, because right now, this was all a ruse. She'd need people like that when everything was said and done. He hoped he'd get to be one of those people.

"Understood," Liam said.

"I need to go see about my house." Dean stepped back and made his way to a police officer.

Samantha stepped out of Liam's embrace, and he immediately

missed her presence. It had been so long since he'd held someone like that. Sophia excluded.

They turned around, and both girls were staring at them, mouths agape.

"What?" Sam stopped in her tracks.

"Are you two dating now?" Isabella looked at Sophia, then glanced between the two of them. "We were getting *vibes* at lunch."

Liam reached down and grabbed Sam's hand. Gave it a little squeeze. "I guess the secret's out."

She looked up at him. Vulnerability filled her face.

This was obviously a big step for her. Even if it was fake.

"We could be sisters!" Sophia turned to Isabella and wrapped her arms around her.

He wasn't going to ruin their excitement with semantics. They needed all the happy they could get right now.

And he needed to figure out who had just tried to kill them. There was no way that a drive-by at Dean's house was a coincidence. This was a targeted attack.

Dating took a back seat to attempted murder.

SEVENTEEN

SAM WAS NUMB. IT WAS LIKE SHE WAS WATCHING a movie. She knew what was going on, but she wasn't actively participating in it. Except she really was. They'd waited until they were given the go-ahead to grab their stuff, and Liam and Sophia helped them pack up what little they owned and load it into his SUV.

They had to leave her car behind because it was blocked in by all of the emergency vehicles. Not to mention it was part of the crime scene. It had sustained a few bullet holes.

Stress upon stress. Now she'd need to make an insurance claim for her car. First her home, then her car.

She shivered. They'd almost died today. For what? The fact the girls had told them about a trash-can fire? Nothing about this made any sense.

Sam was no longer worried that this was connected to the Mob. It had to be the kid from the outlet center.

Liam was certain they hadn't been followed. Given his career and experience, she was confident in his ability to do his job. But how could they have known where to find them otherwise?

She wanted to close her eyes and sleep for a week. Or any amount of time, actually, if when she woke up, she discovered this was a nightmare. It hadn't worked for the Mob. And it probably wasn't going to work for this.

The car stopped moving. She looked out the front window to see that they were parked in Liam's driveway. Wow, she had no recollection of the drive over here. That's what she got for zoning out.

She didn't have the energy to climb out of the car. Her entire body felt like rubber. No matter how many times her brain told her arm to open the door, it wouldn't listen.

Her eyes started to burn, and her breath came in rapid gasps. The sounds in the SUV faded to a ringing, and her vision blurred.

Had the doors just opened and shut?

Her chest constricted. There wasn't enough air.

The atmosphere next to her changed, and she was pulled from the SUV and jostled around until she was sitting in someone's lap, strong arms wrapped around her and holding her tight. She faintly registered the closing of the car door.

She was safe in these arms. She closed her eyes and burrowed into the safety.

A hand rubbed up and down her arm, and words were whispered into her hair. She couldn't hear what was being said.

Breathe in. Breathe out.

Her body relaxed with each breath, and with that, her eyelids grew heavier and heavier until she couldn't fight it anymore. She'd used the last bit of her energy fighting the panic attack, and she couldn't manage to stay awake.

***

Sam breathed in the smells of citrus and sage like she was

standing in an orange grove. Except she wasn't. She was cradled against something warm and firm.

Her head rose and fell with the inhales and exhales of Liam breathing beneath her. His heartbeat steady against her ear. Was this what a real relationship felt like?

Liam's arms tightened around her. "It's okay. You're safe." His voice was gravelly.

They were still in the SUV. Liam had pushed the front seat all the way back and held her in his lap. His seat was leaned slightly back.

She tried to move to get out, but he held her tight against him.

"Slow down, would ya? Your elbow in my chest isn't that comfortable, and my legs are asleep."

"Oh, I'm sorry." She covered her face with her hands as heat crept up her neck.

He gently grasped her fingers and pulled them away so that he could make eye contact. "Are you okay now?"

The compassionate concern in his gaze set flutters in motion in her stomach. This wasn't good. Unable to speak for fear her voice would betray her, she nodded.

"Good. I was worried." He brushed the hair from her face.

Her breath hitched as his fingers lingered on her cheek. She closed her eyes and relished the moment. She'd never felt more cared for than she did right now.

"Sam." Liam's voice was a husky whisper.

She opened her eyes. He stared at her like he felt something too.

It wouldn't take much. Just lean up a couple inches, touch her lips to his.

He cradled her face like he could read her thoughts.

Another time, another place, and she might do it. Throw caution to the wind, lose control in *what could be*. But this wasn't just about her. So she pulled back. "We should go inside."

Liam blinked. The warmth in his face was replaced by the serious marshal she was used to. "Right."

He opened the door. She maneuvered to climb out of the SUV.

"Oof." He grunted as her elbow slipped and jabbed him in the chest.

"I'm sorry." She jerked and hit him in the face with her forearm. "Oh no."

He wrapped his arms around her. "Will you stop moving?" His breath whispered against her cheek, raising goosebumps along her neck. She needed to get as far away from this man as she could.

He helped her out of the vehicle before rotating until his legs hung outside.

"Do you need some help?" He'd sat for however long with her in his lap.

"No. I'll be fine, just a minute." He flexed his feet and rotated his ankles, then bent his knees.

She grimaced. "How long was I out?"

"About thirty minutes."

Her heart raced. He'd held her the whole time. "I'm sorry."

He smiled. "I wish you'd quit saying that."

"Well, I am. I'm such a wreck." She rubbed her forehead with the palm of her hand.

He stood up out of the SUV and grabbed her hand. "I'd say you've handled the past week pretty well, considering. I saw you were about to lose it, so I sent the girls inside."

"Thank you. For"—she nodded at the SUV—"helping with that. And everything else. I'm used to people protecting me. But that's because 69- 3322it's their job. You? You make it feel personal. You don't treat me like a job. You treat me like I'm something worth caring about."

He shoved his hands into his pockets. "Everyone should have someone who looks out for them like that. You've never had that? In a boyfriend?"

She shook her head. "I'm sure you've read my file. You know about my mother and the last man I dated."

He reached out and grasped her hand. "Sam, you are like no other woman I've met. So strong. Resilient. You care deeply. I wish all women were like that."

"I sense an ugly ex hiding in your closet."

"Yeah, she jetted once Sophia became a permanent part of my life."

Sam smiled softly. "That's her loss. You're a great man, and Sophia's worth sticking around for."

Something flashed in his eyes. Before she could decipher it, it was gone. He dropped her hand and took a step back. "Shall we go into the house now?"

"We need to get our things. Let me go get Bella."

"I can help." Liam popped the rear hatch and grabbed the bags.

She followed behind him, carrying the one bag he let her carry.

"While you were sleeping, I texted Sophia and told her to put clean sheets and a blanket on my bed for you."

She stopped dead in her tracks. "I'm not sleeping in your bed."

"Well, the only other option is sharing the couch with the dog." He opened the front door.

"That's perfect."

"She snores." He dropped Bella's things next to the couch.

"It can't be that bad." She clung to her bag.

"I insist on you taking my bedroom. You'll rest more comfortably than on this springy old couch."

"And you can sleep comfortably on it?" She quirked an eyebrow at him.

"I don't sleep that much." He took her bag from her arms, turned around, and waltzed down the hall.

She followed quickly behind him. "You're kind enough to let us stay with you. I can't let you give me your bed."

"Well, that couch isn't big enough for the both of us, but I'm willing to give it a try." He continued down the hall.

They passed a bathroom and came up to Sophia's room, where the girls were sprawled across her bed, watching television. "It's about time y'all came in," Sophia yelled as they passed by.

The room next to Sophia's was a small home office. A giant bookshelf full of books almost took up one wall.

Liam disappeared into the next room.

Her steps slowed as she entered. A queen-size bed with a simple black headboard was pushed to the right side of the room. A dark-blue comforter and matching pillows made the bed. There was a matching nightstand and chest of drawers. Black curtains hung over the lone window.

He tossed her bag onto the bed and turned to face her. "What's it going to be?"

She chewed her bottom lip. "I just don't want to put you out."

He sighed. "You can go ask Sophia about my sleeping habits. She'll confirm that I don't sleep as much as the average person."

"Fine. But promise me the minute you get uncomfortable or can't sleep, you'll take your bed back." She fisted her hands on her hips.

"It won't happen, but I promise." He stuck his hand out, pinkie up.

She narrowed her eyes at his hand. "What are you doing?"

"It's a pinkie promise. You put your pinkie out, and we hook like this." He demonstrated with his other hand. "A pinkie promise can't be broken."

She just stared at his hand.

"You seriously don't know what a pinkie promise is? I thought all girls did. I'm going to have to talk to Kayleigh about this." He shoved his hands in his pockets.

"I didn't even think about how this would affect your girlfriend.

Is she going to be okay with this whole"—she waved her hand around the room—"situation?"

"I don't have a girlfriend. Kayleigh is my sister, Soph's mom."

"Right." She gave a small smile, remembering that he'd told her. "You're doing a good job with her."

Unlike the way she'd grown up. A mother in a prison—not a physical prison like the one Sophia's mom was in, but a prison of addiction. How would Sam's life have been different if she'd had an aunt or uncle to step in like Liam was doing?

"I'm doing the best I can, but sometimes I wonder if I'm going to be enough. You know?"

"Oh, I do." She glanced over her shoulder and out into the hall. "I've been helping raise Bella since she was a newborn."

"Wow. That was a lot to take on for someone so young. You were, what . . . fourteen when she was born?"

"Yeah."

"Uncle Liam," Sophia called from down the hall. "Can we order pizza tonight? I'm starving."

He chuckled. "The savages are getting restless. You and Isabella going to be okay with pizza again?"

"Only if you allow me to buy it."

"But you bought lunch. It's my turn to pay."

"We'll go halfsies." She crossed her arms over her chest.

"Deal."

She turned and made her way down the hall and stopped in front of Sophia's room. "Bella, come get your things out of the front room, okay?" They didn't need to be making a mess.

Sam paused outside Sophia's door, the weight of Liam's words settling deep. This wasn't just about safety or duty. It felt personal.

She clenched her jaw, reminding herself not to get ahead of things. But part of her wondered if letting go—even a little— might be what she needed.

Liam lay on the couch, staring at the ceiling, processing everything that had happened today. How close he'd come to losing his niece and two witnesses. He replayed the day over and over in his head, trying to find what he'd missed. And each time, he came up with nothing.

Lying here second-guessing himself was getting him nowhere. He needed to get some rest so he could start fresh tomorrow.

He rolled over to his side and tried to clear his head. No more thinking about work.

The memory of having Samantha wrapped in his arms came to the forefront. The way she'd felt in his arms.

You don't treat me like a job. You treat me like I'm something worth caring about.

That wasn't part of the job description. He was her handler; his job was to protect. Nothing more. He squeezed his eyes shut. He didn't need to be feeling things. Especially for his witness.

It needed to be pushed down into a box and shoved far out of reach. He had Sophia, and that was all he needed. To focus on raising her and being the best uncle-slash-dad he could be.

Despite what had happened between him and Sam, Liam didn't need to add a romantic relationship into his life while juggling work and parenting. Especially a relationship with a witness.

There were so many rules against that. He wouldn't be able to properly keep her safe if he let her in. But he'd already started letting her in. He needed to keep things professional. Letting his guard down could be disastrous.

Also, if she wasn't a believer, that was an even bigger reason to hit the brakes. No matter how much he might be attracted to her, if they weren't on the same page regarding God, they were ultimately on different paths.

His brain understood; he just needed to get his heart on the same page.

Convinced he wasn't going to get to sleep anytime soon, he flicked on the front-room light, moved the coffee table out of the way, and pushed his body with an intense workout of slow, punishing push-ups, squat holds that set his thighs on fire, and planks that shook his core—every move deliberate, silent, and fueled by the need to burn through the storm in his head.

His muscles ached from pushing his body so hard. A hot shower would relax him, and maybe his mind, so he could get some sleep.

He grabbed underwear, blue-plaid pajama pants, and a T-shirt from the dryer—a chore he'd meant to do tonight—and headed to the hall bathroom. He'd shower in there to avoid disturbing Sam.

He dropped his chin to his chest. This was Sophia's bathroom. Which meant the only available soap smelled like watermelon. Note to self: Hide a bottle of his soap in here for the future. Hopefully, the fruitiness would wear off before he had to go into the office.

Once he was dressed, he opened the bathroom door and padded down the hallway toward the kitchen. The light was on. He was certain he'd turned it off after walking through from the laundry room.

Sam was seated at the kitchen table, a cup of water in front of her. Her dark-blonde hair, which was normally pulled back in a tight braid, was loose and flowed down her back and across her shoulders. Smooth and silky. She looked at him as he entered.

"Couldn't sleep either?" He leaned against the cabinet nearest the door.

She shook her head. "I was worried about you not being able to sleep with all the snoring, but I don't see the dog."

"Yeah, she's in the room with the girls." He chuckled. "I insisted."

"I hope it's okay I got myself a cup of water." She nodded at the cup in her hands.

"It's fine. Help yourself to anything you want. Soph has some chamomile tea she swears helps her sleep. Would you like me to make some for you?" He opened the cupboard and pulled out the box of tea. He'd thought about trying it if the workout didn't relax him.

"You don't have to do that." She fidgeted with the cup. "Water is fine."

He pulled the electric kettle from the cabinet and set it next to the box of tea. Apparently, microwaving water to make tea was sacrilegious. "Well, it's here if you want it."

"Thanks."

He made his own glass of water and took a seat across from her at the small table. They sat in companionable silence. It was comfortable. He hadn't had that in a long time.

"When I found out Kayleigh was going to prison and that I needed to step up and be Sophia's guardian, I was more scared than I'd ever been in my life. And that's bad, considering what I do for a living. I've stared down the barrel of a gun, but that seemed like a cakewalk compared to raising a teenager."

She looked up from her cup.

"That was nothing compared to the fear I experienced today." He was being vulnerable right now, and he couldn't explain why he felt the need to do so.

"I'm sorry." Sam bit her bottom lip.

His heart constricted. "I didn't say that to make you feel bad. I wasn't afraid for just Sophia. I never expected to be in a situation like this, where my personal life mixed with my professional life." He wasn't sure exactly what he was saying, but this was different than anything he'd experienced before. Today had changed his perspective. The line between his duty and his feelings had blurred, shifting the way he saw everything.

"I wish none of this had happened. Sophia would be safe. Maybe Bella and I should find somewhere else to stay. Is there another marshal that can take over?" She returned her gaze to the cup of water in her hand.

He shook his head. "No. I need to see this through. Not just because you're my assigned witness, but because *I* need to know that you and Bella are okay."

There was so much in that statement that he couldn't explain. Why was his need to personally be in control of their safety so strong?

"I mean, God is ultimately in control, but I need to do everything I can to make sure nothing happens to the three of you."

She looked up and studied his face. "God is in control? He's got a loose grip on that control, if my history is any indication."

"That's the god, little *g*, of this world talking. Scripture says his purpose is to steal, kill, and destroy. He doesn't want you to see how truly gracious and full of mercy God is. He's going to do everything he can to keep you as far away from God as he can."

"Well, it feels like little-*g* god is winning—in my life, at least."

"That's what little-*g* god wants you to believe. But God is with us the whole time, and you can rest in the fact that He is working all things out for the good of those that love Him. It's gonna hurt in the moment, but one day, you'll be able to look back and see His fingerprints all over it, leading you to where you were supposed to be. We aren't promised an easy ride, just help during the ride. God is with you in everything."

"I'm not sure I can believe that."

"It's okay to have questions. Dig into that tattered Bible you packed and see if you can find those answers."

She pursed her lips. "I picked it up last night. Started reading the gospel of Mark. But it talks about all these things Jesus did for other people, and all I can think is, why didn't He help me when I needed it?"

"Hmm. The Gospels are a good start, but maybe you should also read about Joseph or Paul, people who went through tough things but still held on to God. I'm not saying it's easy to understand, but remembering their struggles helps me hold on when nothing else makes sense. And I'm here to help you through it too—no pressure, just a hand to hold if you want it."

"Thanks." She stood and placed her cup in the dishwasher, signaling the end of the conversation.

He prayed she'd let go of her anger and see how great God really was.

EIGHTEEN

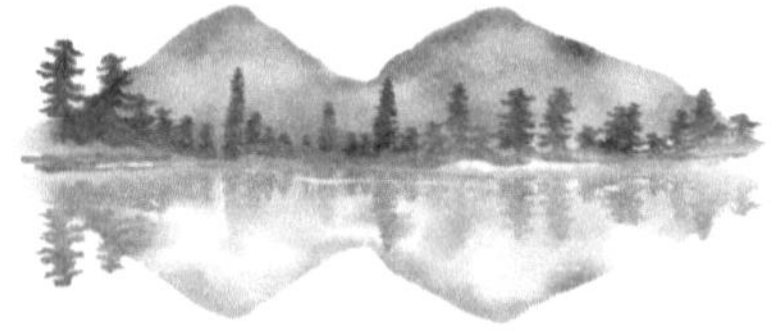

THE BLARE OF THE ALARM STARTLED HER FROM a deep sleep.

5:30 a.m.

She sat up and rubbed the sleep from her eyes. Her body protested, begging for more rest. How traitorous. First, she couldn't sleep, and then it demanded more.

Her mind lingered on the quiet moment with Liam last night. He'd given her some food for thought. Maybe she didn't have to do it alone.

She'd burrowed into the bed and fallen asleep surrounded by the smell she was beginning to crave. Her heart was in trouble. Her brain told her to not read too much into anything with Liam. He was doing his job. He was probably like this with all of his witnesses. Tending to them physically and emotionally. Keeping them relaxed, happy, and safe was his job. It put bad guys behind bars.

She pushed all thoughts of Liam to the back of her mind. She needed to focus on getting ready for work.

Showered and with her hair in a French braid, Sam left the room feeling more refreshed. The scent of Columbian roast coffee filled the hallway. She followed her nose.

Liam sat at the kitchen table, dressed in a soft-blue button-down shirt and black slacks. A Bible lay open in front of him, his hand wrapped around a cup of coffee.

He looked up when she entered the room. "Morning. Help yourself to some coffee." He turned his attention back to the book.

Sugar packets, a small carton of milk, and creamer were situated next to the coffeepot.

"I wasn't sure how you took your coffee, or if you even drank it, so I got everything out." He closed the Bible.

"I didn't mean to interrupt." She nodded at his Bible.

"You didn't. I finished. What do you and Bella usually do for breakfast? I wasn't sure if y'all were eggs-and-bacon kind of people."

A flutter began in her stomach. She was just hungry. "I usually eat a protein bar on the way to the station, and Bella has cereal before school."

"Well, she and Sophia are going to get along, then. Assuming they like the same cereal."

"If it's fruity and covered in milk, she'll be happy."

"Good thing we have that." He smiled. "I thought I'd take you to work this morning since, you know, your car is otherwise unavailable."

"I'd appreciate it. I'm sure I could get a ride on the Renegade Rides app, but they're probably all asleep."

"No need for that. I've got you covered." Liam nodded. "Speaking of the girls, I think it's best if we pull them from school. We don't know who is behind the shooting and if they might try anything at the school. If they're with me at all times, I can keep them safe. We don't want to put any of the other students in danger."

"I think that's a good idea."

Sam hesitated, realizing how much she was beginning to rely on Liam—not just as a handler but as someone she might trust. It was unfamiliar territory, and part of her bristled at it, but another part whispered that maybe, for once, she didn't have to carry the weight alone.

Liam rubbed the back of his neck. "I thought maybe the girls and I could show up at the station for lunch. What time do you guys usually eat?"

She turned and leaned against the cabinet. "That's not necessary. I'm sure you've got lots of work to do."

"Actually, it is necessary. I need to keep an eye on everyone, and since we are, quote-unquote, 'dating,' lunch is the best opportunity to check in."

"What about your job?"

"You are my job, remember?" He stood up and placed his cup in the sink. "If you'd prefer, you can take some time off and we can all hang out here."

"As tempting as that is, I'd rather work." This wasn't her home. She would be more comfortable at the station, where she could be doing things that needed to be done. "Unless you think it's necessary. I'm sure Captain Bennett will be able to find a replacement."

"I figured you'd want to keep working. We don't have a lot to go on, so I don't know that taking time off and holing up is the answer. I also don't know that it's not the answer. The drive-by was the first physical attack. And if it was related to the boy that was following you at the outlet mall, then I think the girls might be the target, not you."

Should she be relieved? "That makes sense."

"Which means the girls will be with me twenty-four seven until this is resolved. Let me go wake them up."

Sam looked at her watch. "Have you seen what time it is?"

"Apology pancakes always work with Sophia." He grinned and started to leave. "Oh. Should you be the one to wake them up? I mean, I know Sophia sleeps in pajama pants and a shirt. I don't want to—" He rubbed the back of his neck.

"Isabella too. But I'll go wake them up."

She flipped on the light and told the girls to get up and get dressed. They moaned and groaned until they buckled into the SUV, then they leaned against the doors and closed their eyes.

Liam pulled the SUV up to the fire station and put it in Park.

Sam grabbed the door handle. "Thanks for the ride. I'll see you about noon?" The station tried to keep a regular schedule as much as possible. Of course, emergencies didn't have a schedule. "I'll let you know if we get called out."

She opened the door and hopped out, tossing the duffel bag over her shoulder. Liam's door clicked shut, and he met her at the hood of his SUV.

Heat climbed her neck. "I can walk myself inside."

"I know you can, but can't a guy get out and tell his girlfriend goodbye?" He slipped the duffel bag off her shoulder with one hand and grabbed her hand in his other.

She stared down at their joined hands. Such a strange feeling. She liked it. She hadn't held hands with anyone lately but Bella. Warmth spread from his hand to her stomach.

"Ready." He squeezed her hand.

"I'm quite capable of carrying my bag. I could actually carry you with ease." She trained for that exact scenario. "What are the guys going to think when they see this? They're not going to trust that I can rescue them if the need arises."

"I highly doubt me carrying your bag one time is going to erase six years of working with you and witnessing what you're capable of from their minds."

"True." They walked hand in hand to the station lobby, the girls leading the way so they weren't alone even for a few minutes while he walked Sam in.

"We'll let you go from here." He handed her bag over and she took it.

Then he leaned forward. She held her breath. He placed a soft kiss on her cheek, then leaned into her ear. "We have an audience."

Her cheeks flamed. Of course it was all for show. This wasn't real.

He pulled back. "See you at lunch." He turned and walked back out to the SUV with the girls. She watched as they drove off before walking into the dayroom.

Greer gasped. "It's true. You're fraternizing with the enemy." He bit his knuckle and turned to the group gathered around the kitchen island. "Sam has gone to the dark side. This calls for an intervention!"

"Why settle for the donut patrol when you could have a real man like me?" Ryan Calloway, the ladder engineer from the night shift, flexed his bicep and waggled his eyebrows.

Sam dropped her chin to her chest and held in her laugh. These guys were too much sometimes.

"All right, knock it off." Dean laughed. "Give her some space. Everyone is allowed to make mistakes in their life." He walked over and gave her a hug.

"Har har." She hugged him back.

"Seriously." Greer's expression sobered. "We're glad you're okay." He gave her a hug.

"And on behalf of Station 4," Captain Bennett said as he stepped up, "we've all chipped in some money to help you and Bella out on your new place." He offered an envelope.

Tears burned her eyes. "You guys didn't have to do that." Emotion filled her voice.

"Of course we did. You're one of us. When you hurt, we hurt." This from Murph. "Fair warning, there are fundraiser plans in the making as well."

This was what family was like. Taking care of each other when things were wrong. She had always been the one taking care of herself or Bella. Having people actually care about her was so foreign. She swallowed hard. She wasn't going to cry. Not here. Not now. "You guys are amazing. Thank you."

The guys each took turns hugging her and offering words of encouragement. Then they split up and went their different ways to start their daily tasks.

"Dean." She jogged after him. "How are Cass and the boys?"

"They're good. I packed them up and sent them to Cass's parents until I can get the damage fixed."

"I'm sorry. I should never have stayed with you guys." Her stomach roiled. She'd put her friends in danger.

"Please don't beat yourself up over this. It was not your fault. Besides, Cass wanted to repaint the front room anyway. I told her one day we would. And look, it's happening, and we don't have to pay for it." He smiled brightly before pulling her to his side. "Seriously, don't stress, okay?"

"I'll try not to." She hugged him back and made a mental note to call Cass later and apologize to her personally.

Even with Liam on the case and the girls protected, it didn't mean that the people Sam cared about wouldn't get caught in the crossfire.

Liam pulled the SUV into the station parking lot at ten 'til noon. Samantha hadn't rung or texted to let him know they'd been called out, so he'd loaded the girls up to have lunch at the station. He held the lobby door open for them and followed them inside.

A man a few inches shorter than Liam, with dark hair and a baby face, greeted them. "Bella. How's it going?" He held up his fist, which Bella bumped with her own.

"Greer, this is my friend Sophia," Bella said.

"Nice to meet you, Sophia." He held his fist up for her, and she bumped it.

"I'm Liam Roberts." Liam stepped forward and held his hand out.

Greer took hold and gave it a too-firm shake. Liam recognized it for what it was. A show of masculinity. He wouldn't be surprised if there was a "don't hurt her" conversation coming.

Greer turned to the girls. "You're just in time. It's Murph's day for lunch, and he brought pulled pork. He's in there now, finishing the potato salad and baked beans. Why don't you two go ahead and get started?"

Isabella nodded, grabbed Sophia by the forearm, and pulled her into the dayroom.

Greer turned his attention to Liam. "So, you're the new boyfriend?" he said as he studied him.

"Yes. I'm the new boyfriend." That sentence tasted weird in his mouth. This was all for the safety of Samantha and Isabella. He needed to play the part and get used to saying it.

The man folded his arms over his chest.

Liam remained relaxed in his stance. He knew what was coming, and he was going to let the man have his say.

"You probably think this is going to be one of those 'hurt her and die' conversations."

"I wouldn't expect less. I know how working closely with a team of people builds a bond and familial relationship."

Greer nodded. "Our jobs may be different in many ways, but they're similar in others. The family thing is one of them. I'm not here to give you that big-brother speech. No matter how much I want to. I know Sam and her capabilities. She can take care of herself just fine. Physically, that is. She has to be strong to do our job. You know she's the only woman employed by the Renegade Fire Department?"

Liam shook his head. "I didn't know that."

"I've only been on the team three years, but I know she has the strength, determination, and grit to do the job. I've seen her carry grown men bigger than she is from buildings."

There was no doubt in Liam's mind that Samantha was capable of doing her job. She wouldn't be here if she wasn't. What he didn't know was what Greer was going for here.

"What I haven't seen is her showing any personal emotional connections outside of the station. There's always some man trying to catch her eye when we're out on calls and community events. She ignores the attention and moves on. There's something different with you." Greer studied him.

He had no idea how right he was—just not in the sense he was implying.

"You should know she's been through some stuff."

Liam narrowed his eyes. She'd said she hadn't told anyone about her past.

"She's got something locked up inside her that she hasn't shared with the rest of us. You can tell by how closed off she is. She tries to cover it but doesn't always do a good job. It's not very often you see a twenty-nine-year-old woman with custody of their younger sister and a past she doesn't talk about."

"Okay, so you're telling me to be careful?" What was Greer's angle? Did he harbor some romantic feelings for his coworker?

"Yes. Be careful with her. Who she dates and why is her business. I want nothing more than to see her happy, and if you're the man to do it, then so be it, even if you're part of the donut patrol." He smirked.

Liam huffed at the nickname.

Greer's face softened. "I'm just saying, tread carefully. When she finally opens her heart up, she's going to love with all of it."

"Understood." Liam crossed his arms. Even though this relationship was fake to the two of them, to those who cared about

Sam, this was real. He would do everything in his power to maintain that professionalism and not lead her to any other conclusion.

"If you ever mention we had this conversation, I will deny it and tell her you've secretly wanted to be a firefighter your whole life but couldn't grow the mustache."

Sam pushed through the door. "There you are." She eyed Greer suspiciously. "What are you two doing?"

Greer held up his hands in fake surrender. "Deputy Marshal Roberts was just asking me if I'd noticed anything unusual around the station." He turned to Liam. "And I was telling him I hadn't."

"Just trying to investigate a little, that's all." Liam shrugged his shoulders and let his arms drop to his side.

She studied the two of them like she wasn't sure she believed the story. "Well, lunch is served. We better eat before another call comes in."

She turned around and walked back to the dayroom.

"Guests first." Greer gestured for Liam to follow Sam.

Everyone was gathered around the kitchen island, making plates. The aroma of tangy barbecue filled the air.

Liam watched as Sophia and Isabella made themselves plates and slumped onto the loveseat in the dayroom.

"Here." Sam handed him a paper plate. "If you don't get in there and get some food, it will disappear." She turned and got in line.

When he'd pulled into the station, he hadn't been all that hungry, but his mouth had started watering once he'd stepped into the dayroom.

Liam stepped into line behind Sam.

"Murphy." She pointed to the firefighter with red hair. "Smoked the meat himself and made the barbecue sauce. He never tells us his secret, but it's amazing."

It sure smelled that way.

"You've already met Greer and Dean." She looked around the room.

"And Captain Bennett and Lieutenant Fischer."

"Right."

She pointed to the man with tattoos crawling up his neck. "That's Zachary Holt." Then she pointed to another man, who probably had a locker full of protein powder and pre-workout supplements. "And that's Logan Tate. They're both firefighters on the ladder truck with Captain Bennett and Dean."

"That means Fischer, Greer, and Murph are on the engine with you?" He knew all of this already. One of the first things he'd done after the fire at her house was to look into her coworkers.

She nodded. "Yeah."

"From what I've seen, you appear to be closest to Dean and Greer." He wanted to learn more about her work dynamic so he could get a bigger picture of the team.

"Dean is like the big brother I never had, and Greer is like the little brother I never wanted."

"I heard that," Greer said through a mouthful of food.

"And?" She gave him a sassy face.

"You know you love me." He batted his eyes at her.

She laughed.

Everyone filled their plates and dispersed into the dayroom. Sam took a seat in a recliner. Liam grabbed a metal folding chair that had been brought out, and pulled it up next to her.

"So, Marshal, what brings you to Renegade?" Tate asked before taking a bite of his pulled-pork sandwich.

"Call me Liam." He looked to Sophia. "I got custody of my niece and transferred jobs. Renegade had an opening."

"Oh." Sam sat up straighter. "I don't know if everyone has met her, but that's Sophia." Sam nodded toward his niece.

The guys all said hello. Sophia's face reddened. She didn't like being the center of attention.

"What do you do for the Marshals?" Dean asked.

"Before moving to Renegade, I was on one of the fugitive

apprehension teams. Now I do courthouse security and transporting inmates to and from the courthouse, along with some witness protection duties." He balanced his plate on his knee. "I'll do apprehension if I'm needed, but my focus is the courthouse security."

"How'd you and Sam meet?"

Liam swallowed his food. They hadn't had time to discuss the logistics of their relationship. It was best to stick as close to the truth as possible. "The first time I met her was at that motel shooting she responded to. We didn't say more than a few words to each other though."

"Oh, wow. That shooting was wild. How's the marshal that was hit?" Greer asked.

"He's fine. Off for a few weeks' healing."

"What about the fugitive?" Sam asked.

He turned to her. She'd been the one to treat him, so her curiosity was natural. "I can tell you he lived."

"That's—" She shook her head.

"A miracle." Liam finished for her. "The trajectory of the bullet missed all of the man's major organs."

She shrugged.

"Sometimes miracles happen. There's no rhyme or reason to it."

The alarms started to blare, dispatch calling a structure fire over the intercom.

Everyone jumped up and tossed their trash or set their plates on the counter.

He stood up and took Sam's plate. "We'll see ourselves out. Be careful."

She nodded and disappeared into the bay with her crew.

"Come on, girls. Let's do some cleanup, then we'll head out."

As he cleaned up the plates and trash, his thoughts turned back to Sam. This was her life. Her world. And somehow, just by stepping into it, he'd caught a glimpse of something he wasn't sure he wanted to give up when this was all over.

But how could he keep it?

NINETEEN

S AM EXITED THE STATION LOBBY AND FOUND Liam leaning against the front of his SUV with his ankles crossed in front of him. As if thinking about him all day had conjured him here in front of the firehouse.

He smiled and stood up when he saw her. "Have a good day?"

He walked up, Mr. Loose-Hipped Marshal with all that federal swagger. He grabbed her hand. The warmth of his touch flooded up her arm and throughout her body. Something in her stomach did a little dance.

She cleared her throat. "The guys wanted me to make sure to tell you and the girls thanks for cleaning up."

Liam held her hand, walked to the passenger side of the SUV, and opened the door for her. "Anytime."

He let her get settled before shutting the door. Greer walked out and waved to them. Sam waved back.

She turned in the seat and looked at the girls. "Did you have a good day?"

They both nodded, not bothering to look up from their phones.

Liam climbed into the SUV and put it in Reverse. "I set some hamburger meat out to thaw this morning and cooked it before coming to pick you up. I thought I'd make spaghetti for dinner tonight. Is that something you ladies would eat?" He glanced in the rearview mirror at Isabella and then to Sam.

"Yes. We like spaghetti." Sam answered for both of them. A man who cooked dinner?

"Oh, can you bake it?" Sophia said from the back seat. "It's so good."

"I don't see why not. Have you had baked spaghetti?" He clicked on the turn signal and glanced at Sam.

"Can't say that I have. How is baked spaghetti different than regular spaghetti?"

"It's like a spaghetti lasagna. With lots of cheese," Sophia explained.

"I can help cook," Sam offered.

"You don't have to. It's pretty easy. Cook the meat, which I've already done, cook the noodles to al dente, mix it all with the sauce, throw some cheese on it, and slap it in the oven."

"That sounds simple enough. And like something that would be perfect for my day to cook lunch at the firehouse, actually. Cheap and easy. And if we get called out, it wouldn't go bad if it was left for hours."

"So, did you guys get called out again after we left?" He kept his attention on the road.

"The call was a small electrical fire. Then we had a couple medical calls, but other than that, it was a slower afternoon." Which had left plenty of time for teasing from the guys about her new boyfriend.

"That's good. So, you're not just a firefighter, you're a paramedic too?"

"Yeah, I got my EMT certification, then entered the fire

academy. I got my paramedic certification while I was working my probationary period with the fire department."

"How long did that take?"

"About two years for all of it."

As soon as Liam stopped in the driveway, the girls jumped out of the car.

Liam got out. "Do your homework first!"

Sophia waved over her shoulder and used her key to let them in, then the girls disappeared.

Sam and Liam followed the girls into the house, crossed through the living room, and into the kitchen.

"Now that they're occupied, we need to talk." He leaned against the counter.

She bit her bottom lip. "Did you find out anything?"

He shook his head. "No, still waiting on Howard to fill me in, but it feels like he's dodging me. I was talking about our *relationship*."

"Oh."

He turned and pulled a pan from one of the bottom cabinets, set it in the sink, and turned on the water.

"I think it's best if we stay as close to the truth as possible." He turned to look at her.

"What do you mean?" She thought the whole point of this relationship was to keep from blowing her cover.

"I mean how we met and how our relationship started." He held the pot under the faucet.

"It'll be easier that way. So we met the first time at the motel shooting," she said.

"Yeah. I think it'll be okay to say we met again when I came with Aubrey looking for her cat. We can just leave out the part about me being your handler. I was just out helping my new coworker because I didn't want her going door to door alone."

"Okay." Sam nodded. "I mean, everything about how we've

interacted since then can be told. The girls started to get into trouble, and we were thrust together."

"And that's when the attraction started." He shut off the water, set the pan on the stove, and turned on the burner. Then he turned the knob to preheat the oven. "Can you grab the bread from the freezer?"

She grabbed the boxed cheese bread from the freezer and started opening it. Liam pulled a cookie sheet from under the stove and set it on the counter. He reached for the box.

She held it out of his reach. "I'll help."

Liam nodded and turned back to the stove, sprinkling some salt in the water.

Sam pulled the bread slices apart and started lining them in the pan. "Then I was in danger, and your protective instincts took over."

"Bingo." He turned around and leaned against the cabinet. "We need some ground rules as well."

"Right. We're supposed to be portraying a couple, and there will be coupley things we need to do."

"I hope you were okay with me holding your hand and walking you to the car. I noticed one of the guys watching us."

"No. That's fine."

An ashamed expression crossed his face. "And I realized I've kissed you twice without your permission. I need to apologize for that."

Her mouth fell open. She hadn't expected an apology.

"I'm not in the habit of doing that, but both times it seemed like an appropriate boyfriend reaction, and I didn't have the option to ask." He looked sheepish.

"I'll admit it took me off guard, but it was necessary."

"Are you comfortable with physical affection, like hand-holding and hugs?"

This was such an odd conversation. "Um. No kissing on the

lips." Not that she was a prude. She'd kissed a few guys in her time, but when she had very real feelings for them. Kissing Liam—that seemed too intimate.

His gaze dropped to her mouth, just for a second, a flicker of heat in his eyes that made her breath catch. He cleared his throat, as if reminding himself of the stakes. "Understood. The mission comes first."

"I think if we stick to hand-holding and hugs, it should be fine. I'm not an overly affectionate person to begin with, so the guys won't think anything about us not being touchy-feely." She walked to the cabinets and started opening them, looking for the spaghetti noodles.

He pointed to the cabinet to her left. "Noodles are in that one."

"Thanks." She handed them to Liam and realized she was now far closer to him than before.

"What about around here? We're pretty much under constant surveillance with Isabella and Sophia."

"I guess we do the same. Isabella has never seen me with a boyfriend other than Matt Marino, and I kept that away from her as much as I could."

He dumped the noodles into the boiling water. "Really?"

"Don't sound so surprised." It was her turn to lean against the counter.

"I didn't mean it that way. It's just—" He ran a hand through his hair. "You're an attractive woman. I just assumed you'd have had a boyfriend or two."

Her cheeks warmed. "Thank you. It's just that I've been taking care of Bella since she was born. Between that and going to school and working, I never had the time or inclination to date. Until Matt Marino. And look how that turned out. Then we joined WITSEC, and I have to be so careful. It's just best to stay single, I guess. What about you?"

He stirred the noodles. "I had a serious girlfriend and was

considering asking her to marry me, then I got guardianship of Sophia. She decided she wasn't ready to be a mother. Especially to a teenager."

"I'm sorry to hear that. You probably don't want to hear it, but it's likely for the best. Some people aren't meant to be parents. It would be doing Sophia a disservice to expect someone to be in her life that didn't want to be there." She could speak from experience.

"I assume you're talking about your mother?"

She nodded. "Unfortunately for me. When I found out she was pregnant with Bella, I was hoping she'd change, you know? She'd want to be a parent, and I'd finally get a mother. It didn't happen. I didn't get a mother; I turned into one."

He set the fork on the stove top. "That's a lot for someone so young to carry. I'm sorry it was something you had to go through."

She shrugged. "When you don't have any other options, you deal with it."

Liam's face softened. "I guess I know that feeling."

Sam tilted her head. "How so?"

"My childhood wasn't the best. Dad had a temper, and I took the brunt of it." He crossed his arms over his chest.

"Where was your mother?"

"She turned a blind eye most times. If he was taking it out on me, he wasn't hitting her."

"I'm sorry. Sounds like we both had useless mothers." There was nothing she could do to change the past, and her words wouldn't do anything to ease the pain of the memories.

"It's all in the past. Now I focus on the future." He stood and turned to check on the noodles. "Enough heavy talk for tonight. Can you grab the pan of meat out of the refrigerator?"

She grabbed the pan from the refrigerator and set it on the stove, bumping Liam's arm. Electricity zapped through her. She stepped back. It was nothing. Just a reaction to her sharing part of her story.

"I talked to my boss today," Liam said. "I'm on full-time

protection duty for now, with some leeway. I thought we'd continue to take you to work and pick you up." He turned the heat down on the stovetop.

"What about your other duties? Courthouse security, was it?"

"Hank, a partially retired marshal, has agreed to work my court shifts for the next couple of days. I have access to our databases from here." He drained the noodles, combined everything, and put it in a glass baking pan. Then he covered it in cheese and slid it into the oven. "It should be ready in ten minutes."

"Great. I'll get the girls, and we can set the table." She turned and walked out of the kitchen.

Liam had watched Sam fall into an easy rhythm over the past two days. He took her to work each morning, met her for lunch, then they spent the evenings together. The girls spent so much of their time in their bedroom that he and Sam didn't have to do much acting at home. So everything had been kept professional since the talk in the kitchen.

The fire station was a different story. They sat next to each other and did the typical new-couple things. Hand-holding and hugs. It had become almost natural.

He'd followed up with RPD a couple of times on the reports regarding the juveniles—the one who'd followed Sam and the girls in the mall, and all of his friends.

So far, they had what appeared to be two separate cases at first glance. The murder of Dr. Torres and the fire to cover it up, and the situation with the girls. But what if they were connected?

An email from the forensic pathologist popped up in his inbox. He clicked the attachment and read her official report. Dr. Torres had died from a single gunshot to the back of the head. He was dead when the fire started.

He saved the report to the case file and clicked over to the fire inspector's report. Based on the burn patterns, an accelerant was used in multiple spots throughout the home. Chemical trace tests confirmed gasoline.

The question was, why had it happened at Sam's house? Had he been lured there and ambushed?

They'd know more when forensics was done with Dr. Torres's phone. It had been damaged during the fire. He prayed that the memory chip was still intact and they'd be able to pull data from it. Unfortunately, that took time. While they waited, he'd obtained warrants and sent them to the cell providers. More waiting.

His phone rang. *Renegade Police Department.*

"Liam Roberts."

"Deputy Marshal Roberts, this is Detective Bridges with the Renegade Police Department. I was calling regarding your request for a criminal check on a juvenile by the name of Aiden Hamilton."

Finally. Now he would have something he could work with.

"I got the clearance needed to give you the file."

"That's great. Email it over." This could have been an email. A telephone call hadn't been necessary.

"Normally I would, but I just got called to a homicide scene."

A prickle raced up his neck.

"Unofficially, it's your juvenile. I thought you might want to meet me there."

His stomach sank. He logged out of the computer. "Give me the address." After jotting it down, he said, "I'll meet you there."

Liam walked down the hall and rapped his knuckles on Sophia's door. "Girls, we gotta go. Come on."

He called Glover while he waited for them in the front room. "Glover."

"Please tell me you're not busy."

"Well, good news is I'm not. What's up?"

"I need to go to a crime scene, but I have my juvenile witness and niece. Can you meet me somewhere, take them, and keep an eye on them while I deal with this?"

"Where we meeting?"

He gave her the address. "I think there's a gas station on the corner a couple blocks up."

"There is. I'll meet you there."

He disconnected the call just as the girls emerged from the room.

"Is everything okay?" Worry etched Isabella's face.

"Yes. I've just been called in for a work thing. You two are going to hang out with my coworker Glover for a bit while I deal with it."

"Okay," they said in unison.

Liam transferred the girls to Glover's vehicle and caught her before she could climb in. "You're aware of the cover that's been woven for this?"

"Yes. You and the witness are dating. How you managed to get Supervisor Howard to sign off on that is beyond me." She smirked.

"I have no clue other than we didn't have many other options. The girls don't know anything other than that." He wanted to make sure that Isabella didn't know the truth. "Samantha thought it would be best if we kept her sister in the dark on the fake relationship."

"Understood." She nodded.

"I'll touch base when I'm done here."

Glover climbed into her SUV and pulled out of the parking lot.

Liam made it to the crime scene and checked in at the perimeter. A narrow gravel alley between two overgrown vacant lots. The ends of the alley were taped off, with officers standing guard. "I'm looking for Detective Bridges."

The officer took Liam's info, then pointed to a man in a black blazer and a pair of slacks, halfway down the alley. "That's him."

"Thanks."

Liam made his way toward the man standing about twenty feet from the inner perimeter. "Detective Bridges."

The detective turned around. He was a man close to retirement age. Salt-and-pepper hair with a receding hairline.

"Deputy Marshal Roberts." Detective Bridges stuck his hand out.

Liam shook it. "Tell me what you've got."

"We've positively identified the body as that of Aiden Hamilton. The forensic pathologist is with the body now." Bridges motioned in that direction.

Dr. Falleur from the coroner's office knelt next to a prone figure clad in black sweats and a hoodie.

The buzzing of insects and the sickeningly sweet aroma of rotten meat intensified as they got closer. The body lay in an unnatural position, limbs askew. Not like a natural fall. He hadn't been killed here.

"What have you got for us?" Detective Bridges asked.

"Based on decomposition and insect activity, I'd estimate our kid's been dead two days." Dr. Falleur looked up at the two of them, then turned back to the body. "Lividity and lack of blood surrounding the body suggests this is a body dump. Of course, that's unofficially."

"COD?" Liam asked.

"Unofficially, gunshot wound to the back of the head." She stood up.

Unofficially was thrown around a lot at crime scenes. Just because it looked one way, didn't mean it ended up actually being that way.

The victim could have been shot in the back of the head, but it could just as easily have been death by poison and a gunshot as assurance the job had been done. He'd seen it happen before.

"You think it could be the same caliber as the one from Dr. Torres?"

"You know ballistics isn't my thing," the forensic pathologist said. "I *can* say it was a medium-caliber weapon. As was the bullet that killed Dr. Torres. There doesn't appear to be an exit wound. If there's anything left, I'll let ballistics handle it."

Liam turned to Detective Bridges. "Keep me in the loop on this one. Not only does this kid connect to one of my witnesses, but my niece is also involved."

"Will do. Let me get that file for you."

Liam followed the detective back out of the alley and to his vehicle.

Bridges retrieved a manila folder and handed it to him. "I also emailed it to you after we hung up."

"Great, thank you."

Back at the office, Liam stuck his head in and checked on the girls. They were sitting at the conference-room table, watching something on Isabella's phone. The table was covered in snacks.

He made his way to Glover's office and knocked on the doorframe.

Glover looked up from the file on her desk. "Have a seat."

Liam took the chair across from her desk. She grabbed a manila folder and stretched it across to him. "Take a look."

"Here's the juvenile file I was given on our dead kid, Aiden Hamilton. The forensic pathologist obviously can't say for certain right now, but his death is similar to that of Dr. Torres, except for the fire." Liam handed her the file he'd gotten from Detective Bridges.

He flipped through the manila folder on Dr. Torres. Glover had ordered a deep dive into his financials and business dealings. He was linked to a few limited liability companies in Colorado. "Okay, so Dr. Torres had some real estate investments in the area."

"Yep. Now look at this." She handed him a sheet of paper with a list of the recent arsons.

"Interesting." Each one of the arsons was owned by an LLC that Dr. Torres was a member of.

"Do we think he was padding his pockets with the insurance money?" It was possible whoever he was working with had gotten greedy and didn't want to share. "There's no way he was actually the one setting the fires."

Maybe a disagreement had gotten him killed.

"It definitely looks suspect," Glover said. "We need to keep pounding the pavement and chase these leads down to find out who murdered our witness."

"Okay." He leaned back in his chair. "We've got arsons being set on buildings owned by a few different LLCs. The only connection between the buildings and LLCs is this Dr. Torres guy. Apparently he had agreed to tell them what he knew about the Shadow Syndicate in exchange for leniency on his other charges."

"Seriously?"

"Then he ends up dead in a property he owns under his real name, not one of the LLCs." Liam shook his head. "Maybe they wanted him silenced."

"It just so happens that the property is rented by a witness of ours, making our jobs harder in the process."

"A witness who has been getting into trouble at school with kids suspected of starting the fires. One of whom is murdered similarly to Dr. Torres."

"This is a tangled mess." Glover looked at him. "Sounds like someone just making it look like it's connected, but they didn't check all the details, so it only seems like the same string of incidents on the surface—until you look deeper."

"Yeah, but hopefully we'll pull the right string and everything will unravel." His mind wasn't just on this as a US marshal. It was personal. He wanted to give Sam and Bella the peace they deserved.

TWENTY

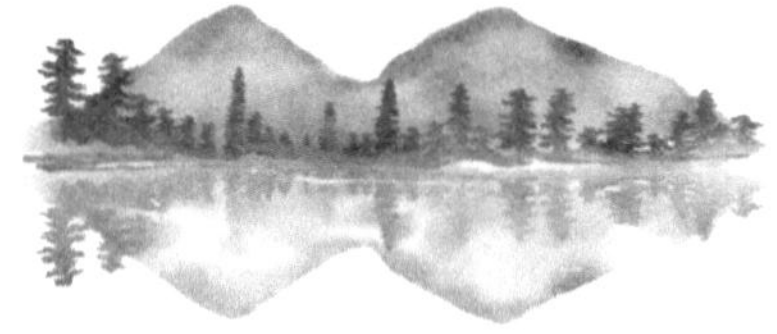

THE FIREHOUSE SMELLED FAINTLY OF COFFEE, the usual morning bustle having died down. Heat pooled behind Sam's ribs as she remembered Liam's attention—how he acted like a doting boyfriend at the station and when the girls were around. The occasional hug, holding her hand. Focusing on her in a room full of people in a way she'd begun to crave. When they were alone, he was professional but not distant or cold. He kept his physical distance but still engaged in conversations with her. Listened like he cared what she had to say.

She'd learned that his favorite television show was a classic black-and-white show about a widowed sheriff raising his boy in a small town.

He prayed over meals, and she'd seen him study his Bible on more than one occasion.

Last night, she'd sat on the bed and again pulled out the Bible that Barbara from the church had given her. Barbara and Liam had both mentioned Joseph, so after quickly googling where to find his story in the Bible, she'd read about how his brothers had sold him into slavery. How he'd been falsely accused and sent to prison. And then she'd read: *But the Lord was with Joseph and showed him steadfast love and gave him favor in the sight of the keeper of the prison.*

God hadn't rescued Joseph. And yet it said the Lord was with him and showed "steadfast love." Honestly, she'd felt a bit indignant on Joseph's behalf, and she wasn't sure what to do with that.

In the end, she'd put the Bible back on the nightstand and gone back out into the front room, where the girls had talked them into watching a rom-com. Liam had sat next to her the entire time, arm laid across the back of the sofa. She hadn't been able to focus on the movie, only on the weight of his presence.

All she could think about was how close his body was to hers and how it would feel if he dropped his arm to her shoulder and held her. Like he really was her boyfriend and this wasn't all some lie concocted to keep her and her sister safe.

The walls around her heart were in danger of crumbling for a man who didn't really have any interest in her outside of a job he had to do. A name in a file.

She'd grown too comfortable with Liam, and that scared her. Of all the people in the world to get comfortable with, her handler wasn't supposed to be one of them.

Six years with the guys at the station, putting their lives on the line together, and those walls had stood. A couple of days with this man and she was losing control of her emotions. She was relying on him too much, and that kind of dependence made her uneasy.

"Earth to Sam." Greer snapped his fingers next to her, cutting through her thoughts.

She shook her head. "What? I'm sorry."

He cocked his head to the side. "You've been staring at the countertop for a while now. Everything okay?"

"Yes. I was just lost in thought."

"Thinking about a certain marshal?" he teased.

Heat climbed up her neck and spread across her face. She ducked her head to keep him from seeing how her face betrayed her. "I have a lot of things on my mind."

"I like this on you," he said softly.

She turned and looked at him. "It's the same thing I wear every day."

"I don't mean your clothes, you weirdo." He laughed. "I meant you've been more relaxed the last couple of days. Not as uptight."

"Uptight?" Was that how everyone saw her?

"Don't take it the wrong way. It's why we love you. You're always in control of your emotions, and even though you joke along with us, you don't let yourself fully go." He stared into her eyes. "You've been so focused on being Samantha Williams the firewoman, and Samantha Williams, Bella's big sister and mother figure, that you haven't been just Sam. I feel like maybe this marshal is helping you realize you're more than just those titles you've given yourself and the responsibilities you've shouldered."

She opened her mouth to say something, but there were no words, because he was right.

"I'll leave it alone for now." He patted her shoulder. "I asked if you've already done the inventory on the medical closet. I need to pull some supplies."

"Oh, not yet. That's next on my list."

"Good. I'll stock the medical bags before you do that, so it won't throw off inventory." He wandered off.

Greer had given her a lot to think about. Most of her life had just been surviving from one day to the next. Was it time she started living? Liam couldn't be a part of that equation, no matter what her feelings were telling her. Once the danger passed, he would be out of her life, no longer her case officer. He'd go back to his job protecting the courthouse. On to the next assignment, the next witness. Leaving her behind, holding the pieces of her heart she hadn't realized he'd been chipping away.

Maybe she'd text Liam and ask him to pick her up later, and she'd get a good run on the treadmill. Clear her head. Her workouts had floundered since the fire destroyed her house.

The station alarm blared.

"Truck 4, Engine 4. EMS. Structure fire at Fourth and Main."

Adrenaline kicked in. She jogged to the engine bay and joined her colleagues. They donned their turnout gear and climbed into the engine. As the sirens wailed, she continued gearing up, listening for the report from Lieutenant Fischer.

"Commercial fire at an abandoned building."

Murph staged the engine while the ladder truck pulled up behind them.

Sam jumped down, grabbed the line, and started running it toward the structure like she'd done a hundred times before. She was first on the hose—her job was to advance the line inside.

Captain Bennett gave his three-sixty report and doled out instructions.

The ladder crew forced entry, cleared the building, then worked on ventilation. Sam entered the building behind them, heat slamming into her as she stepped through the doorway.

She crouched low and aimed the stream at the base of the nearest flames, moving methodically as she pushed forward.

The building was thick with smoke, the kind that clung to the lungs and made the eyes water, even with the SCBA. Pockets of smaller fires had been set throughout the space, but in the middle of the expansive open area just ahead, one massive blaze roared with a fury that her gut said wasn't accidental.

She dropped into a textbook defensive firefighting stance, crouched low and balanced, her body angled behind the nozzle as she aimed the water at the smaller fire in front of her. She needed to put out these flames before moving on to the inferno ahead.

The fire hissed and snapped. A sharp crack from above cut through the roar of the fire. Something heavy gave way somewhere.

Pain exploded across the top of her head, and an unbearable weight piled on top of her. The hose slipped from her hands as her knees buckled and she pitched forward, the world going dark.

***

Liam had spent the last hour with Glover, going over the LLCs and financials of Dr. Torres. "Dr. Torres's membership in the LLCs is the only connection to the arsons. The LLCs don't share any other members or managers. The properties aren't next door to each other or connected in any other way."

Glover leaned back in her chair. "You think Dr. Torres paid someone to set these buildings on fire to collect the insurance money? We'll need to subpoena the insurance companies to determine the scope of the policies."

Liam nodded. "I think something happened between Dr. Torres and whoever he hired. Maybe he decided not to pay out, or maybe their arsonist found out he was going to disappear, but for whatever reason, he or she lured Dr. Torres to Sam's house and killed him, then set the house on fire."

"Without more evidence, we won't know for certain, but it's definitely an angle we need to investigate. The fact that he was killed in Sam's house and that Sam's sister had been involved with the firebugs could all be a coincidence."

He needed to talk to Samantha about all of this. Maybe she could shine some light on it. She'd admitted she'd not had much contact with Torres, but the smallest thing could be what he was looking for.

He pulled his phone from his pocket and called her. The phone rang until voicemail picked up. She was probably out on a call. He'd wait for her to call back. In the meantime, he'd look into the known associates of Dr. Torres. His death proved that whoever was in charge was trying to clean up a mess. That *mess* included Samantha, Isabella, and his niece.

His phone rang, Sam's name filling the screen. "Hey, Sam."

"No. This is Greer." His voice was strained. "She was taken to the hospital by ambulance thirty minutes ago."

Liam was up and running down the hall. "Is she okay?"

"I don't know yet. We just got the fire put out. I went looking for her phone to give you a call. A vent collapsed on top of her. She was unconscious when they pulled her from the building. She's had trauma to the head, resulting in a laceration." Emotion filled Greer's voice.

Liam stopped outside the conference room, where Sophia and Bella were hanging out. "Okay, Greer. Which hospital?"

"She was taken to Renegade Mercy General Hospital. Lieutenant Fischer rode with her while the rest of us worked the fire. I'll text you his number."

"Thank you." Liam opened the door and faced the teens. "Get your things. We've got to go. Sam was hurt at work and has been taken to the hospital."

"What happened?" Bella's face paled.

"I don't know yet. Greer is texting me Lieutenant Fischer's telephone number. As soon as I get it, I'm calling him."

The girls rapidly gathered their things, and they all took off down the hall to the elevator. The doors opened immediately after he pushed the button. They loaded into the elevator, and Liam jammed the close button. "Come on."

He received a text from Samantha's number with Fischer's number. He clicked the telephone number and held the phone to his ear. "Pick up. Pick up." He jammed the close button again.

He should have taken the stairs. He could have been in his car by now.

He lifted his foot to do just that when the elevator doors finally slid shut.

The phone continued to ring until voicemail picked up. He hung up and called again. The doors slid open, and they raced to his SUV.

"Answer the phone." He hung up and dialed again.

"Lieutenant Fischer." The man answered on the second ring.

"Fischer, this is Liam Roberts. Tell me about Samantha." He climbed into his SUV, fired up the engine, and activated the lights and sirens. Once he was sure the girls were buckled and all pedestrians were cleared, he jammed the pedal to the floor. The engine roared as he tore out of the parking lot.

"We don't know anything yet. She was unconscious but stable when she arrived. They're doing a CT scan right now."

Lord.

It was all he could say. God knew his heart and what he wanted.

"I'm on my way with Bella. Call me as soon as you hear anything, but I'll be there in a few minutes," he said, a little more forcefully than he should have.

"Will do."

Liam tossed his phone onto the passenger seat. He looked at Bella in the rearview mirror and relayed to her what Lieutenant Fischer had told him.

Was she okay? She had to be okay. *Lord, she needs You. Be with the doctors. Give them knowledge and discernment. Steady their hands.*

The drive to the hospital took forever. He gripped the steering wheel until his fingers went numb.

The tires squealed as he pulled into the hospital parking lot. He parked the SUV in a space marked for law enforcement and jumped out.

He flew through the doors, Bella and Sophia on his heels, and looked for Lieutenant Fischer. The man was standing by the automatic doors that led to the patient area. A few other men in RFD shirts stood with him. Colleagues he'd yet to meet.

"Fischer." Liam strode up to him. "Any news?"

"Not yet." He shook his head.

"Tell me everything."

Lieutenant Fischer said, "We were called to a fire at an abandoned commercial building. A vent fell on Samantha as she advanced the line."

Bella gasped. Sophia wrapped an arm around her friend.

"Greer was her backup. He called for assistance. Greer and Holt pulled her from the rubble and out of the building. Greer stabilized her neck. The EMTs took over transport and brought her here."

Liam ran his hands through his hair and blew out a breath. A litany of scenarios flew through his mind, ranging from broken bones to death.

The memory of Sam smiling and waving goodbye to them as she walked into the station this morning. So young. So beautiful. His heart ached. He couldn't imagine a world without her.

The automatic doors swung open, and all eyes turned to the nurse who walked out. She looked past them and called out a name that wasn't Samantha Williams.

The group of men sighed in synchrony.

"This could be a while. We should probably stop crowding the door," Lieutenant Fischer said, but he didn't move. Instead, the other guys formed a line against the wall, out of the way.

Liam remained with Fischer.

What was taking so long? They should know something by now. *Lord, calm me.*

He wanted the medical professionals to be cautious and take their time assessing Sam. If they were too hasty, they could miss something.

The automatic doors slid open. This time a doctor stepped out and looked to them. "For Williams?"

Liam and Fischer stepped closer to the doctor.

"I'm her supervisor, Lieutenant Fischer, and this is her boyfriend, Liam Roberts."

"Deputy Marshal Liam Roberts." Liam showed his badge. He didn't like flashing his badge around and expecting special treatment. But if there ever was an occasion to do so, this would be it. "And this is her sister, Isabella Williams."

"I see." The doctor glanced at the badge, then at Bella. "I'm Dr. Yassan. Ms. Williams remains unconscious. CT scans of her head and torso were done to rule out life-threatening injuries. The are no cranial fractures, bleeding, or swelling to the brain. No broken bones in the neck or back. No spinal or organ damage."

Liam took a deep breath. *Thank You, Lord, that there's no serious injury. I pray for ongoing healing of her body.*

The doctor continued, "She does have a two-inch laceration to the back of her head. We've cleaned and stapled it. All of her vitals are stable. We're going to admit her for observation and wait for her to regain consciousness for further evaluation."

"How long will she be unconscious?" Lieutenant Fischer asked.

"Based on what I've been told about the mechanism of her injury, I suspect she has a concussion or other mild head injury. As far as regaining consciousness, I can't give an estimate. Everyone's body responds at its own pace. She could wake up in ten minutes, or it could be another hour. If she doesn't regain consciousness in the next hour or two, we'll order a CT scan."

"When can we see her?" Liam asked.

"Since she's stable and there's evidence that familiar voices can enhance the healing process even when someone is merely unconscious, I'll let one or two people back there. But keep it quiet and calm."

"Yes, ma'am." Lieutenant Fischer and Liam spoke at the same time.

Dr. Yassan waved her badge in front of the electronic pad on the wall and the doors opened. "Follow me."

"I'll be in in a minute. Let me talk to the guys." Lieutenant Fischer gestured to the crew eagerly awaiting news.

Liam nodded, then followed the doctor down the hall, Bella and Sophia right behind him. "She's still in an ER bay. We'll get her moved once a room is ready."

The doctor opened the door. "Bella, go on." She let Bella go first.

"I'll wait right here." Sophia moved and stood to the side of the door.

Liam walked in with Bella.

Sam lay still with her eyes closed. Wires and tubes were everywhere. Her normally fit body looked so small and fragile. Liam swallowed the lump that had developed in his throat.

He pulled a chair close to her bed and let Bella take a seat. She picked up her sister's hand and held it tightly.

"Sam, it's Bella." The teen's voice cracked. "I love you."

He couldn't take it any longer. He walked around to the far side of the bed, where he gently took her other hand in his. It was warm and soft. He brought it to his mouth and placed a small kiss on the back of it.

The line between witness and something more was becoming increasingly blurry. He wanted nothing more than to lean in, hold her, let the rest of the world fade. But he couldn't let that happen. Not yet. Even if he was beginning to pray that there would be a time in the not-too-distant future when he could.

He reached out, his fingers gently brushing a stray strand of hair from her cheek. "Don't you dare leave me," he whispered, his voice rough with an emotion he could no longer hide.

TWENTY-ONE

SOMETHING SOFT AND WARM RUBBED CIRCLES across the back of her hand, pulling her from the dark. Quiet voices filtered through the annoying beeping. She turned her head toward the sounds.

"She's waking up."

Her whole body ached, and all she wanted to do was go back to sleep. It took considerable willpower, but she pried her eyes open, then had to immediately squeeze them shut.

"Kill the lights," the same husky voice said.

The room dimmed. She opened her eyes and focused on the face next to her. Chestnut-brown hair and a square jaw slowly came into focus.

"Sam?" Someone squeezed her hand.

She knew that voice. "Liam?"

He smiled and nodded. "How do you feel?"

"Everything hurts. What happened?" Her mouth was dry, and her throat ached.

"What do you remember?" His brows dipped.

She searched her memory. "I remember you dropping me off this morning." There was more, she knew it, but she couldn't quite grasp it.

"Nothing after that?" Lieutenant Fischer stepped into her line of sight.

What was he doing here?

She shook her head, and sharp pain cascaded through her head. She grimaced.

"It's okay. Just relax." Liam squeezed her hand.

"I'm just so tired." She closed her eyes.

"I'll be right here when you wake up," Liam whispered before she drifted off to sleep.

"Sam, sweetheart, can you wake up for me?" a soft, feminine voice asked.

Sam turned her head and opened her eyes.

"There you are." A brunette woman in hospital scrubs smiled at her. "My name is Neveah, and I'll be your nurse tonight." The woman looked at the machine next to the bed. "How are you feeling?"

Sam could hear whispering behind the nurse. Who else was there?

"I'm a little sore." She vaguely remembered waking up at some point and being in pain, but right now it wasn't as bad.

"That's to be expected. Can you rate your pain for me on a scale of one to ten, with ten being the worst?"

Sam took stock of all the pain. "Um, a three. What happened to me?"

"You were putting out a fire in a commercial building, and a vent fell on you. Your coworkers got you out."

She blinked repeatedly.

"You don't have any serious injuries. Just a cut to the back of your head, bumps and bruises, and a concussion. We're going to keep you overnight for observation." The nurse took her hand. "Okay, can you squeeze my hand?"

Sam did as she was asked.

"Good." She turned around. "I'll let you have your places back." She moved out of the way, revealing the people she had spoken to.

Liam stood against the wall. Flanked by the girls, his arms around their shoulders.

The nurse moved to the foot of the bed and started tapping on a wheeled computer.

"Sam." Bella raced forward and grabbed Sam's hand. "I'm so glad you're awake."

Sam smiled softly at the affection in her sister's voice and squeezed Bella's hand. "I love you." Sam still wasn't sure what she was doing in a hospital bed, but she wanted to make sure that Bella knew exactly how she felt.

"I love you too."

"We'll give you two some time." Liam steered Sophia toward the door.

She didn't want him to leave. "Don't go."

Liam smiled softly and released Sophia before stepping up next to Bella. "I need to go let your friends know you're awake. I'll be right back."

"I can let them know if you'd like," the nurse offered.

"Yes. Please."

"Do you want me to let them come in one at a time?" The nurse pushed her wheeled computer toward the door. "If you're not up for visitors, I'm okay at being the big bad nurse." She smiled.

"I think it'll be okay."

"Okay, I'll send them in. There's a cup of water if you need a drink."

Sam tried to sit up and grab the cup.

"Here." Liam stepped up, grabbed the cup, and placed the straw to her lips.

The cool water was refreshing. "Thank you." She laid her head back against the pillow.

There was a soft knock on the door before it opened, and Captain Bennett stepped inside. "Sam."

"Hey, Cap." Her voice was raspy.

"I'm glad you're okay."

"Thank you."

"Don't worry about work. You focus on getting better. We'll handle all the paperwork."

"I appreciate it."

Captain Bennett looked to Liam and then to Sam. "Is there a way I can have a word with you two. Alone?"

Her heart skipped a beat. What would he want to talk to them about?

Sam looked to Liam. He nodded, concern filling his face.

"Sophia, why don't you and Bella go out to the waiting room with the rest of Sam's friends?" Liam said. "I'll be out there in a minute, and we can go to the cafeteria while they take turns coming in."

"Okay." Bella squeezed Sam's hand again. "I'll be right back."

"I know you will."

Sophia and Bella left.

Captain Bennett waited until the door was shut before addressing them. "The preliminary investigation on the commercial building shows it was another arson."

"Okay." Sam wished she could remember everything that had happened.

He inhaled deeply. "It's also looking like your injury was no accident."

Sam gasped.

Liam gently placed his hand on her shoulder. "Explain."

"The screws holding the vent up appear to have been tampered with. It was rigged to fall."

"Are you certain?"

"It's still being investigated, but the brackets holding the vent up weren't damaged. There were no screws in the brackets or lining the floor. Plus, there's remnants of some type of wire in the ceiling, suggesting it was barely hanging on when the fire started. We'll know more soon. I just thought you two should know."

Bile rose in her throat. "I'm going to be sick."

Liam grabbed the small vomit bucket sitting on the table and handed it to her. "Can I do anything for you?"

She shook her head and held on to the bucket, willing her stomach to calm. Of all the ailments out there, throwing up was the worst. She closed her eyes and focused on breathing and keeping her stomach from revolting.

"Maybe we should talk about this outside," Captain Bennett said.

It was about her. She should argue that it be talked about now, in front of her, but truthfully, she didn't want to know right at this moment. She just wanted to ignore everything around her. "Please."

Liam bent down to her eye level. "I will be right outside those doors. Nothing is going to happen to you. Okay?" His face was stone. He meant what he said.

"Okay." She leaned her head back against the pillow as the two men exited her room. Her stomach started to settle.

Another soft knock sounded on the door before Dean and Greer walked in. The worry on both of their faces was evident.

"Oh, Sam." Greer set a change of clothes on the foot of the bed, then leaned down and gave her a hug. "You don't know how happy I am to see your face. I brought you some department sweats for later. I know how it works and how clothes get cut off."

She hugged him back the best she could, considering all the machines she was tied to. "Thank you for the clothes. Right now, I don't mind the hospital gown, but I'll eventually want to get up and not shine my heinie to the world."

"No full moons for Sam." He smiled. "I'll be back when you're feeling better."

Dean was next. "You gave us quite a scare." He lingered a little longer than Greer. "Cass sends her love."

"Thank you," Sam whispered.

"We know you need your rest, so we're going to let the others come lay their eyes on you and then shoo them out. It's one thing for us to be told you're okay; it's another thing to confirm with our own eyes." Dean patted her hand.

"Love you, girlie," Greer said as he backed out of the room. "We all do."

Tears burned Sam's eyes. They'd never openly expressed just how much they cared for one another in the past. She appreciated it now.

All of Station 4 filed through her room for the next several minutes. Her eyelids were heavy by the time the last visitor, Lieutenant Fischer, left.

Liam and the girls returned. Bella took the seat directly next to the bed and scooted it as close as she could get. Liam and Sophia took the small couch by the window.

"Get some rest." Liam sat forward and leaned his forearms on his legs. "We'll be here when you wake up."

Sam nodded and let herself drift back to sleep.

***

Liam had remained rooted to the loveseat while Sam slept. His mind raced with a myriad of things. His growing feelings for Sam and the fact that the fire had been set with the intention of ending

Sam's life were at the forefront. She had grown to be so much more than just a witness. He cared for her. More than he should as her handler.

Did that make him the best person to keep her safe, or the worst? He could argue both sides. Hopefully, that was an argument he wouldn't need to have any time soon.

Liam's phone vibrated in his hand.

Glover

I'm here.

While Sam had been visiting with her coworkers, Liam had made a few calls. Sam and Bella were under twenty-four-hour protection, and he couldn't be at two places at once, so he asked Glover if she would be available to work the night shift at the hospital while he took the girls home.

Before Sophia, he would have been good to stay at the hospital the entire time. When it came to sleeping and eating, Liam could regulate his body. Now, he had another person to think about. Two people, actually. Until Sam was well and out of the hospital, Isabella was his responsibility.

He stood up and opened the door just as there was a knock.

Glover looked more tired than she had earlier. It had been a long day for all of them.

"Good evening." She smiled at him and then everyone else in the room.

"Glover, this is Samantha. You already know Isabella and Sophia."

"Nice to meet you." Glover nodded at Samantha.

A look of confusion crossed Sam's face.

"Glover is going to sit with you while I take the girls home so they can rest."

"No." Isabella stood up. "I'm not leaving Sam."

"Bella." Sam reached up and grabbed her sister's hand. "Relax.

You heard the doctor. I'm going to be fine. There's no use in you being stuck here sleeping on that uncomfortable sofa."

"We'll come back first thing in the morning. I promise." Liam smiled softly at Isabella.

"She'll be safe," Glover said. "The hospital has security, and I'll be here, standing at the door all night. No one will get past me."

Isabella was quiet. Thinking it over.

Liam took a deep breath. "She should be able to go home tomorrow, and she'll need some clothes and personal items. I could really use your help." It wasn't just an excuse. Liam didn't really want to rummage through Sam's things.

Isabella turned to Sam. "Promise me you'll call if something happens."

"I promise. I plan on going to sleep." Sam yawned.

"Okay." Isabella leaned over and hugged her sister. "I love you."

"I love you too."

Isabella grabbed her stuff and walked to the door.

Liam fought the urge to walk over and give Samantha a hug. A handler wouldn't hug his witness goodbye. "I'll have Isabella get your clothes and toiletries. Is there anything else you'll want or need?"

Sam looked around. "Maybe my phone charger." She reached over and grabbed her cell phone off the hospital bedside table.

"I have a charger that will fit." Glover pulled a charger from her pocket. "Never leave home without it. I brought it up in case anyone needed to use it."

"Thank you. I can't think of anything else I might need."

"Okay. Get some rest." Liam turned his attention to Glover. "Call me if anything changes or there's an issue."

"I will."

Liam kept one eye on the rearview mirror as he drove toward his house. Were they being followed? He was pretty certain the SUV behind him had been there since they left the hospital.

He signaled left and turned onto a random side street. The SUV followed. He continued a couple blocks and signaled to turn. Followed again. He tried a few more evasive turns, and finally the SUV disappeared.

Just to be on the safe side, he took a different route back to his house. He pulled into the driveway and parked.

They climbed from the SUV. Something was off. He studied the house. The porch light was on, and everything was exactly as he'd left it. "Girls, wait."

The girls stopped at the bottom of the porch steps.

He looked up and down the street. There weren't any unknown vehicles or anything else suspicious.

It could just be the stress of the last few days playing with his mind. He unholstered his weapon and held it down by his side.

The girls gasped.

"It's okay. I just want to check everything out." He climbed the stairs and unlocked the door. "I want you two to stay right here. Don't go anywhere."

They nodded.

He opened the door and flicked on the light. Blossom stood at the door, tail wagging. "Grab the dog."

Blossom ran past him.

He turned his attention to the interior. Nothing was out of place. He kept his weapon at the low ready position, finger off the trigger as he made slow, steady steps. He cleared the kitchen and turned his attention to the hallway. Next, he cleared Sophia's bedroom, then moved on to the bathroom.

A click came from his right. The unmistakable click of a gun misfiring.

Liam spun and raised his weapon just as a figure dressed in black from head to toe jumped from his bedroom and knocked him to the ground. The gun fell from his hand into the dark hallway.

The attacker straddled Liam's torso and delivered a blow to his face followed by another. Pain splintered his head.

"You should have left things alone," the attacker growled as he wrapped his hands around Liam's neck.

Liam's training kicked in. He trapped the attacker's hands while he planted his feet on the ground before bucking his hips, knocking the guy off-balance.

He rolled over on top of the man and delivered a few blows of his own. The attacker swung an elbow, connecting with Liam's ribs. Pain shot through his chest. The man twisted free from Liam's grasp.

He pulled his hand up, a metallic object extending forward.

A knife.

Liam wasn't fast enough. The knife sliced across his chest, followed by searing pain.

"Uncle Liam?" Sophia's panicked voice sounded too close.

"Get out of here!" he yelled at his niece. "Sophia, run!"

The man lunged with the knife again. This time, Liam dodged the attack and slammed his forearm on the man's arm. The knife fell from his grip. Liam gritted his teeth and pushed through the pain. He was the only thing standing between Isabella and Sophia and death. Death would not win tonight.

Liam bent low and tackled the man's waist, sending them sprawling on the floor. He grappled with the man, but his hands kept slipping in his own blood.

Lord, let me get the upper hand and keep my family safe.

He hoped one of the girls had called 911. He just needed to hold the man off until backup could arrive. If he had that long. He didn't know the extent of his injuries.

Liam grabbed the attacker by the hair and slammed his head into the ground. The man immediately went limp.

Liam got off the man and rolled him onto his stomach, then

pulled his hands behind his back and secured them with the handcuffs he pulled from his belt.

"Sophia?" He needed to make sure they were okay. He stood up, and a wave of dizziness washed over him. He stumbled down the hall and picked up his gun before turning to the front of the house to look for the girls. "Sophia? Are you safe?"

No answer.

Adrenaline coursed through his veins. He looked up and down the street. No sign of them. Sirens wailed in the distance. Help was coming.

"Sophia!" he yelled louder. "Isabella!"

The girls appeared from behind his SUV. Once they were satisfied he was alone, they raced to him.

"Uncle Liam." Sophia barreled into him, knocking him over.

Pain sliced through his chest. He groaned as he held on to his niece. "It's okay."

Flashing lights reflected off the porch. He gently pushed Sophia up. "You need to back up and keep your hands visible, okay? The police will want to make sure the scene is secure."

She wiped the tears from her face.

"Isabella, you too. They're coming in with limited information. They don't know what to expect." Liam set his gun down on the porch, stood up, and held his hands in the air as a police cruiser pulled in front of his house.

The officer jumped out of the vehicle and pulled his gun but didn't aim it at them.

"Deputy US Marshal Liam Roberts." Liam kept his hands in the air. "The man who attacked me is handcuffed inside. That is my weapon on the porch."

Another car pulled up.

"These girls are with me." He wobbled.

A flurry of activity descended, and it wasn't long until he found himself in the back of an ambulance sitting outside his house, the girls standing right outside, holding each other.

"You're definitely going to need some stitches." The paramedic had cut his shirt away and was cleaning the area on his chest.

Liam looked down at the six-inch gash that ran from his upper right pectoral to his breastbone. "That little thing caused all this blood?"

The paramedic laughed. "It's a deep wound, so yeah."

Liam peered around her to check on the girls. They weren't there. He started to sit.

The woman put her hand to his chest and gently pushed him back down. "Easy there. I need to get this covered."

"I just need to make sure my girls are okay. Sophia?"

She didn't pop out from the side like he expected.

His pulse pounded in his ears.

"Sophia." He started to stand. "Sophia!"

"You really need this stitched up."

He leveled her with a steely gaze. "Slap some butterfly bandages on it, because I'm not going anywhere until I find my girls."

TWENTY-TWO

SAM FOUND IT HARD TO GET THE REST HER BODY needed when people kept coming and going. Two different nurses had already been in to check on her, and it hadn't been all that long ago that Liam and the girls had left.

Pain thrummed through her head. She picked up her phone and checked the time. An hour and a half, to be exact. Glover had been nice enough to plug in Sam's phone and set it on the rolling table while it charged. Then she'd excused herself to stand guard outside.

The hospital room was quiet, other than the annoying beeping coming from the machine to her right. She'd tried to sleep but hadn't had any luck yet, so she turned on the television. Nothing tickled her fancy, so she shut it off.

She'd thought about trying to read an ebook, but focusing on the small screen made her head hurt worse. Sam was half tempted to call Liam just so she could hear his voice.

There were so many conflicting emotions running through her body. Fear about what could happen next. Anger over being attacked. Giddiness that Liam's face had been the first one she'd seen, besides the nurse. How did that even make the top of the list? That should be the farthest thing from her mind. But here she was, wanting to hear his voice.

She should call Cass. Surely she'd be able to talk her through this. But it was late, and she had the boys to take care of.

Maybe Glover would want to come in and chat for a while. She seemed like a nice enough woman. Maybe she would do that. Pick the marshal's brain about everything that'd been happening. It wasn't like she didn't trust Liam. She did. With her life and Isabella's life. But maybe Glover knew something Liam didn't.

Sam moved to stand up and got tangled in the wires. If she was going to get up, she might as well make a pit stop in the restroom. She pressed the nurse call button and waited for someone to answer.

"Can I help you?" A tinny voice sounded from the speaker on the bed rail.

"Yes. I need to use the restroom, but I'm kinda tied to the bed."

"I'll have someone come help you."

"Thank you."

A few minutes passed before there was a knock on the door and a petite woman in scrubs walked in, followed by Glover.

"Good evening. My name is Sara. I'm the CNA for tonight, and I'm here to help you to the bathroom." The woman walked around to the right side of the bed and started to remove the blood pressure cuff and pulse oximeter.

"Thank you."

"Everything still okay?" Glover asked.

"Yes, but if you have a minute, I'd like to talk to you when I'm done."

"Sure thing. I'll wait out here."

Sara lowered the bedrails. "Carefully turn your body and let your feet hang off the side, but don't stand yet."

Sam's muscles protested as she sat up, her head wobbly. A nurse named Nathan entered, performed a quick neuro check, and nodded for Sara to help her to the bathroom—an odd reversal for Sam, who was used to being the one helping others.

She shuffled to the bathroom with her entourage. Sara pushed the IV pole into the bathroom. "I'll let you take it from here, but holler if you need help." Then she shut the door.

Sam did her business, flushed the toilet, and washed her hands. She opened the door and found Sara standing right there, ready to jump in if she needed.

"While you're here, can I put on some pants?"

"Of course." Sara helped her put on the pants and then left the room. Glover entered before the door could shut all the way.

"Feeling better?"

"Not quite as groggy, but definitely still sore." Sam adjusted the blanket over her legs and torso.

Glover stood against the door, propping it open. She split her attention between Sam and the hallway. "You wanted to talk to me?"

"Yeah. I wanted to ask you about my case. I know Liam is handling it, but I thought you might have an opinion or know something maybe I don't yet." She shrugged.

Glover's face softened. "We have had reasons to talk about your case, yes. As a matter of fact, we learned something this afternoon that Liam was going to talk to you about, but he had the call about the accident." Glover was quiet for a moment, like she was weighing what to say. "You're familiar with the arsons going on around Renegade?"

Sam nodded.

"Well, it turns out that every building that was burned down belonged to a limited liability company that was connected to your landlord, Dr. Torres." Glover watched her, probably wanting to know if this was news to Sam.

She blinked a few times. "Really?"

Glover nodded. "And then he was killed in a house that he owned under his real name. Your house. We're still putting the pieces together." Glover folded her arms over her chest. "Do you know anything about Dr. Torres's business dealings?"

"No. We never talked outside of the typical landlord-tenant talk. I rarely saw or talked to him." Sam fidgeted with the blanket in her lap. "I can't believe it happened at my house. It makes no sense."

The phone in Glover's pocket rang. She pulled it out. "Give me a sec." She swiped the screen and put the phone to her ear as she stepped out the door. "Liam?"

Sam sat up straighter. Why would he be calling? Had he found something new?

A flicker of warmth stirred in her stomach. Maybe he was just checking on her.

She shook her head. Wishful thinking. If that were the case, he could've called her directly—unless he thought she was asleep.

"No, the girls haven't called."

Sam sat straight up and grabbed her phone. Nothing new in her notifications. What was going on?

"Are you okay?" Glover listened for a minute. "Okay. I'll keep my eyes peeled. Keep me updated."

Glover walked back into the room. "That was Liam. He was attacked at his house."

Sam's stomach fell. "Is he okay? Are the girls okay?"

"The man that attacked him is in custody. Liam said he's going to need some stitches. He also said the girls took off while he was being checked by paramedics."

Sam threw the covers off her lap and started tugging the tape holding the IV in. The world swam around her, and everything started to tip sideways.

"Whoa, wait a minute." Glover raced to her side.

Adrenaline coursed through her veins, clearing her head enough to say, "I have to go find them. Get me some toilet paper for the blood."

"You were in a serious accident, and you have a concussion. You need to lie back down and let Liam handle this."

Sam deftly pulled the IV from her vein, used the hospital gown to put pressure on the puncture wound, and stood up to face Glover. "You cannot keep me here."

"I could handcuff you to the bed."

"I'm not under arrest, so that would violate my rights." Sam stomped around the woman, grabbed some toilet paper from the bathroom.

"I have to strongly advise against this."

"Look, I understand. Do everything you can to cover your butt and the department. Just know that I am leaving with or without you." She turned around and looked for the T-shirt that Greer had left.

"I'm not the only one who needs to cover my butt." Glover folded her arms. "I'll help you, but only because I would do the same thing if it were me." Glover shut the door, grabbed the shirt from the couch, handed it to Sam, and turned around. "I'll be right outside."

Sam took off the hospital gown and slid the shirt on. Shoes. No one had brought her shoes, and she couldn't run around barefoot. She opened a cabinet, hoping to find some house shoes or something, and found the next best thing. Her work boots. She slid her feet into them and went to open the door when her cell phone rang on the table.

She grabbed it. Unknown caller.

With shaky fingers, she slid the answer button. "Hello?"

Sobbing sounded on the other end.

Was that Bella?

"Hello?"

"Sam." Her sister cried into the phone. "I'm sorry."

There was a man's voice in the background.

"What's going on?" Sam gripped the phone. "Isabella?"

"He said to meet us at the old slaughterhouse on the Ashbend River." A strangled cry echoed across the line. "He said you need to come alone and no one will get hurt."

The line went dead.

Sam stared at the phone. What was she supposed to do?

The smart thing to do was to tell Glover, let her alert the cavalry, and let them do their jobs. Except Liam had been attacked, and now the girls had been kidnapped. It would take too long for them to make a plan and execute it. Time she didn't know if they had.

But it would be completely stupid to go alone. She chewed on her lip. She'd give Glover the location, but she wouldn't let Glover slow her down. She had to go. She couldn't sit around and wait helplessly while the seconds ticked down and something happened to Bella.

"Glover!" Sam yelled.

Glover burst into the room. "Are you okay?"

"No. Bella just called. Someone has taken them." She raced around the bed. "We have to go now."

Glover snapped to attention. "Where are they?"

"The slaughterhouse at Ashbend Industrial Park."

"Let's go."

The two walked down the hall. The nurse who had performed the neuro exam on her stepped out of the nurses' station. "You can't leave."

"Watch me." Sam didn't even stop to talk to the man.

"Ms. Williams, I have to insist that you stay."

"I'm leaving AMA. You're absolved of any responsibility." She kept walking.

There wasn't much a nurse could do to keep a patient in the hospital.

"Okay." Disapproval filled the nurse's tone.

They made it to the elevator bay, and she jammed the button a few times. The doors slid open, and they loaded onto the elevator.

Sam needed to think of a way to ditch her chaperone. How could she distract her long enough to slip away? The marshal was highly trained and would see through just about anything she tried.

So Sam would use that training to her advantage. By distracting her with a potential threat. The doors slid open, and the two stepped out, slowly making their way through the halls toward the exit. She watched the reflections in the doors and windows. Picked out a bystander.

Sam stepped closer to the marshal. "I think we're being followed."

"The man in the hoodie," Glover said. "Keep walking. Do you recognize him?"

"I think he was standing outside the building where I got hurt this afternoon."

"Okay. I'm going to turn around and confront him. I want you to take cover."

"Okay."

"One. Two. Three." Glover spun around and rested her hand on the gun in her holster. "Deputy US Marshal. Put your hands where I can see them."

Everyone around them stopped and gawked. Sam took that opportunity to slip away. Hopefully, Glover would forgive her.

"I don't care who you have to wake up or what you have to do, ping those phones," Liam yelled into the phone as he pounded his hand on the steering wheel. "You need to find my niece and her friend."

The cut across his chest throbbed in time with his heartbeat. How could there be so many cops milling about and not a single one of them saw two teenagers slip off.

Lord, help me find them.

He hit the contact button for Sophia. "Answer the phone, Soph."

Straight to voicemail.

He wanted to throw his phone. He'd tried to use the tracking app, but her phone had gone dark. Most likely turned off. He kept trying to call her on the off chance that she'd answer it.

Lord. Help me.

He drove around the neighborhood. They couldn't have gone too far on foot. Assuming someone hadn't snatched them. He hit the steering wheel with the palm of his hand.

He knew the statistics.

"God, don't let Sophia and Bella become statistics."

Lord.

The RPD was searching for the girls. They were also working on getting an Amber Alert issued. It wasn't a confirmed kidnapping, but given the attack, it was a high probability.

It took some real guts to kidnap two girls with the number of police present at the scene.

The suspect who'd stabbed him was in custody and at the emergency room, being checked out before booking.

The phone in his hand rang. He looked at the screen. Glover.

"Please tell me the girls showed up at the hospital."

"No." She sighed. "We have another problem. Sam is gone."

Liam slammed on the brakes. "What do you mean she's gone?"

"She said Bella called her. Bella said they'd been kidnapped and Sam was to go to the slaughterhouse at Ashbend Industrial Park. We were on the way out of the hospital when she pointed out a man and said he'd been following us and that he'd been at the crime scene this afternoon. As soon as I took care of it, she was gone."

"Why didn't you call me immediately?" The rush of blood pounded in his ears.

"Because I was focused on trying to get us to the SUV, where I would have called you. I didn't expect her to give me the slip." Glover's voice was hard.

"Okay." Being angry with her wouldn't help right now. "So she used the man as a distraction?"

"Yeah. He's just some random bystander she chose to target."

"Any idea why she gave you the slip?"

"None."

"You said the slaughterhouse?" He knew where it was but wasn't too familiar with the area yet.

"Yes. I'll head toward Ashbend and set up a command center."

"I'm on my way. I've got Kennedy working on pinging the girls' phones. I'll call and have her ping Sam's just in case they move from there—"

"Hold on. You were stabbed." Shock filled Glover's voice. "Have you been stitched up? I'll call for backup. We'll handle this."

"I'm not going anywhere until I know my girls are safe." He ground his teeth.

"Don't do anything stupid. We don't need to worry about you while trying to rescue everyone."

"Don't try to stop me."

"Wouldn't dream of it," Glover said in a wry voice.

Liam hung up, then found Sam's number and called it. It rang a couple times and then went to voicemail. Her phone was on, but she'd chosen to ignore him.

He dialed Kennedy and told her to add Sam's number to the ping list.

He tried Sam again. Same thing. A couple rings, then voicemail.

Lead filled his stomach. Why had she given Glover the slip, and why wasn't she answering her phone?

His phone rang. The display on his dash flashed Kennedy at the Marshals' office. "Tell me you got something."

"I'm still not able to ping the girls' phones, but that last number you gave me is on and tracking south on South Highway 23 before it bends east."

They had a current location, but was she actually headed to Ashbend? Liam wanted to believe that she'd told the truth and wasn't causing some type of distraction so she could go out on her own to save the girls. "Would that take her to Ashbend Industrial Park?"

"That's the most direct route, yes."

Good. "Keep an eye on that phone, and let me know if it goes anywhere other than Ashbend. I'll start heading that way." Liam switched on his turn signal and busted a U-turn, then activated the lights and sirens.

What could the suspect possibly want with his niece and Sam and Bella? Dread filled his gut. "We need to find them."

Sam had a twenty-minute head start on him. He pushed the SUV harder. A lot could happen in twenty minutes. All of it bad. His chest tightened at the thought. Liam gripped the steering wheel until his knuckles were white. He veered around cars that refused to yield to emergency lights or just stopped in the middle of the street instead of pulling to the right.

He slowed at intersections, making sure they yielded before speeding through. The last thing Sam and the girls needed was for him to be in a wreck and unable to make it to them. As it was, he wasn't sure he would make it in time.

"Lord, please. I need them."

He'd needed his fugitive apprehension job, and God had taken that away to give him this life. Would God allow him to lose Sam and Isabella—and Sophia? Liam had to trust, no matter what happened.

But he knew what he wanted.

He wasn't sure where or when his relationship with Samantha

and Isabella had changed from handler and witnesses to whatever it was now.

It had probably started the day of the shooting, if not way before that, but seeing Sam unconscious and vulnerable in that hospital bed had undone him. Knowing it was a targeted attack only made it worse, because he had no idea who wanted her and why.

If they made it through—no, *when* they made it through this, he would need to seriously consider whether he should continue to be their handler. But first, he had to find them.

He couldn't bear the thought of losing them before he'd ever really had them. Sam had become so much more to him than just a witness.

And having to tell his sister that something had happened to Sophia would destroy them both.

His phone started to ring. Samantha's name flashed on the dash. He pushed the Answer button. "Sam, where are you?"

"I just got to Ashbend Industrial Park. I'm sure Glover's already told you, but someone has the girls. They told me to come alone."

"You know it's a trap. You need to wait for me. I'm ten minutes out."

"That's too long. What if something happens to them before you can get here? I'm going to go in and try to stall as long as I can."

He gripped the steering wheel. "Why didn't you just answer the phone and tell me where you were heading?"

"Because you'd tell me to stop. And I might have listened." She hiccupped.

"I know me telling you not to go in won't stop you but"—he had to try—"don't go in. Sam, you need to wait for me."

"You're right. Saying that won't stop me. I have to save the girls."

"Please be careful. I couldn't bear it if something happened to you." He was admitting to so much right now.

The line was silent. The timer on the dash indicated the call was still connected. "Sam?"

"Liam." Sam's voice was filled with emotion. "I . . . I . . . feel the same. But we can't lose the girls. I'll be careful. You just get here."

TWENTY-THREE

LIAM'S WORDS BOUNCED AROUND IN HER MIND. *I couldn't bear it if something happened to you.*

So much said in so few words. And she'd just admitted she felt the same way.

This man had come in and upended her whole life. Challenging everything she thought she knew and everything she thought she wanted. She'd let him in, and now she wanted things she'd never thought possible.

But right now, Isabella and Sophia needed her, and she was going to do everything she could to get them out safely.

It had been a stroke of luck that a Renegade Rides vehicle was in the hospital parking lot when she walked out. Now she was standing in the dark, abandoned parking lot at the industrial park.

She walked across the lot and toward the slaughterhouse. Graffiti covered the building, windows were boarded up, and overgrown weeds pushed up the side of the building. It hadn't been operational in decades, but she could still smell the metallic scent of blood. A shiver raced down her side.

How was she going to be able to stall until help could get here? The risk of losing the girls was far too great to just stand here and do nothing. Enough she felt the urge to pray.

Suddenly, something hard was shoved into the back of her head. "Don't move."

Nausea filled her stomach and her vision blurred. It couldn't be. She knew that voice. Knew that the hard thing was the barrel of a gun pointed at her skull.

She knew who had taken the girls.

"Why, Dean?"

"We're going to walk up to that door, and you're going to toss your phone inside. Do you understand?" Dean said from behind her.

She gasped. "Why did you do this?"

He shoved the gun farther into her skull, causing pain to radiate through the cut.

"Where are the girls?"

"You think you have the upper hand here, but you don't. I know it's only a matter of time before your boyfriend shows up. So you can either die here in the parking lot, and I'll take care of the girls, or you can do as you're told, quickly, and be with them."

"Okay." She'd known going into this that the odds they all made it out of this alive were slim to none, but she had to try. She'd give her life as long as Isabella and Sophia lived. "Don't hurt them."

Her heart ached at the thought of her sister being alone in the world, but that was so much better than being dead. She marched forward.

"Good. Now open the door," Dean barked.

She pushed open the rusted metal door to gaping darkness. The pungent smell of gasoline assaulted her nose.

"Now. Throw your phone inside."

Her hand shook. The phone clattered across the floor. The flick of a lighter sounded behind her.

"No!" She spun around just as Dean tossed a metal flip-top lighter to the ground.

Fire whooshed to life, following a trail through the entryway and deep into the building. Toward where he said he'd stashed the girls.

Sam cried out.

Dean grabbed her around the throat with his free hand and turned around. "Let's go."

"What?"

"Let's go." He released his grip on her throat, grabbed her arm, and dragged her away from the building.

Liam and the authorities would be busy looking for them in the fiery blaze, and the whole time they'd be somewhere else. She gasped, coughing and stumbling as he dragged her.

Dean marched her across the parking lot and toward the cold-storage factory.

"Why did you do this?" If she could get him to talk, perhaps she could delay him a bit. "You have a family. You're a good man."

"You know nothing." He shoved her forward. "Shut up and walk."

She stumbled but managed to catch herself before she could fall. The gun jammed into her back.

"If you're going to kill us, you at least owe me the truth. Why are you doing this, Dean? I trusted you! Cass trusts you!" She clenched her fists.

This man had been family. She'd been there for the birth of his twins. Babysat them. They'd taken her in when her life fell apart.

And then someone had shot up the house when his family was out.

"I don't owe you anything," he said.

"Think about Bella." Could she play on his emotions? "She's a kid, just like your boys. You wouldn't hurt them."

"I *am* thinking about her. And the marshal's kid. They've messed everything up, telling the authorities about my Rebels." He swore under his breath. "Now it's up to me to handle the situation. Just like Aiden."

She gasped. Had he been the one to put the bullet in Aiden's head? If so, he might also be responsible for Dr. Torres's death. "Why drag me into this?"

"Why me?" he wailed, then dissolved into ugly laughter.

"It doesn't have to end like this." Sam stumbled. "This isn't you."

"Shows what you know, *Sammy*." He grabbed her arm and jerked her upright. "Loose ends always need to be tied up."

"We can keep your secrets. We won't tell anyone." She gasped. "You have no idea what I've been keeping from you and the rest of the department. We can go. Let us go and we'll disappear. You'll never see us again."

Could she overpower Dean? She knew he was strong. They all had to be to do their jobs. She'd learned to defend herself, but she'd never tried to go on the offensive. And with a man she'd cared about . . .

A man she'd thought was good.

If she'd been wrong about Dean, what else was she wrong about?

If she could just keep him out here long enough for the police to arrive, the girls would be okay. He'd be too focused on her to hurt the girls. Except, the police didn't know where the girls were. What if he was working with someone? Wait, he was. His *Renegade Rebels*. He wasn't running around setting fires alone. He was using the high school kids.

"How could you do this?"

"Keep walking." He shoved her forward. They neared the cold-storage facility. Broken windows with jagged glass lined the exterior. "Get inside."

She opened the door and immediately smelled the gasoline. Everything in her tried to retreat.

He held up another lighter. "I'll start a fire here too, don't tempt me."

"You have me walking to my death. Why wouldn't I try to fight?" She ground her teeth.

"Because believe it or not, I care about you. I don't want you to suffer. This way will be easier. You'll just go to sleep and never wake up. No pain. No agony. Just sleep."

He leaned in suddenly, his breath far too close to her face and a container of gasoline poised over her head. "Or I light you on fire here and now, and the last thing those girls hear is your screams."

This wasn't the same man she'd trusted with her life the last six years. This was a desperate man. A monster.

"Okay. I'll go." She walked slowly forward. "You'll never get away with this."

"Don't worry about me. They'll be so worried looking for you, they won't notice the fireman on scene. Now shut up, or I light you up."

She didn't want to test him.

He directed her through several hallways and into an expansive room lined with walk-in freezers. All of the freezers had two-by-fours jammed under the handles to keep the doors locked.

Even if Liam was able to determine they were in this building, he wouldn't know which freezer they were in. Was he going to be able to save them? Assuming he even made it in time.

Until then, it would be up to her to save them.

"Where are the girls?" She scanned the room, determining the layout. Desperate to find a way to stop him.

"I know what you're doing. I've already done the assessment. Distance. Airflow. Vapor weight." He lifted the gasoline container. "I can set you ablaze and be gone before you hit the ground."

She knew how gasoline vapors behaved. They didn't rise. They sank. Three to four times heavier than air meant they were pooling on the floor. Waiting for the slightest spark.

"That one." He pointed to the third door from the left. "Move the board and get in."

She stepped forward and grabbed the board. A tiny bark sounded from inside the freezer. Sophia must have had Blossom when they were taken.

She gripped the board. She could use it to knock him out. Then she could grab the gun and hold him until help arrived. Except he'd been smart enough to bring a lighter he could simply toss at the gas. If he dropped it, the fight was over.

She'd just have to hope Liam made it on time.

And perhaps pray that the Lord would be with her the same way he had been with Joseph.

Right there in the middle of her troubles.

She opened the door. Light filtered across the space, revealing two figures huddled in the corner.

"Get in there." Dean shoved her, and Sam hit the floor, causing pain to radiate through her body.

The door slammed shut behind her, enveloping them in darkness.

She stood up and pounded on the door. It was no use. Dean had already wedged the two-by-four under the handle.

"Sam!" Isabella yelled.

Sam turned and kneeled down. "I'm coming." There hadn't been enough light or time for her to make out everything in the freezer. She crawled toward the scared teenagers a foot at a time, swiping her hands out and feeling for things as she went. "Talk to me."

If they talked to her, she could follow the sound of their voices.

"I'm sorry, Sam," Bella cried.

"We're going to be okay." She wished she believed what she was saying. She needed to keep the girls calm. Freaking out wouldn't do them any good.

"You were in the hospital, and Liam had been attacked," Sophia croaked.

"Dean was at Liam's house," Bella sobbed. "He said Liam had called him and that he was supposed to take us back to the hospital. We didn't know he was the one behind all of it."

"None of this is your fault." Sam continued her crawl. She reached out her hand and felt denim material.

Her best friend was an arsonist and murderer, and he'd been grooming teens to do his bidding. Was he trying to distance himself from the crimes they were committing? Using kids like pawns?

She wanted to be sick.

Hands reached out and grabbed her. She crawled closer and pulled the girls to her. "I'm here."

"Where's Uncle Liam?" Sophia asked.

"He's on his way." But would he get here in time?

The deep roaring of a fire filtered through the freezer.

Bella screamed. "What is that?"

She wasn't going to lie to them. "Dean has set the gasoline on fire."

"No!" Sophia screamed.

Sam pulled the girls tighter. "You need to calm down. Okay? Conserve air. The freezer will buy us some time for Liam to find us."

"What if he doesn't?" Bella burrowed into her side.

"I'll be honest. If help doesn't come, we're going to die."

The girls sobbed.

She stroked their hair. "Ssshhh. This freezer is old and not airtight. We'll pass out from the carbon monoxide before the flames reach us."

"Oh, God help us." Sophia pleaded.

Panic seized her chest. Liam had said *God is with you in*

everything. If ever there was a time she had needed to believe that, it was now.

Please God.

———

Smoke filled the horizon as Liam neared the industrial area of Renegade. Dread filled him.

He knew Sam hadn't waited. Had gone looking for the girls. Because that's exactly what he would have done.

He could lose everyone he loved in Renegade. Why would God bring him here, give him so much, only to take it away? But faith wasn't just for when things made sense. He'd trusted God this far. He'd trust Him now. Even if he lost everything. God was still in control.

He pushed the telephone button on the steering wheel and waited for the beep. "Call 911."

"911, where's your emergency?"

"This is Deputy Marshal Liam Roberts. I'm en route to the slaughterhouse off Millrace, looking for three kidnapping victims. There's smoke. Please send fire and rescue and officers. It's possible there are other people trapped in the fires."

The dispatcher asked a few additional questions.

The massive buildings came into view, glowing orange in the dark night sky. Smoke billowed out of the building to the right. "The slaughterhouse is on fire. I'm on scene."

He pulled the SUV into the parking lot and jumped out. Flames weren't visible from the outside, but it was only a matter of time.

Movement out of the corner of his eye caught his attention. A figure slinked in the shadows, away from the building that shared a parking lot with the slaughterhouse.

"US Marshals! Stop!" Liam took off running in the same direction.

The acrid smell of gasoline filled his nostrils. He looked to the slaughterhouse and then to this storage building. A faint glow flickered from the windows. The girls had to be in one of these buildings, but which one?

The slaughterhouse had obviously been burning the longest. Would the arsonist have hidden them there, assuming Liam would search the storage building first, or had he thought Liam would try the slaughterhouse first and therefore hidden them in the other?

Which building was he supposed to search?

Lord, lead me. Show me where to go and let me get there before it's too late.

Left.

God had never audibly spoken to Liam, but there had been times in his life that he'd known God was directing him. Like when he'd picked up and moved to Renegade with Sophia. This was one of those times.

He raced to the building.

Flames lined the hallway.

How long until the fire department arrived?

Liam looked over his shoulder. However long it was, it would be too long. Liam pulled his shirt over his nose and followed the trail of flames.

Where were they?

He could follow the trail and hope it led him to where Sam and the girls were being held. But the building was huge, and they could be anywhere. What if the trail had been deliberately set to take him away from the girls?

His gut told him to follow the trail—that and the still, small voice of God. He continued on until it opened up to an expansive room. The wall was lined with walk-in freezers that were all wedged closed with two-by-fours.

Fire separated him from the wall. The flames burned hot, but there were empty spots. He could follow a path to the freezers. *Thank You, Lord.*

He raced through the flames and made it to the other side. But now he had to figure out which freezer they were in.

"Sophia!" he screamed.

If they were still alive, hopefully they could hear him.

He heard something to his right and jogged down the row. "Sophia! Samantha!"

"We're here." Muffled cries could be heard just ahead.

"Sophia!"

"We're here!" The screams were right next to him now. He kicked the two-by-four from where it was wedged under the handle and yanked the door open.

Sophia launched herself into his arms while cradling Blossom. "Uncle Liam."

He wrapped his arms around her and squeezed her as tight as he could. He looked past her to see Samantha and Isabella making their way to the door, holding on to each other. They all looked terrified.

Samantha said, "It was Dean."

Liam inhaled sharply. Dean? A firefighter? Someone who was supposed to be a good guy had tried to kill everyone he cared about? Liam couldn't process that right now. "Let's get out of here. There's fire everywhere." He reached out to take Sophia's hand. "Follow me."

He pulled his niece behind him and led the way to safety. Every so often, he double-checked to make certain that Sam and Bella were following, but he didn't slow his pace.

They emerged from the building to red and blue lights flickering everywhere. Firefighters and police were busy with the slaughterhouse. Paying no attention to the cold-storage facility.

"Over here!" Liam started waving his arms, trying to get the attention of anyone nearby.

Sam and the girls had collapsed into coughing fits on the ground of the parking lot.

"Liam," Sam wheezed.

He looked to her. "I'm getting help." He yelled again. This time a firefighter saw him and made his way to them.

Liam turned his attention to Sam. "Someone is on their way."

Sam shook her head as a cough overcame her. "No." She grabbed him, gasping for breath. "Dean."

He knelt in front of her. "I know, he's the one who did this."

"It's Dean." She coughed, shaking her head. "He's still here. Blending in."

Liam's pulse skyrocketed, and he turned around, every instinct in him on alert. But it was too late.

Something hard connected with his face. Isabella screamed as the pain sent him to his knees.

"Why won't you people die?" Dean bent over Liam and reached for Liam's gun.

Liam responded with a punch of his own, knocking Dean off-balance.

"Get out of here!" He yelled the order at Sam and the girls while he worked to overpower Dean and pin him to the ground.

Dean delivered a well-placed blow to Liam's chest, where the butterfly stitches held his wound closed.

Liam's breath caught, and pain reverberated through his chest.

"Not today." Sam's leg came out of nowhere and connected with Dean's face, sending him sprawling onto the concrete. Knocking him unconscious. He didn't move again.

Sam collapsed in a coughing heap next to Liam.

He scrambled over to Dean and secured the man's hands behind his back. Two officers raced over.

"Deputy US Marshal Liam Roberts." Liam sat back on his heels, panting for breath. "This man is under arrest. Could I borrow some handcuffs? He needs to sit in one of your units until my coworkers get here to take him into custody."

"We've got him." One of the officers shifted into place, and Liam moved out of the way.

He let the officers take care of Dean. In this moment, he wasn't a marshal but a man whose family had been in danger.

But he hadn't been too late.

Thank You, Lord.

Sam lay on the ground. Her coughing spasms had subsided, but she was so pale. He stood up and scooped her into his arms.

"What are you doing?" she asked.

"Getting you help." He carried her over to where Sophia and Isabella were seated in the back of an ambulance, oxygen masks covering their faces while EMTs checked their vitals.

"Here's another one." He set Sam on the rear bumper of the ambulance, stepped back, and let them do their work. He took some deep breaths to try and steady his heart rate, pulled his phone from his pocket, and dialed Glover.

She picked up on the first ring. "Where are you? I just pulled into the slaughterhouse parking lot. It's chaos."

"Over by the ambulance." Liam hung up, and she jogged to them.

"That's a lot of blood." She stared at his chest. "You need to get checked out."

He looked down at his chest. The cut had bled through the gauze the paramedics had applied earlier. Getting punched in the chest hadn't helped. "On my list of things to do."

"It needs to be at the top." She narrowed her eyes at him. "Fill me in on everything else." She quickly glanced at Sam and the girls.

"Caleb Dean, Sam's coworker, is our guy. He kidnapped the girls and lured Sam here, set the buildings on fire with them inside one. I managed to free them, but he attacked us once we were outside. He's in a police cruiser somewhere."

Glover motioned to his front. "Get that taken care of first. I'll take custody of Dean and get him down to the office. You can come in when you're stitched up and help me with the paperwork."

As much as he wanted to argue, he couldn't. She was right. He was already risking infection with the cut being open as long as it had been. He also needed to make sure Sam and the girls were okay.

His cut was deep enough to require internal stitches as well as external. Twenty-six stitches and four hours later, he and Sophia were released from the ER. Sophia had only suffered minor smoke inhalation, and all of her vitals and oxygen levels were normal.

They'd been able to find an emergency vet who'd agreed to pick up Blossom and keep her under observation.

Sophia wrapped her arms around his waist. "I was so scared, but you saved me."

He hugged her tightly. "You think I would ever let you go? I'd do anything for you, Soph."

"I know—" She hiccupped. "But he wanted us to die. We shouldn't have gone with him. But he was Sam's friend."

"You had no way of knowing." He pulled back and looked his niece in the eyes. "This is not your fault. Do you understand me?"

She nodded as tears streamed down her cheeks. "I love you, Uncle Liam."

"I love you too. We're okay. Sam is going to be okay. God protected everyone." He pulled her in tight.

Sam would be admitted since she already had a concussion and wasn't supposed to have left in the first place. Bella was cleared for release.

Liam was glad that he and Sophia had been put in a room next door to Sam and Bella. He spent his time going back and forth between the rooms.

Supervisor Howard showed up with Stanton in tow. They took everyone's statements and headed back to the office to question Dean.

Liam hadn't had a chance to talk to Sam about everything that had occurred. This had to be extremely rough for her. Dean was a friend and a respected firefighter. The frantic search for Sam and the girls tonight had made Liam realize that Sam and Bella meant so much more to him than he had ever thought they would. He didn't know what the future held as far as a relationship with Sam went, but his heart had crossed the line, and there was no way he would be able to reel it back. He had some very important decisions to make.

His life and his career were on the line.

TWENTY-FOUR

SAM LAY IN ANOTHER HOSPITAL BED, SUR-rounded by the smells of antiseptics mixed with smoke. Bella curled into her side. Safe. Sam stroked her hair. "Bella, you don't have to keep anything from me, you know that, right?"

"I was scared." She sniffled.

"I know you were, but whatever it is, we can deal with it together. From now on, come to me right away. Okay?"

"Okay." She nodded.

"I love you."

"I love you too."

As they settled into silence, Sam's thoughts turned to Liam. He'd come for them. Saved them despite being injured. He'd risked his life for them. Then, when it was all said and done, he had bounced between her room in the emergency department and his own. Checking on everyone. Not to mention he had his own wounds to deal with.

Dean had done a number on him. First with the knife wound and then the punch to the face.

Her stomach roiled at the thought of Dean. She couldn't wrap her mind around everything. Her friend, brother, was the one responsible for kidnapping her sister and trying to kill them both. Not to mention everything else that had gone on. The laundry list of crimes Dean was responsible for was most likely growing as they sat here.

Sophia was curled up on the couch, asleep. Out cold now.

Liam had come and gone from the room a few times. Each time he entered, his eyes softened when their gazes connected, and heat consumed her stomach. This man was her hero. He'd saved her and her sister at great peril to himself. *Thank you* would never be enough.

There was someone else she needed to thank as well.

In the dark, minutes from death, God had sent Liam to save the three of them when Sam couldn't do it herself. And for the first time, she could also see the ways God had been with her in the middle of her trouble. Dean didn't have to lock her in with the girls, but she was so glad he hadn't separated them. And as warped as his reasons had been for shutting them in the walk-in freezer in the first place, that had given Liam the time he'd needed to get there and save them.

Thank You, God. I'm sorry I've spent so many years doubting Your goodness.

Liam popped his head in and looked to her first. "Hey." His eyes softened. "You have a visitor. If you're up for it?"

She nodded.

Captain Bennett stepped into the room behind Liam.

"Sam." The older man had aged ten years in the last twelve hours.

"Hey, Captain."

He looked to the two sleeping girls. "Would it be possible to talk to you two alone?" He glanced between her and Liam.

Sam's stomach churned. There was nowhere for the girls to go. Sam was all Bella had, and Liam was all Sophia had.

"Glover is here. Would you be okay if she took the girls to the vending machines down the hall?" Liam leaned against the door-frame, his arms crossed over his chest.

Sam looked at her sleeping sister. She didn't really want the teen out of her sight, but Captain Bennett must have something important to tell them, or he wouldn't have asked.

Sam nodded and then nudged Bella. "Wake up, sleepyhead."

Bella started to stir.

Liam walked over to his sleeping niece and woke her up.

"Can you guys go with Marshal Glover to get some snacks so we can talk with Captain Bennett?"

Bella nodded and rubbed her eyes. The girls slowly made their way outside, Liam on their heels. He wasn't gone but a minute.

"Okay, Captain. What do you have?"

Captain Bennett's Adam's apple bobbed. "I have no words. I thought I knew Caleb Dean." He looked down to his feet. "I never would have thought he was capable of something like this."

Tears stung Sam's eyes. He wasn't the only one.

Liam walked over to her and grabbed her hand in his. The warmth from his palm spread up her arm and enveloped her. "My team has Dean in their custody. We'll get everything figured out." He squeezed her hand.

"That's not why I came though," the captain said. "I wanted to talk to you about the fires."

"Okay." Sam furrowed her brows.

"The slaughterhouse is a total loss. But it's the cold-storage facility that has piqued my interest, and I wanted to ask you two some questions."

"Shoot." Liam reached out and pulled a chair closer to the bed and took a seat.

"Sam, tell me what you saw when you went in."

Sam closed her eyes. The last thing she wanted to do was relive the nightmare.

Liam lifted her hand to his mouth and placed a gentle kiss on the back of it, sending flutters swarming in her stomach.

What was she going to do when this was all over? He was acting like the dutiful guy in her life. Playing the part of a doting boyfriend. Was it all an act? Somewhere along the line, Sam's heart had gotten involved.

She wanted more with Liam.

She swallowed her feelings and turned her attention to Captain Bennett. "Dean had poured gasoline all throughout the halls he led me down, and there was also gasoline puddled in the room where the freezers were."

"How much gas would you guess was there?"

A lot. He had to have made several trips to get all of that gas.

She shook her head. "I'd say at least twenty gallons? Maybe not so much in the hallway, but definitely a lot in the freezer room."

"That matches what we found in his truck. He had half a dozen five-gallon gas containers. He probably doused the slaughterhouse, refilled the containers, and then doused the cold storage." Captain Bennett tapped his thigh with his right thumb. "Deputy Marshal Roberts, when you entered the cold storage, did you have a fire extinguisher or any other aid to put out the fire?"

Sam turned her attention to the man seated next to her.

"No, sir."

Captain Bennett nodded and pulled his phone from his pocket. "I want to show you two some pictures." His tone and demeanor were out of character for him. What was going on?

He turned his phone around and showed them. A blazing inferno filled the screen. "Swipe left."

Liam took the phone and moved so they could look together. "That's the slaughterhouse."

Liam swiped through two similar photos before he landed on

a photo of the cold storage. It was still standing. The flames had been put out.

"Keep going," Captain said.

The next photo was taken in the hallway that Dean had led her down. There were some scorch marks on the ground, where gas had been poured and lit on fire. The damage was inconsistent with what she knew about fires. Her heart thudded in her chest.

The next photo was of the open room containing the freezers. There were still puddles of gasoline all throughout the room.

But there were no burn marks.

Sam gasped. "It should have burned."

Liam's gaze was focused on the photo. "It was God."

Sam shook her head. "What?"

"God protected you and the girls. Just like He led me to you." Liam shrugged. "I'm sure forensics will go through there, and they'll tell us some scientific reason why it didn't burn up and why you all survived. But by natural means or otherwise, God saved you."

"You think so?" Had God been in the midst of it all this whole time?

"I believe He saved you." Liam nodded. "When I got there, both buildings were on fire. I didn't know which one to choose. I was afraid of being wrong. God nudged me to the right building and to the right freezer so that I could get you all out."

There was no use in denying it. She hadn't been alone in that warehouse, just like she hadn't been alone all along.

"Sam, God was looking out for the four of you today," Captain Bennett said.

A tear rolled down her cheek. She looked to Liam. "God really did protect us today. He's been holding on to me this whole time, and I'm finally seeing it."

Liam brushed her tear away with his thumb. Relief softened his face.

Peace that could only come from God settled over her—steady, quiet, real. "I'm so grateful."

Liam handed the phone back to Captain Bennett. "Thank you, sir."

The captain stood. "I'll leave you two alone for now, but there will be an official investigation into both fires. The fire marshal will be in touch."

All she could do was nod.

He let himself out of the room.

"Liam, what does all of this mean?" she asked.

He looked her in the eyes and cupped her face with his free hand. "It means God has a plan for your life, and He wasn't going to let Dean or anyone else interfere."

"I still feel like I have so many questions. So much to learn. And yet, at the same time, somehow I feel . . . peace."

Liam smiled. "That's actually a pretty good description of faith."

She reached over and slid her hand across his cheek. "Will you help me?"

Pain flashed in his eyes, and he gulped like her touch cut him open.

Was it pity? Regret? Or something deeper—something she was too afraid to hope for?

She dropped her hand to her lap and looked away. She'd gone too far. She was asking too much. Why did she have to ask him?

Liam gently turned her face to his. "I can't be your handler anymore."

Tears poured down her face. "I'm sorry. I'm so foolish." She tried to turn away, but he held fast.

"You don't understand. I can't be your handler anymore. Not when I feel the way I do."

Sam swallowed. "How do you feel?"

"I feel like God brought me to Renegade to find you."

Sam's heart swelled in her chest. "Really?"

He nodded. "I love you, Sam."

Emotion clogged her throat.

He studied her face. "I want nothing more than to help you, but I need to get this situation with Dean wrapped up and take care of a few things. Will you wait? If you feel the same, I'll figure out how we can make this work without breaking the rules."

"I will." Her heart soared. God had saved her life, and now He was giving her everything she'd ever wanted. Someone who loved her.

"Good." He squeezed her hand and bent down. "I want to kiss you so bad, but I can't. Not right now."

He was such an honorable man. And he was all hers. She leaned forward and placed a kiss on his cheek. "I can wait."

"Knock, knock," Glover said from Liam's office door.

"Come in." He saved the report he'd been working on. It was going to be a long night.

Kennedy had been assigned to stand guard until Dean could be thoroughly questioned and confirm that the threats against Sam and the girls were over.

Once Liam was sure that everyone was okay and Sam had assured him that Sophia would be fine to stay in the hospital room with her and Bella, he returned to the office to take care of all the paperwork.

His first stop had been Supervisor Howard. For once, Liam had been able to catch him in his office. Even though it was after hours.

He'd gone in ready to quit his job with the Marshals to pursue a relationship with Sam. But God had other plans.

Butler was back and was now officially the marshal in charge of the Williamses' case again. Sam and Isabella were no longer Liam's witnesses. They could be his family.

Then he'd gone to find Dean, only to learn he'd been uncooperative and requested a lawyer. So Liam had headed back to his office and the mountain of paperwork awaiting him. Glover's interruption now was a welcome reprieve.

"I've come bearing good news." Glover tapped her leg. "It seems some alone time in the holding cell has changed Dean's mind. He's waived his right to an attorney and has decided to talk."

Liam pushed away from his desk. "Let's go before he changes it again."

Liam and Glover entered the interview room. Dean sat at a metal table bolted to the floor, his hands cuffed and secured to the metal ring welded to the tabletop.

Liam gritted his teeth. This man had been like a brother to Sam. And then he'd tried to kill her.

Glover took the seat across from Dean, while Liam chose to stand by the door. He leaned against the frame and crossed his arms. He would let Glover handle the interview. Liam was too close to this.

"Mr. Dean. You wanted to talk to us." She leaned forward and stared Dean in the eyes.

"Can these come off?" He lifted his hands.

"No," Liam bit out.

"It was worth a shot." Dean rearranged himself in his seat. "What do you want to know?"

"Before we start, let me read you your Miranda rights." Glover read them verbatim from the card. Reading it from a card left no room for mistakes.

"Now, start at the beginning?" Glover leaned back in her chair.

Dean cocked his head. "Which beginning?"

"Dr. Torres."

"Dr. Torres needed some money, and he had some buildings that would make it for him. He just needed someone to burn 'em down. I was happy to oblige. For a price."

"How would that work?"

"They'd burn. He'd get insurance money and give me a cut. It was a good thing until someone was willing to pay more to make him disappear."

"So you killed him?" Glover asked.

Dean shrugged.

Not actually an admission but not a denial either. Why was he talking now? Was there an angle he was trying to play?

"Who was the someone that wanted Torres dead?"

"I can't tell you that. They'll kill my family." Dean gritted his teeth.

Liam clenched his fists.

"You've got to give us more than that." Glover said.

"Rousseau." Dean's voice was barely above a whisper.

"Who's that?" Glover asked.

Dean shrugged. "That's all I got to say."

"Fine, so how do Aiden Hamilton and the other teens fit into this?" Glover sat back in her chair.

"Bored teenagers with pyromania are easy to buy. As long as they did exactly what I told them to, they'd get paid."

Liam stood up straight. "Were Isabella and Sophia always a part of the plan?"

Dean turned to Liam, sadness filling his face. "No. They never should have been involved."

"Then how did they get involved?" Liam took a step closer to the table.

"The idiot teens decided they wanted to outsource. It was just my luck they had to pick someone with unwanted connections. I told Aiden to clean up his mess, and he failed."

"So you had to clean it up for him?" Glover leaned forward.

Dean gritted his teeth. "Something like that."

"Would you be willing to write out a statement?" Glover slid a notepad and pencil over to Dean.

Dean didn't say a word. He picked up the pencil and started writing.

"Dean." The man's name tasted bitter on Liam's tongue.

Dean looked to him.

"You tried to kill three very important people to me. I need to know, is it over? Are they safe?"

Dean stared at him. Emotion flickered in his eyes before he nodded. "They are safe."

Liam had no reason to believe Dean. They wouldn't just take his word for it. Liam would leave no stone unturned to make sure the people he loved remained safe.

Liam was no longer needed here. Dean had confessed to all of his crimes, citing that debt from fertility treatments had made him desperate and it had snowballed to a point of no return. He was looking at doing hard time for his myriad of crimes.

Liam left Glover to handle the rest of the interview. Right now, he needed to go to the woman he loved.

Deputy Marshal Kennedy was standing outside the hospital door when Liam arrived. "Everything okay?"

She nodded. "It's been quiet."

Giggles erupted from inside the room.

Kennedy rolled her eyes. "Except the giggling."

Liam smiled. Giggling was good. He opened the door.

Sam was sitting up in bed, and the girls were sitting together on the loveseat, looking at their phones.

"Uncle Liam, you have to watch this." Sophia stood and showed him her phone.

He watched a thirty-second video montage of dogs doing funny things. She laughed.

He pulled his wallet from his back pocket and pulled out a twenty-dollar bill. "Why don't you take Bella and Kennedy to the cafeteria and get a snack?"

Sophia took the money. "Sweet."

Sophia and Bella left with Kennedy.

He sat on the edge of the hospital bed and asked Sam, "How are you feeling?"

"Pretty good, considering."

Liam swept a lock of hair from Sam's face and tucked it behind her ear, letting his hand linger on her neck.

Her breath hitched.

His pulse raced.

"Remember that talk we had before I left?" He rubbed his thumb along her jawline.

She looked at his lips and swallowed. "Yes."

"What if I told you that Deputy Marshal Butler is back and is your handler again?"

She reached up and grabbed his shirt, tugging him forward. Her lips met his—soft and steady at first, then suddenly desperate and hungry, like he was the air she needed to survive.

He didn't hesitate. He returned the kiss, pouring every feeling she offered right back at her.

EPILOGUE

Two weeks later

SAM WIPED HER SWEATY PALMS ON HER SHORTS. She had never felt so free and light in her life. She glanced out into the audience of Orange Street Church and found Liam in a mint-colored polo and khaki slacks, seated next to Bella and Sophia in matching floral dresses.

Behind them, Cass sat with the boys and her parents. Sam's friend had been as surprised as everyone else over what Dean had been doing, but Sam hadn't wanted Cass to pull away as if she was responsible for any of it. They'd determined to support each other like family should and were working on forgiveness together. It was going to be a long road, but they would get there.

Next to Cass were all the guys from Station 4. Her found family. The men who would always be with her and for her. Supporting her.

Like God would want her to do—showing love to others.

"Next, we have Samantha Williams."

The preacher looked to her and held out his hand.

Sam stepped out from behind the partition and took his hand.

Warmth started at her toes and worked its way up until she was waist-deep in the baptismal.

"Sam and I have had quite a few long discussions in the last couple of weeks. Haven't we?"

She nodded.

"You told me you had something you wanted to share with the congregation?"

She nodded again.

The preacher handed her the mic.

"Um." Her neck warmed. "I had a rough childhood and a past I'd rather not talk about. Although I became a Christian when I was younger, because of everything I've been through, I came to the conclusion that God didn't care about me. That maybe He wasn't as good as people said he was. Then I met a man who told me about the God he knew." She looked at Liam. "He said that God was always with me and that He would work everything out. I have seen how God has worked in my life in the last several weeks, and now I know that God is good. I know that I am a sinner and don't deserve His grace, but He's freely given it to me through His son Jesus Christ." She handed the mic back to the preacher as the congregation clapped.

"Because of your profession of faith to make Jesus Christ Lord of your life, and in accordance with the walk of a disciple, I baptize you, my sister, in the name of the Father, the Son, and the Holy Spirit."

The preacher lowered her into the water and raised her back up.

She emerged from the water with tears flowing from her eyes. She was new. All the old life, Madison and Samantha, had been washed away, and she was a new creation.

The congregation clapped.

She stepped from the water and into the arms of Barbara, who had been meeting with her twice a week since the fire. "I'm so happy for you."

"Thank you. For everything." Sam gave her a hug.

Sam had been studying Barbara's Bible, and the notes had intrigued her enough that she'd asked Barbara if she'd be willing to meet with her and help her grow in her understanding.

Sam dried off and changed clothes before joining Liam and the girls in the sanctuary.

Liam immediately grabbed her hand and brought it to his lips. "I'm so proud of you." He smiled the smile that melted her heart a little more every time, then slid his arm around her waist. This was home.

Sam knew that Liam was the man God had made just for her, and she would be spending the rest of her life with him. She just had to wait for him to catch up.

"Ready?" He squeezed her hand.

She turned to him and wrapped her arms around his neck. "For anything."

His arms slid around her waist. "Anything?"

"Anything." She leaned forward and pressed her lips to his.

THANK YOU!

Thank you so much for reading *Protector*. We hope you enjoyed the story. If you did, would you be willing to do us a favor and leave a review? It doesn't have to be long—just a few words to help other readers know what they're getting. (But no spoilers! We don't want to wreck the fun!) Thank you again for reading!

We'd love to hear from you- not only about this story, but about any characters or stories you'd like to read in the future. Contact us at www.sunrisepublishing.com/contact.

She's survived twenty years of hiding. Now someone from her past wants to finish what they started.

Aubrey Richardson thought she'd finally found peace in Renegade, Colorado. Working for the US Marshals, spearheading the town's favorite day of the year, and living a safe life she loves. But when the Federal judge who helped her find this life is murdered, Aubrey realizes life in Renegade isn't as safe as she thought.

Some secrets refuse to stay buried.

US Marshal Ethan Butler has been looking into the shadow syndicate operating in town, but even after weeks he doesn't have much evidence. When a federal prison transport plane goes down in the woods outside town, no one knows where the aircraft was going—or who might have been on board. Torn between duty and his growing affection for Aubrey, Ethan is forced to choose between following protocol and breaking every rule to protect the woman who just might be his everything.

When your greatest fear becomes your greatest fight, how far will you go to protect the ones you love?

From the wreckage of the plane crash to the depths of a conspiracy that reaches into the highest levels of law enforcement, Aubrey and Ethan race against time to unmask a killer who knows their every weakness. But when the final confrontation forces Aubrey to choose between her own safety and protecting innocent lives, she'll discover that sometimes the greatest act of courage is learning to trust—in God's plan, in love's power, and in the strength she never knew she had.

ONE

IT HAD EITHER BEEN A COLOSSAL MISTAKE VOLunteering to assist with the annual Fourth of July Renegade Days or a brilliant idea. Right now, Aubrey Richardson was leaning toward the former. She stared at the to-do list on her desk and sighed at the enormity of her effort to give back to the community that had been her safe space for the last six years.

In Renegade, she was simply Aubrey, assistant for the US Marshals Service. This city had become her home, her lifeline, and she owed them the best Renegade Days festival she could organize.

Yet lately, the memories she'd worked so hard to box away seemed determined to break out, taunting her and putting her on edge. Just one of the reasons for the plate of homemade brownies, baked fresh this morning, currently sitting on her desk.

She gave herself a mental shake to banish the nightmare of her childhood. *Focus, girl.*

Old-fashioned stagecoach? Check. Band of outlaws recruited

from the local community theater group? Check. Costumes and horses secured? Check and check.

Only two days until the festival, and everything was falling into line—except she hadn't heard from Judge Stephen Mullinax in three days.

She'd specifically asked him to participate since not only was he a fixture around town and a dear friend of hers, but he also looked the part. Salt-and-pepper hair. Full mustache and beard. That beat-up Stetson he wore whenever he was outside. The judge looked as if he'd stepped out of an old-timey black-and-white photograph from the Wild West. All he needed was a duster and a six-shooter strapped to his side.

She glanced down at her phone one last time before she logged in to work at the US Marshals office.

No messages. No voicemails.

Aubrey had formed a close bond with Stephen after she moved to Renegade six years ago. They'd known each other for years, and he'd looked out for her in a lot of ways, but over the last few years, they'd really gotten to know each other.

These days, he was the closest thing she had to a father figure. After her testimony at a high-profile murder trial had sent her and her family into hiding, her relationship with her parents had become strained, to say the least. Her presence put them in danger, and it had caused a rift. Six years ago, she'd left them to their life in witness protection and moved here to Renegade.

A tall figure opened the door of the Renegade branch of the US Marshals Service, his face obscured by the bright sunlight streaming through the glass windows behind him as he stepped in from the wainscoted hallway of the federal courthouse.

She raised a hand to her eyes, trying to determine if this was a friend or someone more sinister.

She shifted closer to the monitor, one hand on the office phone, one finger on the concealed panic button, ready. Oh, good grief!

Her imagination was getting out of control. It was twenty years since her world had been shaken. The man she had testified against was in prison, and he was never getting out.

"Hey, Aubrey. What's up?"

She squeaked and placed her hand over her heart. "Goodness, Liam. You scared the ever-lovin' wits out of me!"

Liam was the newest member of the US Marshals team in Renegade. Over six feet tall, with expertly styled dark-brown hair, he could charm the worst offender with his blue eyes and that easygoing smile. Even though he'd only been in town a few weeks, he was already one of the people she was comfortable confiding in.

"Guilty conscience." Liam laughed.

All the tension in her back and shoulders released. She sipped the now-cold coffee she'd picked up earlier from the Beanery. "You're in early this morning."

He leaned against the reception desk, a grin on his face. "Yeah, thought I'd come in and take care of some paperwork for my group of protectees." He'd pushed the sleeves of his dress shirt up his forearms.

His gaze locked on the platter of homemade brownies she'd baked earlier this morning. A few weeks ago, Liam had met one of the local firefighters, Samantha Williams. Now that she wasn't his protected witness, they were dating, and Liam's niece and Sam's sister––both in their teens—were best friends. Aubrey loved their new little family, but as far as baking goodies went, Sam was a bit of a disaster. She approached baking the way she approached a training burn—full commitment, lots of optimism, and a willingness to call for backup when things got smoky. She'd once set a pan on the counter and announced, "Good news: Nothing caught fire. Bad news: I'm not sure they're legally brownies."

Aubrey smiled as she picked up the plate. "Would you like a brownie?"

Truthfully, she was saving them for the return of Deputy US

Marshal Ethan Butler, but there was no sense in wasting them. Ethan probably wouldn't eat them anyway. The man was a health nut, usually, with no room for any "fun" food. Though lately, he had been acting out of character, so she was hoping the treats—if he actually indulged—would cheer him up.

"I made them this morning for Butler." She set the plate on the desk and pushed it closer.

"All those for Butler?" He quirked one eyebrow.

"Maybe." She cleared her throat and looked away. "But I have a feeling my efforts will be rebuffed, so you go ahead." Nothing she did seemed to break through Butler's gruff exterior. Maybe she should quit trying.

"Well now, you don't have to twist my arm."

She laughed and watched as he ate the brownie in two bites, wondering how Sam thought he was attractive. To Aubrey, he was more of an annoying brother, but maybe she worked with too many alpha males with guns and badges.

"What?" He wiped away the crumbs with a napkin.

Aubrey shook her head, then waved away the thought. "Never mind. There's a fresh pot of coffee on the credenza." She opened a tab on her computer and clocked in.

"What would this office do without you, Aubrey?" He wandered over to fill an official US Marshals mug with coffee and held it up in a salute.

"Starve. And probably have better dental checkups." She scanned her email, checking for any urgent messages. Nothing. "Anything new with your protectees?"

"Nope. All safe and secure." Liam leaned both forearms on her monitor, his blue eyes intense. "Look, I know I'm the new guy around here, but what's up with Butler?"

Ethan Butler was the one person in this office who seemed immune to her sunny disposition. She'd seen him with his elderly neighbor at the grocery store, witnessed his kindness toward animals. In those rare moments, he'd let down his guard and flash a brief smile. And yet here, he rarely talked to her or any of the others on the team unless it was necessary.

Always the protector, Ethan stepped into danger without a second thought. Between chasing fugitives and his talk of kayaking rapids and tearing across Renegade's mountain trails on his dirt bike—when he did mention personal stuff—it seemed clear that adrenaline wasn't just a rush for him, it was fuel. Given they worked together, he was someone she shouldn't want . . . but couldn't stop thinking about. Infuriating man.

Aubrey rearranged the already neat files on her desk. "I don't know what you mean."

"Oh, come on. All he does is growl at everyone in the office, especially you."

She rested her chin on her fist and sighed. "I don't get it. Most people like me. I mean, I'm easy enough to get along with, right?"

Liam smirked. "You're Little Miss Sunshine to his thundercloud."

"I suppose some people like to be miserable."

"Maybe, but I don't think that's the reason." He glanced over his shoulder, then came around the desk and sat in the extra chair beside her. "Do you think he's in trouble?" He motioned her closer. "I mean, after all, he was suspended."

As the office administrative assistant, she was privy to a lot of personal information. But Ethan's sudden removal from the office two weeks ago didn't make sense to her.

One day he was out visiting their witnesses, and the next day he was gone.

A few weeks back, he'd been on a short administrative leave following a shooting. That was standard procedure when a weapon was discharged by an agent. This suspension had been something entirely different, and it just didn't make any sense to her. Had it been anyone else, maybe. But Ethan?

She stood and grabbed the stack of files from her desk. "I don't know, but something *odd* has been going on lately, both around town and in the office." Goosebumps rose on her arms, and it wasn't the air-conditioned office.

"That's what I'm talking about." He leaned back and crossed his arms over his chest. "Look, I'm just trying to figure out what's going on. From what I've seen, Butler does everything by the book, so a suspension doesn't make any sense."

"And all this tension since he's been gone isn't good for the team." Aubrey nibbled on a brownie. "Butler should be back either today or tomorrow, from what little information I've been given."

"Good. When he shows up, I really need him to fill me in on whether he's discovered more about this shadow syndicate since Dr. Torres was killed. I know he was looking into it, but I haven't heard anything."

She sighed. "I wish I could tell you, but the man is a closed book. The only thing I really know about him is that he transferred from a much larger field office two years ago. Denver, I think."

Did Liam really think Ethan would tell him what he was working on? Especially if it was sensitive.

They should probably quit gossiping about the guy, but Aubrey was the first person to admit she wasn't perfect. Ethan was just so difficult to figure out.

"That's what he told me. Denver." Liam crossed his arms and watched her under hooded eyes.

She opened the file cabinet and stuffed the folders inside. She'd figure out where they were supposed to go later. "In the two years that he's been here, this is how he is. With everyone. Even Supervisor Howard."

"Maybe that was the reason for his suspension. Insubordination." Liam followed her over to the filing cabinets.

Aubrey shook her head. "I don't think that's why he was suspended." She slammed the drawer shut, then sat down behind the desk and shrugged. "The paperwork I saw said that he was suspended for an unintentional and improper discharge of a firearm while on assignment."

"You're kidding me."

"I wish I was."

Liam frowned. "I can't see Butler being careless so soon after he was cleared for a different shooting. The guy is meticulous."

"I know, right? It doesn't make sense. He's one of the best marshals out there." She looked around the office area, hoping no one else could hear them. "There has to be something else, some logical explanation as to why he's been suspended."

"You're right." Liam held up his hands. "If Ethan wants to tell us, he will. But when he does arrive, can you let him know I'd like to sit down and talk with him?" Liam picked up a flyer for Renegade Days from her desk and glanced at it. "Or is that asking you to risk your life?" He smirked and sat on the edge of her desk, his back to the door.

Didn't the guy have any work to do?

"You have no idea." She took his empty mug back to the credenza. "I just wish I knew what his problem is. Renegade's not that bad, is it?" She sighed. "Maybe he needs to get out of Renegade for a bit—take a couple of days and go kayaking. Go visit his friends or family somewhere else."

Someone cleared their throat behind them. "Who needs to get out of Renegade?"

Heat rose up Aubrey's neck as she and Liam looked at each other.

Busted. When would she learn to keep her opinions to herself? She knew better than to talk about a coworker. Every coherent thought in her head stalled, and she slowly glanced up at the man in question.

Ethan's mouth turned down in a grimace, his eyebrows practically touching. Shoot. Mad and *gorgeous.*

Aubrey shot Liam a death glare, but Liam's smile only grew wider, if that was even possible.

"You do, my friend." Liam stood and slapped Ethan's back. "I'm hoping you took your shot to get out of town and into the great outdoors, work out some of that tension you carry."

Ethan's gaze moved between Aubrey and Liam, his eyes shooting sparks, and Aubrey glanced back at her keyboard. "Don't you two have some work to do? Someone else to annoy?"

She looked up and saw him shrug off Liam's hand. "And you"—he turned his dark-blue eyes on Aubrey, his gaze polar-ice-cap cold—"shouldn't gossip."

Was it hot in here? She stood and leaned on her desk, smiled sweetly at him.

Ethan's frown deepened.

Liam snorted, and Ethan's gaze drifted to his coworker. Liam coughed into his hand and stood.

Aubrey bit her lower lip and cleared her throat. "Anyway, welcome back! I made these this morning. Care for a brownie?"

She held out the plate, along with a napkin. Who knew they were destined to be apology brownies?

Ethan stared at her for another long moment before Liam grabbed a napkin and loaded it with two chocolate squares.

"Don't mind if I do." Liam held up the brownies in a salute. "You make the best brownies of anyone I know." He leaned closer. "Just don't tell Sam I said that, or she'll have my hide."

Aubrey laughed, and it felt good to release some of the tension from the past week. She made an X over her chest. "Promise."

"My girlfriend has many talents, but baking isn't one of them." He started to walk back to his office, stopped and pivoted. "Don't tell her I said that either."

Liam whistled on his way back into the old office building, the jaunty tune echoing off the marble floors.

Aubrey shook her head and sat down, staring at the open email inbox on her computer screen. Nothing new.

She felt Ethan's gaze on her, and she looked up into those mesmerizing blue eyes of his. He was a handsome man, if you could get past his grumpy exterior. Short brown hair a little long in the front, and a smattering of freckles.

She gave herself a mental shake. "Something else I can help you with, Deputy Marshal Butler?" She pasted on a smile. She'd kill him with kindness.

If it didn't kill her first.

"Uh, no. Thanks for the brownie." Ethan grabbed one of the bigger squares and headed back to his office, his footsteps drifting away.

Huh. Will wonders never cease?

Aubrey checked her phone one last time. She moved her to-do list into the file folder marked Robbery Reenactment.

It looked like she needed to make a personal visit to Judge Mullinax.

Thankfully, she didn't need to understand Ethan Butler in order to make this year's Renegade Days a success.

Ethan closed the door to his office and leaned against it, staring at the brownie in his hand. Aubrey and her baked goods.

It was better than thinking about the past few months though.

He needed to check in with Sebastian Carlsson, his good friend and the US marshal in charge of the Denver office. They'd met while on assignment over ten years ago, and he was one of the few people Ethan completely trusted.

A few months ago, Detective Michael Martinelli and a private investigator named Luca Saxon had shared with Ethan that they suspected local businessman Roger Rousseau was in the middle of a criminal organization operating in Renegade. But without evidence, neither could do anything about it. Ethan had started to dig into Roger Rousseau, and all too quickly, the threats had begun.

Ethan had put in a request for surveillance on Roger and a warrant to look into the guy's financials, but he'd been turned down. The same day, his elderly neighbor had been roughed up by two men who'd told her that Ethan should back off from looking into Rousseau. And she'd told Ethan that one of the men had been wearing a silver star like his.

After that, Ethan had been forced to come up with a more radical plan. If someone in the office was working for the Shadow Syndicate, he had to keep his investigation under the radar. And do it in a way that kept the people around him safe.

He and Carlsson had devised a ruse to throw off whoever was leaking information to the Shadow Syndicate. They'd agreed to set things up to make it look like Ethan was suspended for improper use of a firearm, to give him the chance to investigate without anyone knowing. He'd spent the past two weeks following Rousseau and trying to unearth the evidence they needed.

Ethan dialed his friend's number.

"Carlsson."

"It's me." Ethan closed the office door and sat behind his desk. Morning light filtered through the double-paned glass, a few dust motes floating in the air.

"What did you find out tailing Rousseau on his trip?"

Ethan ran his free hand through his hair. "Nothing."

He studied his usually tidy office, and a shiver of apprehension raced up his spine. A fine white dust covered his desk and bookshelves. Strange. Two weeks out of the office shouldn't have produced that much dust.

"Martinelli and Saxon were so sure Rousseau's involved in the syndicate."

"I know. I still think he is." Ethan exhaled. "Look, I know we were supposed to connect this morning, but I don't think I should talk about this now."

"Hang on." Muted sounds bled through the line. "You at the office?" Carlsson asked.

"Yeah. Let me get back to you later this afternoon." Ethan disconnected the call.

He fired off an email to private investigator Luca Saxon, asking to meet, and sent the same email to Detective Martinelli.

An automated response came from Luca. *I'm out of town right now. If this is an urgent matter, please contact Detective Martinelli of the Renegade Police Department.* The email included Martinelli's number.

Muted laughter from the reception area drifted down the hallway, and he popped a corner of brownie in his mouth and groaned in appreciation, savoring the rich, chocolatey flavor.

Ethan called Martinelli's number, but the call went to voicemail. "You've reached Detective Martinelli of the Renegade PD. I am unavailable for the next two weeks. If this is a police matter, please contact my lieutenant."

He leaned back in his chair and stared at his phone. What were the odds that both were unavailable?

He closed his laptop with more force than necessary. Everything was messed up, and now his coworkers assumed that he was in trouble with the Marshals. The fewer people involved in this investigation, the better he'd be able to narrow down who was working against them.

He brushed a stray cat hair off his pant leg and grimaced. He'd stopped by his elderly neighbor's house to check on her two spoiled felines. He should've known better than to wear dark dress slacks.

He didn't want to interact with anyone in the office today. Too much weighed on his mind—too much confusing information he'd gathered that didn't make sense. He was convinced Roger Rousseau had to be working with the syndicate, but he just couldn't prove it. Yet. He'd followed the guy during his trip to Denver and, afterward, questioned the shady guy Roger had met with.

No dice.

No one would talk, and Ethan still had no evidence. But the attack on his neighbor couldn't be ignored. Rousseau was connected somehow.

With a loud exhale, he massaged his temples, eyeing the remaining portion of the decadent brownie. Aubrey knew how to push his buttons, sure. But she also knew the way to his heart. He didn't dare tell her he had a sweet tooth that he tried not to indulge. If she continued baking, he'd be as big as a barn.

A small smile lifted his lips as he stared out the multipaned window. He'd never hear the end of it from Liam if he ate the rest of that brownie. Ethan shook his head. Liam seemed like the kind of guy who could easily become a friend. Ethan was reluctant to admit he missed the camaraderie of a close-knit team to lead.

But what he needed right now was silence and a solid lead to break open the case he'd been secretly assigned. Just when he thought he was getting close to ferreting out the mole, another clue surfaced linking his theory to another suspect. If he didn't know better, he'd wonder if there weren't multiple people in charge of the syndicate—or if power kept changing hands.

He raked his fingers through his hair. This was a case he really needed help with. A second set of eyes.

But could he trust Liam?

If he knew Liam a little better, had worked with him more than a few weeks, he might be able to get a better read on the guy. Maybe trust him.

Before his manufactured suspension, Ethan had been invited to join Liam for his weekly pickup game of basketball at the high school. Even invited to his house for a cookout with some of the other marshals. Ethan shook his head. Liam seemed to be a good deputy marshal. Hard-working. Dedicated. But after investing fifteen years into his own career as a marshal, it was easier for Ethan to keep his own counsel than risk facing another career disaster.

He glanced at the brownie on his desk, debating whether to finish it. A knock on his door made him pause, his hand hovering over the baked treat. He cleared his throat. "Come in."

"You busy?" Aubrey stood in the doorway, her dark-auburn hair shimmering around her shoulders. Her deep-green blouse matched her eyes, and man, she was stunning. She held a stack of manila folders.

Ethan shook his head. "What's going on?"

She moved to stand in front of his desk. "Supervisor Howard wanted me to give these to you for review. Looks like we're getting more protectees in a few weeks."

"Thanks."

She placed the stack on his desk, and they locked eyes for a moment. He cleared his throat. "Something else I can help you with?"

She glanced away first. "Uh, no. Just making sure you have everything you need now that you're . . . uh, *back* and all." Aubrey tucked a strand of hair behind her ear.

"Thanks."

"Sure." She gave him a small smile. "I'll see you later, then."

"Yeah."

Butler, you are an idiot.

"Aubrey, wait up." He stood, and she slowly pivoted toward him. He pointed at the brownie. "Thanks again for making the brownies. They're really good."

A smile lit up her face. "Thanks. I tried a new recipe. Less sugar."

"Well, they're great."

They stood there awkwardly, staring at each other. The air shifted and sizzled until the moment was broken by his phone ringing.

Ethan cleared his throat. "Sorry, I have to get that."

She gave him a little wave. Most days, he might go so far as to wish they weren't coworkers so he could ask her out on a proper date. But dating a coworker was a bad idea. He needed to keep her at arm's length.

He glanced at the caller ID and answered, a small smile forming. "Mrs. Hanover, what can I do for you?"

His elderly next-door neighbor was sweet and a little nosy, but he enjoyed their nightly talks. She treated him like a grandson and was the one person in town who had made him feel welcome after his transfer from Denver.

"Oh, Ethan. I'm so sorry I missed you this morning. The girls were glad to see you though. They're always so pleasant after you visit. When did you get back?"

"Late last night." He cradled the phone between his ear and shoulder and opened his laptop, scanning through the documents he'd sent himself. "I didn't want to wake you up, so I just left the cat treats on the front porch."

"Oh, that's so sweet."

If he didn't get control of this phone call, she would go on for hours. He'd love to chat, but he was working on the biggest case of his life. "Is there a problem? Do the cats need to go to the vet?"

"Heavens, no." She laughed, almost a girlish giggle. "You're so thoughtful. No, this is something else."

He pinched the bridge of his nose. "Anything." He'd do anything at this moment to end this call, but his grandmother would tan his hide if he was rude.

"Yes, well," she said. "I don't know if you can or not, what with your schedule, but I need a huge favor."

Mrs. Hanover's sunny personality reminded him so much of his own grandmother, which made it difficult to refuse her requests. Not to mention his work had put her in danger. He didn't want to say yes purely out of guilt, but he was still going to help her. "Of course. What is it?"

"Could you watch Mittens and Simba for me while I'm away this week?"

He exhaled and a smile tugged at his mouth. He should've known this call would have something to do with her "girls."

This week wasn't good though. The cats would want extra attention. "I'd love to, but . . ."

"Oh, thank you, dear. They just adore you. I'm leaving tonight. My granddaughter is having a baby, and I want to be there to hold her."

Ethan shifted in his chair. He cleared his throat, forcing calmness into his voice. "Now how can I refuse that?"

Despite what she'd said, Ethan heard the fear in her tone, the tremor. The same fear he'd heard when she told him about the two masked men who'd shoved her around while she was loading groceries in her car. Ski masks, broad shoulders . . . and one idiot who hadn't bothered hiding he was a marshal.

Did the police follow up with her after? No.

The case had seemingly fallen through the cracks for lack of evidence.

A tight burn settled beneath Ethan's ribs. Mrs. Hanover had been scared enough the first time. No way was he putting her through a voice-ID lineup that would only drag her back into that moment and maybe paint a fresh target on her. He wouldn't take that risk with her. Not ever.

The old woman's voice wavered. "You're a good man, Ethan Butler. God has a special woman just for you."

He'd heard this tune multiple times from his neighbor. "As I told you, I'm content being single."

"Come now. Wouldn't you like to come home to a special someone every night?"

The question hit harder than it should have. Once, he'd thought he had that future. An engagement ring. A promise that should have been ironclad. Turned out he wasn't half as good at reading people as he was at tracking fugitives. If he were, he'd have seen the truth behind his fiancée's words and actions.

And he wouldn't be spending his evenings with an elderly neighbor who baked him casseroles out of pity.

"It's not good for a man to be alone," she continued gently. "Just be patient. God has the perfect woman prepared for you."

Perfect. That word scraped along a raw edge he kept buried deep. He'd chased perfect once. It hadn't ended well.

He cleared his throat. "What time are you leaving?"

"Around four."

"I'll drop by tonight after work, and I'll feed the cats and make sure they're taken care of while you're gone."

"Thank you, dear. I'm praying for you."

She disconnected the call before he could respond or even ask when she was returning.

He shook his head. Prayer. He hadn't been praying about the Roger Rousseau case. Who to bring in to help. Or even if he should. Which was the problem. He was forging ahead in his own strength, his own wisdom, without seeking the Lord's guidance.

The lapse was subtle. If he were honest with himself, ever since he'd been reassigned to Renegade, he'd neglected his relationship with the Lord. Instead of being thankful for the move, he'd allowed bitterness to creep into his daily interactions with his coworkers. He'd done this to himself. No wonder no one wanted to be around him.

A knock on his doorframe jolted him out of his thoughts.

"Glad to see you back in the saddle." Adam Montgomery towered over Ethan's six feet, two inches and looked like he needed to eat a huge plate of pasta. Montgomery had to be ten years younger than him. Shoot, most of the staff were younger than him. Ethan felt like a grandpa most days.

"Thanks." Ethan returned to the encrypted files he'd sent himself. The sound of leather squeaking pulled his concentration away from the monitor. "You're in early."

Adam leaned back in the chair. "Yeah. I thought you might want to know what happened these past two weeks."

"I already have the notes from last week's briefing." Ethan picked up the single sheet of paper and waved it at the kid.

Adam leaned forward, resting his forearms on his thighs. He glanced over his shoulder. "I'm going to close the door."

"Do whatever you want." This guy could be the office traitor for all he knew.

"Testy." Montgomery closed the door and resumed his seat. "Look, dude, I know a lot more than you think I do."

Ethan snorted. "Sure, kid."

Adam pulled the notepad that was sitting on the corner of the desk closer to himself and wrote on it.

YOUR OFFICE IS BUGGED.

All the breath froze in his lungs. Ethan pulled his chair closer to study the man in front of him. Montgomery had a lot of nerve, but he sat there unwavering. Ethan narrowed his eyes and responded on the notepad.

How do you know?

Adam shrugged. "Want to grab a coffee?"

"I could use the caffeine." He picked up the notepad and scribbled another message, then turned it around for Adam to read.

Adam stood and nodded. "Yeah, I need something to counteract all the sugar from Aubrey's brownies."

"Montgomery, you could eat an entire plate of brownies and still not gain an ounce." Ethan chuckled. "Let's go. I'm buying." Ethan locked his laptop. "I need a good, stiff black cup of coffee from the Beanery."

Outside the old courthouse that housed not only the federal

courts but also the US Marshals on the third floor and holding cells for prisoners in the basement, Ethan exhaled.

"What do you know?" Ethan stepped off the curb and turned to Adam.

"Not here. Let's get that coffee." Adam headed for the storefront with the dark-blue awning.

The rich aroma of roasted coffee beans greeted Ethan as he stepped across the threshold of the Beanery coffeehouse. Rich wood floors, small café tables, and wide picture windows added to the charm of the old building. Ethan inhaled and closed his eyes, willing the caffeine into his bloodstream, the fatigue and stress from the past few weeks weighing on him.

"Can I help you?" A barista with pink hair and a nose ring greeted him.

"Hey, Chloe." Ethan resisted the urge to ask for his usual drink. "I'll have a large black coffee with two shots of espresso, and my friend here will have . . ."

Adam stared at the petite woman, mesmerized. "Uh . . ." His Adam's apple bobbed up and down.

Ethan poked him in his ribs. "Speak up, man."

Adam leaned closer to Chloe. "I hope you won't think less of me, but I'll have one of those white chocolate mint iced coffees." He grinned.

Chloe shook her head. "Coming right up, gentlemen."

The whir of the machines made conversation impractical while they waited, but a few minutes later, Ethan paid for their coffees and pointed to a table in the far corner of the shop. "Let's sit and you can fill me in."

Adam grabbed the drinks from the far end of the counter and joined him. "While you were suspended, a tech team came into the offices and were supposedly upgrading the Wi-Fi, some of the phones, you know, that sort of thing."

"Go on." The jolt of coffee soured as it hit Ethan's stomach.

"But the thing is, they were only in your office."

All the customer chatter and noise faded into the background. "And that's your basis for thinking my office is bugged?"

"They replaced the Wi-Fi access point in your office and out front. That's it."

Son of a gun.

Ethan glanced around the shop. Nothing seemed out of place—just the normal, everyday activity of customers needing their coffee fix. *Think, man.* "Okay, thanks for letting me know." Ethan leaned his forearms on the table, gaze focused on his colleague. "Did you mention anything to Supervisor Howard about surveillance?"

Adam shook his head.

"Good." He wrapped his hands around the paper cup, the heat seeping through and almost burning his palms. "Did Aubrey know they were coming?"

"No. She was a little suspicious. Stalled them until Howard got into the office."

"Makes no sense."

Adam shrugged. "I'm just telling you what happened."

"But why bug my office?"

"And the entryway. Someone is fishing for info." Adam sipped his drink. "I had lunch with a Renegade PD detective friend of mine. He heard some gossip around town that Roger Rousseau might be involved in some shady stuff."

Ethan tried to play it off. "Like the syndicate people are talking about?" Seemed a bit coincidental that his coworker wanted to talk about the very thing Ethan was secretly working on. "What do you know about it?"

Adam sipped the last of his drink and tossed the cup into the trashcan by their table. "Nothing, really. It's just word-on-the-street type of chatter. But come on, it's the most interesting thing that's happened around town recently. Some shadow syndicate in Renegade, and witnesses like Torres getting murdered." Adam shrugged. "Your office was bugged for a reason. Is Rousseau really involved?"

"To determine that, I need evidence." Ethan paused a moment, considering his limited options. He didn't want to wonder if Adam was the dirty agent in the office. He'd never have believed that before now and wasn't inclined to think it just because the guy was astute enough to put some of the pieces together, but right now, everyone was a suspect.

"I can't tear apart the life of a guy like Roger Rousseau without cause," Ethan said. Judge Mullinax would never give him a warrant for wiretaps and surveillance without proof something was going on. "So let me know if you hear anything else, because I could definitely use the help."

"I know you were on a special assignment the last two weeks and not really suspended."

Ethan leaned back in his chair and crossed his arms. *This is bad.* "How did you find out?"

"Come on, man. You're a rule follower, and I've never seen you lose control. Word around the office is that it was misuse of a firearm. That's baloney." Adam shook his head. "Besides, it makes sense. I think you're onto something. There are too many inconsistencies in what's happening in town, witnesses and suspects like Torres and old Ralph Rousseau dying, and evidence disappearing. There's more to Roger than meets the eye. If he's a small player, maybe we can flip him for info on the big boss—whoever is in charge of the syndicate."

"I agree." Ethan stood, tossed his half-empty cup in the trash. "Come on, let's get back to the office." He'd need to do a sweep of his room for the bug, but with Adam on board, it felt like a fresh injection of energy into this case.

Adam nodded. "You got it. Thanks for the coffee."

"Anytime."

He paused in front of the three-story federal courthouse that housed multiple departments. Built in the neo-classical style of the early 1900s, the light-gray sandstone created an air of sophistication, while the dormer windows reflected the morning sun, almost blinding him. The old-fashioned globe lights at the entrance were yellowed with age, and an American flag fluttered in the breeze.

Adam stood off to the side, his gaze watchful. "I'll let you know if I hear anything else." He opened the reinforced glass door, and a blast of cold air washed out. "I have courtroom duty today." Adam slid his sunglasses onto the top of his head.

Ethan grinned. "Lucky you."

Adam's tall form passed through the metal detectors and then disappeared down the long hallway. Ethan rubbed the two-day stubble he hadn't bothered to shave before he came in this morning.

Even though Adam was a good guy and wanted to help Ethan with this case, there was no way he would let him. If life had taught him anything, it was that the fewer people involved, the better.

Otherwise, someone else was going to get hurt because of him

NOTE FROM AUTHOR

First and foremost, thank you to God, my Savior, to You be the glory.

I'd be remiss if I didn't acknowledge my husband, kids, and mother, who've cheered me on every step of the way.

Thank you to Pastor Lee Denton at Kibler Baptist Church. I used your baptism speech in the epilogue.

I learned so much about the US Marshals at the United States Marshals Museum in Fort Smith, Arkansas. If you ever get the opportunity to visit, I highly suggest you do.

Thank you to Sunrise Publishing for allowing me to contribute to the Heroes of Renegade.

Jennifer Pierce is a top ten Publishers Weekly bestselling author. She lives in Arkansas, where she's busy raising two children and a husband. She's a paralegal by trade and an author by free time. She's fluent in sarcasm and Princess Bride quotes. Her love of books began with trips to the library with her grandmother. Please don't ask her to name her favorite book—it's like trying to pick her favorite child. And unicorns. She loved unicorns before they were cool.

Learn more at jenniferpiercewrites.com.

Another epic series created by

SUSAN MAY WARREN
and LISA PHILLIPS

We solve the problem of what to read next.

WE THINK YOU'LL ALSO LOVE...

Infiltrating a dangerous militia to save her troubled brother, Jamie Winters finds herself kidnapped. Only Logan Crawford, the man she once broke, can rescue her—but he demands a promise in return. As they navigate peril in the Alaskan wilderness, their unresolved feelings spark a chance for love and redemption.

Burning Hearts **by Lisa Phillips**

Stunt double Vienna Foxcroft's stunt team are the only ones she trusts. Then in walks Sergeant Crew Gatlin and his tough-as-nails military dog, Havoc. When an attack on a film set sends them fleeing into the streets of Turkey, Vienna must face the demons of her past or be devoured by them. And Crew and Havoc will be tested like never before.

***Havoc* by Ronie Kendig**

When an attempt is made on Grey Parker's life and dead bodies begin piling up, suddenly bodyguard Christina Sherman is tasked with keeping both a soldier and his dog safe... and with them, the secrets that could stop a terrorist attack.

***Driving Force* by Lynette Eason
and Kate Angelo**

We solve the problem of what to read next.

WHERE EVERY STORY IS A FRIEND,
AND EVERY CHAPTER IS A NEW JOURNEY...

Subscribe to our newsletter for a free book, the latest news, weekly giveaways, exclusive author interviews, and more!

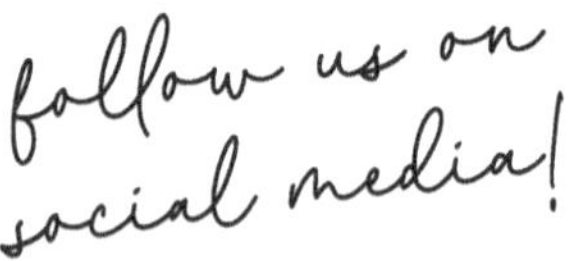

Shop paperbacks, ebooks, audiobooks, and more at
SUNRISEPUBLISHING.MYSHOPIFY.COM

www.ingramcontent.com/pod-product-compliance
Lightning Source LLC
Chambersburg PA
CBHW020908060726
47591CB00004B/1147